SANDRA

hello, darkness

BROWN

Simon & Schuster
New York London Toronto Sydney Singapore

SIMON & SCHUSTER
Rockefeller Center
1230 Avenue of the Americas
New York, NY 10020

SIMON & SCHUSTER and colophon are registered trademarks
of Simon & Schuster, Inc.

Designed by Jaime Putorti

Manufactured in the United States of America

ISBN 0-7432-4552-0

hello, darkness

prologue

Up until six minutes to sign-off, it had been a routine shift.

"It's a steamy night in the hill country. Thank you for spending your time with me here on 101.3. I've enjoyed your company tonight, as I do each weeknight. This is your host for classic love songs, Paris Gibson.

"I'm going to leave you tonight with a trio of my favorites. I hope you're listening to them with someone you love. Hold each other close."

She depressed the button on the control board to turn off her microphone. The series of songs would play uninterrupted right up to 1:59:30. During the last thirty seconds of her program, she would thank her listening audience again, say good night, and sign off.

While "Yesterday" played, she closed her eyes and rolled her head around on her tense shoulders. Compared to an eight- or nine-hour workday, a four-hour radio show would seem like a snap. It wasn't. By sign-off, she was physically tired.

She worked the board alone, introducing the songs she had selected and logged in before the show. Audience requests necessitated adjustments to the log and careful attention to the countdown clock. She also manned the incoming telephone lines herself.

The mechanics of the job were second nature, but not her delivery. She never allowed it to get routine or sloppy. Paris Gibson the person had worked diligently, with voice coaches and alone, to perfect the Paris Gibson "sound" for which she was well known.

She worked harder than even she realized to maintain that perfected inflection and pitch, because after 240 minutes on air, her neck and shoulder muscles burned with fatigue. That muscle burn was evidence of how well she had performed.

Midway through the Beatles classic, one of the telephone lines blinked red, indicating an incoming call. She was tempted not to answer, but, officially, there were almost six minutes left to her program, and she promised listeners that she would take calls until two A.M. It was too late to put this caller on the air, but she should at least acknowledge the call.

She depressed the blinking button. "This is Paris."

"Hello, Paris. This is Valentino."

She knew him by name. He called periodically, and his unusual name was easily remembered. His speaking voice was distinctive, too, barely above a whisper, which was probably either for effect or disguise.

She spoke into the microphone suspended above the board, which served as her telephone handset when not being used to broadcast. That kept her hands free to go about her business even while talking to a caller.

"How are you tonight, Valentino?"

"Not good."

"I'm sorry to hear that."

"Yes. You will be."

The Beatles gave way to Anne Murray's "Broken Hearted Me."

Paris glanced up at the log monitor and automatically registered that the second of the last three songs had begun. She wasn't sure she'd heard Valentino correctly. "I beg your pardon?"

"You will be sorry," he said.

The dramatic overtone was typical of Valentino. Whenever he called, he was either very high or very low, rarely on an emotional level somewhere in between. She never knew what to expect from him, and for that reason he was an interesting caller. But tonight he sounded sinister, and that was a first.

"I don't understand what you mean."

"I've done everything you advised me to do, Paris."

"I advised you? When?"

"Every time I've called. You always say—not just to me, but to everybody who calls—that we should respect the people we love."

"That's right. I think—"

"Well, respect gets you nowhere, and I don't care what you think anymore."

She wasn't a psychologist or a licensed counselor, only a radio personality. Beyond that, she had no credentials. Nevertheless, she took her role as late-night friend seriously.

When a listener had no one else to talk to, she was an anonymous sounding board. Her audience knew her only by voice, but they trusted her. She served as their confidante, adviser, and confessor.

They shared their joys, aired their grievances, and sometimes bared their souls. The calls she considered broadcast-worthy evoked sympathy from other listeners, prompted congratulations, and sometimes created heated controversy.

Frequently a caller simply needed to vent. She acted as a buffer. She was a convenient outlet for someone mad at the world. Seldom was she the target of the caller's anger, but obviously this was one of those times, and it was unsettling.

If Valentino was on the brink of an emotional breakdown, she couldn't heal what had led him to it, but she might be able to talk him a safe distance away from the edge and then urge him to seek professional help.

"Let's talk about this, Valentino. What's on your mind?"

"I respect girls. When I'm in a relationship, I place the girl on a pedestal and treat her like a princess. But that's never enough. Girls are never faithful. Every single one of them screws around on me. Then when she leaves me, I call you, and you say that it wasn't my fault."

"Valentino, I—"

"You tell me that I did nothing wrong, that I'm not to blame for her leaving. And you know what? You're absolutely right. I'm not to blame, Paris. *You* are. This time it's *your* fault."

Paris glanced over her shoulder, toward the soundproof door of the studio. It was closed, of course. The hallway beyond the wall of windows had never looked so dark, although the building was always dark during her after-hours program.

She wished Stan would happen by. Even Marvin would be a welcome sight. She wished for someone, anyone, to hear this call and help her get a read on it.

She considered disconnecting. No one knew where she lived or even what she looked like. It was stipulated in her contract with the radio station: She didn't make personal appearances. Nor was her likeness to appear in any promotional venues, including but not limited to all and any print advertising, television commercials, and billboards. Paris Gibson was a name and voice only, not a face.

But, in good conscience, she couldn't hang up on this man. If he had taken to heart something she'd said on air and things hadn't turned out well, his anger was understandable.

On the other hand, if a more rational person disagreed with something she had said, he simply would have blown it off. Valentino had vested in her more influence over his life than she deserved or desired.

"Explain how it's my fault, Valentino."

"You told her to break up with me."

"I never—"

"I heard you! She called you the night before last. I was listening to your program. She didn't give her name, but I recognized her voice. She told you our story. Then she said that I had become jealous and possessive.

"You told her that if she felt our relationship was constricting, she should do something about it. In other words, you advised her to dump me." He paused before adding, "And I'm going to make you sorry you gave her that advice."

Paris's mind was skittering. In all her years on the air, she'd never encountered anything like this. "Valentino, let's remain calm and discuss this, all right?"

"I'm calm, Paris. Very calm. And there's nothing to discuss. I've got her where no one will find her. She can't escape me."

With that statement, sinister turned downright scary. Surely he didn't mean literally what he'd just said.

But before she could speak her thought aloud, he added, "She's going to die in three days, Paris. I'm going to kill her, and her death will be on your conscience."

The last song in the series was playing. The clock on the computer monitor was ticking toward sign-off. She cut a quick glance at the Vox Pro to make certain that an electronic gremlin hadn't caused it to malfunction. But, no, the sophisticated machine was working as it should. The call was being recorded.

She wet her lips and took a nervous breath. "Valentino, this isn't funny."

"It isn't supposed to be."

"I know you don't actually intend—"

"I intend to do *exactly* what I said. I've earned at least seventy-two hours with her, don't you think? As nice as I've been to her? Isn't three days of her time and attention the least I deserve?"

"Valentino, please, listen—"

"I'm over listening to you. You're full of shit. You give rotten advice. I treat a girl with respect, then she goes out and spreads her legs for other men. And you tell her to dump me, like I'm the one who ruined the relationship, like I'm the one who cheated. Fair's fair. I'm going to fuck her till she bleeds, then I'm going to kill her. Seventy-two hours from now, Paris. Have a nice night."

chapter *one*

Dean Malloy eased himself off the bed. Groping in darkness, he located his underwear on the floor and took it with him into the bathroom. As quietly as he could, he closed the door before switching on the light.

Liz woke up anyway.

"Dean?"

He braced his arms on the edge of the basin and looked at his reflection in the mirror. "Be right out." His image gazed back at him, whether with despair or disgust, he couldn't quite tell. Reproach, at the very least.

He continued staring at himself for another few seconds before turning on the faucet and splashing cold water over his face. He used the toilet, pulled on his boxers, and opened the door.

Liz had turned on the nightstand lamp and was propped up on one elbow. Her pale hair was tangled. There was a smudge of mascara beneath her eye. But somehow she made deshabille look fetching. "Are you going to shower?"

He shook his head. "Not now."

"I'll wash your back."

"Thanks, but—"

"Your front?"

He shot her a smile. "I'll take a rain check."

His trousers were draped over the armchair. When he reached for them, Liz flopped back against the heaped pillows. "You're leaving."

"Much as I'd like to stay, Liz."

"You haven't spent a full night in weeks."

"I don't like it any better than you do, but for the time being that's the way it's got to be."

"Good grief, Dean. He's sixteen."

"Right. Sixteen. If he were a baby, I'd know where he was at all times. I'd know what he was doing and who he was with. But Gavin is sixteen and licensed to drive. For a parent, that's a twenty-four-hour living nightmare."

"He probably won't even be there when you get home."

"He'd better be there," he muttered as he tucked in his shirttail. "He broke curfew last night, so I grounded him this morning. Restricted him to the house."

"For how long?"

"Until he cleans up his act."

"What if he doesn't?"

"Stay in the house?"

"Clean up his act."

That was a much weightier question. It required a more complicated answer, which he didn't have time for tonight. He pushed his feet into his shoes, then sat down on the edge of the bed and reached for her hand. "It's unfair that Gavin's behavior is dictating your future."

"*Our* future."

"Our future," he corrected softly. "It's unfair as hell. Because of him our plans have been put on indefinite hold, and that stinks."

She kissed the back of his hand as she looked up at him through her lashes. "I can't even persuade you to spend the night with me, and here I was hoping that by Christmas we'd be married."

"It could happen. The situation could improve sooner than we think."

She didn't share his optimism, and her frown said as much. "I've been patient, Dean. Haven't I?"

"You have."

"In the two years we've been together, I think I've been more than accommodating. I relocated here without a quibble. And even though it would have made more sense for us to live together, I agreed to lease this place."

She had a selective and incorrect memory. Their living together had never been an option. He wouldn't even have considered it as long as Gavin was living with him. Nor had there been any reason to quibble over her relocation to Austin. He had never suggested that she should. In fact, he would have preferred for her to remain in Houston.

Independently, Liz had made the decision to relocate when he did. When she sprang the surprise on him, he'd had to fake his happiness and conceal a vague irritation. She had imposed herself on him when the last thing he needed was an additional imposition.

But rather than opening a giant can of worms for discussion now, he conceded that she had been exceptionally patient with him and his present circumstances.

"I'm well aware of how much my situation has changed since we started dating. You didn't sign on to become involved with a single parent of a teenager. You've been more patient than I had any right to expect."

"Thank you," she said, mollified. "But my body doesn't know patience, Dean. Each month that passes means one less egg in the basket."

He smiled at the gentle reminder of her biological clock. "I acknowledge the sacrifices you've made for me. And continue to make."

"I'm willing to make more." She stroked his cheek. "Because, Dean Malloy, the hell of it is, you're worth those sacrifices."

He knew she meant it, but her sincerity did nothing to elevate his mood, and instead only increased his despondency. "Be patient a little longer, Liz. Please? Gavin is being impossible, but there are reasons for his bad behavior. Give it a little more time. Hopefully, we'll soon find a comfort zone the three of us can live within."

She made a face. "'Comfort zone'? Keep using phrases like that and, next thing you know, you'll have your own daytime TV talk show."

He grinned, glad they could conclude the serious conversation on a lighter note. "Still headed to Chicago tomorrow?"

"For three days. Closed-door meetings with folk from Copenhagen. All male. Robust, blond Viking types. Jealous?"

"Pea green."

"Will you miss me?"

"What do you think?"

"How about I leave you with something to remember me by?"

She pushed the sheet away. Naked and all but purring, lying on the rumpled bedding on which they'd already made love, Elizabeth Douglas looked more like a pampered courtesan than a vice-president of marketing for an international luxury-hotel chain.

Her figure was voluptuous, and she actually liked it. Unlike most of her contemporaries, she didn't obsess over every calorie. She considered it a workout when she had to carry her own luggage, and she never denied herself dessert. On her the curves looked good. Actually, they looked damn great.

"Tempting," he sighed. "Very. But a kiss will have to do."

She kissed him deeply, sucking his tongue into her mouth in a manner that probably would have made the Viking types snarl with envy. He was the one to end the kiss. "I've really got to go, Liz," he whispered against her lips before pulling back. "Have a safe trip."

She pulled up the sheet to cover her nudity and pasted on a smile to cover her disappointment. "I'll call you when I get there."

"You'd better."

He left, trying to make it look as if he wasn't fleeing. The air outside settled over him like a damp blanket. It even seemed to have the texture of wet wool when he inhaled it. His shirt was sticking to his back by the time he'd made the short walk to his car. He started the motor and set the air conditioner on high. The radio came on automatically. Elvis's "Are You Lonesome To-night?"

At this hour there was virtually no traffic on the streets. Dean slowed for a yellow light and came to a full stop as the song ended.

"It's a steamy night in the hill country. Thank you for spending your time with me here on 101.3."

The smoky female voice reverberated through the interior of the car. The sound waves pressed against his chest and belly. Her voice was perfectly modulated by eight speakers that had been strategically placed by German engineers. The superior sound environment made her seem closer than if she'd been sitting in the passenger seat beside him.

"I'm going to leave you tonight with a trio of my favorites. I hope you're listening to them with someone you love. Hold each other close."

Dean gripped the steering wheel and rested his forehead on the back of his hands while the Fab Four yearned for yesterday.

As soon as Judge Baird Kemp retrieved his car from the Four Seasons Hotel parking valet and got in, he wrestled loose his necktie and shrugged off his jacket. "God, I'm glad that's over."

"You're the one who insisted we attend." Marian Kemp slipped off her Bruno Magli sling-backs and pulled off the diamond clip earrings, wincing as blood circulation was painfully restored to her numb earlobes. "But did you have to include us in the after party?"

"Well, it looked good for us to be among the last to leave. Very influential people were in that group."

Being a typical awards dinner, the event had run insufferably long. Following it, a cocktail party had been held in a hospitality suite, and the judge never passed up an opportunity to campaign for his reelection, even informally. For the remainder of their drive home, the Kemps discussed others who had been in attendance, or, as the judge derisively referred to them, "the good, the bad, and the ugly."

When they arrived home, he headed for his den, where Marian saw to it that the bar was kept well stocked with his favorite brands. "I'm going to have a nightcap. Should I pour two?"

"No thank you, dear. I'm going up."

"Cool the bedroom down. This heat is unbearable."

Marian climbed the curved staircase that had recently been featured in a home-design magazine. For the photo, she'd worn a designer ball gown and her canary-diamond necklace. The portrait had turned out quite well, if she did say so herself. The judge had been pleased with the accompanying article, which had praised her for making their home into the showplace it was.

The upstairs hallway was dark, but she was relieved to see light beneath the door of Janey's room. Even though it was summer vacation, the judge had imposed a curfew on their seventeen-year-old. Last night, she had flouted the curfew and hadn't come in until almost dawn. It was obvious that she'd been drinking, and, unless Marian was mistaken, the stench that clung to her clothing was that of marijuana. Worse, she'd driven herself home in that condition.

"I've bailed you out for the last time," the judge had bellowed. "If you get another DWI, you're on your own, young lady. I won't pull a single string. I'll let it go straight on your record."

Janey had replied with a bored, "So fucking what?"

The scene had grown so loud and vituperative that Marian feared the neighbors might overhear despite the acre of manicured greenbelt between their property and the next. The quarrel had ended with Janey stomping into her room and slamming the door, then locking it behind her. She hadn't spoken to either of them all day.

But apparently the judge's most recent threat had made an impression. Janey was at home, and by her standards, it was early.

Marian paused outside Janey's door and raised her fist, about to knock. But through the door she could hear the voice of that woman deejay Janey listened to when she was in one of her mellow moods. She was a welcome change from the obnoxious deejays on the acid rock and rap stations.

Janey tended to throw a tantrum whenever she felt her privacy was being violated. Her mother was disinclined to disturb this tenuous peace, so, without knocking, she lowered her hand and continued down the hallway to the master suite.

Toni Armstrong awoke with a start.

She lay unmoving, listening for a noise that might have awakened her. Had one of the children called out for her? Was Brad snoring?

No, the house was silent except for the low whir of the air-conditioning vents in the ceiling. A sound hadn't awakened her. Not even the soughing of her husband's breath. Because the pillow beside hers was undisturbed.

Toni got up and pulled on a lightweight robe. She glanced at the clock: 1:42. And Brad still hadn't come home.

Before going downstairs, she checked the children's rooms. Although the girls got tucked into their separate beds each night, they invariably wound up sleeping together in one. Only sixteen months apart, they were often mistaken for twins. They looked virtually identical now, their sturdy little bodies curled up together, tousled heads sharing the pillow. Toni pulled a sheet up over them, then took a moment to admire their innocent beauty before tiptoeing from the room.

Toy spaceships and action figures littered the floor of her son's bedroom. She carefully avoided stepping on them as she made her way to the bed. He slept on his stomach, legs splayed, one arm hanging down the side of the bed.

She took the opportunity to stroke his cheek. He'd reached the age where her demonstrations of affection made him grimace and squirm away. As the firstborn, he thought he had to act the little man.

But thinking of him becoming a man filled her with a desperation that was close to panic.

As she descended the staircase, several of the treads creaked, but Toni liked a house with the quirks and imperfections that gave it character. They had been lucky to acquire this house. It was in a good neighborhood with an elementary school nearby. The price had been reduced by owners anxious to sell. Parts of it had needed attention, but she had volunteered to make most of the repairs herself in order to fit the purchase into their budget.

Working on the house had kept her busy while Brad was getting settled into his new practice. She'd taken the time and effort to do necessary repairs before finishing with the cosmetic work. Her patience and diligence had paid off. The house wasn't only prettier in appearance, but sound from the inside out. Its flaws hadn't been glossed over with a fresh coat of paint without first being fixed.

Unfortunately, not everything was as easily fixable as houses.

As she had feared, all the rooms downstairs were dark and empty. In the kitchen, she turned on the radio to ward off the ominous pressure of the silence. She poured herself a glass of milk she didn't want and forced herself to sip it calmly.

Maybe she was doing her husband a disservice. He might very well be attending a seminar on taxes and financial planning. He had announced over dinner that he would be out for most of the evening.

"Remember, hon," he'd said when she expressed her surprise, "I told you about it earlier this week."

"No you didn't."

"I'm sorry. I thought I did. I intended to. Pass the potato salad, please. It's great, by the way. What's that spice?"

"Dill. This is the first I've heard of a seminar tonight, Brad."

"The partners recommended it. What they learned at the last one saved them a bundle in taxes."

"Then maybe I should go, too. I could stand to learn more about all that."

"Good idea. We'll watch for the next one. You're required to enroll in advance."

He'd told her the time and location of the seminar, told her not to wait up for him because there was an informal discussion session following the formal presentation and he didn't know how long it would last. He had kissed her and the kids before he left. He walked to his car with a gait that was awfully jaunty for someone going to a seminar on taxes and financial planning.

Toni finished her glass of milk.

She called her husband's cell phone for the third time, and as with the previous two calls, got his voice mail. She didn't leave a message. She thought about calling the auditorium where the seminar had taken place, but that would be a waste of time. No one would be there at this hour.

After seeing Brad off tonight, she had cleaned up the dinner dishes and given the children their baths. Once they were in bed, she had tried to go into Brad's den, but discovered that the door to it was locked. To her shame, she'd torn through the house like a woman crazed, looking for a hairpin, a nail file, something with which she could pick the lock.

She had resorted to a screwdriver, probably damaging the lock irreparably, but not caring. To her chagrin, there had been nothing in the room to validate her frenzy or her suspicion. A newspaper ad for the seminar was lying on his desk. He'd made a notation about the seminar on his personal calendar. Obviously he had been planning to attend.

But he was also very good at creating plausible smoke screens.

She had sat down at the desk and stared into his blank computer screen. She even fingered the power button on the tower, tempted to turn it on and engage in some exploration that only thieves, spies, and suspicious wives would engage in.

She hadn't touched this computer since he had bought one exclusively for her. When she saw the labeled boxes he'd carried in and placed on the kitchen table, she had exclaimed, "You bought another computer?"

"It's time you had your own. Merry Christmas!"

"This is June."

"So I'm early. Or late." He shrugged in his disarming way. "Now that you have your own, when you want to exchange email with your folks, or do some Internet shopping, or whatever, you won't have to work around me."

"I use your computer during the day when you're at the clinic."

"That's my point. Now you can go online anytime."

And so can you.

Apparently he had read her thought because he'd said, "It's not what you're thinking, Toni." Here he had propped his hands on his hips, looking defensive. "I was browsing in the computer store this morning. I see this bright pink number that's small, compact, and can do just about everything, and I think, 'Feminine and efficient. Just like my darling wife.' So I bought it for you on impulse. I thought you'd be pleased. Obviously I was wrong."

"I am pleased," she said, instantly contrite. "It was a very thoughtful gesture, Brad. Thank you." She looked askance at the boxes. "Did you say *pink?*"

Then they'd laughed. He'd enfolded her in a bear hug. He'd smelled like sunshine, soap, and wholesomeness. His body had felt comfortable, familiar, and good against hers. Her fears had been assuaged.

But only temporarily. Recently they had resurfaced.

She hadn't booted up his computer tonight. She'd been too afraid of what she might find. If a password had been required for access, her suspicions would have been confirmed, and she hadn't wanted that. God, no, she hadn't.

So she had done her best to restore the busted doorknob, then had gone to bed and eventually to sleep, in the hope that Brad would awaken her soon, brimming with knowledge about financial stratagems for families in their income bracket. It had been a desperate hope.

"I've certainly enjoyed your company tonight," the sexy voice on the radio was saying. "This is your host for classic love songs, Paris Gibson."

No seminar lasted until two o'clock in the morning. No therapy-group meeting lasted until the wee hours either. That had been Brad's excuse last week when he had stayed out most of the night.

His explanation had been that one of the men in his group was having a difficult time coping. "After the meeting, he asked me to go get a beer with him, said he needed an understanding shoulder to cry on. This dude has a *real* problem, Toni. Whew! You wouldn't believe some of the stuff he told me. I'm talking *sick*. Anyhow, I knew you would understand. You know what it's like."

She knew all too well. The lying. The denials. The time unaccounted for. Locked doors. She knew what it was like, all right. It was like this.

chapter two

This was creeping her out. Like, *really* creeping her out.

He'd been gone for a while now, and she didn't know when he would be coming back. She didn't like this scene and wanted to leave.

But her hands were tied. Literally. And so were her feet. The worst of it, though, was the metallic-tasting tape he had secured over her mouth.

Four—maybe five—times in the past several weeks, she had come here with him. On those occasions they had left drained of energy and feeling mighty good. The expression "screwed their brains out" sprang to mind.

But he had never suggested bondage or anything kinky. Well . . . nothing *too* kinky. This was a first and, frankly, she could do without it.

One of the things that had first attracted her to him was that he seemed sophisticated. He had been a definite standout in the migratory crowd comprised mostly of high school and college students looking for drink, dope, and casual sex. Sure, now and then you had your pathetic old geezer lurking in the bushes wagging his weenie at anybody unfortunate enough to glance his way. But this guy was nothing like that. He was way cool.

Apparently he had thought she was a standout, too. She and her friend Melissa had become aware of him watching them with single-minded interest.

"He might be a cop," Melissa speculated. "You know, working undercover."

Melissa had been on a real downer that night because she had to leave for Europe the following day with her parents, and she couldn't imagine anything more miserable. She was trying like hell to get glassy-eyed stoned, but nothing had taken effect yet. Her outlook on everything had been sour.

"A cop driving that car? I don't think so. Besides, his shoes are too good to be a cop's."

It wasn't merely that he had looked at her. Guys always looked at her. It was the *manner* in which he had looked at her that had been such a major turn-on. He'd been leaning against the hood of his car, ankles crossed, arms casually folded over his midriff, perfectly still and, despite his intensity, seemingly relaxed.

He didn't gawk at her chest or legs—consistently the objects of gawking—but looked straight into her eyes. Like he knew her instantly. Not just recognized her, or knew her by name, but knew *her*, knew everything there was to know about her that was important.

"Do you think he's cute?"

"I guess," Melissa replied, self-pity making her indifferent.

"Well, I think he is." She drained her rum and Coke, sucking it through the straw in the provocative way she had perfected by practicing for hours in front of her mirror. Its suggestiveness drove guys crazy and she knew it, and that's why she did it.

"I'm going for it." She reached behind her to set the empty plastic cup on the picnic table where she and Melissa had been sitting, then came off it with the sinuous grace of a snake sliding off a rock. She shook back her hair and gave the hem of her tank top a tug while drawing a deep, chest-expanding breath. Like an Olympic athlete, she went through a preparatory routine before each big event.

So it had been she who had made the first move. Leaving Melissa, she had sauntered toward him. When she reached the car, she moved in beside him and leaned back against the hood as he was doing. "You have a bad habit."

Turning only his head, he smiled down at her. "Only one?"

"That I know of."

His grin widened. "Then you need to get to know me better."

With no more invitation than that—because, after all, that was the reason they were there—he took her arm and ushered her around to the passenger side of his car. In spite of the heat, his hand was cool and dry. He politely opened the door and helped her into the leather-upholstered seat. As they drove away, she shot Melissa a triumphant grin, but Melissa was rummaging through her pouch of "mood enhancers" and didn't see.

He drove carefully, with both hands on the wheel, eyes on the road. He wasn't gaping at her and he wasn't groping and that was certainly a switch. Ordinarily, the minute she got into a guy's car, he'd start grabbing at her, like he couldn't believe his good fortune, like she might vaporize if he didn't touch her, or change her mind if he didn't hurry up and get on with it.

But this guy seemed a bit detached, and she thought that was kinda cool. He was mature and confident. He didn't need to gape and grope to assure himself that he was about to get laid.

She asked his name.

Stopping for a traffic light, he turned to look at her. "Is it important?"

She raised her shoulders in an exaggerated shrug, the rehearsed one, the one that pushed her breasts up and squeezed them together better than any Wonderbra could have. "I guess not."

He left his eyes on her breasts for several seconds, then the light changed and he went back to driving. "What's my bad habit?"

"You stare."

He laughed. "If you consider that a bad habit, then you really need to get to know me better."

She had placed her hand on his thigh and in her sultriest voice said, "I look forward to it."

His place was a major letdown. It was an efficiency apartment in a guest hotel. A tacky red banner strung across the front of the two-story building advertised special monthly rates. It was in a seedy neighborhood that didn't live up to his car or clothes.

Noticing her disappointment, he'd said, "It's a dump, but it's all I could find when I first moved here. I'm looking for something else." Then he added quietly, "I'll understand if you want me to take you back."

"No." She wasn't about to let him think she was a stupid, prissy high school girl with no spirit of adventure. "Shabby chic is in."

The apartment's main room served as both living area and bedroom. The galley kitchen was barely shoulder width. The bathroom was even smaller than that.

In the main room was a bed and nightstand, a four-drawer bureau, an easy chair with a floor lamp beside it, and a folding table long enough to accommodate an elaborate computer setup. The furnishings were garage-sale quality, but everything was neat.

She went over to the table. The computer was already booted up. With only a few clicks of the mouse, she found what she anticipated finding. She smiled at him over her shoulder and said, "So you weren't out there tonight by accident."

"I was out there tonight looking for you."

"Specifically?"

He nodded.

She liked that. A lot.

The Formica bar separating the kitchen from the living area was used as shelving for photographic equipment. He had a 35-millimeter camera, several lenses, and various attachments including a portable tripod. It all looked intricate and expensive, out of place in the crummy apartment. She picked up the camera and looked at him through the viewfinder. "Are you a professional?"

"It's only a hobby. Would you like something to drink?"

"Sure."

He went into the kitchen and returned with two glasses of red wine. Cool. Wine showed that he had refined tastes and class. It didn't jibe with the apartment either, but she figured that his explanation for it was a lie. This probably wasn't his main residence, only his playground. Away from the wife.

Sipping her wine, she glanced around. "So where are your pictures?"

"I don't display them."

"How come?"

"They're for my private collection."

"'Private collection'?" Grinning at him slyly, she twirled a strand of hair around her finger. "I like the sound of that. Show me."

"I don't think I should."

"Why not?"

"They're . . . artistic."

He was looking at her in that straightforward way again, as though measuring her reaction. His stare caused her toes to tingle, her pulse to race, and that hadn't happened in a long time in the company of a guy. It was usually she who created tingles and racing hearts. It was rare and wonderful to be the one unsure of exactly what was about to take place. Exciting as shit.

Boldly she declared, "I want to see your private collection."

He hesitated for several seconds, then knelt down beside the bed and pulled a box from beneath it. He removed the top and took out a standard photo album bound in faux black leather. As he came to his feet, he hugged it close to his chest. "How old are you?"

The question was an affront because she prided herself on looking much older than she was. She hadn't been carded in years—but a glimpse of the butterfly tattoo on her right breast usually made a bouncer too stupid to ask for an ID. "What the hell difference does it make how old I am? I want to see the pictures. And anyway, I'm twenty-two."

Clearly he didn't believe her. He even tried unsuccessfully to hide his smile. Nevertheless, he set the album on the table and stepped away from it. Trying to appear nonchalant, she walked over to it and flipped open the cover.

The first photo was graphic and startling. From the angle at which the close-up had been taken, she assumed—correctly, she discovered later—that it was a self-portrait.

"Are you offended?" he asked.

"Of course not. Do you think I've never seen one erect?" Her response wasn't nearly as blasé as she made it sound. She wondered if he could hear her pounding heartbeat.

She turned the page to the next shot and then to the next, until she had gone through the entire album. She studied each photograph, pretending to be as analytical as an art critic. Some were in color, some in black and white, but all except the first one were of naked young women provocatively posed. Anyone else might have considered them obscene, but she was too sophisticated to get uptight over exposed genitalia.

But by no stretch were they "artistic" studies of nudes. They were nasty pictures.

"Do you like them?" He was standing so close behind her now she could feel his breath in her hair.

"They're okay."

Reaching around her, he flipped back through several of the pages until he came to a particular shot. "This one's my favorite."

She didn't see anything that made this girl so special. Her nipples looked like mosquito bites against a flat, bony chest. You could count every rib and her hair had split ends. She had zits on her shoulders. A veil obscured her face, probably for good reason.

She closed the album, then turned to him and gave him her most seductive smile. Slowly she pulled her tank top over her head and dropped it to the floor. "You mean it's been your favorite up till now."

He caught his breath, then released it on a staggering exhalation. Moving slowly, he took her hand and placed it beneath her breast so that she was cupping it in her palm as though offering it to him.

He gave her the sweetest, most tender smile she'd ever seen. "You're perfect. I knew you would be."

Her ego soared. "We're wasting time." She unzipped her shorts and was about to remove them when he stopped her. "No, leave them there, low on your hips. Just like that." Quickly he reached for his camera. Apparently it was loaded with film and ready to fire, because he put his eye to the viewfinder.

"This is going to be great." He moved her closer to the floor lamp near the easy chair and adjusted the dingy shade, then backed away and looked through the camera again. "Lower the shorts just a little more. There. Right there."

He clicked off several shots in rapid succession. "Oh, lady, you're killing me." He lowered the camera and looked at her with pure delight. "You're a natural. You must've done this before."

"I've never posed professionally."

"Amazing," he said. "Now go sit on the edge of the bed."

He knelt on the floor in front of her and positioned her the way he wanted her. Legs. Hands. Head. Before he picked up the camera again, he kissed her inner thigh, sucking her skin against his teeth and leaving a mark.

For another hour, the picture taking continued along with the foreplay. By the time they actually did it, she was past ready. Afterward he refilled their wineglasses and lay beside her, stroking her gently all over and telling her how beautiful she was.

She had thought, *Now, here's a guy who knows how to treat a woman.*

When they finished their wine, he asked if he could take more pictures. "I want to capture your afterglow."

"So you'll have the before and after?"

He laughed and kissed her quickly and with affection. "Something like that."

He dressed her—yes, he had personally dressed her as she used to dress her dolls. He returned her to the park on the lake where they'd met and saw that she got safely into her car. As he closed the door, he kissed her lips softly. "I love you."

Whoa! That had taken her aback. A hundred guys had told her they loved her, but usually as they were fumbling to get a rubber on. More often than not these professions of love took place within the steamy interior of their cars or pickups.

But love had never been proclaimed softly, tenderly, and meaningfully. He'd even kissed the back of her hand before he let her go. She'd thought that was awfully sweet and gentlemanly.

They'd been together several times since that first night, and it was always good kicks. But soon, and predictably, he'd started whining. Where were you last night? Who were you with? I waited for hours, but you never showed up. When can I see you again?

His possessiveness took the fun out of being with him. Besides, the newness and novelty had begun to wear off. His photography didn't seem exotic anymore, just weird and often creepy. It was time to bring this to a halt.

Maybe he sensed that she'd decided to break it off tonight, because it had started off badly. They'd quarreled immediately after he picked her up. From there things had grown progressively worse.

He'd gone bizarre and scary on her with this bondage shit. Leaving her tied up for what was going on hours now. What if this dump caught on fire? What if there was a tornado or something?

She didn't like it. She wanted out of here. The sooner the better.

Before he left, he had at least turned on the radio and tuned it to Paris Gibson's program. That provided her with some company. She didn't feel quite as abandoned as she would have felt in a total silence that accompanied the total darkness.

So she lay there listening to Paris Gibson's voice and wondering when the hell he was coming back and what other fun and games he had in mind.

chapter three

The red light on the control board went out. Valentino had hung up.

It was several seconds before Paris realized that the only sound she heard was that of her own heartbeat. The music had stopped. On the log monitor she saw a series of zeros where descending numbers should be counting down the time remaining on a song. How long had she been broadcasting dead air?

With twenty-three seconds left in her program, she depressed her microphone button. She tried to speak. Couldn't. Tried again.

"I hope you've enjoyed this evening of classic love songs. Please join me again tomorrow night. I'll be looking forward to it. Until then, this is Paris Gibson on FM 101.3. Good night."

By depressing two control buttons, she was off the air. Then she was off her tall swivel stool like a shot, yanking open the heavy studio door, racing down the dark hallway, and barreling into the engineering room.

Except for a box of take-out fried chicken on Stan's desk, the room was empty. She continued running down the hall, turning right at the first intersection of corridors and literally slamming into Marvin, who was dragging a dirty rag along an interior windowsill.

She gasped, "Have you seen Stan?"

"No." One thing you could say about Marvin—he was a man of few words. If he spoke at all, it was in monosyllables.

"Has he already left?"

This time, he didn't even give her a verbal reply, only a shrug.

Leaving the janitor, she ran to the men's rest room and pushed open the door. Stan was at the urinal. "Stan, come here."

Stunned by the interruption, he whipped his head around. "What— I'm sorta busy here, Paris."

"Hurry up. This is important."

She rushed back to the studio and wheeled her stool over to the Vox Pro. It recorded each incoming call for optional playback. There was also a mandatory recording made of everything that went out over the air. But that was another machine and another matter. Right now, she was interested only in the telephone call.

"What's going on?" Stan strolled in, looking at his wristwatch. "I've got plans."

"Listen to this."

"Remember, my shift ends when you sign off."

"Shut up, Stan, and listen."

He leaned against the edge of the control board. "Okay, but I really need to be leaving soon."

"Shh." Valentino had just identified himself. "This is a repeat caller."

Stan appeared more interested in the crease of his linen trousers. But when Valentino told her she would be very sorry, her co-worker's eyebrows shot up. "What's that mean?"

"Listen."

He was quiet through the remainder of the recording. When it ended, Paris looked at him expectantly. He raised his narrow shoulders in a quick shrug. "He's a kook."

"That's it? That's your assessment? He's a kook?"

He snuffled. "What? You don't think he's *serious?*"

"I don't know." Turning, she punched the hot-line button on the board. That was the telephone line provided for the deejays' personal use.

"Who're you calling?" Stan asked. "The cops?"

"I think I should."

"Why? Nutcases call you all the time. Wasn't there one just last week who wanted you to be a pallbearer at his mother's funeral?"

"This is different. I talk to a lot of people every night. This one . . . I don't know," she added uneasily.

When her 911 call was answered, she identified herself and gave the operator a brief description of what had happened. "It's probably nothing. But I thought someone should hear this conversation."

"I listen to your program on my nights off, Ms. Gibson," the operator said. "You don't sound like the type to panic. There'll be a squad car there shortly."

Paris thanked her and hung up. "They're on their way."

Stan winced. "Do I have to hang around?"

"No, go on. I'll be fine. Marvin's still here."

"Actually he's not. He split. I saw him leaving on my way here from the men's room, where I was rudely interrupted midstream. A surprise like that, a guy could get hurt, you know."

She was in no mood for Stan tonight. "I doubt you'll suffer any damage." She waved him out. "Go on. Just lock the door behind you. I can let the police in."

Her nervousness must have conveyed itself and made him feel like a deserter. "No, I'll wait with you," he said glumly. "Go brew yourself some tea or something. You look rattled."

She *was* rattled. Tea sounded like a good idea. She headed for the employee kitchen, but never made it. An obnoxious buzzer sounded throughout the building, announcing that someone was at the main entrance.

Reversing her direction, she rushed toward the front of the building and was relieved to see two uniformed policemen on the other side of the glass door. Never mind that they appeared to be fresh out of the academy. One of them looked too young to shave. But they were all business and introduced themselves with stiff-lipped laconism.

"Thank you for coming so quickly."

"We'd been out this way and were headed back when we got the call," one explained. He and his partner were looking at her strangely, as most people did when they first met her. The sunglasses made them instantly curious.

Without acknowledging either her glasses or their curiosity, she led Officers Griggs and Carson through the labyrinth of dark corridors. "There's a recording of the call in the studio."

The unremarkable exterior of the building hadn't prepared them for the electronic sophistication of the studio. They gazed about them with curiosity and awe. She brought them back on track by introducing Stan. Their acknowledgments were clipped. No one shook hands. Paris used the mouse on the Vox Pro computer to play Valentino's recorded call.

No one spoke while they listened. Officer Griggs stared at the ceiling, Carson at the floor. When it ended, Griggs raised his head and cleared his throat, seemingly embarrassed by Valentino's crude language. "Do you get calls like this often, Ms. Gibson?"

"Weird and kooky sometimes. Heavy breathers and dirty propositions, but nothing like what you've just heard. Never anything threatening. Valentino has called before. He tells me about a wonderful new girlfriend, or a recent breakup that left him heartbroken. He's never said anything like this. Never anything even close to this."

"You think it's the same guy?"

They all turned to Stan, who had ventured the idea.

He continued, "Somebody else could have borrowed the name Valentino because they've heard him on your show and know that he's a regular caller."

"I guess it's possible," Paris said slowly. "I'm almost positive that Valentino's voice is disguised. It never sounds quite natural."

"That's not a common name either," Griggs said. "Do you think it's legit?"

"I have no way of knowing that. Sometimes a caller is reluctant to give even a first name, preferring to remain totally anonymous."

"Do you have a way of tracing calls?"

"Ordinary caller ID. One of our engineers added software to the Vox Pro that would give us a readout of the number, if it was available. Each call is also date and time stamped."

She brought up the information on the computer screen. There was no name, but a local telephone number, which Carson jotted down.

"This is a good start," he said.

"Maybe," Griggs said. "Considering what he called to say, why would he use a traceable number?"

Paris read between the lines. "You think it was a hoax?"

Neither of the policemen answered her directly. Carson said, "I'll call the number, see if anyone answers."

He used his cell phone, and after listening through numerous rings concluded that no one was going to pick up. "No voice mail either. Better call it in." He punched in digits, then while he was giving Valentino's number to whomever was on the other end, Griggs told her and Stan that the number would be traced.

"But my guess is that it was a guy using a name he'd heard on your program and just trying to get a reaction out of you."

"Like the sickos who make obscene phone calls," Stan said.

Griggs bobbed his cropped head. "Exactly like that. I bet we find a lonely drunk or a group of bored kids trying to have some fun by talking dirty, something like that."

"I hope you're right." Paris hugged herself and rubbed her arms for warmth. "I can't believe someone would do this as a joke, but I certainly prefer a joke to the alternative."

Carson disconnected. "They're on it. Shouldn't take long."

"You'll let me know what they find out?"

"Sure thing, Ms. Gibson."

Stan offered to follow her home, but it was a halfhearted offer and he seemed relieved when she declined. He bade them good night and left.

"How can we contact you when we know something?" Griggs asked as they wended their way through the building, toward the entrance.

She gave him her home telephone number, emphasizing that it was unlisted. "Of course, Ms. Gibson."

It surprised the two policemen that she was the one to lock up the building for the night. "Are you here alone every night?" Carson asked as they walked her to her car.

"Except for Stan."

"What does he do and how long has he worked here?"

He doesn't do much of anything, she thought wryly. But she told them that he was an engineer. "He's on standby if anything should go wrong with the equipment. He's been here for a couple of years."

"Nobody else works the night shift?"

"Well, there's Marvin. He's been doing our janitorial service for several months."

"Last name?"

"I don't know. Why?"

"Never can tell about people," Griggs said. "Do you get along with these guys all right?"

She laughed. "Nobody gets along with Marvin, but he's not the type to make a scary phone call. He only speaks when spoken to, and then he more or less grunts."

"What about Stan?"

She felt disloyal talking about him behind his back. If she spoke candidly, it wouldn't be a flattering description, so she told them only what was relevant. "We get along fine. I'm sure neither of them had anything to do with that call."

Griggs smiled at her and closed his small notebook with a decisive snap. "Doesn't hurt to follow up."

Her home telephone was ringing when she let herself in. She rushed to answer. "Hello?"

"Ms. Gibson, it's Officer Griggs."

"Yes?"

"Did you get in okay?"

"Yes. I just disengaged my alarm. Have you learned anything?"

"That number belongs to a pay phone near the UT campus. A squad car was dispatched to check it out but nobody was around. The phone's outside a pharmacy that closed at ten. Place and parking lot were deserted."

In effect, they were back to where they had started. She had hoped they would trace the number to a sad and lonely individual like Griggs had described, a lost soul who had threatened her and an imaginary captive in a dire attempt to get attention.

Her initial misgivings returned. "So what now?"

"Well, there's not really anything to be done unless he calls again. I don't think he will, though. It was probably someone just trying to rile you. Tomorrow night, we'll have squad cars patrolling the area around that phone booth, watching for anyone lurking in the vicinity."

That wasn't satisfactory, but it was all she was going to get. She thanked him. He and his partner had done what was expected of them, but she wasn't ready to concede that Valentino's call was a prank and nothing to worry about. Even the origin of the call was worrisome. Wouldn't someone seeking attention leave obvious clues so that he could be traced and identified, chastened by the police, maybe even written up in the newspaper?

Valentino had used a public telephone so the call couldn't be traced. He didn't want to be identified.

That disturbing thought was uppermost in her mind as she made her way through the living area of her house, down the hallway, and into her bedroom. As always when she returned home from work, the rooms were dark and silent.

The houses neighboring hers were also dark and hushed at this hour, but there was a difference. In those houses, the prayers of children had been heard before they were tucked in. Husbands and wives had kissed good night. Some had made love before settling beneath their blanket. They shared a bed, body heat, dreams. They shared their lives. Darkness was relieved by nightlights, small beacons of comfort that shone in rooms littered with toys and shoes, with the accoutrements of busy family life.

The nightlights in Paris's house only emphasized the sterile neatness of the rooms. Her movements were the only source of sound.

She slept alone. That wouldn't have been her first choice, but that's the way it was, and she had come to accept it.

Tonight, however, the solitude was unnerving. And the cause was Valentino's call.

She'd had years of experience listening to voices, picking up nuances in speech, detecting underlying messages, separating truth from lies, and hearing more than what was said out loud. She was able to draw several conclusions about a person based strictly on his or her inflections. Calls had left her feeling happy, sad, reflective, annoyed, and, on occasion, downright angry.

None had left her feeling afraid. Until tonight.

chapter *four*

*H*er limbs were beginning to cramp from being held in one position for so long, and an itch on the sole of her foot was driving her nuts. Her face hurt and she could feel it swelling. She ached all over.

That son of a bitch, she thought, unable to curse him out loud because of the tape over her mouth.

Why had she ever thought he was so special? It wasn't like he took her to fabulous places and spent money on her. They'd never been anywhere together except this place, and it was a rathole.

She didn't know anything about him, not where he worked, not even his name. She'd never learned his name even by accident. It wasn't printed on anything in the apartment, no subscription magazines or mail, nothing. He remained nameless, and that should have been her first clue that he wasn't classy and intriguing, but just flat-out, freaking weird.

The second time they were together, he had defined the nature of their relationship. Laid down the ground rules, so to speak. He had opened the conversation while spreading baby oil over her, hoping to achieve a special effect in a series of photographs.

"Your friend . . . the one you were with the night we met."

"You mean Melissa?" she'd asked, feeling a stab of jealousy. Was he wanting to invite Melissa to join them in a ménage à trois? "What about her?"

"Have you told her about us?"

"I haven't had a chance. Her folks made her go to France with them for vacation. I haven't seen or talked to her since the night I met you."

"Have you told anyone about me and what we do here?"

"Oh, sure. I announced it over breakfast to my parents." His poleaxed expression made her giggle. "No, silly! I haven't told anyone."

"That's good. Because this is so special, I like thinking that you and I are each other's best-kept secret."

"We are each other's secret. I don't even know your name."

"But you know me."

He stared deeply into her eyes, and she was reminded of her first impression of him, that he could see straight into her innermost being. He apparently had felt the instantaneous connection that she had. After all, he'd told her that first night that he loved her.

The secrecy was probably necessary because of a wife who knew nothing about his "hobby." She envisioned his missus as a missionary-position-only prude who would never understand, much less consent to, his need for variety and excitement. Pictures of Mrs. No-name masturbating? Get real. Never in a million. Probably not even a bare-boob shot.

That night his lovemaking had been especially ardent. He was focused, you might say, not just his camera. She lost count of the number of times they did it, but it was always different, so it never got boring. He couldn't get enough of her and told her so. It was a heady experience, being practically worshiped by a man so classy he could probably have any woman. She had thought she would never want it to end.

But that had been then.

Each time she saw him, his jealousy increased, until it began to irritate her and rob her of the pleasure of being with him. No matter how good the sex was, it wasn't worth the hassle he gave her about other men.

She had thought about standing him up tonight, but then changed her mind. He was going to take it hard whenever she told him she didn't want to see him anymore. She dreaded a scene, but better to put him out of his misery sooner rather than later.

He had been waiting for her at the appointed place. And, unlike the night they'd met, he didn't look at all cool and relaxed. He was agitated and edgy. The moment she joined him in his car, he started in on her. "You've been with somebody else, haven't you?"

She supposed she should be flattered that he was jealous, but she had a headache and was in no mood for the third degree. "Do you have a joint?" Having learned that she was fond of smoke, he always had some for her.

"In the glove compartment."

There were three in a Ziploc bag. She lit one and inhaled deeply. "Best thing for a headache." Sighing, she laid her head on the headrest and closed her eyes.

"Who was he?"

"Who was who?"

"Don't jerk me around."

His tone brought her head up.

"You've already been with someone tonight, haven't you?" His fingers were clenching the steering wheel. "Don't bother lying about it. I know you've just had sex with someone else. I can smell him on you."

At first she was surprised and a bit unnerved that he knew. Had he been spying on her? But the uneasiness soon gave way to anger. Why was it any of his business who and when she screwed?

"Look, maybe getting together tonight isn't a good idea," she'd said. "I'm PMSing and I don't need any shit from anybody. Okay?"

His anger dissolved instantly. "I'm sorry I raised my voice. It's just . . . I thought . . ."

"What?"

"That we had something special here."

That's when she should have told him that she didn't want to see him again. Right then he'd given her an opportunity, but, damn it, she hadn't taken it. Instead she'd said, "I don't like you ragging me about where I go, what I do, and who I do it with. I get enough of that at home." She leaned back and pulled deeply on the joint. "Either chill or take me back to my car."

He chilled. He was subdued, even a little sullen, when they reached the apartment. "Want some wine?"

"Don't I always?"

She was already high from the weed. Might as well go all out and get really wasted. One mercy fuck, then she'd tell him they needed to cool it for a while—read *forever*—then she'd get the hell out of here and never come back.

His computer monitor was the only source of light in this room where the shades were always drawn. One of the more graphic photos of her was on his screen saver.

Seeing it, she said, "Tsk, tsk. That's definitely one of the 'afterglows,' isn't it? I'm such a naughty girl. Naughty but nice, right?" She winked at him as she accepted the glass of wine he brought from the kitchen.

She drank it like water, burped loudly and wetly, then extended the empty glass toward him in an impertinent request for a refill.

"You're acting like a slut." He calmly took the glass from her and set it on the nightstand. Then he slapped her. He slapped her so hard that tears came to her eyes even before the rocket of pain from her cheekbone reached her brain.

She cried out, but was too shocked to articulate a word.

He pushed her back onto the bed. She landed hard. The room seemed to tilt. She was more wasted than she'd thought. She struggled to get up. "Hey! I don't—"

"Oh, yes, you do."

He splayed his hand over her chest, holding her down while he wrestled with his belt and fly. Then he began tearing at her clothing. She swatted his hands, kicked at him, and called him every name in the book, but he wouldn't be stopped.

He pushed himself into her with such force that she screamed. He covered her mouth with his hand. "Shut up," he hissed, so close to her face she felt a shower of spit.

She bit into the flesh beneath his thumb. He yelped and withdrew his hand. "You bastard," she yelled. "Get off me."

To her astonishment, he began to laugh softly. "You fell for it. You thought I was serious."

She stopped struggling. "Huh?"

"I was just fulfilling your rape fantasy."

"You're crazy."

"Am I?" He thrust hard into her. "Can you honestly say you don't like it?"

"Damn right. I hate it. I hate you, you son of a bitch."

That caused him to smile, because in spite of what she said, she was responding. When it was over, each was exhausted and glistening with sweat.

He recovered first and went for his camera. "Stay just as you are," he said as he clicked off the first shot.

The flash seemed exceptionally bright. She was good and truly stoned.

"Don't move," he told her. "I have an idea."

Move? She was too lethargic to move. Her entire body throbbed, starting with her cheekbone—how was she going to explain a bad bruise?—and all the way down to her splayed thighs. Christ, she still had her sandals on. How funny was that? But she was too tired to trouble herself with taking them off. Besides, he had told her not to move.

Maybe she dozed for a minute or two. Next thing she knew he was back, bending over her, pulling her wrists together.

"What's that?" She roused herself and saw that he was using a necktie to bind her wrists together.

"A prop for a photograph. You've been a bad girl. You need to be punished." He climbed off the bed and picked up his camera and adjusted the focus.

That's when it began to get creepy and she felt the first twinges of apprehension. She had struggled to sit up. "Have I mentioned that I'm not into bondage?"

"This isn't bondage, this is punishment," he said absently as he moved to the lamp. He adjusted the shade, setting it first at one angle, then another, causing shadows to shift across her body.

Okay. Enough of this. She'd had it. After tonight, no more of him. Posing for him had been fun. It had been something different and, admittedly, it had been a kick to later look at the pictures of herself.

But he was getting too possessive and too . . . too out there.

"Look," she recalled saying sternly, "I really want you to untie my hands now."

Finally satisfied with the lighting, he began setting up the tripod.

Taking another tack, she softened her tone. "I'll do anything you want. You know I will. All you have to do is ask. Anything."

He still didn't seem to be listening. While he was distracted, she had inched toward the edge of the bed, calculating the distance to the door. But when she looked at it, something struck her as odd, and a cold dart of fear went through her when she realized that there was no doorknob on this side. Only a brass disk where the doorknob should have been.

That's when he had stopped tinkering with the camera. No doubt sensing her alarm, he had smiled down at her. "Where do you think you're going?"

"I want you to untie me."

"You moved and spoiled the lighting," he chided gently.

"Lighting, my ass, I'm *leaving*."

Her cheerleading days had paid off. She came off the bed with surprising strength and agility. But she didn't get far. He caught her by the hair and yanked her back, then shoved her down onto the bed.

"You can't keep me here," she'd cried.

"You just had to ruin it, didn't you?"

"Ruin what?"

"Us."

"There isn't any 'us,' you sick wacko."

"You had to cheat on me. Just like the others. Didn't you think I'd find out? I listen to Paris Gibson, too, you know. She put your call on the air. Thousands of people heard you telling her that you felt smothered by my possessiveness. You were going to take her advice and dump me, weren't you?"

"Oh, Jesus."

He'd stood over her, both fists clenched at his sides as though he were forcibly suppressing his rage. "You can't treat people like toilet paper and get away with it, you know."

And because he had become so freaking scary, she had wisely shut up.

He had taken a few more photos, then decided that her feet also needed to be tied. She had fought him as if her life depended on it, but he'd eventually slapped her so hard her ears rang. That was the last thing she heard.

When she came to, she was spread-eagled, her hands and feet tied to the bed frame beneath the box springs, her mouth taped shut. The apartment was empty. He was gone. She was alone, and no one knew where she was.

Over the passing hours, she had devised a dozen means of escape, but dismissed the ideas almost as soon as she conceived them. None was workable. She was helpless to do anything but wait for him to come back for more of his sick sex games.

Jesus, she thought, *what have I gotten myself into?*

"I hope you've enjoyed this evening of classic love songs. Please join me again tomorrow night. I'll be looking forward to it. Until then, this is Paris Gibson on FM 101.3. Good night."

Great. Now she didn't even have Paris to keep her company.

chapter *five*

Gavin Malloy was awfully drunk. The pleasant buzz from the cheap tequila wasn't quite so pleasant any longer. It was too hot to be drinking tequila shots. He should have stuck to beer. But he had needed something strong and nasty to drown his depression.

The hell of it was, he was still depressed.

The evening had been spoiled for him early on. His drinking had accomplished nothing except to make him light-headed, sweaty, and nauseous. Blearily he looked toward a clump of scraggly cedar trees and wondered if he could cover the distance over the rocky ground before he puked. Probably not.

Besides, he'd seen a couple disappear behind the trees a while ago. If they were still doing what they'd gone there to do, they wouldn't appreciate him hurling on them. Talk about coitus interruptus.

He chuckled at the thought.

"What're you laughing at?" his new friend asked, nudging him in the gut, which caused the tequila to slosh. The guy's name was Craig something. If he'd ever heard his last name, he'd forgotten it. Craig drove a Dodge Ram pickup, the biggest one made. Jet black. Fully loaded. It was one badass truck.

Gavin, Craig, and several others had been hanging out in the bed of the pickup for hours, waiting for something to happen. A group of girls had come by earlier, drunk some of their tequila, showed them just enough skin to get them excited, then wandered away with promises to return. So far they hadn't.

"What's funny?" Craig asked again.

"Nothing. Just thinking."

"'Bout what?"

What had he been thinking? He couldn't remember. Must not've been very important. "My old man," he said around a belch. Yeah, his old man had been in the back of his mind all night, bothering him like an itch he couldn't reach.

"What about him?"

"He's gonna shit 'cause I went out tonight. He grounded me."

"That sucks."

"You got grounded?" another guy jeered. "What are you, twelve?"

Gavin didn't know his name, only that he was an asshole with bad skin and worse breath who thought he was a lot cooler than he was.

Gavin had moved to Austin from Houston a week after the spring semester ended. Finding a new crowd during summer break hadn't been easy, but he had joined this group, who accepted him once they learned he was a guy who liked to party as much as they did.

"Awww, Gavin's scared of his daddy," the jerk taunted.

"I'm not scared of him. I just dread having my ass chewed again."

"Save yourself the hassle." This from the optimist who'd showed them earlier his inventory of condoms. "Wait till he goes to bed before you sneak out."

"I tried that already. He's a freaking bat. He's got like built-in radar or something."

This conversation was making the lousy evening lousier. Nothing could cheer him up tonight, not more tequila, not even the return of the girls, and chances were excellent that they weren't going to come back as promised. Why would they waste their time on losers like this bunch, like him?

He stood up, swaying dangerously. "I'd better split. If I'm lucky, he won't be home yet. He's with his girlfriend."

He waded through the others, then jumped off the tailgate. But he miscalculated the distance to the ground as well as the weakness in his knees and wound up facedown in the dirt.

His new buddies howled. Weak with laughter himself, he struggled to get upright. His T-shirt was so wet with sweat that when he tried to dust himself off, he left streaks of mud across the front of it.

"Tomorrow night," he told his friends as he staggered away. Where had he left his car?

"Don't forget tomorrow is your turn to bring the booze," Craig called.

"I'm broke."

"Steal it from your old man."

"I can't. He checks the bottles."

"Jesus, is he a cop in his spare time?"

"I'll see what I can do," Gavin mumbled as he turned in the general direction of where he'd parked.

"What if Miss Hotpants comes looking for you?" It was the asshole, calling to him in a singsong voice. His grin was ugly and goading. "What should we tell her? That you had to go home to your daddy?"

"Get fucked."

The obnoxious kid hooted. "Well, it's for sure you won't. Not tonight anyway."

One of the others muttered, "Shut up, dickhead."

"Yeah, give it a rest," the condom guy said.

"What? Wha'd I do?"

Craig spoke softly. "She dumped him."

"She did? When?"

Gavin moved out of earshot, which was just as well. He didn't want to hear any more.

He located his car. It wasn't that difficult to spot among all the others because it was a piece of shit. No badass pickup or sports car for him. Oh, no, nothing like that for Gavin Malloy. And you could forget a motorcycle. That wasn't going to happen as long as his old man was in charge, and probably not as long as he was drawing breath.

His car was a snore. It was a sensible, good-mileage means of transportation that would spoil the racy image of a Mormon soccer mom. And he was expected to be grateful for it.

He'd gotten a lecture when he expressed his low opinion of it. "A car isn't a toy, Gavin. Or a status symbol. This is a reliable first car. When you've proved that you're responsible enough to take care of it and use it safely, I'll consider an upgrade. Until then . . ." Blah-blah-blah.

The thing was an embarrassment. When the fall semester started at his new school, he would probably be laughed off campus for driving this heap. The dorkiest of the dorks wouldn't want to be seen with him.

In his present condition, he had no business driving anything and was just sober enough to realize it. He concentrated hard on keeping the center stripe in focus. But that only seemed to increase his dizziness.

He was still several blocks from home when he was forced to pull over, get out, and vomit. He spewed a torrent of tequila on some poor sucker's flower bed that formed a neat circle of color around the mailbox. Someone would have a disgusting surprise when they came out to get the mail tomorrow. To say nothing of the mailman.

Coordination shot, he climbed back into his car and drove the remainder of the way to the new house his dad had bought for them. It wasn't bad. In fact, Gavin kinda liked it. Especially the pool. But he didn't want his dad to know he liked it.

He was relieved to see that his old man's car wasn't in the driveway. But Gavin wouldn't put it past him to have laid a trap, so he slipped into the house through the back door and paused to listen. His dad would love to catch him sneaking in so he could ground him for longer, take away his cell phone, his computer, his car, and make his life even more miserable than it was.

That was his parents' main mission in life—to make *him* miserable.

Satisfied that the house was empty, he went to his room. His old man must still be with Liz. Screwing like rabbits, no doubt. They never did it here in his dad's bed. Did they think he was stupid, that he didn't know they were having sex when they spent the evening at her place?

It was easy to imagine Liz in bed. She had a hot body. But his old man? Rutting? No way. Gavin couldn't imagine anything more gross.

In his bedroom he turned on his computer even before he switched on the desk lamp. He couldn't fathom life without a computer. How had people survived before them? If his dad really wanted to punish him, that's the privilege he would revoke.

He checked for email. There was one from his mom, which he deleted without reading. Anything she had to say was salve for her conscience and he didn't want to hear it.

You'll come to realize that this is best for all of us.

You and your future are our main concerns, Gavin.

Once you have adjusted to the change . . .

Sure, Mom. Whatever you say, Mom. Bullshit, Mom.

He sat down at the desk and began composing an email letter. But not to his mother. His anger with her was mild compared to the animosity he felt for the recipient of this letter. Not that he planned on sending it. And because he didn't, he poured out all the anger that had been roiling inside him for days.

"What makes you think you're so hot anyway?" he wrote. "I've seen better. I've *had* better."

"Gavin?"

When the overhead light flashed on, he nearly jumped out of his skin. He quickly exited his email before his old man could read what was on his screen. He pivoted in his chair, hoping he didn't look guilty. "What?"

"I'm home."

"So?"

"You okay?"

"Why wouldn't I be? I'm not a kid."

"Did you eat some dinner?"

"Oh yeah," he said, smacking his lips. "Microwaved leftover pizza."

"You were invited to join Liz and me. You chose not to."

"Bet that broke your heart."

In the even, unruffled voice Gavin hated, his dad said, "If I hadn't wanted you to come along, I wouldn't have invited you." He came into the room. Gavin thought, *Oh, great.* "What've you been doing all evening?"

"Nothing. Surfing the net."

"What's that on your shirt?"

Perfect. He'd forgotten about the filth on his T-shirt. Dirt. Probably vomit, too. Ignoring the question, he turned back to face the computer. "I'm busy."

His dad took him by the shoulder and turned him around. "You went out. Your car isn't in the same place it was when I left and the hood is warm."

Gavin laughed. "You're checking the temperature of my car's engine? You need to get a life."

"And you need to get with the program." His father said this in a raised voice, which was rare. "You stink of vomit and you're drunk. Driving drunk, you could've killed somebody."

"Well, I didn't. So relax and leave me alone."

Dean stuck out his hand, palm up. "Give me your car keys."

Gavin glared at him. "If you think taking my keys will keep me cooped up in here, you're wrong."

Dean said nothing, just kept his hand extended. Gavin fished the keys from the pocket of his jeans and dropped them into his father's palm. "I hate the damn car anyway, so no big loss."

His dad pocketed the keys but didn't leave. He sat down on the edge of the unmade bed. "Now what?" Gavin groaned. "One of your famous lectures on how I'm pissing my life away?"

"Do you think I enjoy punishing you, Gavin?"

"Yeah, I think you do. I think you get off on being the big, bad father, having me to boss around. You enjoy telling me everything I'm doing wrong."

"That's ridiculous. Why do you say that?"

"Because you've never done anything wrong in your whole goddamn life. Mr. Perfect, that's you. It must be boring as shit to be so right all the time."

He was surprised to see his dad smile. "I'm far from right all the time and nowhere near perfect. Ask your mother. She'll tell you. But I know I'm right about one thing."

His dad paused and looked at him hard, probably hoping he would ask what that one thing was. He could wait till hell froze over. Finally he said, "It's right that you're living with me now. I'm glad you are. I want you here with me."

"Right. I'm sure you're just thrilled over the new living arrangements. You love having me around, cramping your style, getting in the way."

"In the way? Of what?"

"Of everything." The exclamation caused his voice to crack. He hoped his dad didn't mistake it for emotion, which it sure as hell wasn't. "I'm in the way of your life. Your new job. Liz."

"You're not in the way, Gavin. You're my family, my son. Liz and I wanted you with us tonight."

He scoffed. "For a cozy dinner? Just the three of us. Your new family. Then what? What was I supposed to do when you took her home? Wait in the car while you went inside for a quick blow job?"

He knew instantly that he'd gone too far. His dad wasn't one to fly off the handle when he got angry. He didn't lose his temper, rant and rave, stomp around, yell, or throw things. Instead, Mr. Self-control went very still. His lips narrowed and something funny happened to his eyes that made them seem to harden and sharpen and go right through you like steel picks.

But apparently there was a limit to his old man's restraint, and he'd just reached it.

Before he had even processed all this, his father was on his feet, and he was on the receiving end of a backhanded smack that caught him hard across the mouth and split his lip.

"You don't want to be treated like a kid? Fine. I'll treat you like an adult. That's what I would have done to any grown man who said something like that to me."

Gavin struggled to hold back tears. "I hate you."

"Well, too bad. You're stuck with me." He went out, soundly pulling the door shut behind him.

Gavin launched himself out of the chair. He stood in the center of his messy room, bristling with anger and frustration. But realizing he had nowhere to run, and no means of running if he had somewhere to go, he threw himself onto his bed.

He made swipes at the snot, tears, and blood that had mingled on his face. He felt like blubbering. He wanted to draw himself into the fetal position and cry like a baby. Because his life sucked. All of it. He hated everything and everybody. His dad. His mom. The city of Austin. Women. His stupid friends. His ugly car.

Most of all he hated himself.

chapter *six*

Without making it too obvious, Sergeant Robert Curtis was trying to see past the dark lenses of her sunglasses. Catching himself staring, he hastily held a chair for her. "Forgive my lack of manners, Ms. Gibson. I'll admit to being a little starstruck. Have a seat. Can I get you some coffee?"

"I'm fine, thanks. And I'm hardly a star."

"I beg to differ."

Curtis was a detective for the Austin Police Department's Central Investigative Bureau. He was fiftyish, compactly built, and neatly turned out, down to a polished pair of cowboy boots, the heels of which added a couple of inches to his stature. Although he was still no taller than she, he gave off an air of authority and confidence. A sport jacket was hanging on a coat tree, but his necktie was tightly knotted beneath a starched collar. His cuffs were monogrammed with his initials.

On the walls of the small enclosure were a detailed map of the state, another of Travis County, and a framed diploma. The built-in desk was nearly completely covered with paperwork and computer components, but somehow avoided looking messy.

Curtis sat down at his desk and smiled at her. "It's not every morning of the week I get visited by a radio personality. What can I do for you?"

"I'm not sure you can do anything."

Now that she was here, ensconced with a detective in his compact cubicle where he doubtless worked long hours, serving the public by snaring felons, she was second-guessing her decision to come.

Things that happened at two o'clock in the morning took on a different complexion in daylight. Suddenly, coming here seemed like a melodramatic and somewhat self-centered reaction to what probably amounted to a crank phone call.

"I called in a 911 last night," she began. "Actually early this morning. Two patrolmen, Griggs and Carson, responded. I have a case number for your reference." She gave him the number that Griggs had left with her.

"What kind of 911, Ms. Gibson?"

She gave him an account of what had happened. He listened attentively. His expression remained open and concerned. He didn't fidget as though she were wasting his time on something trivial. If he was faking his interest, he did it very well.

When she finished, she removed a cassette tape from her handbag and passed it to him. "I went to the station early this morning and made a copy of the call."

Insomnia had claimed her until dawn, when she finally surrendered to it. She got up, showered and dressed, and was back at the radio station by the time Charlie and Chad, the morning drive-time deejays, were reading the seven o'clock news headlines.

"I'll be happy to listen to your tape, Ms. Gibson," Curtis said. "But this department investigates homicide, rape, assault, robbery. Threatening phone calls . . ." He spread his hands wide. "Why'd you come to me?"

"I read your name in yesterday's newspaper," she admitted with chagrin. "Something about your testifying at a trial. I thought I'd get more personal attention if I asked to speak with a particular detective rather than just showing up without an appointment."

Now he looked chagrined. "You're probably right."

"And if my caller does what he threatens to do, it will fall to this department to investigate, won't it?"

Sobering instantly, Curtis left his chair and stepped outside the cubicle. He called across the room at large, asking if anybody had a cassette recorder handy. Within moments another plainclothes detective appeared with one. "Here you go."

He regarded Paris with patent curiosity as he handed the machine to Curtis, whose brusque, "Thanks, Joe," was as good as a dismissal. The other man withdrew.

Sergeant Curtis had been a random selection, but she was glad she'd come to him. He obviously had some clout and wasn't reluctant to use it.

He returned to his seat and inserted the tape into the recorder, saying in an undertone, "I see word has gotten around as to who you are."

Maybe, Paris thought. Or maybe the detective was simply wondering why she hadn't removed her sunglasses. This wasn't a particularly bright environment. In fact, it was a room without windows.

Curtis and the other detective probably assumed that she wore the sunglasses like a celebrity would, to conceal her identity in public or to add to her mystique as a media personality, that she wore them to shut others out. It would never occur to them that she wore the glasses to shut herself in.

"Let's see what Mr. . . . what was it? Valentino? . . . has to say for himself." Curtis pressed the Play button. *This is Paris. Hello, Paris. This is Valentino.*

When the tape ended, Curtis tugged thoughtfully on his lower lip, then asked, "Mind if I play it again?"

Without waiting for her consent, he rewound the tape and restarted it. As he listened, he frowned with concentration and rolled his University of Texas class ring around his stubby finger.

At the end of the tape, she asked, "What do you think, Sergeant? Am I reading too much into a crank call?"

He asked a question of his own. "Did you try to call the number?"

"I was so stunned, I didn't think of calling back immediately, but I suppose I should have."

He dismissed her concern with a wave. "He probably wouldn't have answered anyway."

"He didn't when Carson called later. No voice mail either. Just an unanswered ring."

"The number on the caller ID, you say it was traced to a pay phone?"

"I'm sure the details are in the report, but Griggs told me that a patrol car in that area had been dispatched to check out the phone booth. But by that time—at least half an hour, maybe more—whoever placed the call was gone."

"Somebody could have seen him at the phone booth. Did the patrolmen ask around?"

"There was nobody to ask. According to Griggs, the area was deserted when the patrol car arrived." Curtis's questions were validating her concern, but that only increased her anxiety. "Do you think Valentino was telling the truth? Has he kidnapped a girl he plans to murder?"

Curtis made balloons of his ruddy cheeks before expelling a long breath. "I don't know, Ms. Gibson. But if he has, and if he sticks to his three-day deadline, we don't have time to sit around and talk about it. I don't want another kidnap-rape-murder case on my desk if I can possibly avoid it." He stood up and reached for his jacket.

"What can we do?"

"We start by trying to determine if he's for real or just a nut trying to win the attention of his favorite celebrity." By now he was ushering her through the maze of similar cubicles toward the set of double doors through which she'd entered the CIB.

"How do we make that determination?"

"We go to the authority on the subject."

Just as Dean was leaving the house, Liz called from the Houston airport. "You're already in Houston?"

"My flight from Austin was at six-thirty."

"Brutal."

"Tell me." After a short pause, she asked, "What happened with Gavin when you got home last night?"

"Your basic open warfare, both sides scoring hits and suffering casualties."

He balanced the cordless phone between chin and shoulder and poured himself a glass of orange juice. He'd lain awake for hours last night, and when he finally did fall asleep, he'd gone comatose. His alarm had been going off for half an hour before it awakened him. No time to brew coffee this morning.

"Well, at least he was home when you got there," Liz said. "He hadn't disobeyed."

Not wanting to recount his argument with Gavin, Dean harrumphed a nonverbal agreement. "What time is your first meeting in Chicago?"

"As soon as I arrive at the hotel. I hope O'Hare isn't too hairy and I can get through it quickly. What have you got on tap today?"

He outlined his day. She said she needed to run, that she'd just wanted to say hi before her flight to Chicago. He told her he was glad that she'd caught him and wished her a safe flight. She said, "I love you." And he replied with, "Love you, too."

After disconnecting, Dean bowed his head, closed his eyes, and tapped his forehead—hard—with the telephone as though he were paying some kind of unorthodox self-flagellating penance.

Rather than getting his day off to the good start that Liz had obviously intended, her call put him out of sorts. Add the blasted heat and Austin's rush-hour traffic, and he was in a testy mood when he reached his office fifteen minutes late.

"Good morning, Ms. Lester. Any messages?"

Dean shared the secretary with several other people. She was competent. And friendly. His first day on the job, she had informed him that she was the divorced mother of two daughters and that it was okay for him to call her by her first name.

Unless his eyes were deceiving him, and he didn't think they were, since his arrival her necklines had gotten progressively lower and her hemlines higher. This gradual reduction of textiles could be in correlation with the rising summertime temperature, but he doubted it. Just to be safe, he had stuck to calling her Ms. Lester.

"Messages are on your desk. A fresh pot of coffee is brewing. Soon as it's ready, I'll bring you some."

Fetching him coffee wasn't in her job description, but this morning he was glad she'd volunteered. "Great, thanks."

He went into his office and closed the door, discouraging further conversation. He slung his jacket onto the wall rack, loosened his tie, and unbuttoned his collar button. He sat down at his desk and riffled through his messages, happy to see there were no urgent ones. He needed a few minutes to decompress.

He swiveled his desk chair around and adjusted the window blind so he could see out. The sunlight was glaring, but that wasn't why he dug his fingers into his eye sockets, then wearily dragged his hands down his face.

What was he going to do about Gavin? How many times could he ground him? How many more privileges could he revoke? How many more scenes like the one last night could they withstand? Arguments such as that inflicted damage that was often irreparable. Could any relationship survive constant onslaughts like that?

He sorely regretted smacking him. Not that Gavin hadn't deserved it for the insulting crack he'd made. Still, he shouldn't have struck him. He was the grown-up and he should have behaved as such. To lose his temper like that was juvenile. And dangerous. Loss of control could wreak havoc, and he knew that better than anyone.

Besides, he was determined to be a positive role model for Gavin. He didn't want to preach to him, but to set a good example. Last night, he had sent the wrong message on how to manage anger, and he was sorry for it.

He ran his fingers through his hair and wondered what was taking the coffee so freaking long.

Should he send Gavin back to his mother? "Not an option," he muttered out loud. No way. For a long list of reasons that included welshing on the agreement he and Pat had reached about their son, but the main one being that Dean Malloy deplored failure. At anything. He threw in the towel only when absolutely forced to.

Gavin had told him—more like *accused* him—of always being right. He'd said that it must be boring as shit to be so right all the time. *Hardly, Gavin,* he thought cynically. He didn't feel right about anything. Obviously he wasn't doing right by his son.

Or by Liz. Not by a long shot was he doing right by Liz. How long could he put off doing something about that?

"Dr. Malloy?"

Thinking that Ms. Lester was bringing the long-awaited, high-octane coffee, he kept his back to the door. "Just set it on the desk, please."

"There's someone here to see you." Dean swiveled his chair around. "Sergeant Curtis from CIB asked for a minute of your time," the secretary told him. "Is it all right if he comes in?"

"Certainly." He'd met the detective only once, but he'd seemed like a stand-up kind of guy. Dean knew that he was a hard-working and well-respected member of the Austin PD. He stood up as Curtis walked in. "Good morning, Sergeant Curtis."

"Just plain Curtis. That's what everybody calls me. Do you prefer Doctor or Lieutenant?"

"How about Dean?" They met in the center of the office and shook hands.

"Is this a bad time?" Curtis asked. "I apologize for barging in on you unannounced, but this might turn out to be important."

"No problem. Coffee is on the way."

"Make that coffee for three. I'm not alone." Curtis stepped back into the open doorway and motioned someone forward.

Despite her sunglasses, Paris feared that her expression was no less revealing than Dean's.

He appeared to be as dumbfounded as she'd been a few moments ago when she read his name on the office door she was about to enter, unaware, unprepared, unbolstered, and unable to stop the inevitable.

He gaped at her for several seconds before managing to articulate a startled, "Paris?"

Curtis divided a surprised look between them.

"Should I bring more cups, Dr. Malloy?"

That from the secretary.

Dean's gaze remained fixed on Paris as he replied, "Please, Ms. Lester."

The secretary withdrew, leaving Paris, Dean, and the detective standing frozen in an awkward tableau like actors who had forgotten their lines. Finally Curtis placed his hand beneath her elbow and nudged her forward. Unwillingly she went farther into the office, into Dean's space.

And like any space Dean had ever occupied, he dominated it. Not just physically, with his above-average height and broad shoulders, but with the strength of his personality. Immediately one sensed that this was a man of principle, unshakable conviction, and unwavering determination. He could be your staunchest ally or your most feared adversary.

Paris had experienced him as both.

Her throat had constricted, as though every blood vessel leading from her heart had converged there. The oxygen in the room seemed insufficient. She was breathing with difficulty while striving to appear perfectly composed.

Dean wasn't doing so well either. When it became obvious that shock had robbed him of manners, Curtis motioned Paris into the nearest chair. That snapped Dean out of his daze. "Uh, yeah, please, sit. Both of you."

As they were taking their seats, Curtis said, "I'm not a detective for nothing. I gather you two know each other."

She relied on her voice to earn her living, but it had deserted her. She left it to Dean to do the talking.

"From Houston," he said. "Years ago. I was with the PD and Paris . . ."

He looked at her expectantly, leaving her no option but to take up the explanation. "I was a reporter for one of the television stations."

Curtis raised his pale eyebrows in surprise. "Television? I assumed you'd always been on radio."

She glanced at Dean, then shook her head. "I moved from TV to radio."

Curtis murmured an acknowledgment that said he understood the transition when clearly he didn't understand at all.

"Excuse me." Ms. Lester came in carrying a tray. As she set it on Dean's desk, she asked, "Cream and sugar, anyone?"

They all declined. She filled three mugs from a stainless-steel carafe, then asked Dean if there would be anything else. He shook his head and thanked her.

Curtis watched her leave. When he turned back around he remarked, "I'm impressed. They don't spring for personal assistants in CIB."

"What?" Dean looked at him with confusion, then at the empty doorway. "Oh, Ms. Lester. She's not my personal assistant. She just . . . She's just very efficient. Treats everybody over here like that."

"Over here" referred to the annex next door to the main building of police headquarters. It was accessible through a connecting parking garage, which was the route Paris and Curtis had taken. The detective didn't seem to buy Dean's explanation for the secretary's attention any more than Paris did, but he didn't comment on it further.

Paris wrapped both hands around the steaming mug of coffee, grateful for the warmth it provided. Dean took a gulp of his that probably blistered his tongue.

Curtis said, "I had no idea that I would be reuniting two long-lost friends."

"Paris didn't know about my transfer here," Dean said, watching her closely. "Or if she did—"

"I didn't. I assumed you were still in Houston."

"No."

"Hmm."

Curtis filled the ensuing gap in conversation. "Up until Dr. Malloy joined us, we used civilians and paid them a consulting fee. But for a long time, we'd been needing and wanting a psychologist on staff, a member of the department, someone with experience and training as a cop as well as a psychologist. Early this year, the funding was finally approved and we were lucky enough to lure Dr. Malloy here."

"How nice." She included both of them in her perfunctory smile.

After another short silence, Dean cleared his throat again and addressed the detective. "You mentioned a matter that could be important."

Curtis sought a more comfortable position in his chair. "Are you familiar with Ms. Gibson's radio program?"

"I listen to it every night."

Her head came up quickly and she looked at Dean with surprise. Their eyes connected for several seconds before he turned back to Curtis.

"Then you know she takes call-in requests and such," the detective said. Dean nodded. "Last night, she received a call that disturbed her. With cause." Curtis went on to explain the nature of Valentino's call, then concluded by saying, "I thought you might take a listen and give us your professional opinion."

"I'll be glad to. Let's hear it."

Curtis had brought the cassette player with him. He set it on the desk, rewound the tape, and after several false starts for which he apologized, her voice filled the taut silence: *This is Paris.*

By now she knew the dialogue word for word. As it played, she stared into her coffee mug, but in her peripheral vision she observed Dean. Individual parts of him. All of him. Surreptitiously she looked at his hands resting on the edge of his desk, fingers laced. He was slowly rubbing his thumbs together, and that, just that, caused a quiver deep in her belly.

Only once did she allow herself to look at his face. He'd been gazing into near space, but he must have felt her eyes on him because he focused on her sharply. His eyes still had the capability of making her feel like a butterfly pinned to a corkboard.

At one time, years ago, it had been thrilling to be looked at with that kind of intensity. Now it only made her remember things that should have been long forgotten. It resurrected sensations and emotions she had tried to bury and, until a few minutes ago, thought she had. She returned her gaze to her coffee mug.

When the tape ended, Dean asked if he could have a duplicate made.

"Of course," Curtis replied.

Dean ejected the tape and left the office only long enough to dispatch Ms. Lester on the errand. When he returned, Curtis said, "So you don't think this guy is just blowing smoke?"

"I want to listen to the recording several more times, but my first impression is that it's worrisome at the very least. Ever get a call like this before, Paris?"

She shook her head. "Listeners have reported UFOs, terrorist infiltration, asbestos in their attics. One night a woman called to tell me she had a snake in her bathtub and asked if I knew how to tell if it was poisonous. I get at least one proposal of marriage a week. I've had one offer of donor sperm. Hundreds of obscene propositions. But nothing like this. This . . . this *feels* different."

"Although he's called you before."

"A man identifying himself as Valentino calls periodically. I believe this is the same man, but I can't swear to it."

"Do you think he's someone you know?"

She hesitated before answering. "Honestly? I couldn't sleep last night for thinking about that. But I don't recognize the voice, and I believe I would."

"You would have an ear for voices," Dean said thoughtfully. "But it sounds to me as though he's trying to disguise his."

"To me, too."

"So it *could* be someone you know."

"I suppose. But I can't think of anyone who would play such a horrible prank."

"Have you recently made someone angry?"

"Not that I know of."

"Exchanged words?"

"I don't recall an incident like that."

"Have you said anything that would come across as an affront? To a coworker. Bank teller. Waiter. Grocery sacker. The guy who dries your windows at the car wash."

"No," she snapped. "I don't make a habit of provoking people."

Ignoring her annoyance, he pressed on. "Have you quarreled with a boyfriend? Ended a relationship? Broken someone's heart?"

She glared at him for several ponderous moments, then shook her head.

Serving as a tactful referee in a conflict he didn't understand, Curtis coughed behind his fist. "Couple of rookies, Griggs and Carson, handled this last night," he told Dean. "They were going to check out the radio station personnel first thing this morning. I'll follow up with them right now, see if they've learned anything. Excuse me."

Before she could protest—and how could she?—Curtis pulled his cell phone from the holster clipped to his belt and left the office.

Instead of warming her hands, the ceramic coffee mug had grown cold within them. She leaned forward and placed it on the edge of Dean's desk, giving the mug and the surface of the desk more focus than either warranted.

Unable to avoid it any longer, she looked at him. "I didn't plan this, Dean. When I came here this morning, I had no idea . . . I didn't know you were in Austin now."

"I could have told you at Jack's funeral. You wouldn't talk to me."

"No, I wouldn't."

"Why not?"

"It would have been inappropriate."

Leaning toward her, he said, softly but angrily, "After seven years?"

Jack had been the first to say that nobody could get to Dean the way she could. She seemed to be the only person on the planet with a knack for gouging a chink in his rigid self-control.

Still sounding angry, he said, "I thought the sunglasses were only for the funeral. Have you still got—"

"I'm not going to talk about this, Dean. I'd leave if I could. If I'd known who Sergeant Curtis was bringing me to see—"

"You'd have turned tail and run. That's your MO, isn't it?"

Before she could form a reply, Curtis returned. "They're checking out the janitor, Marvin Patterson. Nothing solid so far. There appears to be some confusion that they're trying to sort through. Should have some info soon. Stan Crenshaw . . ." Here he paused and looked at Paris. "He's related to the station's owner?"

"He's Wilkins Crenshaw's nephew."

"A nepotistic hiring?"

"To be sure," she said candidly. "Stan does as little as possible and isn't very good at what little he does. His laziness is irritating and often inconvenient for those of us who work with him, but on a personal level we get along. Besides, it couldn't have been either him or Marvin, even if one of them would do such a thing. They were in the building when the call came in."

"Telephones being the high-tech gadgets they are these days, I've got the department's electronics wizard working on that angle. Officers are also talking to the people who work in the nearby pharmacy, seeing if they can pick up something there. Either an employee or a customer who's got a fixation on you. But . . ." He paused to tug on his ear. "We don't actually have the commission of a crime here. Just the threat of one."

"It's a serious threat."

"Right," the detective conceded thoughtfully. "Valentino said he heard the woman talking about him on your show. Do you remember a call like the one he describes?"

"Not off the top of my head. It must have been fairly recent, though, and it was a call that I played on the air. That narrows it down considerably. But I never would have told a caller to 'dump' someone."

"He could've been lying about that," Dean said. She and Curtis looked at him for clarification. "The call from the girlfriend could be an invention to justify—even to himself—what he plans to do to her."

It was a grim surmise. During their reflective silence, Ms. Lester returned with the original tape and the requested duplication. Dean played it again. "Something really bothers me," he said when it ended. "He refers to 'girls,' not women."

"Diminishing a female's status," Curtis remarked.

"In his estimation, it does. That gives us a clue into this guy's mind-set. His basic dislike and mistrust of women comes through loud and clear. If I had to profile him based on no more than this conversation, I'd categorize him as an anger-retaliator rapist."

Apparently Curtis was acquainted with the clinical term. "He's angry with women in general over real or perceived injustices."

"Yes. Possibly a result of sexual abuse, even incest. A dangerous motivation," Dean said. "Sex is his method of punishment. That usually translates to violent rape. If he wants to make his victim bleed, as he told Paris, then he'll have no qualms about killing her." His lips formed a grim line, which expressed the apprehension that all were feeling. "Another thing, the only other Valentino I ever heard of was Rudolph."

"The silent-film star," Paris said.

"Right. And his best-known film was *The Sheik*."

"In which he kidnaps and seduces, rather forcibly, a young woman." She knew the movie. She and Jack had seen it at a classic-film festival. "Do you think that's why he's using that name?"

"It could be a coincidence, but I'm not prepared to dismiss it as such." He thought about it only a second longer. "In fact, Curtis, I'm not prepared to dismiss any of this. My recommendation is that you take him at his word."

The detective agreed with a somber nod. "Unfortunately, I agree."

"I'd like to work with you on the case."

"I welcome your input. We'll take Valentino's threat seriously until it proves to be a hoax."

"Or proves to be real," Paris added softly.

chapter *seven*

Judge Kemp granted the defense attorney's request for a thirty-minute recess to consult with his client, hopefully to urge him to accept a plea bargain that would end the trial and free up the judge's afternoon.

He used the half hour to retire to chambers and clip hairs from his nostrils with a tiny pair of silver scissors. He used a mirror with a magnifying power of five times actual size. Nevertheless, it was a delicate procedure. The sudden ringing of his cell phone almost cost him a punctured septum.

A bit irritably, he answered his wife's call.

"Janey's not in her room," she stated without preamble. "She hasn't been there all night."

"You told me she was in when we got home."

"I thought she was because I could hear the radio through her door. It was still on this morning. I thought that was odd, because you know what a late riser she is, but I figured she was sleeping through it.

"I knocked on her door around ten. I wanted to take her to that new tearoom for lunch. That would be something we could do together. And it's a lovely little place, really. Bea and I were there last week and they have an exceptional gazpacho."

"Marian, I'm in recess."

Reigned in, she continued, "She didn't answer my knock. At quarter to eleven, I decided to go in and wake her. Her room was empty and the bed hadn't been slept in. Her car isn't in the garage and none of the help has seen her."

"Maybe she got up early, made her bed, and left the house."

"And maybe the sky will fall this afternoon."

She was right. It was an absurd assumption. Janey had never made a bed in her life. Her refusal to do so was one of the reasons she'd been sent home from summer camp the one and only time they had ignored her protests and insisted she go.

"When did you last see her?"

"Yesterday afternoon," Marian replied. "She'd been lying out by the pool for hours. I persuaded her to come indoors. She's going to ruin her skin. She refuses to wear sunscreen. I've tried to tell her, but of course she won't listen. She says sunscreen is the stupidest thing she's ever heard of because it defeats the purpose.

"And, Baird, I really think you should say something to her about sunbathing topless. I realize it's her own backyard, but there are always workmen around here doing one project or another, and I refuse to allow them a free peep show. It's bad enough she wears a thong, which, if you ask me, looks not only distasteful and unladylike, but terribly uncomfortable."

This time she stopped herself from going off on a tangent. "Anyway, yesterday I coaxed her to come inside during the hottest part of the day. I reminded her that we were going to the awards dinner and that she was restricted to the house. She flounced upstairs without speaking to me, slammed her door, and locked it. Apparently, she left last night sometime after we did, and she hasn't been home since."

He hadn't noticed that Janey's car was missing because he'd left his out front overnight, not parked in the garage. The next time he grounded Janey he would remember to confiscate her car keys. Not that that would stop her from sneaking out of the house and meeting up with those wild friends of hers, whose influence was doubtless the cause of her misbehavior.

"Did you call her cell phone?"

"I get her voice mail. I've left repeated messages."

"Have you checked with her friends?"

"Several of them, but none claims to have seen her last night. Of course, they could be lying to cover for her."

"What about that tart, that Melissa she's been spending so much time with?"

"She's in Europe with her parents."

His secretary knocked softly, then poked her head in and told him that everyone was back in the courtroom.

"Listen, Marian, I'm sure she's just punishing us for punishing her. She wants to give you a scare, and she's succeeding. She'll turn up. It's not as if this is the first time she's stayed out all night."

The last time Janey had failed to come home, she'd come close to being booked into the Travis County jail for public lewdness. She and a group of friends had availed themselves of a hotel's outdoor hot tub. Guests had complained of noise. When hotel security officers checked on the nature of the disturbance, they discovered a bubbling cauldron of young people in varying degrees of drunkenness and nakedness, engaging in all manner of sexual activity.

His daughter was among the drunkest. She was definitely the most naked, according to the Austin policeman who had personally fished her out of the water and separated her from the young man with whom she was coupled.

He had wrapped her in a blanket before transporting her home rather than to jail. He'd done it as a favor to the judge, not out of kindness toward the girl who had hurled invectives at him when he delivered her to her parents' doorstep.

The officer had been thanked with a hundred-dollar bill, which had tacitly bought his promise to exclude Janey's name from the incident report.

"Thank God the media didn't get wind of that story," Marian said now, reading the judge's mind. "Can you imagine the damage your reputation would have suffered?" She sniffed delicately and asked, "What are you going to do, Baird?" Thereby effectually dumping the problem into his lap.

"I'm in court all day. I haven't got time to deal with Janey."

"Well, you can't expect me to drive all over Austin looking for her. I'd feel like a dogcatcher. Besides, you're the one with the contacts."

As well as the hundred-dollar bills, he thought sourly. Over the last few years, he'd liberally doled out C-notes to ensure that his daughter's shenanigans remained a private matter.

"I'll see what I can do," he grumbled. "But when she does reappear—as I'm certain she will—don't forget to page me. I'll have my pager on vibrate if I'm in court. Punch in three threes. Then I'll know she's at home and won't waste anyone's time looking for her."

"Thank you, dear. I knew I could depend on you to handle this."

Curtis invited Dean to join him for lunch and he accepted, but not naively. He figured the detective was after background information on Paris. He could hardly blame Curtis for being curious, especially after the charged atmosphere they'd created in his office this morning.

He wouldn't give him anything, nothing that Curtis couldn't learn for himself by reading a published bio, but it would be interesting to watch the detective in action.

They were on their way down the steps in front of the building when Curtis was hailed from behind. The young uniformed cop who had called after him had just emerged from the glass doors. He offered a breathless apology.

"I hate to hold you up, Sergeant Curtis."

"We're only going to lunch. Do you know Dr. Malloy?"

"Only by reputation. I'm a little late welcoming you to the Austin PD. Eddie Griggs." He extended his hand. "A pleasure, sir."

"Thank you," Dean said as they shook hands. "You two take your time, I'll wait over here in the shade."

"I don't think Sergeant Curtis will mind you hearing this, seeing as how you're working with him on that Paris Gibson call. That's what this is about. Well, sorta. Indirectly."

"Let's all get in the shade," Curtis suggested.

They moved closer to the building to take advantage of the sliver of shadow it cast on the blazing sidewalk. Traffic whizzed past on nearby Interstate 35, but the rookie made himself heard.

"You issued a heads-up memo?" he said to Curtis. "About missing persons reports?"

"That's right."

"Well, sir . . . Judge Baird Kemp?"

"What about him?"

"He's got a daughter. High school age. Wild as a March hare. Every now and then she gets a little too wild and crosses the line. She's real well known by cops on patrol after midnight."

He glanced around, checking to see if anyone entering or exiting the building was within hearing distance. "The judge is real generous to any officer who takes her home, keeps her out of jail and her name out of print."

"I get the picture," the detective said.

"So today," Griggs continued, "the judge called in a special request to some of his friends on the force. Seems that Janey—that's her name—didn't come home last night. Everyone's been asked to be on the lookout, and if she's spotted, the judge would be very appreciative to the officer who brought her home."

Dean hadn't yet met the judge, but he knew him by name. One

of his first duties in Austin had been to try to talk a prisoner into helping the police apprehend his partner in crime, who, by comparison, was the more evil of the two and was still at large.

The prisoner had refused to cooperate. "I'm not giving them shit, man."

"Them," as opposed to "you," because Dean had placed himself on the prisoner's side, becoming his friend, sympathizer, and confidant. The good cop.

"My trial was rigged! Fuckin' rigged," the prisoner ranted. "You hear what I'm saying, man? That judge swayed the jury. Smug motherfucker."

His regard for his trial judge didn't differ from that of most convicted criminals. They rarely had a kind word for the robed individual who, with a final bang of the gavel, sealed their bleak futures.

Eventually Dean got information from the prisoner that resulted in his partner's arrest, but the man had maintained his low opinion of Judge Kemp, and, based on what Griggs had just told them, Dean thought it might have been justified.

Curtis said, "In this county alone, there could be a hundred teenagers who didn't come home last night, and whose current whereabouts are unknown to their parents. And that would be a conservative estimate."

Dean was thinking of his own teenager, who had alarmed his mother on more than one occasion by not returning home until well into the next day. "I agree. It's too soon to jump to conclusions about one unaccounted-for girl, especially if she makes a habit of staying out."

"Judge Kemp would shit a brick if his 'special request' became an all-points bulletin," Curtis remarked, his distaste showing. "All the same, thanks for telling us about this, Griggs. Good follow-up and good hustle. How come you came in so early today?"

"Putting in overtime, sir. Besides, I hoped I could, you know, help Paris Gibson. She was pretty shook up last night."

"I'm sure she will appreciate your diligence."

Curtis's statement was made tongue in cheek. Apparently, he'd noticed the same thing Dean had—the kid was smitten with Paris.

"Let's give Miss Janey Kemp a few more hours to sober up and find her way home before we link her to Ms. Gibson's caller," Curtis said.

"Yes, sir." The young policeman's manner was so militarily correct, Dean almost expected him to salute. "Have a good lunch, sir. Dr. Malloy."

Curtis continued down the sidewalk, but Dean hung back, sensing that Griggs still had something on his mind. If it concerned Paris, he wanted to know what it was. "Excuse me, Griggs? If something's nagging at you, we'd like to hear it."

It was clear the rookie didn't want to step on the toes of a detective with rank or an officer with an alphabet soup of degrees behind his name and a Dr. in front of it. All the same, he seemed relieved that Dean had invited him to speak his mind.

"It's just that this girl goes looking for trouble, sir." He lowered his voice to a confidential pitch. "One of our undercover narcs at the high school? He says she's great looking and knows it. A . . . a real babe. Says she's made moves on him that almost made him forget he was a badge." Griggs's ears had turned red. Even his scalp was blushing through his buzz haircut.

Hoping to relax the younger man, Dean quipped, "I hate when that happens. One of the reasons I never worked undercover."

Griggs grinned as though happy to learn that Dean was just a guy after all. "Yeah, well, what I'm saying is, she might've placed herself in a situation where something bad could happen."

"Flirted with danger and got more than she bargained for?" Curtis asked.

"Something like that, sir. From what I know of her, she does what she wants to, when she wants to, and doesn't account to anybody. Not even to her folks. Perfect candidate to be slipped some Rohypnol. If she crossed paths with this Valentino, and he's done what he claims, nobody would know it for a while. And that could be bad."

Curtis asked if anyone had looked for Janey Kemp in places where she was known to hang out.

"Yes, sir. That's what the judge wanted done. Covertly, of course. Couple of intelligence officers are on it as well as the regular patrolmen. But it's summer, so the Sex Club meets outdoors more nights than not, and the meeting place changes every few nights to keep narcs and parents—"

"Sex Club?" Dean looked over at Curtis for an explanation, but the detective shrugged. Both looked back at Griggs.

Nervous again, the young officer shifted his weight from one polished shoe to the other. "You don't know about the Sex Club?"

● ● ●

Paris arrived home exhausted. This was normally the time of day she was getting up. Customarily she ate breakfast when everyone else was having lunch. Today she was off her schedule. If she didn't sleep a few hours this afternoon, she would be a zombie by sign-off time tonight.

But after her unexpected reunion with Dean, sleep was unlikely.

She made herself a peanut butter sandwich she didn't really want and sat at the kitchen table, a napkin in her lap, pretending it was an actual meal. As she ate, she sorted her mail.

When she came to the pale blue, letter-sized envelope with the familiar logo in the upper-left-hand corner, she stopped her methodic chewing. She washed down the bite of sandwich with a whole glass of milk, as though fortifying herself for the contents of the envelope.

The three-paragraph letter was from the director of Meadowview Hospital. Politely but firmly, in language that could not be misunderstood, he requested that she retrieve the personal belongings of former patient the late Mr. Jack Donner.

"Since you haven't responded to my numerous attempts to reach you by telephone," the letter read, "I can only assume that you never received those messages. Therefore, let this letter serve to notify you that Mr. Donner's belongings will be removed from the facility if you do not collect them."

Her deadline to comply was tomorrow. Tomorrow. And he meant it. The date was underlined.

While Jack was a patient at Meadowview, Paris had been on a first-name basis with everyone on staff, from the director to the custodian. This read like a letter to a stranger. He'd reached the limit of his patience with her, no doubt because she had ignored his telephone messages.

She hadn't been back to the private nursing facility since the day Jack died inside room 203. In the six months since then, she hadn't had the wherewithal to return, not even to pick up his personal belongings. With very few exceptions, she'd gone to the hospital every day for seven years, but after leaving it that final day, she'd been unable to make herself return.

Her reluctance to do so wasn't entirely selfish. She didn't want to dishonor Jack by remembering him lying in that hospital bed, his limbs withering even though they were exercised every day by Meadowview's capable staff of physical therapists. He'd been no more self-sufficient than a baby, unable to speak anything except gibberish, unable to feed himself, unable to do anything except take up space and rely on dedicated health care professionals to tend to even his most personal needs.

That was the condition in which he'd lived—existed—the last seven years of his life. He deserved better than to be remembered like that.

She folded her arms on the table and laid her head on them. Closing her eyes, she envisioned Jack Donner as he'd been when she met him. Strong, handsome, vital, self-confident Jack . . .

"So you're the new one who's causing such a sensation."

He had spoken from behind her. When she faced him, her first impression was of the cockiness of his grin. Her assigned cubicle in the news room was barely large enough to turn around in. It was crammed with boxes that she was in the process of unpacking. Jack had pretended not to notice that he was contributing to the crowded conditions.

Coolly she repeated, " 'New *one.*' "

"You're being talked about in the front offices. Don't force me to repeat what I've heard and risk a sexual harassment charge."

"I've just joined the news team, if that's what you mean."

"The 'award-winning' news team," he corrected, his grin stretching wider. "Don't you pay attention to our station's promos?"

"Are you in the promotions department?"

"No, I head the official host committee. In fact, I *am* the official host committee. It's my job to welcome all newcomers."

"Thank you. I consider myself welcomed. Now, if you'll—"

"Actually I'm in sales. Jack Donner." He stuck out his hand. They shook.

"Paris Gibson."

"Good name. Stage or yours for real?"

"Mine for real."

"You want to go to lunch?"

His audacity didn't give offense. Instead it made her laugh. "No. I'm busy." She raised her arms to indicate the boxes surrounding her. "It'll take me all afternoon to get this stuff organized. Besides, we just met."

"Oh, right." As he mulled over that dilemma, he gnawed on his lower lip in a manner he probably knew was cute and endearing. Then he brightened. "Dinner?"

She didn't go to dinner with him that night. Or the next three times he asked. In the ensuing weeks she worked her tail off, covering as many stories as the assignments editor would give her. She vied for as much airtime as she could get, knowing that exposure was the only way to build audience recognition of her name, voice, and face.

She was aiming for the evening anchor spot. It might take her a year or two to get there. She had a lot to learn and much to prove, but she saw no reason to set her sights on anything lower than the top. So she was way too busy getting herself established in the Houston television market to accept dates.

And Jack Donner was way too confident that she would ultimately submit to his charm. He was all-American-boy handsome. His personality was engaging, his humor infectious. Every woman in the building, from the college interns to the grandmother who ran the accounting department, had a crush on him. Surprisingly, men liked him, too. He'd held the top sales record for several consecutive years, and it was no secret that he was being groomed for management.

"Upper management," he confided in her. "I want to be GM and then, who knows? One day I might own my own station."

He certainly had the ambition and charisma to achieve whatever he set out to do, and getting a date with her was his primary short-term goal. Finally he wore her down and she accepted.

On their first date, he took her to a Chinese restaurant. The food was dreadful and the service even worse, but he kept her laughing throughout the meal by creating histories for each of the dour wait staff. The more rice wine he drank, the funnier the stories became.

When he opened his fortune cookie, he whistled. "Wow, listen to this." He pretended to read. "Congratulations. After months of trying to seduce a certain lady, tonight you get lucky."

Paris broke open her cookie and pulled out the fortune. "Mine says, 'Disregard previous fortune.'"

"You won't sleep with me?"

She laughed at his crestfallen expression. "No, Jack, I won't sleep with you."

"You're sure?"

"I'm sure."

But after four months of dating, she did. After six months, everyone at the TV station acknowledged them as a couple. By Christmas Jack had asked her to marry him, and by New Year's Day she had accepted.

In February it snowed. Houston, where snow was as infrequent as the Hale-Bopp comet, ground to a halt, which meant that the news teams worked overtime to cover all the weather-related stories, from school closings, to shelter for the homeless, to the myriad hazards of icy roadways. Paris worked for sixteen hours straight, going in and out of the weather, riding in a drafty news van, drinking lukewarm coffee, meeting deadlines.

When she finally got home, Jack was in her kitchen stirring a pot of homemade soup. "If I never loved you before," she said, lifting the lid on the pot and taking a deep whiff, "I do now."

"I'd cook for you every night if you'd move in with me."

"No."

"Why not?"

"We've been over this at least a thousand times, Jack," she said wearily as she pulled off soggy boots.

He knelt down to massage her frozen toes. "Let's go over it again. I keep forgetting your lame excuses. As you know, my dick is longer than my attention span. And aren't you glad?"

She withdrew her foot from between his warm hands. The massage felt entirely too good to be getting while they were having this oft-repeated argument.

"Until we're married, I'm maintaining my independence." Seeing that he was about to press his argument, she added, "And if you keep bugging me about it, I'll postpone the wedding for another six months."

"You're a hard woman, Paris Gibson soon-to-be Donner."

They ate their soup and finished the bottle of wine Jack had opened before her arrival. He didn't even suggest that he spend the night, and she was grateful for his sensitivity to her exhaustion.

As she bade him good night at her door, she noticed that the inch and a half of snow that had immobilized the city was already beginning to melt. All that ass-busting news coverage was made history by a few degrees on the thermometer.

"Thank God tomorrow is Saturday," she said with a sigh as she leaned against the doorjamb. "I'm going to sleep all day."

"Just wake up in time for tomorrow night."

"What's tomorrow night?"

"You're meeting my best man."

Recently he'd told her that his best friend from college was moving back to Houston after getting an advanced degree in something, from an out-of-state university somewhere that right now she couldn't remember. She knew only that Jack was very excited to have his friend returning to the area and couldn't wait to introduce them.

"How's he liking the Houston PD?" she asked around a wide yawn.

"Still too early to tell, he says, but he thinks he's going to like it. We're gonna try to scare up a game of basketball at the gym while you're snoozing the day away. We'll pick you up around seven tomorrow evening."

"I'll be ready." She was about to close the door when she called after him, "I'm sorry, Jack, what's his name again?"

"Dean. Dean Malloy."

Paris sat up, gasping.

She was in her own kitchen, but it took her a moment to orient herself. Revery had given way to dreaming. She'd been in a deep sleep. The angle of the sunlight coming through the window had changed. Her arms were tingling from the lack of circulation that lying on them had caused. Shaking them only heightened the prickling sensation. With a numb hand, she reached for the ringing telephone—the cause of her waking up so abruptly.

Out of habit, she said, "This is Paris."

chapter *eight*

"When was the last time you saw a dentist, Amy?"

"I don't remember. A few years maybe."

Dr. Brad Armstrong gave his patient a stern frown. "That's much too long between checkups."

"I'm scared of dentists."

"Then you haven't been to the right one." He winked at her. "Until now."

She giggled.

"You're lucky I've found only one cavity. It's small, but it needs to be filled."

"Will it hurt?"

"Hurt? I'll have you know that in this office, pain is a four-letter word." He patted her shoulder. "My job is to fix your tooth. Your job is to lie back and relax while I'm doing it."

"The Valium sure helps. I'm already getting sleepy."

"It doesn't take long."

His staff had cleared it with Amy's mother before giving her a low-dosage tranquilizer to relieve her anxiety and make the procedure less stressful for both patient and doctor. Her mother was coming back in a while to drive her home. In the meantime, he was free to look his fill as she drifted into la-la land.

According to her chart she was fifteen, but she was well formed. She had good legs. Her short skirt revealed smooth, tan thighs and muscled calves.

He loved summer. Summer meant skin. Already he dreaded the onset of fall and winter when women gave up sandals for boots, and bare legs for opaque tights. Skirts got longer, and shoulders bared in the summer by halters and narrow straps were covered with sweaters. The only good thing about sweaters was that some-times they clung, and the suggestion of what was underneath could be wonderfully enticing.

His patient took a deep breath that shifted the paper bib to one side of her chest. He was tempted to lift it and look at her breasts. If she protested, he could always say he was returning the bib to its proper place, nothing more.

But he restrained himself. His nurse might come in, and, unlike his patient, she wasn't loopy on Valium.

He surveyed the girl's legs again. Relaxation had caused them to roll outward, leaving several inches of space between her knees. The stretchy fabric of her skirt fit like a second skin. It molded to the dip between her thighs and delineated the vee. Was she wear-ing panties? he wondered. The possibility that she wasn't inflamed him.

He also wondered if she was a virgin. Beyond the age of four-teen, few were. Statistically, the odds were good that she had been with a man. She would know what to expect from a man who was aroused. She wouldn't be that shocked if—

"Dr. Armstrong?" His assistant appeared, interrupting the day-dream. "Is she ready for the deadening?"

He never let his patients even hear the word "shot."

He came off the low stool on which he'd been sitting, pretend-ing to study the patient's X rays. "Yes. Go ahead. Let's give it ten minutes."

"I'll have everything ready."

He disposed of his latex gloves and went into his private office, closing the door behind him. His skin was feverish. His heartbeat was accelerated. If not for his lab coat, his assistant would have seen his erection. If not for her timely interruption, he might have made a dreadful mistake. And he couldn't afford to make another.

That last time, though—now, that had *not* been his fault.

That girl had been in his chair three times within two months, and with each visit she had become a little friendlier. Friendlier, hell, she'd flirted with him outright. She had known exactly what she was doing. The way she smiled up at him provocatively when-ever she was reclined in his chair—hadn't that practically been an invitation to fondle her?

Then when he did, she had raised such a hue and cry it had brought his partners, all the hygienists, and most of the patients running down the hallway and into the treatment room where she stood screaming accusations at him.

If she had been the twenty-five-year-old she appeared to be, instead of the minor she was, those accusations would have been dismissed. As it was, they'd been believed, and he'd been invited to leave the practice. The following morning when he arrived at the office, his partners had met him at the door with a severance agreement that included a check amounting to three months' earnings. Under the circumstances, they considered that fair. Good-bye and good luck.

Sanctimonious pricks.

But the repercussions hadn't stopped there. The girl's parents, incensed that a normal, heterosexual male had responded to the inviting signals transmitted by their sexpot of a daughter, had filed charges of indecency with a child. As if she was a child. As if she hadn't asked for it. As if she hadn't liked having his hand slide between her thighs.

He was dragged into court like a criminal and, on the advice of his inept attorney, forced to apologize to the conniving little bitch. He'd pled guilty to the humiliating allegations in order to receive a "light sentence" of mandatory counseling and probation.

The judge's ruling was much lighter than Toni's, however. "This is the last time, Brad," she'd warned.

Since he had dodged incarceration, wouldn't you assume a celebration was in order? Oh, no. His wife had other plans, which included beating the subject of his "addiction" to death.

"I can't go through another ordeal like this," she told him. Then for hours she'd harped on his "destructive pattern of behavior."

Okay, there had been a few other incidents, like the one at the clinic where he'd first practiced. He had shown a dental hygienist some photographs. It was a joke, for godsake! How was he to know she was a Bible beater who probably thought babies should be born with fig leafs attached to their belly buttons. She had spread such vicious gossip about him, he'd left of his own accord. But Toni still held him responsible.

Finally she had concluded by saying, "Let me make this even clearer, Brad. I *won't* suffer through another ordeal like this. I won't allow our children to suffer through it. I love you," she declared tearfully. "I don't want to divorce you. I don't want to break up our home and family. But I will leave you if you don't get help and control your addiction."

Addiction. So what if he had a strong sex drive? Was that an *addiction?* She'd made him sound like a pervert.

He wasn't a complete fool, though. He knew he had to adapt to the world in which he lived. If society was going to be puritanical, then he must adjust to the accepted rules. He must walk the straight and narrow as defined by church and state, and they were in league on this issue. One misstep beyond their silly boundaries of so-called decency, and you were not only a sinner but an out-law.

Even the mildest flirtation with another patient could cost him his career. It had taken him eight months to land this job in Austin, long after the severance check had been spent and the savings accounts depleted.

This clinic wasn't as prosperous as the previous one. His current partners weren't as specialized and renowned as his former associates. But the job paid the mortgage. And his family liked Austin, where no one knew the reason for their move here.

For weeks after that courtroom nightmare, Toni had flinched each time he touched her. She had continued sharing a bed with him, although he figured that pretense had been for the kids' benefit.

Eventually she had allowed him to hold her and kiss her, and then, after his group therapy leader had given him a gold star for the progress he'd made toward "healing," she had resumed having sex. She had seemed reasonably content . . . until a few nights ago when he'd been careless enough to stay out all night.

He'd devised a plausible story, and she might have continued believing it if he hadn't been so late getting home last night. The story about the tax seminar didn't fly. He had gone to the seminar and signed in, so there would be a record of his attendance. But he had never intended to stay and had left after the first boring hour.

He'd caught hell for it this morning. Toni shooed the kids from the breakfast table and sent them upstairs to do chores. Then, without any warning, she demanded, "Where were you last night, Brad?"

No lead-in, just that angry, surprise attack that immediately pissed him off. "You know where I was."

"I was up until after two o'clock this morning and you weren't home yet. No tax seminar lasts that long."

"It didn't. It was over around eleven. I met a few guys there. We went out for a beer. Realized we were hungry. Ordered food."

"What guys?"

"I don't know. Guys. We exchanged first names. Joe, I think it was, is an executive at Motorola. Grant or Greg, something like that, owns three paint and body shops. The other one—"

"You're lying," she exclaimed.

"Well, thanks for giving me the benefit of the doubt."

"You haven't earned it, Brad. I tried to go into your office last night. The door was locked."

He stood up, pushing his chair away from the table so angrily it scraped loudly against the floor. "Big deal. The door was locked. I didn't lock it. One of the kids must have. But why were you going in there in the first place? To see what you could find to hold against me? To snoop? To spy?"

"Yes."

"At least you admit it." He expelled a long breath, as though taking time out to get a grip. "Toni, what's wrong with you lately? Every time I leave the house, you put me through a royal grilling."

"Because you're leaving the house more often and you stay away for long periods of time that you can't, or won't, account for."

"Account for? What, I'm not an adult? I'm not allowed to come and go of my own free will? I have to check in with you if I decide to stop for a beer? When I need to take a piss, shall I call you first and ask permission?"

"It won't work, Brad," she'd said with maddening composure. "I'm not going to let you turn the tables and make me feel bad for asking why you were out until early this morning. Go to work. You're going to be late." That had been her exit line. She had stalked from the kitchen, her spine as straight as if she had a girder up her ass.

He'd let her go. He knew her. Once she reached that stage of righteous indignation, he could grovel for hours and nothing he said or did would appease her. She would stay frosty for days. Eventually she would thaw, but in the meantime . . .

Jesus! Was it any wonder that he wasn't eager to go home tonight? Who wanted to cozy up to a Popsicle? If he erred tonight, Toni was to blame, not him.

Thankfully he had discovered a new outlet for his "addiction." Sex in all its variations was his for the taking. Thinking about what was now available to him, he smiled.

Reaching beneath his lab coat, he stroked himself. He liked to stay semierect, so throughout the day he took sneak peeks at the photographs he kept locked in his credenza drawer, or, if he felt safe from intrusion, he visited favorite websites. Only a minute or two would do the trick. Some people drank coffee for a quick pick-me-up. He'd discovered something a hell of a lot more stimulating than caffeine.

It would be a long afternoon, but the anticipation alone was delicious.

Hurry, nightfall.

chapter nine

When Paris entered the room where they were waiting for her, Dean and the other two men stood up. They had convened in a small meeting room within the CIB that was ordinarily used to interview witnesses or question suspects. It was cramped quarters but confidentiality was assured.

Curtis pulled a chair from beneath the table for Paris. She nodded her thanks to him and sat down. She was still wearing sunglasses. Dean could barely detect her eyes behind the dark gray lenses. He hated to speculate as to why she never removed them.

"I hope it wasn't too inconvenient for you to come back downtown," Curtis said to her.

"I got here as quickly as I could."

In unison they all looked at the wall clock. It was coming up on two P.M. None needed to be reminded that twelve hours of Valentino's deadline had already expired.

The detective motioned to the third man in the room. "This is John Rondeau. John, Paris Gibson."

She leaned forward and extended her hand across the table. "Mr. Rondeau."

As they shook hands, he said, "A pleasure, Ms. Gibson. I'm a huge fan."

"I'm glad to hear that."

"I listen to you all the time. It's a real honor to meet you."

Dean drew a bead on the officer, whom he had met only minutes before Paris's arrival. Rondeau was young, trim, and good looking. A weight lifter, from the looks of his biceps. His face was lit up like a Christmas tree as he gazed at Paris. Plainly, like the rookie Griggs, Rondeau was instantly infatuated with her.

Dean suspected that Sergeant Curtis was, too. They'd gone to lunch at Stubb's. The Austin landmark, famous for its barbecue, beer, and live music, was only a few blocks from police headquarters. They'd walked.

During the lunch period there was no band playing in the amphitheater beneath the live oaks out back, but hungry state capitol personnel and downtown office workers lined up by the dozens to order cuts of smoked meat slathered with fiery sauce.

Opting to not wait for a table, he and Curtis had ordered chopped beef sandwiches and had taken them out onto the wood porch, where they stood in the shade to eat.

Dean had expected Curtis to ask him about Paris, but he'd thought the detective's approach would be subtle. Instead Curtis had dug into his sandwich, then asked him bluntly, "What's with you and Paris Gibson? Old flames?"

Maybe it was Curtis's candor that made him such a crackerjack investigator. He caught suspects off guard. Striving for nonchalance, Dean took a bite of his sandwich before answering. "More like water under the bridge."

"Lots of water, I'm guessing."

Dean continued chewing.

"You don't want to talk about it?" the detective probed.

Dean wiped his mouth with a paper napkin. "I don't want to talk about it."

Curtis nodded as though to say, Fair enough. "You married?"

"No. You?"

"Divorced. Going on four years."

"Kids?"

"One of each. They live with their mother."

"Has your wife remarried?"

Curtis took a drink of iced tea. "I don't want to talk about it."

They'd left it at that and moved the conversation back to the case, which actually wasn't a case yet, but which they feared would become one. But now Dean knew that Curtis was single, and the detective never let pass an opportunity to treat Paris to some show of chivalry.

Paris elicited that kind of attention from men. In all the time he'd known her, he'd never seen her play the coquette. She didn't simper. She didn't flirt or deliberately draw attention to herself or dress provocatively. It wasn't anything she *did*. It was something she *was*.

One glance at her and you wished you had a long time to study her. Her figure wasn't voluptuous like Liz's. In fact, hers was rather angular and boyish, and she was taller than average. Her hair, light brown streaked with several shades of blond, always looked slightly mussed, which was certainly sexy, he supposed. But that alone wasn't enough to rouse male interest.

Maybe it was her mouth. Women got painful collagen injections to achieve that pout. Paris had come by it genetically. Or was it her eyes? God knows they were pretty damn spectacular. Blue and fathomless, they invited you to dive in and splash around, see if you could ever plumb their depths. Not that you could tell anything about her eyes now, hidden as they were behind the sunglasses.

Young John Rondeau didn't seem to mind, though. He was practically transfixed.

"Have you learned something else since this morning?" she asked.

"Yes, but we don't know how significant it is." She had posed the question to Curtis, but by answering, Dean forced her to look at him, which she had studiously avoided doing since she entered the room. "We're here to discuss its validity."

Curtis chimed in, "Rondeau works in our computer crimes unit."

"I don't understand," Paris said. "How do computer crimes relate to what you requested of me?"

"We'll get to that," the detective replied. "I know it appears to have no relevance, and maybe it doesn't."

"On the other hand," Dean said, "it could all tie in together. That's what we're trying to determine. Are those the cassettes?" He gestured at the canvas tote she had carried in along with her handbag.

"Yes. The Vox Pro holds one thousand minutes of recorded material."

"So when a call comes in, it's automatically recorded?" Curtis asked. "That's how you screen calls, keep people from shouting obscenities to your audience?"

She smiled. "Some have tried. That's why each call is recorded. I then have the option of saving it and playing it on the air, or deleting it."

"How do you transfer the recordings onto cassette?" Dean asked.

"It isn't easy. As a favor to me, one of the engineers figured out a way. Periodically, he dumps—his term, not mine—the recordings off the Vox Pro computer onto cassettes for me."

"Why?"

She shrugged self-consciously. "Nostalgia, maybe. The more interesting conversations could also be useful if I ever put together a demo tape."

"Well, whatever your reasons for saving them, I'm glad you have them now," Curtis told her.

"I hope you understand that you lose quality in the duplication process," she said. "These tapes won't be as clear as the original."

"Doesn't matter," Dean said. "Quality might become an issue later if a voice print becomes necessary. But right now all we want to know is if the call Valentino referenced was real or a fabrication.

"That's why we asked to hear the calls you received during the past week. If there *was* such a call, and if hearing it on your program lighted Valentino's fuse, then we need to trace that call to the woman who placed it."

"If it's not too late," she murmured.

Judging by the expressions around the table, everyone in the room echoed her grim thought.

"Can you remember a call similar to the one Valentino described?" Curtis asked her.

"Possibly. I've been thinking about it since our conversation this morning. I got a call three nights ago. As I was driving here, I listened to it on the cassette player in my car. I marked the cassette and cued the call."

Dean found the marked cassette among the others in the bag, inserted it into the machine, and pressed Play.

This is Paris.

Hi, Paris.

What's on your mind tonight, caller?

Well, see, I met this guy a few weeks ago. And we really hit it off. I mean, it's been hot, hot, hot between us. (A giggle.) Sorta exotic.

That's probably all the detail we need on a family show.

(Another giggle from the caller.) But I like being with other guys, too. So now he's getting jealous all the time. Possessive, you know?

Do you want to take the relationship to another level?

You mean like do I love him? Hell, no. The whole thing has been about fun. That's it.

Perhaps not to him.

Then that's his problem. I just don't know what to do about him.

If you feel that the relationship is constricting, you probably shouldn't be in it. My advice is to make the break as quick and painless as possible. It would be cruel to string him along when your heart is no longer in it.

Okay, thanks.

"That's all," Paris said. "She hung up."

Dean switched off the recorder. For several moments there was a heavy silence, then everyone began talking at once. Curtis pointed to Paris, giving her the floor.

"I was just going to say that this call may have absolutely no connection to Valentino. It was a rather silly conversation. I only put her on the air because she was so animated. I gathered from her voice that she was young. My audience are mostly baby boomers. I've wanted to expand it to include the younger crowd, so when a call from someone obviously younger comes in, I generally use it."

"Did you get the phone number?"

"I checked the Vox Pro. The caller ID said 'unavailable.'"

"Did other listeners respond to your conversation with her?"

"You'll hear a few on the tape. Several offered interesting advice on how she should handle the breakup. Others I thanked for calling but didn't put them on the air and deleted their calls from the Vox Pro.

"I don't remember talking to anyone else this week about a breakup, even off the air. But I talk to dozens of people every night. My memory isn't one hundred percent."

"Do you mind if we keep these tapes for a while?" Curtis asked.

"They're yours. I had duplicates made."

"I think I'll have someone listen to all—how many hours is it?"

"Several, I'm afraid. I went back three weeks. That's fifteen nights on the air, but of course I delete more calls than I save."

"I'll have someone listen, see if there's a similar call that's slipped your mind."

"Did Valentino call in response?" Dean asked.

"That night, you mean? No. He always identifies himself by name. Last night was the first time I'd heard from him in a while. I'm definite on that."

Curtis stood up. "Thank you, Paris. We appreciate your help. I hope coming back downtown wasn't too much of an imposition."

"I'm as concerned as you are."

Apparently, he intended to escort her out, but she remained seated. Curtis hesitated. "Is there something else?"

Dean knew why Paris was reluctant to leave. Her news-gathering instinct had kicked in. She wanted the full story and didn't want to stop until she had it. "I'm guessing she'd like to know what's going on," he said.

"I would, yes," she said with a nod.

Curtis hedged. "It's really a police matter."

"For you it is. But it's a personal matter to me, Sergeant. Especially if Valentino turns out to be someone I know. I feel responsible."

"You're not," Dean said, speaking more sharply than he intended. Everyone looked toward him. "If he's for real, he's a psychopath. He would be doing something like this whether or not he talks to you on the radio."

Curtis agreed. "He's right, Paris. If this guy is wound as tight as he sounds, he would've snapped sooner or later."

Rondeau said, "You're just providing him with a forum, Ms. Gibson."

"And because of that, you're our only link to him." Dean looked over at Curtis where he still stood beside her chair. "That's why I think she has a right to know the leads we're following."

Curtis frowned, but he resumed his seat. Then he looked directly at Paris and, with his characteristic bluntness, stated, "We might have a missing girl."

"'Might'?"

Dean watched her while she listened to Curtis's summary of what Griggs had told them about Judge Baird Kemp's daughter. He already knew the facts, so he was able to tune them out and concentrate on Paris, who was hanging on every word.

Obviously she had cultivated a sizable radio audience, but he wondered if she missed her TV news reporting. Like greasepaint for a stage actor, didn't it get into a person's blood?

She'd been a natural, earning the viewers' confidence with her solid and impartial reporting. She'd been smart enough to know that if she was too cutesy or glamorous they would regard her as an airhead who had probably slept her way into her job. Taken to the other extreme, she would've been thought of as a ball-breaking bitch with penis envy.

Paris had struck the perfect balance. She had been as aggressive a reporter as any of her male counterparts, but without any sacrifice to her femininity. She could've taken her career as far as she chose to take it.

If only.

Her soft exclamation brought him back into the present. "This girl hasn't been seen or heard from for almost twenty-four hours, and her parents are just now becoming worried?"

Dean said, "Hard to believe, isn't it? They haven't formally notified the police, so Janey's disappearance isn't official. But there've been no other missing persons reported. It's a long shot, but it's a coincidence that Curtis and I thought we should investigate."

She quickly connected the dots. "And if it turned out that this caller was the judge's daughter—"

"That's why we asked for the tapes," Dean said. "Did she give you her name?"

"Unfortunately, no. You heard the recording. And the name doesn't ring a bell. If I'd recently heard the name Janey, or Kemp, which is more unusual, I think I would remember. Besides, isn't this a stretch? It's an awfully broad coincidence on which to base an investigation."

"We thought so, too. Until we heard about this Internet club. The Sex Club."

"The *what?*"

Rondeau came to life. "That's where I come in." He glanced at Curtis as if asking permission to continue.

Curtis shrugged. "Go ahead. It's not as if she couldn't find out for herself."

Rondeau launched into his description. "The website has been online for a couple of years. Janey Kemp was one of the . . . founders, I guess you'd say. It started out as a message board where local teens could communicate, more or less anonymously. Using only their user names and email addresses.

"Over time the messages got more explicit, the subject matter racier, until the purpose of it has evolved into what it is now, which is, basically, an Internet personals column. They flirt via cyberspace."

"Flirt?" Dean scoffed. "The messages they exchange are more like foreplay."

The younger cop said, "I didn't want to offend Ms. Gibson."

"She's a grown-up and this isn't Sunday school." Dean looked at her directly. "The Sex Club's sole purpose is to solicit sex. Kids post messages advertising what they've done and what they're willing to do with the right partner. If they want more privacy with someone, they enter chat rooms and talk dirty to each other. Here's a sample." He opened a folder and removed the sheet he'd printed off the computer in Curtis's office.

She scanned it, registering her dismay. When she looked up, she said, "But these are kids."

"High school mostly," Rondeau told her. "They congregate at a designated spot each night. It's a huge swap meet."

Curtis said, "Part of the fun, it seems, is trying to match individuals with their user names, see if you can figure out who's who."

"And if a couple who've been chatting over the Internet find each other, they have sex," Dean said.

"Or not," Rondeau said, correcting him. "Sometimes they don't like what they see. The other person doesn't live up to expectations. Or someone better comes along in the meantime. No one's obligated to follow through."

"The computer crime guys discovered the website," Curtis said, "and since most of the users are minors, they brought it to the attention of the child abuse unit, which investigates sex offenses against children and child pornography, which falls under the auspices of the CIB." He folded his arms across his stocky torso. "It's a bleed-over investigation, meaning we can put a lot of people on it."

"That's the good news," Rondeau said. "The bad news is that stopping it is virtually impossible."

Paris was shaking her head with incredulity. "Let me make sure I understand. Girls like Janey Kemp go to a designated place and meet up with strangers whom they've teased, via the Internet, into believing they'll have sex."

"Right," Rondeau said.

"Are they insane? Don't they realize the risk they're taking? If they meet their chat room partner, who turns out to be less than a Brad Pitt, and say, 'No thanks,' they're placing themselves at the mercy of a man whom they've inflamed and who is . . . disappointed, to say the least."

"They're hardly at anyone's mercy, Ms. Gibson," the young cop said quietly. "We're not talking nuns here. These are party girls. They frequently charge the men for their favors."

"They ask for money?"

"Not ask. Demand," Rondeau told them. "And they get it. Plenty of it."

This information stunned them into silence. Eventually Curtis said, "What troubles us, Paris, beyond the obvious, is that anybody who applies for membership in this so-called club gets it. Getting a password and access to this website requires only a few clicks of a mouse. That means any sexual predator, any deviate, would know where to go to look for his next victim."

"What's more," Dean said, "his victim would probably go with him willingly. He'd have to put forth very little effort."

"This is alarming whether or not it has a connection to Valentino," she said.

"And we're fighting a losing battle," Rondeau said. "We bust up the kiddie porn rings. But for each one that's busted, dozens more spring up and thrive. We work with the feds, with Operation Blue Ridge Thunder, a nationwide information network that deals specifically with Internet crimes against children. That's more than we can handle. Teenagers consensually exchanging dirty email is a low priority."

Curtis said, "It's like writing tickets for jaywalking, while across town, gang members are shooting each other."

"What about Janey's parents?" Paris asked. "Have they been made aware of this?"

"They've had trouble with her," Curtis replied. "She has a history of misbehavior, but even they probably don't know about all her activities. We didn't want to alert them to a possible connection between her unknown whereabouts and Valentino's call until we had more to go on. We were hoping your audiotape would shed some light."

"It doesn't shed much, does it?" she said. "I'm sorry."

After a discreet knock, the door was opened and another detective poked his head in. "Sorry to interrupt, Curtis. I have a message for you."

He excused himself and left the room.

Paris consulted her wristwatch. "Unless I can be of further help, I should be going."

Rondeau nearly broke his neck getting out of his chair and helping her with hers. "What time do you have to be at the radio station, Ms. Gibson?"

"Around seven-thirty. And please call me Paris."

"Do you have to do a lot of preparation ahead of time?"

"I select the music myself and prepare my log—that's the order in which songs are played. Another department, called 'Traffic,' has already logged the commercials.

"However, a lot of my programming occurs spontaneously. I never know what song someone from the audience is going to request. But I can insert that song into the log instantly, because we have a computerized library of music."

"Are you ever nervous when you go on the air?"

She laughed and shook her head, making the shaggy hairdo even shaggier and more attractive. "I've been doing it too long to get butterflies."

"Do you operate the equipment all by yourself?"

"If you're referring to the control board, yes. And I man my own telephone lines. I turned down having a producer. I like being a one-woman show."

"When you started, did you have to learn a lot of technical stuff?"

"Some, but, honestly, you probably know much more about the workings of a computer than I know about the physics of radio waves."

The implied compliment brought a silly grin to his face. "Does working alone ever get boring?"

"Not really, no. I like the music. And the callers keep me on my toes. Each broadcast is different."

"Don't you get lonely working alone every night?"

"Actually, I prefer it."

Before Rondeau asked her to father his children, Dean interceded. "I'll walk you out, Paris."

As he ushered her toward the door, she said, "I'd like to stay updated. Please ask Sergeant Curtis to call me when he knows something." Sergeant Curtis. Not him. The snub couldn't be more blatant, and it irritated the hell out of him. He was as much a cop as Sergeant Robert Curtis. *And* he outranked him.

He reached around her to grab the doorknob. But the door opened without his help and Curtis was on the other side of it. His complexion was several shades ruddier than usual. What was left of his pale hair seemed to be standing on end.

"Well, it's hit the fan," he announced. "Somehow a courthouse reporter learned that cops were looking for Janey Kemp. He confronted the judge about it as he was returning from lunch recess. His Honor is *not* happy."

"His daughter's life could be at risk and he's worried about media exposure?" Paris exclaimed.

Dean said, "My thought exactly. I don't give a shit if he's happy or not."

"Fine. You'll have an opportunity to tell him that to his face. We've been ordered by the chief to meet with Kemp and try to smooth his feathers. Right now."

chapter ten

Paris wheeled into the Kemps' circular driveway directly behind Sergeant Curtis's unmarked Taurus. She got out of her car at the same time he got out of his. Before he had a chance to speak, she said, "I'm coming with you."

"This is a police matter, Ms. Gibson."

If he was back to using her last name, he was irked. She held her ground. "I started this ball rolling when I came to see you this morning. If I never hear from Valentino again and the call last night turns out to be a hoax, then I owe you, the Austin police, and especially this family a profound apology. And if it isn't a hoax, then I am directly involved and so are they, which entitles me to speak with them."

The detective looked across at Dean as though seeking guidance on how to handle her when she took a stubborn stance. Dean said, "It's your call, Curtis. But she's good at talking to people. That's what she does."

Coming from a trained negotiator, that was quite a compliment. Curtis considered it for only a moment, then said grudgingly, "All right, but I don't know why you'd want to involve yourself in this any more than you already are."

"I didn't choose to be. Valentino involved me."

She and Dean followed him toward the door. For Dean's ears only she said, "Thanks for backing me up."

"Don't thank me yet." He nodded toward the wide front door, which was being opened as they made their way up the veranda steps. "Looks like he's been lying in wait."

Judge Baird Kemp was tall, distinguished looking, and handsome, except for his scowl, which he directed toward Curtis, whom he obviously knew by name. "I'm trying to keep a lid on this, Curtis, and what does the Austin PD do? Trot extra cops out to my house. What the hell is going on with you people? And who are they?"

To Curtis's credit, he kept his cool, although his face and neck flushed to a deeper hue. "Judge Kemp, Dr. Dean Malloy. He's the department's psychologist."

"Psychologist?" the judge sneered.

Dean didn't even bother extending the judge his hand, knowing it would be rebuffed.

"And this is Paris Gibson," Curtis said, motioning toward her.

If her name meant anything to the judge, he didn't show it. After giving her a cursory look, he glared at Curtis. "Are you the one who started the false rumor that my daughter is missing?"

"No, Judge, I didn't. You did. When you called one of the cops you've got on the take and told him to start looking for her."

A vein ticked in Kemp's forehead. "I told the chief that I demanded to know who was responsible for leaking that story, which has been grossly exaggerated. He sends me you, a shrink, and a—" He glanced at Paris. "Whatever. Why the hell are you here?"

"Baird, for godsake." A woman emerged from the house and upbraided him with a stern look. "Can we please do this inside where fewer people will have the opportunity of overhearing?" She gave their guests a collective once-over, which was just shy of hostile, then said stiffly, "Won't you come in?"

Again Paris and Dean followed Curtis. They were shown into an elaborately appointed living room that might have been a salon in Versailles. The decorator had padded her budget with an overload of brocades, gilt, beading, and tassels.

The judge marched over to a dainty liquor cart, poured himself a drink from a crystal decanter, and tossed it back as if it was a shot. Mrs. Kemp perched on the delicate arm of a divan as though she didn't intend to stay very long.

Curtis remained standing, looking as out of place as a fireplug in this room of froufrou. "Mrs. Kemp, have you heard from Janey?"

She glanced at her husband before answering. "No. But when she gets home, she'll be in serious trouble."

Paris couldn't help but think the girl could be in much more serious trouble now.

"She's a teenager, for christsake." The judge was still standing, too, glaring down at them as though about to sentence them to twenty years of hard labor. "Teenagers pull stunts like this all the time. Except when *my* daughter does it, it makes headlines."

"Don't you realize that negative publicity only makes a situation worse?"

For whom? Paris was dismayed that Mrs. Kemp's primary concern was publicity. Shouldn't she be more worried about the girl's absence rather than what would be said about it?

Curtis was still trying to be the diplomat. "Judge, I don't know who within the Austin PD spoke to that reporter. We'll probably never know. The culprit isn't going to come forward and admit it, and the reporter is going to protect his source. I suggest we move past that and—"

"Easy for you to say."

"Not at all easy." Dean spoke for the first time, and his tone was so imperative that all eyes turned to him. "I wish the three of us had come here, hat in hand, to beg your forgiveness for an error in judgment, a slip of the tongue, a false alarm. Unfortunately, we're here because your daughter could be in grave danger."

Mrs. Kemp moved off the arm of the divan and onto the seat cushion.

The judge rocked back on his heels. "What do you mean? How do you know?"

"Maybe I should tell you why I'm here," Paris said quietly.

The judge's eyes narrowed. "What was your name again? Are you that truancy officer who kept hassling us last year?"

"No." She reintroduced herself. "I have a radio program. It's on each weeknight from ten to two."

"Radio?"

"Oh!" Mrs. Kemp exclaimed. "Paris Gibson. Of course. Janey listens to you."

Paris exchanged glances with Dean and Curtis before turning back to the judge, who apparently was unfamiliar with her and her show. "Listeners call in and sometimes I put them on the air."

"Talk radio? A bunch of left-wing radicals spouting off about this, that, or the other."

He had to be the most unpleasant individual Paris had ever met. "No," she said evenly, "my show isn't talk radio." She was in the process of describing her format when he interrupted her.

"I get the picture. What about it?"

"Sometimes a listener calls to air a personal problem."

"With a total stranger?"

"I'm not a stranger to my listeners."

The judge raised a graying eyebrow. Apparently he wasn't used to people contradicting or correcting him. But Paris wasn't intimidated by someone she had already formed such a low opinion of.

Being flagrantly rude, he dismissed her and turned back to Curtis. "I still don't understand what a radio deejay has got to do with any of this."

"I think this will help explain." The detective set the portable tape recorder on a coffee table. "May I?"

"What is this?"

"Sit down, Baird," his wife snapped. Paris saw traces of apprehension in the other woman's eyes. Finally the severity of the situation was beginning to sink in. "What's on the recorder?" she asked Curtis.

"We want you to listen, see if you recognize your daughter's voice."

The judge looked down at Paris. "She called you? What for?"

She, along with the others, ignored him as the recording began.

Well, see, I met this guy a few weeks ago.

Paris noticed that Dean was watching Mrs. Kemp closely. Her reaction was immediate, but was it from recognizing the voice, or from the young woman's description of a short-lived but hot, hot, hot fling?

When it ended, Dean leaned toward Mrs. Kemp. "Is that Janey's voice?"

"It sounds like her. But she rarely talks to us with that much animation, so it's hard to tell."

"Judge?" Curtis asked.

"I can't tell for dead certain either. But what the hell difference does it make if it is her? We know she's got boyfriends. She flits from one to the other so fast we can't keep up. She's a popular girl. What's that got to do with anything?"

"We hope nothing," Curtis replied. "But it might tie in to another call that Paris received from a listener." While talking, he exchanged one cassette for another. Before he played the second tape, he said to Mrs. Kemp, "I apologize in advance, ma'am. Some of the language is rather crude."

They listened in silence. By the time Valentino wished Paris a nice night, the judge had his back to the room and was gazing out the front window. Mrs. Kemp was mashing a pale fist against her lips.

The judge came around slowly and looked at Paris. "When did you receive this call?"

"Just before sign-off last night. I called 911 immediately."

Curtis picked up from there and brought them up-to-date. "Janey's the only missing person who's been reported. If that's her talking to Paris earlier in the week, it could correlate."

"If I heard evidence that flimsy in my courtroom, I'd dismiss it."

"Maybe you would, Judge, but I won't," Curtis declared. "After the reporter confronted you, I understand you called off the unofficial search for your daughter. Well, sir, you should know that as we speak, patrolmen are intensifying their search and intelligence officers are tapping every resource."

The judge looked ready to implode. "Upon whose authority?"

"Mine," Dean said. "I made the recommendation and Sergeant Curtis acted on it."

Mrs. Kemp turned to him. "I'm sorry, we weren't formally introduced. I don't know who . . ." He introduced himself again and explained how he had become involved.

"Very possibly this will turn out to be a hoax, Mrs. Kemp. But until we know it is, we should take this caller seriously."

She stood up suddenly. "Would anyone like coffee?" Then before anyone could answer, she rushed from the room.

The judge muttered a string of curses. "Was that necessary?" he asked Dean.

Dean was barely restraining himself. Paris recognized the tension in his posture and the hardening of his jaw as he stood up and confronted the judge. "I hope to God you can file a formal complaint against me. I hope Janey comes waltzing in here and makes me look like a colossal fool. You'll then have the pleasure of calling me one, possibly even getting me fired.

"But in the meantime, your rudeness is unforgivable and your obstinance is stupid. We've been given a seventy-two-hour deadline, and so far you've wasted twenty minutes of it by being a jerk. I suggest we all set aside our egos and focus on finding your daughter."

The judge and Dean stared each other down. Neither submitted to the other in a silent contest of wills. Finally Curtis cleared his throat. "Uh, when was the last time you saw Janey, Judge?"

He actually seemed relieved to have an excuse to break eye contact with Dean. "Yesterday," he replied briskly. "At least Marian saw her then. In the afternoon. We got home late last night. Thought she was in her room. Didn't discover until this morning that her bed hadn't been slept in." He sat down and crossed one long leg over the other, but his insouciance appeared affected. "I'm sure she's with friends."

"I have a son about Janey's age," Dean told him. "He can be a challenge. There are times when you'd think we hated each other. Discounting the normal ups and downs of living with a teenager, would you say you're basically on good terms with Janey?"

The judge looked ready to tell Dean that his relationship with his daughter was none of his business. But he relented and said stiffly, "She's been difficult at times."

"Breaking curfew? Experimenting with alcohol? Going out with kids you'd rather she not associate with? I speak from experience, you understand."

By placing them on common ground, he was gradually breaking down the judge's barriers and Curtis seemed content to let him continue.

"All of the above," the judge admitted before turning to Paris. "Sergeant Curtis said this degenerate has called you before."

"A man using that name has, yes."

"Do you know anything about him?"

"No."

"You have no idea who he is?"

"Unfortunately, no."

"Do you intentionally provoke this kind of lewdness from your listeners?"

The implicating question took her aback. Before she could form a reply, Dean said, "Paris can't be held responsible for the actions of her listening audience."

"Thank you, Dean, but I can speak for myself." She met the judge's censorious stare head-on. "I don't care what you think of me or of my program, Judge Kemp. I don't need or desire your approval. I'm here only because I heard Valentino's message first-hand, and I share Dean—Dr. Malloy's—concern. I respect his opinion both as a psychologist and a criminologist. Sergeant Curtis's investigative skills are unsurpassed. You'd be wise to give serious consideration to what they're telling you.

"As for my opinion, it's based on years of experience. I listen to people in every possible human condition. They talk to me through laughter and tears. They share their joy, sorrow, grief, heartache, exhilaration. Sometimes they lie. I usually can tell when they're lying, when they're faking an emotion in an attempt to impress me. They do that sometimes, thinking it will increase their chances of being put on the air."

She pointed toward the recorder. "He didn't even hint at being put on the air. That wasn't the reason he called. He called with a message for me, and I didn't get the sense that he was lying or faking it. I don't think it was a crank call. I think he has done, and is going to do, what he said.

"Insult me if it makes you feel better, but, regardless of anything you say, I'm going to do everything within my power to help the police get your daughter returned safely to you."

The taut silence that followed Paris's speech was relieved by the reappearance of Marian Kemp. It seemed she had timed it for just that purpose. "I decided on iced tea instead."

She was followed into the room by a uniformed maid carrying a silver tray. On it were tall glasses of iced tea garnished with lemon and fresh mint. Each glass rested on an embroidered linen coaster. A silver bowl of sugar cubes was accompanied by dainty sterling tongs.

Once they were served and the maid had withdrawn, Curtis awkwardly set his glass of tea on the coffee table. "There's another element to this that you should be made aware of," he told the Kemps. "Does your daughter have a computer?"

Marian replied, "She's on it all the time."

Judge and Marian Kemp listened in stony silence as Curtis told them about the Sex Club. When he finished, the judge demanded to know why his wife had been subjected to hearing about such filth.

"Because we need access to Janey's computer."

The judge erupted with vehement protests. He and Curtis launched into a heated argument over investigative procedure, privacy, and probable cause.

Finally Dean entered the fray. "Doesn't this girl's safety supersede points of law?" His shout silenced them, so he pressed his advantage. "We need a copy of everything on Janey's hard disk."

"I will not permit it," the judge said. "If such a thing as this Sex Club exists, my daughter has nothing to do with it."

"Soliciting to have sex with strangers," Marian Kemp sniffed. "Revolting."

"And speaking as a parent, terrifying," Dean said to her. "But I would rather be informed than ignorant, wouldn't you?"

Apparently not, he thought when neither the judge nor his wife answered. "We don't want to invade Janey's privacy, or yours. But her computer could yield clues to her whereabouts."

"Such as?" the judge asked.

"Friends and acquaintances you don't know. People who send her email."

"If you did discover anything incriminating, it would never be admissible in a court of law because it will have been illegally obtained."

"Then what have you got to worry about?"

The judge had laid that trap for himself and he realized it.

Dean continued, "If Janey has an email address book, which I'm sure she does, we could send out a blanket message to everyone on it, asking if they've seen her, and if they have, urge them to contact you."

"In effect announcing to the world that her mother and I can't keep track of our daughter."

Dean had no love for these people, but he didn't have the heart to state what was glaringly obvious: They wouldn't be here if the Kemps had kept better track of their daughter.

"Her friends will recognize her email address and open the letter," he said. "We'll sign the message from you, not the police, and promise that anyone coming forward with information can remain anonymous."

"Mrs. Kemp," Paris said gently, "an email would reach a lot of people much more efficiently than policemen canvasing Janey's hangouts. Besides, young people get nervous when cops approach even if they're doing absolutely nothing wrong. Janey's friends would be reluctant to talk to a policeman about her. They'd be much more likely to reply to an email."

It was a persuasive point lent even more potency by her mellow voice. Mrs. Kemp looked over at her husband, then back to Paris. "I'll show you to her room." The invitation seemed to include only Paris, who stood when Mrs. Kemp did and followed her out.

Without a word, the judge turned on his heel and stalked toward an adjacent room. From what Dean could see through the doorway before the judge slammed the door behind him, it appeared to be a library or study.

Curtis lightly slapped his thighs as he came to his feet. "That went well, don't you think?"

Dean grinned at the ironic remark, but he sure as hell didn't feel like smiling. "I guess His Honor is divesting himself of the whole ugly matter."

"I'll bet you my left nut he's in there on the phone giving the chief hell about the department's new shrink."

"I don't care. I meant everything I said, and I'd say it again."

"Yeah, well, occasionally I have to testify in his court. I have to play both ends against the middle. But I figure the next time I'm in the witness box, my testimony will be discredited." He ran his hand over his thinning hair. "I'm going outside to make a few calls, see if there's been any news that would make all of us sleep better tonight."

Dean followed him as far as the grand staircase. "I'll wait here for Paris."

"I thought you might."

He didn't have a suitable comeback for the detective's parting shot, so he let it pass. Sliding his hands into the pockets of his trousers, he took in the formal foyer. The floor was marble tile. Overhead was a lavish crystal chandelier that was reflected in the polished wood surfaces of twin consoles facing each other across the wide hall.

Above one of the tables hung an oil portrait of Marian Kemp. And on the opposite wall above the matching table was a painting by the same artist of a girl about seven years old. She was wearing a summer dress of white gauzy fabric. Her feet were bare. The artist had captured sunlight shining through pale blond curls. She looked angelic and achingly innocent.

Dean's cell phone vibrated inside his jacket pocket. He checked the LED and recognized Liz's cell number. He didn't answer, telling himself that now wasn't a good time. She had called twice before. Those hadn't been good times either.

Hearing footsteps in the deep carpeting of the staircase, he looked up to see Paris and Marian Kemp descending. Paris subtly nodded at him. In her hand she was carrying a Zip disk, which she handed over as soon as she reached him. He slid it into his pocket. "Thank you, Mrs. Kemp."

Even though she had cooperated, she hadn't warmed to them. "I'll see you out."

She opened the front door, and when she saw the young woman standing in the driveway with Curtis, she exclaimed, "Melissa! I thought you were in Europe."

Upon hearing her name, the girl turned toward them. She was tall and lanky and was probably attractive underneath the makeup that had been applied with all the finesse of a brave preparing for the warpath.

"Hey, Mrs. K. I just got back."

"She's a friend of Janey's?" Dean asked Marian Kemp.

"Her best friend. Melissa Hatcher."

Behind Paris's car was a snazzy, late-model BMW convertible, but you would never guess by her clothing that this girl came from affluence. She was wearing a pair of denim cutoffs that left ragged strings trailing down her thighs. The waistband had also been cut off, leaving nothing but fringe to hold the shorts on her hipbones. Twin sapphires winked from her pierced navel. The neck and armholes of her T-shirt were oversized, making it no secret that she was wearing nothing beneath it.

Her striped knee socks looked unseasonably heavy, and the black boots laced to her ankles would have been more appropriate on a lumberjack or a mercenary who meant business. Incongruously, the large handbag hanging from her shoulder was a Gucci.

"Have you spoken to Janey since your return?" Marian Kemp asked.

"No," she replied, as though put out by the question. "This guy here's been asking me all these questions. What's going on?"

"Janey didn't come home last night."

"So? She probably just crashed at somebody's place. You know." She shrugged, which slid her T-shirt off one shoulder. She sent a look Dean's way that was unmistakably flirtatious.

"Could you give us some names?"

She turned back to Curtis and eyed him up and down. "Names?"

"Of people Janey might've gone home with?"

"Are you heat?" The detective opened his sport jacket and showed her the ID clipped to his belt. "Oh shit. What's she done?"

"Nothing that we know of."

"She could be in danger, Melissa." Paris moved down the steps to join them.

The girl regarded her curiously. "Danger? What kind of danger? You a cop, too?"

"No, I work for a radio station. I'm Paris Gibson."

Melissa Hatcher's lips were painted a red so dark it was almost black. They fell open in astonishment. "Get out! You're fucking kidding, right?"

"No."

"Oh my God." Her delight was probably the most honest reaction the girl had shown in months. "How cool is this? I listen to your show. When I'm not listening to CDs. But sometimes, you know, you're just not in the mood for CDs. So that's when I turn on your program. Sometimes the music you play sucks, but you are totally bitchin', girl."

"Thank you."

"And I like your hair. Are those highlights?"

"Melissa, do you know if Janey has ever called me while I was on the air?"

"Oh, yeah. Coupla times. It's been a while, though. We called you on Janey's cell and talked to you but we didn't give our names and you didn't put us on the radio. Which was cool, 'cause we were wasted and you could probably tell."

Paris smiled at her. "Maybe next time."

"Has Janey called Paris recently?" Dean asked. Dark eyes lined in darker kohl slid over to him. Paris introduced him to the girl as Dr. Malloy. He stuck out his hand.

She seemed nonplused by the polite gesture, but she shook his hand. "What kind of doctor are you?"

"Shrink."

"Shrink? Jesus, what'd Janey do? OD or something?"

"We don't know. She hasn't been heard from in over twenty-four hours. Her parents are worried about her and so are we."

"We? You a cop, too?"

"Yes. I work for the police department."

"Hmm." Melissa shot them each a suspicious look, and Dean sensed her cautious withdrawal. They were losing her. Despite her being a Paris Gibson fan, her first loyalty would be to her friend. She'd be stingy with information about Janey.

"Like I said, I don't know anything about where Janey is or who she's called 'cause I just got back from France. I've been up for like thirty hours straight, so I'm gonna go home now and crash. When Janey shows up, tell her I'm back, will ya, Mrs. K.?"

Her Gucci bag slung a wide arc as she turned and sauntered toward her car. But just short of reaching it, she suddenly came back around, slapping her forehead with a hand weighed down by sparkling bangles and numerous rings.

"Holy shit, I just got it!" She pointed at Dean. "No wonder you're such a hottie. You're Gavin's dad."

chapter *eleven*

"Wake up, sleepyhead."

Janey opened her eyes. He was bending over her, his face close to hers, his breath ghosting over her face. He kissed her forehead. She moaned pitiably.

"Did you miss me?"

When she nodded, he laughed. He didn't believe her, and he would be wise not to. Because the first chance she got, she was going to kill the son of a bitch.

She tried to keep the malice she felt from showing in her eyes, having concluded that her best option was to appear submissive. The psycho wanted to play games, wanted her to beg, wanted to dominate her.

So, fine. She would be his contrite little plaything—until he turned his back on her, and then she was going to bash in his skull.

"What's this?" He noticed the stained bedsheet and tsked.

She'd peed herself. What did he expect? He had abandoned her here for God knows how long. She had held her bladder for as long as she could, but ultimately she'd had no choice except to wet the bed.

"You'll just have to change the sheets," he told her.

Okay, I'll remake the bed. Untie me and give me a fresh sheet and I'll strangle you with it.

He brushed aside a strand of her matted hair. "You smell like piss and sweat, Janey. Have you been exerting yourself? Doing what, I wonder?" His gaze roved until it settled on the wall behind the bed. "Hmm. Scars in the paint. You've been rocking the bed so the headboard would knock against the wall, haven't you?"

Damn! She had hoped to annoy a neighbor who would eventually get so angry over the monotonous knocking that he'd come over and demand a stop to it. Then, when he was ignored, he would complain to the manager until the manager checked out the source of the noise.

She would be found and her father would be notified, and he would make certain this asshole never saw the light of day again. They'd lock him in a cell *beneath* the prison and give visitation rights to all the bull queers in the place.

Her daydream of rescue and vengeance died when he pulled the bed several feet away from the wall. "We can't have that, Janey." He bent down and kissed her forehead again. "Sorry to spoil your clever little plan, sweetheart."

She looked at him with a desperation that wasn't entirely feigned. She moaned imploringly.

"Do you need the toilet?"

She nodded.

"All right. But I need your promise that you won't try to get away. You would only get hurt, and I don't want to hurt you."

I promise, she said behind the awful tape.

He unbound her feet first. She had thought the instant they were free she would start kicking and fighting him, but, to her alarm, she discovered that her limbs were rubbery. Her legs were reluctant to move at all, and when they did, they did so sluggishly.

He untied her hands, then lifted her into his arms and carried her into the bathroom. He set her on her feet near the toilet, raised the lid, then gently lowered her onto the seat.

She reached for the tape across her mouth.

"You can remove it," he told her softly. "But if you scream, you'll regret it."

She believed him. It was painful to peel off the tape, but when she had done so, she sucked large drafts of air through her mouth. "I'd like a drink of water, please," she said, her voice a croak.

"Finish here first."

He made no move to leave. To her mortification tears came to her eyes. "Go out and close the door."

He frowned down at her impatiently. "Oh, please. This sudden modesty is absurd. Hurry up before I change my mind and make you wet yourself again."

When she was finished, she asked again for a drink of water.

"Certainly, Janey. As soon as you change your bed. You've left it so nasty. Dreadfully nasty."

She was dying of thirst, so she submissively exchanged the

damp sheets for fresh ones. By the time she had completed the task to his satisfaction, she was exhausted and had broken out in a cold sweat.

He made her sit in the armchair, where he could watch her while he stepped into the kitchen and uncapped a plastic bottle of water. She'd hoped for a glass. She could have broken it and shoved a shard of glass into his throat. If she could've found the strength. She was abnormally weak even for someone who'd been lying in bed for hours. Had he drugged her last night? Was he doing so again now? Had he put something in her water?

Actually she didn't care. She was so thirsty, she drank the water greedily.

"Are you hungry?"

"Yes."

He made a pimiento cheese sandwich, then hand-fed it to her, pinching off small pieces one at a time and placing them in her mouth. She thought about biting his fingers, but that would still leave one of his hands free. She hadn't forgotten the slap that had made her vision blur and her ears ring. She didn't want to invite another.

Causing him even momentary pain would give her enormous satisfaction. She would love to sink her teeth into his flesh, draw blood. But in her present condition, it would be impossible to follow that up with a full-fledged attempt to overpower him. The satisfaction she would derive from it would be all too brief and would cost her dearly. Until she could achieve more than just getting him angry and retaliatory, she had best conserve her strength and try to devise a foolproof plan of escape.

When she'd finished the sandwich, he said, "I like you this way, Janey." He stroked her head and used his fingers to comb the tangles out of her hair. "Your submission is very arousing." He touched her nipples lightly. "It makes you so desirable."

He turned away from her only long enough to get his camera. The despised camera. It was the camera that had so intrigued her and made her think he was special. A special pervert, maybe. She hated the sight of that camera now and would like nothing better than to grind it into his face until both his facial bones and the camera had broken apart.

But she was too frightened to resist as he posed her for a series of obscene pictures.

"Get on the bed."

She considered begging, pleading, promising him money, swearing she'd never tell anyone about this, if only he would let her go. But maybe she would have more bargaining power if she did him one more time.

So she lay down on the bed and did exactly what he told her to do. When he was finished, she didn't even have the energy to raise her head. He had drugged her. She was sure of it now.

She watched in dread as he opened the nightstand drawer and removed a roll of duct tape. "No," she whimpered. "Please."

"I hate having to do this, Janey, but you're a whore. Your love isn't pure. You're dishonest. You can't be trusted even to remain quiet."

"I will. I swear."

That was all he allowed her to say before clamping a strip of tape over her mouth. This time he also used the tape to secure her wrists and ankles to the bed frame, winding it so tightly there was absolutely no give.

He showered before he dressed. Standing beside the bed, he calmly threaded his belt through the loops of his trousers. "Are you crying, Janey? Why? You used to be the ultimate party girl."

He stuffed the soiled bed linens into a laundry bag and picked up his keys. He was almost to the door when he snapped his fingers and turned back. "I almost forgot. I have a surprise for you."

He took an audiocassette from the pocket of his jacket and placed it in the player that was built into his sound system. "I recorded this last night. I think you'll find it interesting." He pressed the Play button, then blew her a kiss and left. He locked the door from the outside.

There were thirty seconds of silence on the tape, then a ringing telephone. It rang several times before Janey heard a familiar voice say, "This is Paris."

"Hello, Paris. This is Valentino."

His name is Valentino?

That was her first thought, because she instantly recognized his voice. It wasn't his normal speaking voice, but the other one, the one he sometimes used when they were in bed. She had thought it was amusing, the way he could lower the pitch of his natural voice, make it whispery, make it sound as though it went with doing something naughty—as it usually had.

Now, hearing that voice in stereo only gave her chills.

Listening as he told Paris Gibson their story from his perspective, Janey breathed rapidly through her nose, watching the machine in fascination, listening to the recording with an anxiety that soon escalated into terror. When he told Paris Gibson his plans for her, she began screaming into the hollow chamber of her taped mouth.

But of course no one could hear her.

Toni Armstrong arrived at her husband's dental office just before closing. One of the other dentists in the practice paused on his way out to speak with her. He apologized for not yet having had her and Brad over for dinner. They exchanged promises to get a date on the calendar soon.

Seemingly Brad had no trouble keeping up appearances. She would do the same for as long as she could.

When she walked into the office, the receptionist was surprised to see her. "I got a baby-sitter and thought I'd treat Brad to an un-scheduled dinner out," she explained.

"Oh, golly, Mrs. Armstrong, Dr. Armstrong left a couple of hours ago."

At least to the other woman, her dismay would look like disap-pointment. "Oh, well, so much for my surprise evening. Did he tell you where he was going?"

"No, but I'm sure he has his cell phone."

"I'll give him a call. Will I be keeping you if I use his office?"

"Not at all. Take your time. I've got some filing to do before I leave."

Since Brad was the newest partner, his was the smallest office, but Toni had done her best to make it attractive. Degrees and diplomas in matching frames formed an attractive arrangement on the wall. Family photographs were tucked among the dental health books on the shelves behind his desk. His desktop was neat.

She hoped the setting was as benign as it appeared.

Sitting down in his desk chair, she commenced her search. All his drawers were locked, but she had anticipated that and had come prepared. A bent bobby pin opened them with minimum ef-fort.

Truthfully, she *had* secured a baby-sitter for tonight. She had taken care with her hair and makeup and had dressed up in the hope of surprising Brad with an evening out—to make amends for this morning.

Throughout the day, their quarrel had haunted her. Brad had left the house angry. She had been hurt as well as angry. House-cleaning, menu planning, and the myriad other chores that filled her days had kept her busy. But nothing could take her mind off their argument and the possibility, however slight, that she might have been wrong.

What if Brad hadn't been lying about where he'd been last night?

Maybe she had gone looking for trouble where none existed. If he had been telling her the truth, how frustrating it must have been for him to try to make himself believed, knowing that she would think the worst.

Chances were slim that he had attended a seminar and gone for a beer afterward, but in order to hold her family together, she was desperate enough to act on that chance.

So this afternoon, she had hoped to intercept him at the office with a pleasant surprise, an olive branch of a dinner reservation at an Italian restaurant he'd been wanting to try. By spending an evening alone with him, away from the house and kids, with a bottle of wine and lovemaking later on, she had hoped to win his forgiveness for misjudging him and be able to put the ugly episode behind them.

But he wasn't where he was supposed to be. He had left work early without an explanation and without informing anyone of his destination. It was a familiar pattern, a recognizable signal, that made her heartsick and justified her picking the locks on her husband's desk drawers.

A few moments later, her suspicion was validated. Inside the lower drawer of his credenza was a treasure trove of pornography.

The printed material ranged from relatively mild to extremely graphic. Some of the crudest pictures, both in subject matter and composition, surely had been taken by amateur photographers.

Brad was an addict. Like all addicts, he was susceptible to bingeing. And it was during a binge that an addict was capable of doing something he or she wouldn't ordinarily do, like sexually harassing a coworker or fondling a patient who was a minor.

And God only knew what else.

chapter *twelve*

There was a wet swimsuit on the utility room floor when Dean passed through it on his way into the house. He found Gavin semireclined on the sofa in the den. He was desultorily punching the TV remote, changing stations every ten seconds. He was wearing only a towel around his waist and his hair was wet.

"Hi, Gavin."

"Hi."

"Have you been in the pool?"

Without taking his eyes off the television screen, he replied, "No. I just like to sit around in a towel."

"When you take the wet towel to the utility room, you can also pick up the swimsuit you left on the floor."

Gavin punched through another few stations.

Dean said, "Shower, then we'll go eat."

"I'm not hungry."

"Shower, then we'll go eat," he repeated.

"And if I don't, are you going to hit me again?"

The look Dean shot him apparently conveyed his shrinking patience. Gavin threw down the remote and stalked from the room. Just before moving through the door, he whipped off the towel, baring his ass to Dean, literally as well as figuratively. In spite of himself, Dean gave Gavin two points for the symbolic gesture.

Without asking Gavin's preference, he drove to a chain restaurant that was one of their staples. Gavin sulked, responding in monosyllables to Dean's attempts at conversation.

When their order arrived, Dean asked him if his burger was cooked the way he liked it.

"It's fine."

"I apologize for not having more dinners at home."

"Doesn't matter. Your cooking sucks."

Dean smiled. "I can't argue that. You probably miss your mom's homemade pasta sauce and pot roast."

"Yeah, I guess."

"But all you ever seem to want is burgers or pizza anyway."

Immediately on the defensive, Gavin said, "Something wrong with that?"

"No. I had the same diet when I was your age."

Gavin snorted as though to say he didn't realize they had burgers and pizza that far back in ancient history.

Dean tried again. "I saw an old friend today. Do you remember Paris Gibson?"

Gavin looked at him scornfully. "Do you think I'm retarded?"

"It was a long time ago and you were just a boy. I wasn't sure you would remember her."

"'Course I do. Her and Jack. They were gonna get married, but he got killed."

"He didn't get killed. He survived the accident. He didn't die until a few months ago."

"Huh. She's on the radio here now."

Dean was surprised. "So you knew that?"

"Everybody knows that. She's popular."

"Yeah, I understand she has quite a following. She told me today she's trying to cultivate a younger audience. Do you ever listen to her program?"

"I have. Not every night. Sometimes." Gavin dipped a french fry into a glob of ketchup. "Did you call her up, or what?"

"Uh, no. She had a crank call last night from a listener."

"Seriously?"

"Hmm," Dean said around a bite of his grilled chicken. "She reported it to the police. I was consulted. She and the detective wanted my take on it."

"Detective? Was it that bad?"

"Pretty bad."

He signaled the waitress and asked her to bring Gavin another Coke. For someone who wasn't hungry, he had wolfed down his cheeseburger in record time. "And bring us an order of queso and chips, too, please." Gavin would never ask for more, but Dean knew he was probably still hungry.

"I also saw a friend of yours today," he remarked casually.

"I don't have any friends here. All my friends are in Houston.

Where I used to live. In my own house. Until my mother married that jerk."

Here we go, Dean thought. "She had been single for a long time, Gavin."

"Yeah, 'cause you divorced her."

"Funny. Last night you said she divorced me. Actually, you're right on both accounts. We agreed to divorce because we knew it would be best."

"Whatever," Gavin said with a bored sigh and turned his head to gaze out the window.

"Don't you think your mother has a right to be happy?"

"Who could be happy with him?"

Dean wasn't overly impressed with Pat's choice either. Her husband was rather bland, so lackluster that one had to work at having a conversation with him. But he seemed besotted with Pat and she with him.

"So what if he doesn't have a dynamic personality, can't you just be glad that your mother has found someone she cares about, who also cares for her?"

"I'm glad, I'm glad. I'm ecstatic, okay? Can we drop it now?"

Dean could have reminded him that he'd been the one to bring up the topic, but he let it pass. The waitress came with their additional order.

"Anything else?"

She had addressed Gavin, not him, and for the first time, Dean tried to see his son through a young woman's eyes. Parental bliss notwithstanding, Gavin was a good-looking kid. His brown hair had the wavy texture of his mother's and he must secretly like it because—thank God—he hadn't had it sculpted into a bizarre style or had it dyed a color that glowed in the dark.

His eyes were whiskey colored and slightly brooding. You couldn't tell it now when he was slouching, but he was already over six feet tall, and had the strong, lean build and supple grace of a natural athlete.

Dean smiled at the waitress. "We're fine now, thanks." As she moved away, he said, "She's cute."

Gavin glanced at her indifferently. "She's okay."

"Cuter than the young woman I met today." Regarding Gavin closely, he said, "Melissa Hatcher."

Unmistakably, the name registered. Dean was sure of it. But Gavin played dumb. "Who?"

"She said she knew you."

"She doesn't."

"Then why would she say she did?"

"How should I know? She got the name wrong, or mixed me up with someone else." He was fiddling with the drinking straw in his glass of Coke, avoiding eye contact.

"I introduced myself to her and after we had talked for a while, she said, 'You're Gavin's dad.' She knew you."

"Maybe she'd been warned off me 'cause you're a cop."

"You mean, who wants to be friends with a cop's kid?"

He looked at Dean resentfully. "Something like that."

"Janey Kemp?"

This time Gavin couldn't as easily hide his reaction. His expression became guarded instantly. "Who?"

"Janey Kemp. From what I've heard about her, she wouldn't want to be friends with a cop's kid. Do you know her?"

"I've heard of her."

"What have you heard?"

Gavin scooped up a bite of queso and through a mouthful said, "You know. Stuff."

"Like what? That she's wild? Easy?"

"It's been said."

"Have you ever met her?"

"I may've bumped into her a couple of times."

"Where?"

"Jeez, what is this? The Spanish Inquisition?"

"No, I'm saving the thumbscrews for later. Right now I'm just curious to know where you've bumped into Janey Kemp and her friend Melissa. It must have been enough times that my name meant something to her. Even before that, she recognized me because you and I favor each other."

Gavin squirmed in his seat, shrugged his shoulders. "They hang out with all those rich, snooty kids. I've seen them around, is all. At the movies. The mall. You know."

"The lake?"

"Which one? Town or Travis?"

"You tell me."

"I've seen 'em a few times, okay? I don't remember where."

Dean laughed. "Gavin, don't bullshit me. If I were your age, and I had met Melissa Hatcher, and she was dressed anything like she was today, I would remember it in minute detail." He pushed his plate aside and leaned forward. "Tell me what you know about the Sex Club."

Gavin kept his expression blank, but again his eyes gave him away. "The what?"

"Last night, when you disobeyed and went out, did you go to Lake Travis?"

"Maybe I did. So what?"

"I know that kids congregate in specified spots around the lake. Did you see Janey Kemp among the crowd last night? And before you give me some bullshit answer, you should know that she's been missing for over twenty-four hours."

"Missing?"

"She didn't come home after going out last night. No one's heard from her. Late this afternoon, just before I left headquarters, patrol officers discovered her car. It was parked near a lakeside picnic area in a clump of cedar trees. No sign of Janey. Apparently she met someone last night and left with that person. Did you see her? Was she with someone?"

Gavin lowered his eyes to his ravaged plate and stared at it for several moments. "I didn't see her."

"Gavin," he said, lowering his voice, "I know the ironclad rule against ratting on your friends. The same rule applied when I was growing up. But this isn't a matter of loyalty or betrayal. It's much more serious.

"Please don't try to protect Janey or anyone else by holding back information. Drinking, drugs, whatever else was going on last night, I'm not interested in right now. If Janey left with the wrong guy, her life could be in jeopardy. With that in mind, are you absolutely certain you didn't see her?"

"Yes! God!" He glanced around, realizing he'd drawn attention to himself from people at nearby tables. He slumped in the booth and mumbled to his lap, "Why're you picking on me?"

"I'm not picking on you."

"You're being a cop."

Dean took a deep breath. "Okay, maybe. I'm coming to you as a source of information. Tell me what you know about the Sex Club."

"I don't know what you're talking about. I gotta pee." He slid to the end of the booth and was about to leave, but Dean ordered him to stay where he was.

"You've been potty trained since you were three. You can hold it for a few more minutes. What do you know about the Sex Club?"

Gavin rocked back and forth, staring angrily through the window, his expression hostile. Dean thought he would refuse to answer him, but eventually he said, "Okay, I've overheard guys talking about this website where they swap email with chicks. That's all."

"Not quite all, Gavin."

"Well, that's all I know about it. I didn't go to school with these kids, remember? I got ripped up by the roots and transplanted here, so they're not—"

"You've been hanging out with a group of kids almost since the day we moved here. Your 'Oh woe is me, I had to leave my friends' refrain is getting a little tired. You need to think of something else to bitch about.

"In the meantime, this girl may be fighting for her life, and I'm not exaggerating. So stop sulking and feeling sorry for yourself and give me a straight answer. What do you know about this Internet club and Janey Kemp's participation in it?"

Gavin held out for several more moments, then, as though resigned, laid his head against the back of the booth. "Janey meets up with guys she's met over the Internet, and they have sex. She'll do anything. Her and that Melissa."

"So you do know them."

"I know who they are. Lots more girls are in the club. I don't know all their names. They come from schools all over the city. There's this message board and the members talk about what they do."

"Have you joined this club, Gavin?"

He sat up. "No! You have to know how to get in, and I haven't asked 'cause I'd feel like a dork for not knowing already."

"It's not that much of a secret. The department's computer crime unit is on to it."

The boy laughed. "Yeah? What are they gonna do about it? They can't stop it, and everybody knows that."

"Soliciting sex is a crime."

"You would know," he muttered resentfully. "You're the cop."

He parked in a grove of live oak trees where others had left their cars. He had a Styrofoam chest of beer and wine coolers in the trunk. He selected a beer and carried it with him as he strolled toward the lakeshore and the wood-plank fishing pier that extended thirty yards out over the water.

This was tonight's meeting place.

He had come to check things out.

He had dressed to blend into the crowd. The baggy shorts and T-shirt were Gap issue, exactly like the younger people wore. Nevertheless, he kept the bill of his baseball cap pulled down low so it would shadow his face.

Some of the people here tonight were familiar. He'd seen them before at similar gatherings, or in the clubs on Sixth Street and around the university campus. Others were new to him. There were always fresh new faces.

Name your pleasure—drink, drugs, sex—it was available. And tonight you could even indulge in gambling. On the beach, a girl wearing only bikini trunks and a straw cowboy hat was on her knees fellating a guy. Bets were being placed on how long the guy could hold out before climaxing.

He joined the ring of cheering onlookers that had formed around the couple and wagered five bucks. One had to admire the guy's self-control because the girl had know-how. He lost his bet.

Unhurried, he strolled along the pier. He didn't invite attention, but ordinarily he didn't have to, and tonight proved to be no different. He was soon approached by two girls who were acting so lovey-dovey that right away he knew they were on Ecstasy.

They hugged him, stroked him, kissed him on the mouth, told him he was gorgeous, the moon was awesome, the night air was divine, and life was beautiful.

They asked him to hold their clothes while they went skinny-dipping. He watched from the pier as they cavorted like water nymphs, occasionally pausing to wave and throw kisses up to him.

When they came out of the water and dressed—well, partially— he took them to his car and gave them each a beer.

One of the girls fixed her glassy eyes on him. "Do you like to party?"

"I'm here, aren't I?" Clever answer. Noncommittal. Affirmation was only implied.

She fondled him through his shorts and giggled. "I believe you do."

"We *love* to party," the other drawled.

They did, too. Over the course of the next hour, in the backseat of his car, they showed him just how much the party girls they were. When he finally told them he must go, they were reluctant to say good-bye. They kissed and caressed him and begged him to stay for more fun and games.

He finally disentangled himself and made his departure. As he was steering his car through the makeshift parking lot toward the main road, he noticed a couple of guys looking at him with blatant envy. They must have seen him getting out of his backseat with the two babes, extricating himself from their clinging limbs and drug-induced affections.

Did these losers wish they were as lucky in love as he was? You bet your ass they did.

But he also marked a guy he recognized as an undercover narcotics officer. The cop was thirty, but didn't look a day over eighteen. He was transacting with a known drug dealer through the open window of a car.

What's the difference in the narc buying drugs and what I'm doing? John Rondeau asked himself.

Not a damn thing. To effectively fight a crime, you had to understand the nature and mechanics of it. Ever since his unit had discovered the Sex Club, he had appointed himself to do some research. After hours and on-site, of course.

His ambition was to get promoted to CIB, which was the pulse of the department. That's where all the exciting police work was done, and that's where he wanted to be.

Toward that promotion, he could really distinguish himself with this Kemp case. It had elements that received notice, namely, a celebrity, sex, and minors. Put them together and you had yourself a humdinger of an investigation.

To the computer crime unit, the Sex Club was old hat. They'd known about it for months and, realizing the futility of trying to shut it down, had more or less forgotten about it.

But the messages left on the discussion boards continued to blow Rondeau's mind. He'd made it his duty to check out the situation, see if the members really did what they boasted or simply exchanged their wildest fantasies via email. He had discovered that most of the claims were not exaggerations.

And it was a good thing he had done the research. If he hadn't had hands-on knowledge, he wouldn't have been able to answer intelligently and thoroughly all the questions put to him by Curtis, Malloy, and Paris Gibson this morning. So it really was for the benefit of the PD that he'd been putting in this unpaid overtime, wasn't it?

However, more investigative work was required. It was all about his getting a promotion to CIB. It was his job, his sworn duty. He was working undercover, that's all.

● ● ●

Not surprisingly, Brad Armstrong wasn't at home when Toni returned from his dental office. She explained to the startled babysitter that she didn't feel well and that she and Dr. Armstrong had canceled their plans for an evening out. She paid her for five hours.

Three times she had called Brad's cell phone. Three times she'd left voice-mail messages to which he hadn't responded. She fixed the children hot dogs for dinner. After they'd eaten, she played a game of Chutes and Ladders with the girls while her son watched a *Star Trek* rerun.

They were trooping upstairs to take their baths when Brad came in with chocolate bars and bear hugs. For Toni there was a bouquet of yellow roses, which he sheepishly presented to her. "Can we be friends again? Please?"

Unable to look at the insincere apology in his eyes, she lowered her head. He took that as acquiescence and kissed her quickly on the cheek. "Have you eaten?"

"I was waiting for you."

"Perfect. I'll put the kids to bed. You get something on the table. I'm famished."

What she had on the table when he returned to the kitchen wasn't what he expected. The unappetizing display stopped him dead in his tracks. "Where'd you get all that?" he demanded angrily. "Never mind. I know where you got it."

"That's right. I found it this afternoon when I went to your office. Where you were conspicuously absent, Brad. You didn't tell anyone where you were going, and you haven't answered your cell phone for hours. So don't put *me* on the defensive. I refuse to apologize for violating your privacy when this is what your privacy is protecting."

As soon as he was confronted with the evidence of his sickness, the fight went out of him. It was a physical diminishing, a deflation both of spirit and body. He pulled out a chair and sat down at the table, his shoulders slumping, his hands falling listlessly into his lap.

Toni took a plastic trash bag from the pantry and scooped the collection of sordid photographs and magazines into it. Then she closed it with a twist tie and carried it to the garage.

"I'll take it to a Dumpster in the morning," she told him when she came back in. "I would hate for the bag to come open accidentally and our neighbors, or even the garbage collectors, to see what's inside."

"Toni, I'm . . . There's really no defense I can offer, is there?"

"Not this time."

"Are you going to leave me?" He reached for her hand and clasped it damply. "Please don't. I love you. I love the kids. Please don't destroy our family."

"I'm not destroying anything, Brad," she said, pulling her hand free. "You are."

"I can't help myself."

"Which is all the more reason for me to leave and take the children. What if one of them had found those pictures?"

"I'm careful about that."

"You're careful to conceal it the way a drug addict hides his stash or the alcoholic keeps a hidden bottle in case of an emergency."

"Oh, come on," he cried.

His contrition was gradually dissipating. Hostile defensiveness was setting in. Next would come an air of superiority. They'd played this scene many times before. His transition from penitent to martyr was virtually scripted and Toni knew to anticipate each phase of it.

He said, "Comparing a harmless hobby to drug addiction is ridiculous and you know it."

"Harmless? Some of those pictures are of underage girls. They're exploited by corrupt and depraved people for your entertainment. And how can you call it harmless when it affects your career, our family life, our marriage?"

"Marriage?" he sneered. "I don't have a wife anymore, I've got a jailer."

"If you continue, you may well wind up in jail, Brad. Is that what you want?"

He rolled his eyes. "I'm not going to jail."

"You could, unless you admit to yourself and to others that you're a sex addict and get the help you need to combat it."

"Sex addict." He snuffled a laugh. "Do you hear how absurd that sounds, Toni?"

"Dr. Morgan doesn't think it sounds absurd."

"Jesus. You called him?"

"No, he called me. You haven't been to the therapy group in three weeks."

"Because it's a waste of time. All those guys talk about is whacking off. Now, I ask you, is that a productive way to spend an evening?"

"It's court mandated that you attend the meetings."

"I guess you're going to tattle to my probation officer. Tell him I've been a bad boy. I haven't been going to therapy with the other pervs."

"I don't have to tell him. Dr. Morgan already did."

"Dr. Morgan is the worst sicko in the group!" he exclaimed. "He's a recovering 'addict' himself. Did you know that?"

She continued unflappably. "Dr. Morgan is required to report more than two consecutive absences to your probation officer. You have an appointment with him tomorrow morning at ten o'clock. It's compulsory."

"I guess it doesn't matter if I cancel patient appointments and get my partners pissed at me."

"That's a consequence you'll have to pay."

"Along with sleeping on the sofa, I suppose."

"I would prefer that you did."

His eyes narrowed into a glare. "I bet you would. Since you obviously don't like anything we do in bed."

"That's not fair."

"Fair? I'll tell you what's not fair. It's having a wife who'd rather snoop than fuck. When was the last time we did? Do you even remember? No, I doubt you do. How can you think of sex when you're so busy spying?"

He came to his feet and advanced on her. He curved his hand around the back of her neck and gave it a squeeze that was too hard to be mistaken for affection.

"Maybe if you put out more often, I wouldn't have to resort to looking at my dirty pictures."

He yanked her forward. She turned her head to avoid his kiss and tried to push him aside. But he backed her against the counter and pinned her there. Shocked, she cried out, "Stop it, Brad. This isn't funny."

Her anger only seemed to excite him. His face suffused with color as he ground his lower body against hers. "Feel that, Toni? Feel good?"

"Leave me alone!"

She pushed him hard enough to send him reeling backward and crashing into the table. Covering her mouth with her hand, she tried to stifle her sobs. She was equally outraged and frightened. She'd never seen him this way. Her husband had become a stranger.

He regained his footing and collected himself, then snatched up his jacket and keys. The house shook with the impact of the slamming door. Toni staggered to the nearest chair and sank onto it. For several minutes she wept softly, not wanting the children to hear.

Her life was falling apart and she was incapable of doing anything about it. Even now she loved Brad. He refused to get help to rid himself of this illness. Why was he intent on destroying the love they'd once had? Why would he willfully choose his "harmless hobby" over her, over his children? Weren't they worth more to him than his—

In a heartbeat, she was out the door to the garage. The trash bag in which she had placed the pornography was gone.

Brad had taken his first love with him.

chapter *thirteen*

Paris had an office at the radio station, which she worked in when she wasn't on the air. Although "office" was an aggrandizing word for the small room. It couldn't claim a single redeeming feature, not even a window. Decades ago the plaster walls had been painted an ugly manila color. The acoustic ceiling tiles sagged and bore generations of water stains. Her desk was made of ugly gray Formica, chunks of which had been gouged out, probably by a previous occupant who was hopelessly depressed over his surroundings.

Nothing in the office belonged to her. There were no framed diplomas on the walls, or posters of vacation destinations fondly remembered, no candid snapshots of grinning friends, or posed family portraits. The room was barren of anything personal, and that was intentional. Pictures and such invited questions.

Who's that?

That's Jack.

Who's Jack? Your husband?

No, we were engaged, but we didn't get married.

Why? Where's Jack now? Is he the reason you wear sunglasses all the time? Is he the reason you work alone? Live alone? Are alone?

Even the friendly prying of coworkers could bring on severe heartache, so she tried to prevent it by keeping her relationships with them strictly professional and her office space devoid of any hints about her life.

The office wasn't without clutter, however. The unsightly surface of her desk was covered by mail. Bags of it were dumped onto it daily—fan letters, ratings charts, inner-office memos, and the endless reams of material sent to her by record companies promoting their newest releases. Since there was no space for even a file cabinet in the room, she sorted and tossed as efficiently as possible, but it was an unending task.

She had attacked the pile of correspondence after making her music selections for that night's show and entering them into the program log. She'd been at it for an hour when Stan materialized in the open doorway. His expression was petulant. "Thanks a lot, Paris."

"For what?"

He came in and closed the door. "Guess who came to see me today?"

"I hate guessing games."

"Two of Austin's finest."

She laid aside her letter opener and looked up at him. "Policemen?"

"And I have you to thank for it."

"They came to your house?" She had thought that either Carson or the eager Griggs would have called Stan only to ask follow-up questions.

He moved aside a stack of envelopes and sat down on a corner of the desk. "They interrogated me and jotted down my answers in little black notebooks. Very gestapoesque."

"Stop dramatizing, Stan."

Because of her return trip to the police station, followed by the upsetting visit with the Kemps, she'd had no time to sleep. Before she could rest, she had to do a four-hour radio program and do it as though nothing was wrong. It was a daunting prospect.

Dealing with Stan's wounded pride wasn't the best use of her limited stamina or the time remaining before the evening deejay turned the broadcast studio over to her.

"This morning, I reported Valentino's call to a detective," she explained. "As it turns out, a young woman from this area is unaccounted for. The police are investigating to see if there's a connection between her disappearance and Valentino's call. They're conducting routine background checks on everyone who's involved, even remotely. So don't take offense. They didn't single you out. Marvin is also on their list of people to talk to."

"Oh, great. I rank right up there with a *janitor*. I feel much better now."

For once she felt his sarcasm was warranted. "I'm sorry. Truly. The police are being thorough because they're as convinced as I am that this was no crank call. I hope we're all overreacting and it turns out to be nothing. But if our hunches are right, a girl's life is at stake. Nevertheless, I regret that you were dragged into this by happenstance."

He was mollified, but only slightly. Stan's first consideration was always Stan. "The police also talked to our general manager. Of course, he immediately called Uncle Wilkins, who in turn called the chief of police and, from what I understand, gave him an earful."

"Then I'm sure you've been cleared of all suspicion."

"I was actually under suspicion?" he exclaimed.

"Figure of speech. Forget it. Go out and buy a new gadget. There's bound to be one on the market you don't have yet. Treat yourself. You'll feel better."

"It's not that easy, Paris. My uncle was even more incensed than I was. He's been talking to the GM off and on all afternoon, wanting to know 'what the hell is going on.' I paraphrase, of course. You can count on being summoned into the inner sanctum yourself."

"I already have been."

The station's general manager had called her on her cell phone as she was leaving the Kemp estate. He had asked for a meeting, but he'd put it in the form of a mandate, not a request. She'd received a dressing-down for not telling him about Valentino's call before notifying the police. His primary concern was the station's reputation.

"I played him the recording of the call," she told Stan. "It disturbed him, as it's disturbed everyone who's heard it. He spoke with Sergeant Curtis, the detective who's heading the investigation."

The GM had talked to Curtis via speakerphone, making Paris privy to their conversation. He had agreed that Paris and everyone at 101.3 should cooperate with the police to the fullest extent, but stipulated that if Janey Kemp's disappearance became a big news story, he wanted the radio station's involvement to be minimized.

Curtis's response had been, "Frankly, sir, I'm more worried about this girl's life than I am your radio station's call letters showing up in the press."

Before she left the GM's office, he had peevishly reminded her that her precious anonymity might soon be blown. She had already thought of that, and hoped it didn't come to pass. For years she had safeguarded her privacy with the fanaticism of a miser protecting his stockpile of gold. She never again wanted to be the pivotal figure in a sensational news story.

But she agreed with Curtis—rescuing Valentino's victim superseded everything else. By comparison, the impact it would have on her life was trivial.

To further pacify Stan, she said, "Rest assured that I received a proper scolding for jumping the chain of command. You weren't the only one who had his hands slapped today. Now, can I please get back to work?"

"It was a wristwatch with a built-in GPS."

"What was?"

"The gadget I bought myself today."

She laughed as he blew her an air kiss and headed for the door. Over his shoulder he said, "Oh, by the way, Marvin called in sick."

"Sick?"

"Switchboard left a message on my voice mail," he called back. "That's all it said."

To her knowledge Marvin had never called in sick before, making her curious about the nature of his sudden illness. She left the mail sorting for another time and headed toward the small employee kitchen at the back of the building.

At this time of night, the building was hushed and dimly lighted. Other station personnel were long gone, their offices dark. Paris was accustomed to the silence, the darkness, and the pervasive odors of dust scorched by electronic equipment, burned coffee, and carpet that had absorbed decades of tobacco smoke before smoking was outlawed in the workplace.

FM 101.3 was owned and operated by the Wilkins media conglomerate, which included five newspapers, three network-affiliated television stations, a cable company, and seven radio stations. The corporate offices occupied the top three floors of an Atlanta skyscraper that was upscale and sleek, with glass pods for elevators and a two-story waterfall in the sterile granite lobby.

This facility, rescued from a bankrupt previous owner, was as far from upscale and sleek as a woolly mammoth. There was no waterfall in the lobby, only a water cooler that gurgled and occasionally leaked.

The unattractive, single-story brick structure was situated on a hill on the outskirts of Austin, several miles from the state capitol dome. The building hailed from the early fifties and looked it. It had passed through the hands of twenty-two penny-pinching owners.

Rundown and tacky, it was virtually overlooked by the corporate suits—except when they reviewed the ratings charts. Appearance wise, FM 101.3 was an unsightly wart on the glossy corporate image. But it was healthfully in the black, a reliable producer of revenue.

Despite the building's shortcomings, Paris liked it. It had soul. It bore up well despite its scars.

After the dark hallways, the flickering fluorescent light in the kitchen seemed excessively bright. It took several seconds for her eyes to adjust to the glare even behind her tinted lenses. She took a teabag from her personal stock in the cabinet and put it in a cup of water she heated in the vintage microwave. The water had barely begun to color when she heard voices.

Looking into the hallway, she was stunned to see Dean trailing several steps behind Stan, who was saying to him, "She didn't tell me she was expecting a visitor."

"She isn't expecting me."

Spotting her, Stan said, "He was tapping on the front door. I didn't let him in until he showed me his cop's badge."

Trying to hide her consternation from her coworker, she said, "Dr. Malloy works with the Austin PD. He was consulted for a psychological assessment of Valentino's tape."

"So he said." Stan looked Dean up and down. "Two for the price of one. A cop and a shrink."

"Something like that," he replied, smiling tightly.

Stan looked from one to the other, but when neither spoke, he must have realized that his company was no longer wanted. He said to Paris, "If you need me, I'll be in the engineering room."

Dean watched as Stan retreated down the hallway. When he was out of earshot, he turned back to Paris. "That's Crenshaw? The owner's nephew? Is he gay?"

"I have no idea. What are you doing here, Dean?"

He stepped into the kitchen, immediately reducing its already limited floor space. "Someone should be here with you during your shift."

"Stan's with me."

"You would trust him with your life?"

She smiled wanly. "You have a point."

"Until we know more about this character calling himself Valentino, you should have police protection."

"Curtis offered to send out Griggs and Carson. I said no."

"I've met Griggs. He seems to be on his toes and a real Boy Scout, but neither he nor . . ."

"Carson."

" . . . has hostage-negotiation training. I should be here if Valentino calls again. If I sense that he's close to losing it, I could talk to him, hopefully persuade him to identify his captive and tell us where he's keeping her."

That being his field of expertise, it was a plausible excuse for his being there. Nevertheless, she questioned his motive. "He may not call. You will have wasted your whole evening."

"It wouldn't be wasted, Paris. I'm also here because I wanted to see you."

"You've seen me."

"Alone."

She set the mug of tea on the stained counter, turning her back to him. "Dean, please don't do this."

He moved up close behind her, and she held her breath, fearing he would touch her. She was unsure as to what her reaction would be if he did, so she didn't want to be tested.

"Nothing has changed, Paris."

She gave a rueful laugh. "Everything has changed."

"When you walked into my office this morning, it came back. All of it. I got slam-dunked just like I did the first time I saw you. Remember? It was the night after the snow."

Houston's snowfall had been reduced to a cold rain that gusted inside when she opened her front door to admit Jack and Dean.

She waved them inside hastily so she could close the door. Jack's introduction got lost in the flurry of their shedding damp overcoats and trying to close stubborn umbrellas that were dripping on her entry floor.

Once she had hung their coats on the coat tree and propped their umbrellas in the corner, she turned and smiled up at her fiancé's best friend. "Let's start over. Hello, Dean. I'm Paris. It's a pleasure to meet you."

"The same goes for me."

His handshake was firm, his smile warm and friendly. He was a couple inches taller than Jack, she noticed. His brown hair was showing signs of premature gray at his temples. He wasn't classically handsome like Jack, but ruggedly so. Jack had told her that Dean had to beat women off with a stick. She could see why. The asymmetric features of his face were arresting. They were counter-balanced by his eyes, which were pale gray and outlined by dark, spiky lashes. An absorbing combination.

He said, "I thought Jack was lying."

"Jack lie? Never!"

"When I asked him what you looked like, he said you would take my breath away. I thought he was exaggerating."

"He does tend to do that."

"He didn't this time."

From across the room, Jack grinned at them. "While you two are discussing my character flaws, I'm going to fix a round of drinks."

They enjoyed a convivial dinner at Jack's favorite steak house. After the meal they migrated to the adjacent bar, where they sat in front of the fireplace and sipped after-dinner coffees. The men regaled her with stories about their college days. Of course, Jack dominated the conversation, but Dean seemed willing to yield him center stage. Jack was a talented, witty storyteller.

Dean was an excellent listener. He asked her about her work, and while she was describing a normal workday, he never broke eye contact. He gave her the attention he would give an oracle divulging the future of mankind. He hung on every word and asked pertinent questions. That was Dean's special gift—making the other person feel as if they had become the center of his universe.

Jack's enjoyment of the evening included imbibing too much brandy. He was sleeping in the backseat when Dean pulled his car to a stop in front of her town house.

"I think we've lost him," he remarked.

She looked back at her fiancé, who was snoring softly through his open mouth. "I think you're right. Will you see him home safely and into bed?"

"As long as I don't have to kiss him good night."

She laughed. "I had heard so much about you from Jack, I already considered you my friend, too. Promise me that you'll join us for another evening soon."

"That's a promise."

"Good." She reached for the door handle.

"Wait. I'll see you in."

Despite her protests, he got out and came around with an umbrella as she alighted from the passenger seat. He walked with her to the front door. He even took her key from her, unlocked the door with his free hand, and waited until she had disengaged the alarm system.

"Thank you for seeing me in."

"You're welcome. What's the date?" he added.

"The date?"

"Of the wedding. I need to put it on my calendar. The best man's gotta be there, you know."

"I haven't set the date yet. Sometime in September or October."

"That long? Jack gave me the impression it would be sooner."

"It would be if he had his way, but I want to use fall colors."

"Yeah, that'd be nice. Church wedding?"

"Presbyterian."

"And the reception?"

"Probably a country club."

"A lot of planning."

"Yes, a lot."

"Hmm."

He seemed not to notice that rainwater dripped off the metal tips of the umbrella frame and splashed onto his shoes. She didn't notice that rain was being blown inside and onto her floor. Even that first night, the look they shared was perhaps several moments too long.

Dean had been the one to eventually break the stare, saying huskily, "Good night, Paris."

"Good night."

Often when future spouses are introduced to long-standing best friends, they despise one another on sight, making it awkward for the one in the middle who loves them both. She had liked Dean from the start.

She hadn't known any better than to consider that a good omen.

Now Dean reached for her hand and turned her around to face him. He looked at her with the same disturbing penetration as he had the night they'd met, and it had the same magnetic effect. She felt her will dissolving and knew that if she didn't fight it immediately, she would be lost.

"Dean, I beg you. Leave this alone."

She tried to step around him, but he blocked her path. "Our circumstances may have changed, Paris, but not what counts."

"What counts is what always has counted. Jack."

"He went through hell," he said. "I know that."

"You couldn't possibly know the hell his life was after that night."

He lowered his face to bring it closer to hers. "That's right, I don't. Because you made it clear I was not to come and see him. Ever."

"Because he wouldn't have wanted you—especially you—to see him that way," she said, her voice cracking. "But take my word for it, his was a living death for seven years before his heart made it official and stopped beating."

"I regret what happened to him as much as you do," he whispered urgently. "Don't you know that? Do you think I could blithely forget? Jesus, Paris, do you think I'm that callous? I've had to live with what happened, just as you have."

He expelled a long breath and pushed his fingers through his hair. He gazed at a spot above her head for a moment before his eyes moved back to her. "But at the risk of making you angry, I have to say this. What happened to Jack was his fault. Not yours, not mine. His."

"The accident wouldn't have happened if—"

"But it *did*. And we can't go back and undo it."

"Guilt management 101, Dr. Malloy?"

"Okay. Yeah. Simply put, I'm not going to let regret eat me alive. I've let it go."

"How nice for you."

"So your method of guilt management is better? Emotionally healthier? You think it preferable to dig a hole and hide in it?" He gave the untidy kitchen a scornful glance. "Look at this place. It's a dark, dirty, dreary rathole."

"I like it."

"Because it's no better than you think you deserve."

When he moved a step closer, her reaction was to hug her elbows tighter as a means of self-defense against his nearness. It was also a defense against the truth of what he was saying. She knew he was right, which only made her more determined not to listen.

"Paris, God knows you're good at what you do here. Your listening audience loves you. But you could've written your own ticket in TV news."

"What do you know about it?"

"I know I'm right. Furthermore, *you* know I'm right."

Unable to look into his persuasive eyes, she lowered her head and stared at the sliver of linoleum flooring between his shoes and hers. She curbed the impulse to grab his lapels and plead with him either to drop the subject or to convince her that she had paid her penance. "I did what I had to do," she said softly.

"Because you felt it was your duty?"

"It was."

"'Was,'" he repeated with a soft emphasis. "What duty do you owe Jack now that he's dead?" He took her by the shoulders. It was the first time in seven years that they had touched. A tide of heat surged through her and she struggled against the compulsion to lean into him and press her body to his.

Instead she said, "Dean, please, don't. I had to make some hard choices, but I made them. As you said, it's done. In any case, I won't argue with you about this."

"I don't want to argue either."

"Or talk about it," she added.

"Then we won't."

"I don't even want to think about it."

"I'll never stop thinking about it."

The timbre of his voice lowered. His fingers closed more tightly around her shoulders. Barely but noticeably he came closer, close enough for their clothing to touch and for her to feel his breath on her hair.

The subject had shifted from Jack's death to a topic that was even more unsettling and better avoided. She dared to raise her head and meet his gaze.

"Why do you hide in the dark, Paris?"

"I don't."

"Don't you? I could barely find my way down that hallway."

"You get used to it."

"'Hello, darkness, my old friend.'"

"You're quoting Simon and Garfunkel?"

"Is that your theme song these days?"

"Maybe you should have been the deejay." She smiled, hoping to lighten the tone of the conversation, but he wouldn't be deterred.

His eyes moved over her face. "You're beautiful, but no one in your listening audience knows what you look like."

"It isn't necessary. Radio is an aural medium."

"But normally radio personalities promote themselves. You have no identity beyond your voice."

"Which is all the identity I need. I don't want to focus attention on myself."

"Really? Then maybe you should dispense with the sunglasses."

"She can't. Her eyes are sensitive to light."

Neither realized that Stan was there until he spoke. As they turned toward him, Dean dropped his hands from her shoulders.

Stan eyed him mistrustfully, but his message was for Paris. "It's five to ten. Harry's going into the news update and final commercial break. You're up."

chapter *fourteen*

"*H*ey, Gav!"

Gavin glanced over his shoulder, saw who had hailed him, then waited for Melissa Hatcher to catch up with him. When she got close enough to read his expression, her smile dissolved.

Foregoing any greeting, he said, "Way to go, Melissa. Were you trying to ruin my life, or were you just too stupid to not keep your mouth shut?"

"You're pissed?"

"You bet your ass I'm pissed."

"What for? What'd I do?"

"You told my dad we knew each other."

"So, what's the big deal?"

"The big deal is that we're having a burger at Chili's tonight and he starts in on the Sex Club."

She propped her hand on her hip. "Oh, like I'd tell your dad about the Sex Club. Duh!"

"Well, he heard about it from somebody."

"Probably that other cop. The short, bald one." She puffed on a lighted joint, then offered it to him. "Here. You look in need of some major chilling out."

He pushed the marijuana aside. "What do you know about Janey?"

"She's in deep shit. With her folks. The cops. Everybody." Spotting a group of acquaintances beyond Gavin's shoulder, she waved, calling out, "Hey, y'all, I'm back from France, and have I got stories!"

Gavin sidestepped, blocking her view of the others and forcing her to look at him. "Is Janey really missing?"

"I guess. I mean, that's what your dad told me. By the way, he's hot. Does he have a girlfriend?"

The dope alone couldn't be blamed for her being a mental zero. She hadn't started out with enough gray matter to brag about. "Melissa, what do you know about Janey?"

"Nothing."

"You're her best friend," he argued.

"I've been out of the frigging country," she said crossly. "I haven't seen Her Highness in weeks. All right?" She took another hit of weed. "Look, I've got people waiting for me. Chill, why don't you."

She left him to join a group who had attached a garden hose to a keg of beer and were taking turns guzzling from it. A lot was lost on the ground, but no one seemed to notice or care. There was always more where that came from.

Gavin joined his friends, who were once again congregated in and around Craig's pickup. He surrendered the unopened bottle of Maker's Mark he'd stolen from his dad's liquor cabinet. As busy as his old man was tracking down Janey Kemp, it might be several days before he noticed he was short a bottle of bourbon.

Craig went to work on the red wax seal with his pocketknife. "Did you catch hell last night?"

"And then some." Gavin put his back against the rear fender while his eyes scoured the crowd in search of a familiar face and form.

"You were so wasted."

"Hurled on the way home."

"Oh, man."

"I shit you not." He recounted the incident at the mailbox. "I'm talking projectile vomiting."

Their laughter was interrupted when another of the boys brought up Janey's name. "Y'all hear about her disappearance?"

"It was on the local news," another said. "My mom asked if I knew her."

"Bet you didn't tell her how well you know her."

"Yeah, bet you didn't tell your mom that you know Janey in the biblical sense."

"What do you know about anything biblical?"

"My cousin's a preacher."

"So what happened to you?"

"He tried to save me. It didn't take. Pass the bottle."

The others continued to swap insults along with swigs of the whiskey. Craig climbed out of the truck and came to stand beside Gavin. "What's with you tonight?"

"Nothing."

"Just bummed, huh?" Craig gave him an opportunity to explain his mood, but then gave up with a shrug and joined Gavin's perusal of the crowd. Suddenly, in an excited whisper, he said, "Hey, see that guy over there?"

Gavin looked in the direction Craig indicated and saw a man climbing from the backseat of a car, rearranging his clothes and pulling on a baseball cap. Two girls got out behind him. They were lookers. Barbie-doll types, blond and chesty, although their bony sternums suggested implants.

"Their tits are fake," Gavin remarked.

"Who cares?"

Obviously not Craig, who continued to ogle. "Wonder if the girls know he's a badge?"

Gavin reacted with a start. "A cop? No way."

"I've heard it rumored."

As they watched, the trio engaged in a group hug. Then the man shooed away each girl, but not before giving her an affectionate smack on the butt and a promise to see her again soon.

The girls ambled away, unfortunately in the opposite direction from Craig and Gavin. The man got back into his car, this time in the driver's seat, and as he maneuvered it around Craig's Ram, he and Gavin made eye contact.

"Smug SOB," Craig muttered.

"You're *sure* he's a cop?"

"Ninety-nine point nine percent."

"Then what's he doing here?"

"Same thing we are, and tonight he scored big."

"Yeah, times two."

"Lucky prick." They watched until the taillights disappeared, then Craig said, "I saw you talking to Melissa."

"That's what she's good at. Talking." He told Craig about his dad's chance meeting with her at the Kemp house. "He knows about the Sex Club."

"Don't worry about it," Craig said with a disdainful sniff. "What are they gonna do, seize all the computers?"

"Exactly what I asked my old man. They're pissing in the wind."

Gavin was talking tougher than he felt. Worry gnawed at him like a hunger pain. That's why he had defied his dad once again by leaving the house tonight. He was going to be in trouble anyway, so what the hell? It was a matter of degree.

Weeks ago, planning for an emergency like this, he'd had a spare car key made. As soon as his dad had dropped him off at home and left for the radio station, he was outta there, too. But he didn't feel as cavalier as his defiance implied. He was sick with apprehension over what the next few days might yield.

"Where do you think she is?"

Craig's question broke into his thoughts as though he'd been reading them. "Who, Janey? How the hell should I know?"

"Well, I thought you might."

"Why?"

Craig looked at him with annoyance. "Seeing as how you were with her last night."

As the last few bars of "I'll Never Love This Way Again" faded into silence, Paris spoke into her microphone. "That was Dionne Warwick. I hope you have someone in your life who can look inside your fantasies and make each one come true."

The studio felt claustrophobic tonight and Dean was the reason why. He'd sat for the last three hours and sixteen minutes on a tall, swivel stool identical to hers, far enough away to give her freedom of movement and access to all the controls, but close enough for her to be constantly aware of him. He sat motionlessly and for the most part silently, but his eyes followed her every move.

She felt them especially now when she mentioned fulfilling fantasies. "It's a toasty eighty-two degrees at one-sixteen, but I'll be playing cool classics until two o'clock here on 101.3. Let me know what's on your mind tonight. Call me.

"I've had a request from Marge and Jim, who are celebrating their thirtieth wedding anniversary. This was their wedding song. It's from the Carpenters. Happy anniversary, Marge and Jim."

As "Close to You" began to play, she punched the button to turn off her mike, then glanced across at Dean as she depressed one of the blinking telephone lines. "This is Paris."

"Hi, Paris. My name's Roger."

Throughout the program, each time she had answered one of the phone lines, she and Dean had feared, and yet hoped, that Valentino would be the caller. He'd brought a portable cassette recorder with him. It was loaded and ready to record.

His shoulders relaxed along with hers as she said, "Hello, Roger."

"Can you please play a song for me?"

"What's the occasion?"

"Nothing. I just like the song."

"That's occasion enough. What song would you like to hear?"

Facilely she inserted the requested number into the log, substituting it for one already on deck. Then digging her fists into her lower back, she stood up and stretched.

"Tired?" Dean asked.

"I got virtually no sleep last night and never caught a nap today. You must be tired, too. You're not accustomed to these hours."

"More accustomed than you think. I rarely sleep through a whole night anymore. I doze while listening for Gavin to come in."

"Is he with you for the summer?"

"No, more or less permanently."

She registered her surprise. "Nothing's happened to Pat?"

"No, no, she's good," he said in quick response to her concern. "Doing great, in fact. She finally remarried. He's a nice guy in everyone's opinion except Gavin's."

Paris had met Dean's ex-wife at one of Gavin's Little League games, and she and Jack had once been invited to her house for Gavin's birthday dinner. She remembered her as a petite and pretty woman, but rather serious and structured.

Without her having to ask, Jack had confided to her that Dean had married straight out of college. The union had lasted less than a year. "Really only long enough for them to get Gavin home from the hospital. They were unsuited and knew it and agreed it would be best, even for the kid, if they cut their losses and made a clean break when they did."

Although Gavin had lived with Pat, Dean saw him several times a week and had been actively involved in all phases of his life. He joined Pat at teacher conferences, coached T-ball and soccer teams, participated in and contributed to every aspect of Gavin's development. Following a divorce, a child's upbringing was most often abdicated to the custodial parent. Paris had admired Dean for taking his responsibilities as a father so seriously.

"He and his stepfather weren't getting along?" she asked.

"Gavin's fault. He had moved beyond misbehaving to being downright impossible. Pat and I agreed that he should live with me for a while." He described their tenuous coexistence. "The hell of it is, Paris, I was looking forward to having him with me. I want this arrangement to work."

"I'm sure it will, given time. Gavin is a sweet kid."

He laughed. "Lately, I would beg to differ. But I hope that sweet kid you remember is still in there somewhere behind all that hostility and surliness."

At half past the hour she read a few headlines of news off the information monitor. Following that came several minutes of commercials, during which she took calls. One caller asked her for a date. She graciously declined.

"Maybe you should have accepted," Dean teased. "He sounded desperate."

"Desperately drunk," she said, returning his smile as she deleted the call from the Vox Pro.

The next call came from a giddy couple who'd just become engaged. "He asked me to open a bottle of wine and then handed me a glass with the ring in it." Even her squeal couldn't disguise a charming British accent. "My friends in London won't believe it! We faithfully watched *Dallas* when we were girls and dreamed of someday meeting a handsome Texan."

Laughing because of the young woman's obvious delight, Paris asked what song they wanted her to play.

"'She's Got a Way.' He says Billy Joel could've written it about me."

"And I'm sure he's right. Is it okay if I share our conversation with the listening audience?"

"Fantastic!"

She jotted down their names and answered a few more calls. After the sequence of commercials, she replayed the conversation with the engaged couple and followed it with their requested song, then "Precious & Few," which segued into "The Rose."

Operating the board was second nature to her, so she was able to do all this while continuing her conversation with Dean about Gavin. "What did he say when you told him about meeting Melissa Hatcher?"

"He pretended not to know her."

Paris looked at him inquisitively and he read her thought.

"Yeah, that bothers me, too. Why didn't he want to admit that he knew her? He didn't admit to knowing Janey Kemp either, until I pressed him on it."

"How well does he know her?"

"Not very. At least that's what he told me, but these days I don't always get the truth."

"Not like the time he bent the wheel on his bicycle."

"You remember that?"

"Jack and I had come over to your house for a cookout. Gavin was staying with you that weekend. He'd been riding bikes with neighborhood kids, but came home pushing his. The spokes of his front wheel were bent almost in half. You asked if he'd been popping wheelies and when he confessed, you sent him to his room for the rest of the evening."

"Which might have been punishment enough because he loved being around you and Jack. But I also made him do chores to earn enough money to replace the wheel."

"Tough but good parenting, Dean."

"You think?"

"I do. You made your point about the value of property, but it wasn't the damage to the bike that upset you."

He smiled ruefully. "I'd told him a thousand times not to pop wheelies or jump curbs because it was dangerous. I didn't want him to become an organ donor."

"Right. He could just as easily have busted his head or broken his neck. You were upset over what could have happened, and that's why you were angry."

"I guess I should have explained that to him."

"He knew," she said softly.

He looked across at her and the connection was more than just visual. It lasted through the remainder of the Bette Midler song. As it wound down, Paris turned back to the control board and engaged her mike.

"Don't forget to join Charlie and Chad tomorrow morning. They'll keep you company as you drive to work. In the meantime, this is Paris Gibson with a romantic lineup of classic love songs. The phone lines will be open right up till two o'clock. Call me."

When the next series of songs began, she glanced up at the log monitor. "Only nine minutes left in the program."

"Isn't this about the time he called last night? Right before sign-off?" When she nodded, he said, "Will you be able to talk to him uninterrupted if he does call?"

She pointed to the countdown clock on the screen. "That's the amount of time remaining for everything that's logged to play. Two more selections follow this one."

He calibrated. "So after the last song ends, you'll have barely enough time to say good night and sign off."

"Right."

He glanced at the phone lines on the control board. Three were blinking. "If it's not Valentino, don't engage the caller in a lengthy conversation. Keep the lines open. And if it is him, remember to ask to speak to Janey."

She took a deep breath, checked to see that Dean's finger was on the Record button of the portable machine, then answered one of the phone lines. Rachel wanted to request a song for her husband, Pete, "It Might Be You."

"Ah, Stephen Bishop."

"It was the first song we danced to at our wedding reception."

"It's such a good choice, it deserves a prime spot." Paris promised to play it the following night in the first half hour of her program.

"Awesome. Thanks."

Paris glanced again at Dean before depressing another of the blinking buttons. "This is Paris."

"Hello, Paris."

Her blood ran cold at the sound of his voice. Frantically she cut her eyes to Dean, who started the portable recorder. The Vox Pro screen registered a phone number, which he scribbled down. He stared into the screen as though willing it to give up not just the telephone number but also the image and identity of the caller.

"Hello, Valentino."

"How was your day? Busy?"

"I managed."

"Come now, Paris. Share. What did you do today to keep yourself occupied? Did you think of me at all? Or did you write me off as a crank? Did you talk to the police?"

"Why would I? Unless you let me speak to the girl, I have no reason to believe that she exists and that what you told me last night is true."

"Stop playing silly games, Paris. Of course she exists. Why would I make such a claim if it weren't true?"

"To get my attention."

He laughed. "Well, did it? Will you pay attention this time?"

"This time?"

"You ignored me when I warned you before, and look what happened."

She looked at Dean and shook her head with misapprehension. "What are you talking about, Valentino?"

"Wouldn't you like to know?" he taunted. "Ask me nicely and I may give you a few hints. But you have to ask me *very* nicely. Now, that's an exciting thought." He inhaled deeply, loudly, so she could hear it. "Your voice alone is enough to arouse me. I think about us together, you know. Someday soon, Paris."

She shuddered with repugnance but continued in a bland tone. "I don't believe you have a girl with you. You're all talk and this is a hoax."

Dean nodded approval.

"More games, Paris? I advise against them. You've already squandered twenty-four of your seventy-two hours. The next forty-eight are going to be much more fun for me than for you. As for my captive, she's a little tired, and all her whining and pleading is beginning to grate on my nerves. But she's still a hot fuck, and I'm due."

The line went dead.

"It's not the same number he called from last night," Dean said as he reached for his cell. "Did you notice anything different tonight, Paris? Any change in his inflection or tone from last night?"

Dean was a policeman, she wasn't. Revolted by the call, she was finding it harder to launch into the mode of crime solver. "No," she replied hoarsely. "He sounded the same."

"To me, too, but I thought you might've picked up— Hey, Curtis, he just called," he said into his cell phone. "Different number. Ready?"

As he reeled it off to the detective, Stan pushed open the sound-proof door. "Uh, Paris, we've got dead air."

She hadn't realized the music had stopped. Quickly she signaled for quiet and engaged her mike. "Be safe, be happy, love someone. This is Paris Gibson wishing you a good night." She punched a few buttons, then announced, "We're off."

"The creep called again?" Stan asked.

Dean had turned his back to them while he continued his telephone conversation with Curtis.

To Stan she said, "Leave a note for the morning engineers. Ask them to dump the last call on the Vox Pro onto a cassette and make several copies. They'll be better than the one Dean's portable made."

He looked affronted. "I know how to transfer it to cassette, Paris. I could do it right now."

She hesitated, uncertain of his skill. But he looked so crestfallen, she added, "Thanks, Stan, that would be a help."

Dean ended his call, then turned around and grabbed his jacket off the back of the stool and picked up the portable recorder, all in one fluid motion. "The number belongs to another pay phone. Units are already rolling."

"I'm going, too," Paris said.

"Damn straight you are. No way would I leave you alone now."

He pulled open the door. As they rushed out, she called back to Stan. "Could you drop those cassettes off at my house?"

Dean pushed her through the door before Stan had time to answer.

chapter *fifteen*

Melissa Hatcher was jealous of Janey Kemp for all the reasons that customarily inspire jealousy. Janey was wealthier, prettier, smarter, more popular, and more desired. However, there was one attribute Melissa had that Janey did not: shrewdness.

Had Melissa made Janey her rival, she automatically would have fallen into a distant second place in a two-woman contest. Instead, she had been cunning enough to make Janey her best friend.

But on her first night back from France, when she should have been the center of attention, all anyone wanted to talk about was Janey and her mysterious disappearance. Melissa was miffed. She had tales of the nude beaches on the Côte d'Azur, of the wine she'd drunk and the drugs she'd done. How she'd come to obtain a nipple ring in St. Tropez was a story that would hold an audience captive for half an hour.

But no one was interested in her recent adventures abroad. Janey was the name on everyone's lips, the topic of every conversation.

Melissa didn't believe any of the wild speculations being circulated about her friend's whereabouts. They ranged from her eloping with the Dallas Cowboys rookie quarterback whom she'd met in a club on Sixth Street, to having been kidnapped for ransom that her old man refused to pay, to being snatched by a pervert and made his sex slave.

My ass, Melissa thought resentfully.

If Janey was honeymooning with one of the Dallas Cowboys, she would've made sure that everybody knew about it. Melissa wouldn't put it past the judge to refuse to pay a ransom to kidnappers, but he would do so in front of lights and cameras and use it to campaign for his reelection. And if anybody was being made a sex slave, it was probably the guy who was shacked up with Janey.

Janey was getting stoned. She was getting balled. End of story. When she felt good and ready, she would reappear and gloat over the stir she'd created. She would milk it for all it was worth. That was Janey. She thrived on shocking and agitating people.

How like her so-called best friend, Melissa thought, to steal the limelight on her first night back from Europe. The evening had turned into a real drag, and she was in a sour mood. Having heard enough about Janey to last a lifetime, Melissa decided to go home and submit to jet lag.

But when she spotted the older guy, she changed her mind.

She had seen him before. Her memory wasn't 100 percent reliable, but she was almost positive that Janey had been with him at least once. As galling as it was to admit, he probably would choose Janey over her if Janey was here. Which she wasn't.

So Melissa sauntered over to where he stood leaning against the driver's door of his car, observing. "You going or coming?"

He looked her up and down, then formed a slow grin. "Right now, neither."

She slapped his arm playfully. "I think you took my meaning wrong."

"You didn't intend the double entendre?"

She wasn't sure what that was, so she shrugged and gave him her most beguiling smile. "Maybe."

He was nice looking. Around thirty-five, she'd guess. A little old and geeky, but so what? At least he would be impressed by her travels.

"I just got back from France."

"How was it?"

"Frenchy."

He smiled in appreciation of her wit.

"It was a total blast. I didn't know what the hell they were saying, but I liked listening to them talk. I saw this guy drinking wine with breakfast. Parents give it to their kids, can you believe that? And people sunbathe nude on public beaches."

"Did you?"

She grinned slyly. "What do you think?"

He reached out and brushed her arm. "Mosquito."

"They're vicious tonight. Maybe we should get in your car."

He ushered her to the passenger door and opened it for her,

then went around and got in on the driver's side. He started the motor and turned on the air conditioner.

"Hmm, this is much better," she said, wiggling against the cool leather upholstery. "Nice car," she said, taking in the interior. Glancing into the backseat, she asked, "What's that?"

"A plastic trash bag."

"Duh! I know that. What's in it?"

"Want to see?" He reached between the seats and picked up the bag, then set it in her lap.

"It's not dirty laundry, is it?" she asked, and he laughed.

Melissa undid the twist tie and peered inside, then took out a magazine. The title and cover couldn't have been more explicit, but she feigned nonchalance. "In France, you can buy fetish mags like this on every street corner. Nobody thinks anything about it. Can I look?"

"Be my guest."

By the time she'd gone through the magazine, his fingers were strumming the inside of her thigh. He lowered his head to nuzzle her breast. "What's this?"

"My souvenir from France." She raised her top and proudly showed him her nipple ring. "I met this guy on the beach who knew this dentist who does body piercing on the side."

He began to laugh.

"What's funny?"

He flicked the silver ring with the tip of his finger. "Inside joke."

There were seven calls from Liz on Dean's home telephone voice mail. He listened to all seven.

"I can't imagine why you haven't called me," the last message began. "I've gone beyond angry, Dean. I'm scared. Has something happened to you or Gavin? If you get this message, please call. If I don't hear from you within an hour, I'm going to start calling the Austin hospitals."

The message had been left at 3:20 A.M. There was a similar one on his cell phone voice mail. The last thing he wanted was to talk to Liz. No, the last thing he wanted was to have her start calling the hospitals.

He dialed her cell phone, which she answered on the first ring. "I'm okay," he said immediately. "No one's in the hospital, and you have every right to be mad as hell. Let fly."

"Dean, what is going on?"

He slumped into a chair at his kitchen table and plowed his fingers through his hair. "Work. We've got a crisis situation."

"I haven't heard any news about—"

"Not a national crisis. Not a plane crash, standoff, mass murder, nothing like that. But it's a tricky case. I got involved early this morning . . . yesterday morning, rather. I was consulted as soon as I got to my office, and I've been on it all day. I just got home and I'm beat. None of which is an excuse for not returning your calls."

"What kind of case?"

"Missing girl. Egotistical suspect. He's called and told us what he plans to do to her unless we can locate her before his deadline." He didn't have the energy to tell her more than that. Besides, the details would have included Paris. Liz didn't know about Paris, and this wasn't the time to try to explain a situation of that complexity.

"I'm sorry you had such a hellish day."

"Jesus, Liz, I'm the one who's sorry."

He had much to be sorry for. Sorry for pretending to return her love, and pretending so well that she believed he did. Sorry for not telling her to remain in Houston as she should have done. Sorry for wishing that her trip to Chicago would last longer than a few days.

Lamely he asked, "How did the meetings with the Swedes go?"

"Danes. They accepted my proposal."

"Good. Not surprising, though."

"How's Gavin?"

"He's all right."

"No more arguments?"

"We've avoided bloodshed."

"You sound exhausted. So I'm going to hang up and let you get some rest."

"Again, about today—"

"It doesn't matter, Dean."

"The hell it doesn't. I caused you a lot of unnecessary worry. It matters."

He was angry with her for not being angrier with him. It would have eased his conscience if she'd been royally pissed off. He didn't want her to be understanding. He didn't want to be let off the hook gently. He wanted her to be mad as hell.

But a full-fledged fight would have required energy he didn't have, so he let it drop with a feeble, "Well, anyway, I apologize."

"Accepted. Now go to bed. We'll talk tomorrow."

"I promise. Good night."

"Good night."

He took a long drink straight from the bottle of water in the fridge, then moved through the dark house, toward the bedrooms. There was no light beneath Gavin's door, not even the glow of his computer monitor. He paused to look in.

Gavin was asleep. Wearing only his underwear, he was lying on his back, long limbs flung wide, covers kicked away. He was almost as long as the bed. He was breathing through his mouth, as he'd done since he was a baby. He looked very young and innocent. At sixteen, he was on the borderline between boy and man. But asleep, he seemed much more like a child than a grown-up.

Dean realized, as he stood looking down at his son, that the painful twinge he felt deep inside his chest was love. He hadn't loved Gavin's mother, nor she him, really. But both had loved Gavin. From the day they knew he'd been conceived, they had channeled the love they should have had for each other into the person they had created.

Obviously they had failed to communicate the depth of that love to Gavin. He still didn't believe that correction was for his protection and that discipline wasn't a pleasant pastime for them, but a demonstration of how important he was to them.

Damn it, Dean had wanted to be a good parent. He'd wanted to get it right. He hadn't wanted his son to doubt for one moment of his life that he was loved. But somewhere along the way he must have tripped up, done something wrong, omitted doing something he should have. Now his son held him in contempt and made no secret of it.

Feeling the weight of his failure, Dean backed away from Gavin's bed and quietly closed the door behind him.

The master bedroom was a large room with a high cove ceiling, wide windows, and a fireplace. It deserved better decorating than what he'd done, which amounted to nothing more than basic furnishings and a bedspread. When he'd moved in, he'd told Liz he was saving the decorating for her to do after they married. But he'd been lying to her as well as to himself. He'd never even invited her to spend the night in this bed.

He plugged his cell phone battery charger into a wall socket in the bathroom so it would be handy in case of a call, then stripped and got into the shower and let the hot water pound into him while he mentally reviewed everything that had taken place after Valentino's call.

The race to the pay telephone had been a wasted effort for all concerned—for the cops in the three squad cars who had converged on it, for Sergeant Robert Curtis, who had arrived as neatly dressed as he was during daylight hours, and for Paris and him.

They had arrived shortly after it was confirmed that Valentino was no longer anywhere in the vicinity of the pay phone from which his call had originated. The Wal-Mart store had been closed for hours. The parking lot was a vast desert of concrete. There were no witnesses except for a stray cat who had helped himself to the remnants of a hot dog someone had tossed toward a trash bin, but missed.

"And the cat's not talking," Curtis said wryly as he summed up the situation for them.

He and Paris had joined the detective in his car to conduct a postmortem on the aborted effort to catch Valentino. Paris climbed in the back. He sat in the passenger seat. "I made a cassette recording as the call came in," he told Curtis.

"Let's hear it."

He played the tape once, then rewound it and they listened to it a second time. When it ended, Curtis remarked, "He doesn't seem to know we're after him."

"Which could work in our favor," Dean said.

"Only until tomorrow when it shows up in the newspaper." Curtis turned to Paris. "What does he mean when he says you didn't heed him the last time?"

"Just as I told him, I have no idea."

"You don't recall a previous warning?"

"If I had ever received a call like this, I would have reported it to the police."

"Which is what she did last night." Dean didn't like the way the detective was looking at Paris. "What are you getting at?"

"Nothing. Just thinking."

"Then do us the courtesy of thinking out loud."

Curtis turned to him and seemed ready to take issue with his tone of voice, then must have remembered that Dean outranked him. "I was just thinking about Paris."

"Specifically?"

"How she's gone out of her way to remain anonymous. Which, frankly, I don't get," he said, turning back to her. "Other people in your field are extroverts. Publicity hounds. Their pictures are on billboards. They make personal appearances, stuff like that."

"I'm not like the wild and crazy drive-time jocks. My program isn't hyper like theirs. The music is different, and so am I. I'm the disembodied voice in the dark. I'm the sounding board when no one else will listen. If my listeners knew what I looked like, it would compromise the confidentiality I share with them. It's often easier for people to talk to a stranger than to a trusted friend."

"It's certainly easier for Valentino," he remarked. "If he *is* a stranger to you."

"He may be now, but he doesn't want to remain a stranger," Dean said. Paris and Curtis were sharp enough to know he was referring to Valentino's suggestion that he and Paris would soon be lovers.

Curtis, however, was still following his original train of thought. "You know," he said, "some of those phone sex people are very ordinary looking. Fat, ugly, a far cry from what their voices suggest about them."

Dean knew this wasn't a random observation. "Okay, you've tossed out the bait. I'll bite."

"Instead of lounging on a bed of satin sheets in skimpy lingerie, like they want their callers to fantasize, they're actually in sweats and sneakers, working out of their untidy kitchens. It's all about imagination." He turned to address Paris. "Folks hear your voice and conjure up a mental image of you. I did it myself."

"And?"

"I wasn't even close. I envisioned you dark haired and dark eyed. A fortune-teller type."

"I'm sorry to disappoint."

"I didn't say you disappointed me. You're just not as exotic looking as your voice indicates." He shifted more comfortably in his seat so he wouldn't have to crane his neck to talk to her. "All this is to say that some people may have formed an unwholesome image of you. Valentino appears to be one of those people."

"Paris can't be responsible for a listener's imagination," Dean said. "Especially if he suffers from mental, emotional, or sexual problems."

"Yeah, you said that before." More or less dismissing Dean's comment as irrelevant, the detective continued to address Paris. "Is there a personal reason you want to remain anonymous?"

"Absolutely. To protect my privacy. When you're a television personality, you're always in the public eye, even when you're not on the air. I didn't like that aspect of my work. My life was an open book. Everything I said or did was subject to criticism, or speculation, or judgment from people who didn't know anything about me.

"Radio enables me to stay in the business but out of the spotlight. It allows me to go anywhere without being recognized and scrutinized and to keep my private life just that."

Curtis's harrumph implied that he knew he wasn't hearing the whole story but was willing to let it go for now. "How long did you say you keep the recordings of your phone calls?"

"Indefinitely."

He grimaced. "That's a lot of phone calls."

"But remember, I only save the ones that I feel are worth saving."

"Even at that, we're talking what? Hundreds?" She nodded. He said, "We'd use up a chunk of our remaining forty-eight hours listening to all those calls, trying to find the one Valentino referred to tonight. But if we go in by the back door—"

"By looking at cold cases," Dean said, seeing suddenly where Curtis was headed.

"Right. I called a friend over there." The cold-case unit worked out of a separate building a few miles from headquarters. "He promised to check, see if any of their cases have a similarity to Janey Kemp's."

"And if so, we can check to see if Paris received a call from Valentino around that time."

"Don't get too excited," she cautioned them. "I might not have saved that call. Besides, how could I have dismissed a warning of murder?"

"I doubt he was so blatant the first time," Dean told her. "It's symptomatic of serial rapists to get progressively bolder. They start out cautiously and get more daring with each offense until they're practically courting capture."

Curtis agreed. "That's been my experience."

"Some actually want to get caught," Dean said. "They're begging to be stopped."

"Somehow I don't think Valentino fits into that category," she said. "He sounds very self-assured. Arrogant."

Dean looked across at Curtis and could tell that the veteran detective agreed with her. Unfortunately, so did Dean.

"On the other hand," he said, "he could be manipulating us. Maybe you don't remember any such call because there wasn't one. Valentino could be trying to distract us with a red herring."

"Could be," Curtis said. "I get the distinct feeling he's laughing up his sleeve." He asked Paris, "What do you know about Marvin Patterson?"

"Until yesterday, only his first name."

"Why?" Dean asked the dectective.

"He's split," Curtis said. "Officers called his place to see if he was at home, told him they were on their way to talk to him. By the time they arrived, Marvin Patterson was gone. Vacated in a hurry. Dirty breakfast dishes in the sink and his coffeepot still warm. That's how fast he cleared out."

Paris asked, "What's he got to hide?"

"We're investigating that now," Curtis replied. "The Social Security number he put on his job application at the radio station was traced to a ninety-year-old black woman who died in a rest home several months ago."

"Marvin Patterson was an alias?" Dean asked.

"I'll let you know when we know."

Paris said, "Marvin, or whatever his name is, may have something to hide, but I don't believe he could possibly be Valentino. He uses that creepy whisper, but he's articulate. If Marvin speaks at all, it's a mumble."

Dean asked her what Marvin looked like. "How old is he?"

"Thirtyish. I've never really paid much attention to his looks, but I would describe him as nice looking."

Curtis said, "Let's wait and see what turns up."

"Has anything useful been found on Janey's computer?" Dean asked.

"Smut. Lots of it. Written by other kids."

"Or predators."

Curtis conceded Dean's point. "Wherever it originated it's raw stuff, especially coming from high school kids. Rondeau printed out her email address book and is in the process of tracing the users."

After that, they'd parted company. Paris's protests against having police protection were overruled. Curtis had already dispatched Griggs and Carson to her house.

"They're both starstruck. If they were guarding the president, they couldn't be taking it more seriously. They'll be parked at your curb all night."

Dean drove her home. "What about my car?" she asked when he refused to return her to the radio station so she could pick it up.

"Ask one of your admirers to retrieve it in the morning."

She directed him to her house. It was located in a wooded, hilly area on the outskirts of downtown. The limestone house was tucked into a grove of sprawling live oaks and garnished with well-maintained landscaping. A curved walkway lined with white caladiums led up to a deep porch. Twin brass light fixtures glowed a welcome from either side of a glossy-black front door.

Incongruous with the coziness of the property was the patrol car parked at the curb. The two young policemen practically leaped from it when Dean and Paris pulled up behind them.

Dean waved back the ever-ready Griggs. "I'll see her in."

He'd insisted on going inside with her, and even though her alarm control panel hadn't registered a disturbance since she set it, he went through every room of the house, looking inside closets, behind shower doors, and even beneath the bed.

"Valentino doesn't strike me as the type who would hide under a bed," she said.

"A rapist often hides in his victim's house, waiting for her to return home. That's part of the thrill."

"Are you trying to frighten me?"

"Definitely. I want you good and scared, Paris. This guy wants to punish women, remember? He's angry with Janey—at least we're still presuming it's Janey—for cheating on him. He's angry with you for taking her side."

"I didn't even know there were sides to be taken."

"Well, that's his skewed perception of it and perception is—"

"Truth. I know."

"The suggestion that you and he would soon be together as lovers actually meant that you would be his next victim. He doesn't differentiate between the two."

She pulled her lower lip through her teeth. "When he's finished with Janey, he'll come after me."

"Not if I can help it." He went to her then and placed his hands on her shoulders. "But until we have him in custody, be afraid of him."

She smiled wanly. "I'm not actually afraid. But I'm not stupid either. I'll be careful."

When she'd tried to move away, he hadn't let her go. "This is the first time in our friendship that we've been in a bedroom together."

"Friendship?"

"Weren't we friends?"

She hesitated for several beats before saying quietly, "Yes. We were friends."

"Good friends."

That's when he had reached up and removed her sunglasses, tossed them into a nearby chair, then anxiously searched her eyes. They were as beautiful as he remembered. Deeply blue, intelligent, expressive. They gazed back at him steadily and with seeming clarity.

He exhaled a deep sigh of relief. "I was afraid that you'd lost sight in one eye, or suffered a serious injury, and that was the reason for the sunglasses."

"No permanent damage was done," she said huskily. "I wasn't even left with noticeable scars. But my eyes are still very sensitive to bright light."

Without breaking their eye contact, he leaned forward to reach behind her for the wall switch. He flicked it down and the room went dark. He remained inclined forward, so they were touching from chest to knees, and when she didn't move away, he slid his hands around her neck and up into her hair. He tilted her face up as he lowered his.

"Dean, don't."

But the words were no more than an uneven sigh against his lips as he settled them upon hers. They parted simultaneously, and when their tongues touched, her groan echoed the hunger behind his own. He backed her against the wall, wanting to feel her and taste her. Wanting.

He curved his arm around her waist and drew her lower body up against his, increasing the pressure where already the pressure was intense. She broke off the kiss and moaned his name.

He brushed his lips across her eyes, her cheekbones, whispering, "We've waited long enough for this, Paris. Haven't we?"

Then he returned to her mouth and kissed her even more passionately than before. He worked his hand between their bodies and covered her breast. Her nipple was erect even before his thumb found it. He felt her hands tensing on the muscles of his back, felt the upward and forward angling of her hips.

He remembered muttering something unintelligible, even to himself, as he lowered his head, his mouth blindly seeking her breast.

"Ms. Gibson? Dr. Malloy?"

Dean jerked as though he'd been shot. Paris froze, then squeezed out from between him and the wall.

He saw red. "That goddamned rookie. I'm gonna kill him."

And at that moment he had meant it. He might have stormed

down the hallway and throttled Griggs with his bare hands—as he'd wanted to do—if Paris hadn't grabbed his arm and held him back. She stepped around him and, straightening her hair and clothing as she went, made her way through the house and into the living room.

Griggs was standing on the threshold of the front door. "You left the front door standing open," he said to Dean, who was only half a step behind Paris. "Everything all right?"

"Everything is fine," Paris told him. "Dr. Malloy was kind enough to check my house."

Griggs was staring at her strangely. Either he had noticed that her color was high and her lips were swollen, or he was surprised by her breathlessness, or he was shocked to see her without her sunglasses, or a combination of all of that.

At that moment Dean was incapable of diplomacy and stated bluntly, "You can leave now." He had never liked cops who pulled rank, but this was one time he did and didn't feel bad about it.

Paris was more gracious. "Dr. Malloy will be leaving momentarily. We both appreciate your diligence."

"Uh, some guy . . . Stan? Dropped these off for you." He extended several cassettes.

"Oh, right. Thank you."

"Just leave them there on the table."

Griggs did as Dean ordered. He took another apprehensive glance in his direction, then scuttled out, pulling the door closed behind him.

Dean reached for Paris again, but she avoided his touch. "That shouldn't have happened."

"The interruption? Or the kiss?"

She shot him a baleful look. "It was more than just a kiss, Dean."

"You said it, not me."

She wrapped her arms around her middle. "Don't read anything into it. It won't be repeated."

He looked at her for several moments, taking in her tense expression, her taut posture, and said quietly, "Don't do this, Paris."

"What? Come to my senses?"

"Don't withdraw. Close up. Shut me out. Punish me. Punish yourself."

"You need to go. They're waiting for you to leave."

"I don't care. I've waited for seven years."

"For what?" she asked angrily. "What were you waiting for, Dean? For Jack to die?"

The words hurt, as she'd known they would. She'd said them deliberately to hurt and provoke him, but he'd be damned before he allowed himself to become either. Tamping down his own anger and keeping his voice calm, he said, "I've waited for a chance to get even this close to you."

"And then what did you expect to happen? Did you expect me to fall into your arms? To forget everything that happened and—"

When she broke off, he raised his brow inquisitively. "And what, Paris? And love me? Is that what you were going to say? Is that what you're so goddamn afraid of? That we might actually have loved each other then and still do?"

She had refused to answer him. Instead she'd marched to her front door and pulled it open.

With watchdogs at the curb, he'd had no choice but to leave.

By now the water in his shower had grown cold, but his body was still feverish with a burning desire to know—if he had been able to wring it out of her—what her answer to his question would have been.

chapter sixteen

Janey had abandoned her plans for retribution and was focusing strictly on survival.

Her attempts to escape from this room seemed as remote as her memories of childhood birthday parties. She'd seen photographs taken at those parties, but felt no connection with the little girl wearing the silver paper tiara and blowing out candles on a bakery-made cake. Likewise, her memories of trying to escape from her captor, of plotting his punishment, seemed to be vague recollections of someone else. Such courageous strategizing was unimaginable to her now.

She was so weak that even had her arms and legs not been restrained, she couldn't have moved. He hadn't given her food or water the last two times he'd been there. She could live with the hunger but her throat was raw from thirst. She had implored him with her eyes, but her silent pleas were ignored.

He was cheerful and talkative, blasé even. He tilted his head to one side and regarded her with renewed interest. "I wonder if you're missed, Janey. You've treated so many people badly, you know. Especially men. Your special talent, certainly your hobby, has been to get men to desire you and then to humiliate them with a public rejection.

"I'd been watching you for a long time before you approached me that first night. You didn't know that? I had. I figured out your email name: pussinboots. Right? Very clever. Especially since you enjoy wearing western boots. Your favorites are the red ones, aren't they? You even wore them here one night. Wait! Hold on."

He rummaged around the room until he found the photo album

he was seeking. "Yes, here you are in your boots. Only your boots, in fact," he added with a sly grin.

When he turned the photograph toward her, she averted her head and closed her eyes. Which made him angry. "Seriously, do you think anybody is really sorry that you're missing?"

He'd left shortly after that. She had been relieved to see him go but terrified that he would never return. In spite of the tape across her mouth, she sobbed noisily. Or maybe her weeping only sounded loud to her own ears. When she choked, she panicked, wondering if a person could drown in tears.

Get a grip, Janey!

She could do this. She could survive him. She could hold out until rescue came, and it would come soon. Her parents would be turning Austin upside down looking for her. Her daddy was rich. He would hire private investigators, bring in the FBI, the army, whatever it took to find her.

She'd hated some of the diehard cops on the Austin PD force, the ones who gave her a hard time about driving drunk, and disorderly conduct, and the illegal substances often in her possession. If she hadn't been Judge Kemp's daughter, the cops who went by the book would have busted her too many times to count.

But she had also balled a few of Austin's finest, the younger, good-looking officers who had a more liberal outlook than the veterans, like the narcotics officer who worked undercover at her high school. He'd been a challenge to seduce, and when he'd finally surrendered, a letdown.

Nevertheless, she wasn't entirely without friends in the police department. They would be searching, too.

And her tormentor had called Paris Gibson. Why he had, Janey couldn't imagine and didn't care. He was obviously proud of that call, because he had recorded it just so he could play it for her. Had he wanted her to know that he was on a first-name basis with a well-known radio personality? The egotistical idiot. Didn't he know that Paris was on a first-name basis with anybody who called her?

Whatever. The important thing was that he had involved her. She could pull a lot of strings. No one was going to ignore Paris Gibson.

But Janey's burst of optimism quickly fizzled. Time was running out. Her captor had told Paris that he was going to kill her within seventy-two hours. But when had he made that call? How much of that time had already expired? She'd lost all track of the days and rarely even knew if it was daylight or dark. What if she was in hour seventy-one of the seventy-two?

Even if he didn't murder her, she could die of neglect. What if he simply never came back? How long could she survive without food and water? Or what if—and this was her greatest fear—what if he was right and nobody gave a damn that she was gone?

He hadn't enjoyed the comfort of his own bed last night, but Dr. Brad Armstrong was feeling sprightly when he arrived at the dental clinic a half hour before his first appointment.

He'd had a busy night and had snatched no more than a couple hours of sleep. But sleep wasn't the only way one could get energized. A girl with a silver ring through her nipple—now, that could get a man supercharged.

He was chuckling to himself as he entered the building and greeted the receptionist.

"Good morning, Doctor. I assume Mrs. Armstrong located you last evening. She was so disappointed that her surprise date was spoiled."

"We had a quiet dinner together after the kids went to bed, so it worked out okay. Any messages for me?"

"A Mr. Hathaway has called twice, but he didn't leave a message either time. He only asked that you return his call. Shall I get him on the line for you?"

Mr. Hathaway was his probation officer. On his best day, Hathaway was a humorless tight ass who loved peering at people over the top of his granny glasses. His idea of intimidation, Brad supposed. "No thanks, I'll try him later. No other messages?"

"That's it."

Toni must really be upset this time. Ordinarily she would have tried to reach him by now if only to assure herself that he hadn't had a head-on with an eighteen-wheeler, suffered a heart attack, or been mugged and murdered. It was always she who took the initial steps toward making up. Isn't that what a loving, supportive wife was supposed to do when her husband stormed from the house after a quarrel?

So he really couldn't be blamed for anything he'd done last night, could he? He'd broken vows, but his backsliding was more Toni's fault than his. She hadn't even tried to be compassionate and understanding. Instead she had scolded him.

He had a collection of erotic magazines and pictures. Big deal. Some might call the material pornographic, but so what? And maybe his collection was more extensive than the next guy's. Was that grounds for making it into a federal case?

After last night, her next accusation would be that he had played too rough. He could hear her now. *Where is that aggression coming from, Brad? I don't know you anymore.* Toni had many fine qualities, but she lacked a spirit of adventure. Anything novel or experimental frightened her. He'd seen the fear in her eyes last night.

She should take lessons from that girl he'd met at the lake. Melissa, her name was. That's what she'd told him anyway. He certainly hadn't given her his name, but he didn't remember her asking. To an adventurous girl like her, names were unimportant.

He'd seen this one around a lot, with many different partners, so, not surprisingly, she hadn't been shocked by his graphic pictures. In fact, she had demonstrated a sincere appreciation for them. They had really steamed her up. She'd been all over him. That girl was something else, her and her nipple ring. Toni would probably have him committed if he suggested a body piercing. But, damn, what a turn-on.

He settled into his desk chair and booted up his computer. Other people in the office had been curious as to why he'd placed his monitor with the back of it facing out into the room rather than up against a wall so all the cables wouldn't show. He'd contrived an explanation, but the real reason was that it was nobody's business but his what was on his monitor.

He visited his favorite websites, but was disappointed that the material hadn't been updated since yesterday morning. Even so, he scanned them all, looking specifically for women with nipple rings. He didn't find any.

He would do some research later, surf the Internet until he located some new, exotic websites. Maybe a Sex Club member had discovered some interesting ones that he didn't yet know about. Leave it to kids to be at the forefront of discovery.

He entered his password and went into the site. He went straight to the message board and was about to type in an inquiry when someone knocked on his office door, then immediately pushed it open.

"Dr. Armstrong?"

"What?" he said brusquely.

"Sorry," an assistant said. "I didn't mean to disturb you. Your first patient has been prepped."

He forced himself to smile. "Thank you. I'll be there as soon as I finish this email to my mom."

She ducked out. He glanced at the clock. He'd been in the office for over a half hour, but it had seemed like five minutes. "Time flies . . . ," he chuckled to himself. Some men read the stock-market report over their morning coffee, some the sports page. He had another interest. Was that a crime?

He returned to his home page and, just to be on the safe side, engaged the service that deleted all his Internet connections so they couldn't be traced.

He'd treated three patients before he was able to take a break. A newspaper had been left at the coffee bar. He carried it, a doughnut, and a cup of coffee into his office with him. He sipped the coffee, took a bite from the doughnut, and flipped up the front page of the newspaper . . . nearly choking when he saw her picture.

It was a serious portrait, probably last year's school photo. Laughably ironic, she looked demure. She seemed to be staring straight at him in a way that made him want to look away. He couldn't.

Accompanying the picture was a story about her: county judge's daughter—Jesus; high school senior; previous malfeasances; a three-day suspension from school last semester; her mysterious disappearance.

The reporter went into detail about her membership in an Internet club, the purpose of which was to solicit sex partners. It was all there in black and white. The writer described how it worked, the chat rooms, the sexually explicit messages left on the website, the secret gatherings—which were no secret to the members—and the licentious acts that ensued at these meeting places. Anyone with whom Janey had had contact was being pursued and questioned by the police. A reference was made that hinted at a possible connection to Paris Gibson's radio program.

Brad placed his elbows on his desk and clasped his head between his hands.

Sergeant Robert Curtis, who has organized a team of investigators, wouldn't comment on Ms. Kemp's alleged connection to the Sex Club, although Officer John Rondeau of the Computer Crimes Division said that such a connection had not been ruled out.

"We're still exploring that," Rondeau said.

The officers declined to comment when asked about the possibility of foul play.

The write-up also said that Austin PD personnel had refused to comment when asked why a homicide detective was overseeing a missing persons case. The more loquacious Rondeau did tell the reporter, "At this point in time, we've had absolutely no indication of foul play and are assuming that Ms. Kemp is a runaway." Good answer, but it didn't address the question.

There was one quote from Judge Kemp. "Like all teenagers, Janey can be inconsiderate and irresponsible when it comes to notifying us of her plans. Mrs. Kemp and I are confident that she'll soon return. It's much too soon for alarming speculation."

Brad actually jumped when his phone rang. With a shaking hand, he reached for the intercom button. "Yes?"

"Your wife is on line two, Dr. Armstrong. And your next patient has arrived."

"Thanks. Give me five minutes."

He wiped the sweat off his upper lip and took several deep breaths before lifting the telephone receiver. It was time to play meek.

"Hi, hon. Look, before you say anything, I just want you to know how sorry I am about last night. I love you. I hate myself for saying the things I did. That trash bag of stuff? History. I threw it away. All of it. As for the . . . the other . . . I don't know what came over me. I'm—"

"You missed your appointment."

"Huh?"

"Your ten o'clock appointment with Mr. Hathaway. He called here because he's been unable to reach you at your office."

"Christ. I forgot about it." The truth was, he had. He'd come into his office, killed a half hour on the Internet, seen three patients, read the front-page story.

"How could something that important slip your mind, Brad?"

"I had patients," he replied testily. "They're pretty damn important, too. Remember our mortgage? Car payment? Grocery bill? I have a job."

"Which won't matter if you get sent to prison."

He glanced down at the picture of Janey Kemp. "I'm not going to prison, not for missing one appointment with my probation officer."

"He's being lenient. He rescheduled you for one-thirty this afternoon."

She was back on her high horse, talking to him like he was no older than their son. He was a grown-up, by God. "Apparently I'm not getting through to you, Toni. I've got work."

"And an addiction," she snapped.

Jesus, she was cutting him no slack whatsoever. "I told you I got rid of the magazines. I tossed the bunch of them in a Dumpster. Okay? Happy now?"

Rather than sounding happy, her laugh sounded terribly sad. "Okay, Brad, whatever. But you're not fooling anybody. Not Hathaway, and certainly not me. If you don't keep this appointment, he'll have to report it, and you'll have to face the consequences."

She hung up on him.

"And the horse you rode in on, sweetheart!" he shouted to the telephone receiver as he slammed it down. He sent his chair rolling back on its casters as he shot to his feet. Placing one hand on his hip and rubbing the back of his neck with the other, he began to pace.

Any other time, he would be really pissed off at Toni for taking such a high-handed tone with him. And he was pissed off. Matter of fact, he was mad as hell. But Toni would keep. Today he needed to focus on a much more serious problem.

When you lined it all up, things didn't look so good for him. He was a convicted sex offender. The charge had been a complete falsehood and the trial a farce. Nevertheless, it was there on his personal record.

Last night he'd had sex with a young woman. God help him if she was under seventeen. Never mind that she was as experienced as a ten-dollar whore—ten dollar, hell. For round two he'd given her a fifty-dollar "gratuity." Despite her experience, if she was a minor, he'd committed a crime. And his wife, who had the ear of his group therapist and his probation officer, was probably already yapping to them about his recent violent tendencies.

But what really had him concerned, what was causing his bowels to spasm, was that he couldn't remember if he'd ever seen Melissa in the company of Janey Kemp.

chapter seventeen

Sergeant Curtis called Paris while she was spreading a piece of toast with peanut butter. "I mentioned cold cases last night?"

"There's one that's similar?"

"Maddie Robinson. Her body was discovered three weeks after her roommate reported her missing. A cattleman found it in a shallow grave in one of his pastures. Middle of nowhere. Cause of death, strangulation with a ligature of some kind. Decomposition was advanced. Scavengers and the elements had done significant damage."

Paris set aside her breakfast.

Curtis continued, "But the coroner was able to determine that the body had been washed with an astringent agent." There was a significant pause before he added, "Inside and out."

"So even if it had been found sooner—"

"The perp had made damn sure any DNA evidence would be compromised to the point of making it negligible. Also no sign of either shoe prints or tire tracks. Probably weather eroded. No clues on clothing because there was none."

Paris felt heartsick for the victim who had suffered such a horrible and ignominious death. She asked Curtis what he knew about her.

"Nineteen. Attractive but not a stunning beauty. She was a student. Her roommate admitted that they weren't exactly nuns. Partied a lot. They went out nearly every night. Here's where it gets really interesting. According to her, Maddie had been seeing someone she referred to as 'special.'"

"In what way?"

"She didn't know. Maddie was vague about what set this guy

apart. The girls had been friends since junior high school. Usually confided everything. But Maddie wouldn't tell her anything about this mystery guy except that he was cool and wonderful and special."

"The roommate never saw him?"

"Didn't come to their apartment. Maddie would meet him. The roommate didn't know where. He never even called their apartment phone, only Maddie's cell. The roommate's theory was that he was married, and that was the reason for the secrecy. For all their exploits, she and Maddie had drawn the line at sleeping with married men. Not for moral reasons, but because there was no future in it, she said.

"One day Maddie was in love, the next she announced that she was breaking off the relationship. She told her roommate that he was getting too possessive, which irritated her since he never took her on a real date. The only place they ever went was to his apartment—which she described as dreary—where they'd have sex. She hinted that it had become bizarre, even for her, and she enjoyed novelty. The roommate pressed her for details, but she refused to talk about it. All she'd say was that the affair was over.

"To cheer her up, the roommate prescribed getting laid by someone else. Maddie took her advice. They went out, drank a lot, and Maddie brought a guy home with her. He was later cleared as a suspect.

"Maddie Robinson was last seen on the shore of Lake Travis, where a large group of young people were celebrating the start of summer break. She and the roommate got separated. The roommate went home alone, assuming that Maddie had found a partner for the night. This was nothing unusual. But when Maddie hadn't come home twenty-four hours later, she notified the police.

"I wasn't assigned the case, so it didn't spring immediately to my mind. The trail got cold for the CIB detectives who were investigating, and the case got turned over to the other unit." Summary complete, he took a deep breath.

"So this happened roughly around the time spring semester ended?"

"Late last May. The body was found June twentieth. Do you have recorded calls from that far back?"

"In my files. Shall I bring you duplicates?"

"ASAP. Please."

•   •   •

"Stan?"

He jumped when Paris walked into her office and caught him seated behind her desk. He recovered quickly and greeted her with a glum, "Hey."

She tossed her handbag onto the pile of printed material on her desk. "You're in my seat."

Before coming into her office, she had gone to the storage room and retrieved several CDs containing recorded call-ins that she'd had transferred off the Vox Pro. She'd left them with an engineer and asked him to duplicate their contents onto audiocassettes.

"Cassettes? That's working backward, isn't it?" he'd grumbled.

Without wanting to explain that the CIB was still working with audiocassettes, she simply said, "Thanks," and left before he had an opportunity to refuse her odd request.

"What are you doing in my office?" she asked Stan now as she replaced him in her chair. As he'd done the night before, he cleared a corner of her desk and perched there, uninvited.

"Because I don't rate an office, and this was the most private place to wait."

"For what?"

"My uncle Wilkins. He's in a conference with the GM."

"About what?"

"Me."

"Why, what'd you do?"

He took exception. "How come everybody automatically assumes that I screwed up?"

"Did you?"

"No!"

"Then why is your uncle Wilkins having a conference about you with our GM?"

"Because of that goddamn phone call."

"Valentino's phone call?"

"It churned up some stuff. My uncle flew out here in the company jet early this morning, called and woke me up, ordered me to meet him here, and he meant immediately. So I break my neck to get here, and he's already behind closed doors. I haven't even seen him yet."

"What 'stuff'?"

Rather than answer her question, he asked one of his own. "Do I do a good job around here, Paris?"

She shook her head with amusement and dismay. "Stan, you don't do any job around here."

"I'm here every single weeknight until two o'clock in the freaking morning."

"You're here in body. You occupy space. But you don't do any work."

"Because nothing ever goes wrong with any of the machines."

"If it did, would you know how to correct it?"

"Maybe. I'm good with gadgets," he said petulantly.

"'Gadgets' isn't exactly the word I would use to describe millions of dollars' worth of electronics. Do you even understand radio technology, Stan?"

"Do *you?*"

"I don't have the title of engineer."

He was a spoiled brat, prone to whining. On any given night she felt like throttling him for his incompetence and casual approach to his job. Ineptitude was forgivable, but indifference wasn't. Not in her book, anyway.

Every time she spoke into her microphone, she was aware that hundreds of thousands of people were listening to her. She was touching them with her voice, in their cars and where they lived. She became a partner in whatever they were doing at the time.

To her the listening audience wasn't just a six-digit number on which to base an advertising rate. Each number represented an individual who was giving her his time and to whom she owed the best programming she could provide.

Stan had never considered the human factor of their audience. Or if he had, it hadn't been translated into work. He'd never shown any initiative. He put in his time, counting the minutes until sign-off, and then rushed out to do whatever it was that he did.

But in spite of all that, she couldn't help but feel sorry for him. He wasn't here by choice. His future had been dictated the second he was born into the Crenshaw family. His uncle was a childless bachelor. Stan was an only child. When his father died, he became the heir apparent to the media empire, like it or not.

No one in the corporation seemed willing to accept or admit that he was uninterested and ill-equipped to assume control when his uncle Wilkins stepped down, which probably wouldn't be until he was pronounced dead.

"I'm learning the business from the bottom up," he told Paris sulkily. "I need to know a little about every aspect of it so I'll be ready when it's time for me to take over. At least that's what Uncle Wilkins thinks."

"What stuff did Valentino's call churn up?"

His mouth twisted into a scornful frown. "It's nothing."

"It was enough to get your uncle Wilkins in a spin."

He heaved a huge sigh. "Before I was assigned—read 'banished'—to this swell radio station, I was working at our TV station in Jacksonville, Florida. Compared to this dump, it was paradise. I had a fling with one of the female employees."

"Then you're not gay?"

He reacted as if he'd been jabbed in the spine with a hot poker. "Gay? Who says I'm gay?"

"There's been speculation."

"Gay? Jesus! I hate these stupid rednecks around here. If you don't drive a dual-axle pickup, drink Bud from a bottle, and dress like the Sundance Kid, you're queer."

"What about the woman in Florida?"

He picked up a paper clip and began reshaping it. "We got carried away in the office. Next thing I know, she's crying sexual harassment."

"Which was untrue?"

"Yes, Paris, it was untrue," he said, enunciating each word. "The charge was as bogus as her thirty-six-C cups. I didn't coerce her into having sex with me. In fact, she was on top."

"More information than I needed, Stan."

"Anyhow, she filed suit. Uncle Wilkins settled out of court, but it cost him a bundle. He got pissed at *me,* not her. Can you believe that? Said, 'How stupid do you have to be to take your dick out at work?' I asked him if he'd ever heard of Bill Clinton. A remark he didn't appreciate, especially since all our newspapers had endorsed him for president.

"Anyway, that's why I'm here, serving time." He tossed the now-misshapen paper clip into the wastebasket. It made a soft ping when it struck the metal bottom. "And that's why he hopped the company jet and flew here this morning."

Paris could guess the rest. "After you told him about being questioned by the police, Wilkins thought he should come to Austin and make certain this unfortunate episode in Florida didn't rear its ugly head."

"He called it damage control."

"Spoken like a true corporate godfather."

She now had the picture. Stan had been foisted onto 101.3 as punishment for mixing business with pleasure. Uncle Wilkins had omitted telling management about the incident with the company employee, but felt he should explain it now before the Austin PD uncovered it and suspicion was cast on his nephew.

"Was that the only incident, Stan?"

His eyes narrowed as he looked down at her from his lofty angle. "What do you mean?"

"The question was simple enough. Yes or no?"

The starch went out of him then. "That was the only time, and, believe me, I learned my lesson. I'll never touch another employee."

"As an owner, that could make you vulnerable to litigation."

"I wish somebody had warned me about that before I went to Jacksonville."

Paris passed up telling him he shouldn't have had to be warned. That was a policy he should have adopted without being told. She also refrained from calling him a creep for doing it under any circumstances.

He looked across at her with a wounded expression. "Everybody thinks I'm gay?"

How like Stan to prioritize the least important point. "You dress too well."

The electrician who'd duplicated the recordings stepped in to tell her that the cassettes were ready and that he'd left them for her at the lobby desk.

"More cassettes?" Stan said.

"This may not be the first time Valentino heralded a murder by calling me."

"What happened last night after you and Malloy raced out of here? I gather you didn't catch Valentino."

"No, unfortunately." She told him about the pay phone at the Wal-Mart store. "Patrol cars were there within minutes, but no one was around."

"I heard about the missing girl on the news this morning. Front page of the paper, too."

She nodded, recalling the quote from Judge Kemp. Janey's parents were holding fast to their belief that her absence was by choice, which, to Paris's mind, was a monumental mistake. On the other hand, she hoped they were right.

She stood up and gathered her handbag, preparing to leave. "I'll see you tonight, Stan."

"Who's Dean Malloy?"

The question came from out of the blue and caught her off guard. "I told you. Staff psychologist for the APD."

"Who moonlights as a bodyguard?" He gave her a sardonic look. "When I dropped off those cassettes at your house last night, the cop told me that Malloy was inside with you."

"I'm missing your point."

"Deliberately, I think. Who is Malloy to *you*, Paris?"

If she didn't tell him, he might go digging on his own and learn more than she preferred him to know. "He and I knew each other in Houston years ago."

"Mmm-hmm. I'm guessing you knew each other pretty well."

"Not pretty well, Stan, *very* well. He was Jack's best friend."

Closing the conversation with that, she stepped around him and moved toward the door. But at the threshold, she paused and turned back. "What do you know about Marvin?"

"Only that he's a jerk."

"Is he into computers, the Internet?"

He snuffled. "Like I would know. I haven't exchanged more than a few grunts with him. Why the sudden interest?"

She hesitated, not knowing if Marvin's apparent flight was information that Curtis would want to be shared. "No reason. See you tonight."

Paris and Sergeant Curtis sequestered themselves in a small interrogation room and sat across from each other at a scarred table. On it were the portable recorder he had used the day before and the cassette tapes she had brought from the radio station.

They began their search for Valentino's calls by listening to tapes recorded up to a week before Maddie Robinson's disappearance. Yesterday she and Dean had agreed that Valentino was altering his voice. The affectation made it distinctive and instantly recognizable, thereby allowing her to fast-forward past voices obviously not his.

Curtis left briefly to get them fresh coffees. When he returned, Paris told him excitedly, "I think I've found it. We don't have a date-and-time stamp like we would on the Vox Pro, but it's on a cassette of recordings made about that time. He was especially morose that night, but I aired this call anyway. His statements provoked follow-up calls that kept my phone lines busy for hours."

Curtis resumed his seat. "You made him a celebrity for the evening."

"Unwittingly, I assure you. Ready?" She started the tape.

Women are unfaithful, Paris. Why is that? You're a woman.

*When you've got a man practically eating out of your hand, why
would you want another? Isn't quality better than quantity?*

I'm sorry you're unhappy tonight, Valentino.

I'm not unhappy, I'm angry.

Not every woman is unfaithful.

That's been my experience.

*You just haven't found the right woman yet. Would you like to
hear a special song tonight?*

Like what?

*Barbra Streisand sings a wonderful rendition of "Cry Me a
River." It's a cliché, but what goes around comes around.*

*Play the song, Paris. But even if she gets dumped the way she
dumped me, it won't be the retribution she should receive.*

Paris stopped the cassette and looked across at Curtis, who was
thoughtfully twirling his ring around his finger again. He said, "I
guess the retribution he felt she deserved was to choke her to death
and bury her body in a goddamn cow pasture. Excuse my
French."

Paris lowered her head into her hands and massaged her temples. "I never would have gathered from what he said that he was
plotting to kill her."

"Hey, don't beat yourself up over this. You're not a mind
reader."

"I didn't detect a real threat in what he said."

"No one would have. And anyway, we're still guessing. Valentino may have no connection whatsoever to Maddie Robinson."

She lowered her hands and looked at him. "But you think
they're connected, don't you?"

Before he could answer, John Rondeau pushed open the door.
He smiled brightly at Paris. "Good morning."

"Hi, John."

He seemed pleased that she remembered his name. "Making
progress?"

"We think so."

"So am I." He looked at Curtis. "Can I see you outside for a
minute?"

Curtis got up. "Back in a sec."

"I'll see if I can find any other calls from Valentino."

The detective left with the younger man and was gone much
longer than a sec. By the time he returned, she had scored again.
"This call is on the same cassette, which means they couldn't have
come in more than a few days apart.

"He's a totally different Valentino. Very upbeat. He claims that the unfaithful lover is 'out of his life' and he stresses the word 'forever.' You'll hear on the tape the difference in his mood." Sensing that Curtis was only half-listening and seemed distracted, she paused to ask, "Is something wrong?"

"Maybe. I hate to think this might be bad, but . . ." He ran his hand around the back of his thick neck as though it had suddenly begun to ache. "I suppose you know that Malloy has a son."

"Gavin."

"You know him?"

"I knew him as a little boy. I haven't seen him since he was ten." Curtis's anxiety was evident. She felt a stab of fear for Dean. "Why, Sergeant? What about Gavin? What's happened?"

chapter *eighteen*

"Gavin?"

"Yeah?"

Dean pushed open his son's bedroom door and went in. "Boot up your computer."

"Huh?"

"You heard me."

Gavin was lying on his bed watching ESPN. He should have something more constructive to do than watch a replay of a soccer game between two European teams. Why wasn't he up and dressed, doing something rather than lazing in bed?

Because I haven't made him, Dean thought.

He had a lazy son because he'd been a lazy parent. Trying to make Gavin get off his butt hadn't been worth the quarrels that invariably followed. Lately, to avoid a hassle, he'd let a lot of things go. He shouldn't have. He wasn't trying to win a popularity contest with Gavin. He wasn't his buddy, his pastor, or his therapist. He was his father. It was past time for him to start exercising stricter parental authority.

He snatched the remote control from Gavin's hand and switched off the television set. "Boot up your computer," he repeated.

Gavin sat up. "What for?"

"I think you know."

"No I don't."

The disrespectful tone and insolent expression stoked Dean's temper. He felt it smoldering like a nugget of coal inside his chest. But he wouldn't yield to it. He would not.

He said tightly, "We can go straight to the police station, where they're waiting to interrogate you about Janey Kemp's disappearance, or you can boot up your goddamn computer so at least I'll know what we're up against when I get you down there. Either way, your days of jerking me around are over."

He had stayed home this morning to organize and type his notes on a suspect he had interviewed several days ago. The detective overseeing that case was growing impatient with the delay.

He knew that if he went to his office, he couldn't have concentrated on anything except Paris and the case in which she was involved. He couldn't have kept himself out of the CIB, where he knew she and Curtis would be listening to her tapes.

So he'd called Ms. Lester, told her he would be working at home, and forced himself to tackle the overdue report. He had just finished it when Robert Curtis called and gave him what could be life-altering news.

"The police want to question me?" Gavin asked. "How come?"

Dean had been clinging to a thread of hope that John Rondeau had made a grave error, but Gavin's worried expression was a dead giveaway that the information was correct.

"You lied to me, Gavin. You're an active member of the Sex Club. You've exchanged numerous email letters with Janey Kemp, and, based on what you two wrote back and forth, you know her a hell of a lot better than you led me to believe. Do you dispute any of this?"

Gavin was now seated on the edge of his mattress, his head hanging between hunched shoulders. "No."

"When was the last time you saw her?"

"The night she disappeared."

"What time?"

"Early. Eight or so. It was still light."

"Where?"

"At the lake. She's always there."

"Had you arranged to meet her there that night?"

"No. She'd been giving me the leper treatment for the last few weeks."

"Why?"

"She's like that. Gets you to like her and then, you know, you're history. I heard she's been seeing this other guy."

"What's his name?"

"Don't know. Nobody does. Rumor is he's older."

"How old?"

"I don't know," Gavin whined, becoming impatient with all the questions. "Thirty-something, maybe."

"So what happened the other night?"

"I went up to her and we started talking."

"You were mad at her." Gavin looked up at him, silently asking how he knew that. "In your last email to her, you called her a bitch. And worse."

Gavin swallowed hard and dropped his head again. "I didn't mean anything by it."

"Well, that's not how the police are going to see it. Especially since she's been missing since that night."

"I don't know what happened to her. Swear to God I don't. Don't you believe me?"

Dean desperately wanted to, but he resisted the urge to go easy on him. Now wasn't the time to turn soft. Gavin needed him to be tough, not Mr. Nice Guy. "We'll get to the part about believing you later. Boot up your computer. I need to see how bad it is."

Reluctantly Gavin moved to his desk. Dean noticed that he typed in a user name and a password to get in, which would've been unnecessary if he had nothing to hide.

The home page of the Sex Club had been designed by amateurs. It was the cyberspace-age version of rest room wall graffiti. Dean motioned Gavin aside. He sat down in the desk chair and reached for the mouse.

"Dad," Gavin groaned.

But Dean ignored him and went straight to the message board. Curtis had given him the names Gavin and Janey had used: blade and pussinboots, respectively. For ten minutes, he scrolled through the messages, stopping to read the ones written by his son and the judge's daughter. It was difficult reading.

The last message Gavin had emailed her was crude, insulting, and, now, incriminating. Sick at heart, Dean closed the website and turned off the computer. For several moments he stared into the blank monitor screen, trying to link the writer of what he'd just read with the little boy he had taught to use a baseball glove, the kid with the gap-toothed smile and sprinkling of freckles across his nose, the youngster whose biggest problem used to be foot odor.

Dean couldn't afford the time to indulge in his personal despair now. He must save it for later. More imperative was clearing his son of all suspicion.

"This is one time you had better come clean with me, Gavin. I want to help you, and I will. But if you lie to me, I'll be hamstrung and unable to help you. So no matter how bad it is, is there anything else I should know?"

"Like what?"

"Anything about Janey and you. Did you actually ever have sex with her?" He nodded toward the computer. "Or was this only talk?"

Gavin looked away. "We did it once."

"When?"

"Month ago, six weeks," he said, raising his shoulders. "Not long after I met her. But we'd already been exchanging emails. I was the new kid in town. I think that's the only reason she was interested in me."

"Where did this take place?"

"A whole bunch of us met at some park. I can't remember the name of it. She and I broke away from the group, got in my car." Resentfully, he added, "Didn't you ever do it in the backseat of a car?"

He was trying to pick a fight. The transference of guilt was a classic distraction tactic that Dean recognized and refused to buy in to. "Did you use a rubber?"

"Of course."

"You're sure?"

"I'm sure. Jeez."

"And you were with her only that one time?"

Gavin rolled his shoulders, pushed back a hank of hair that had fallen over his forehead, looked everywhere except at Dean.

"Gavin?"

He sighed theatrically. "Okay, one other time. She went down on me."

"Same questions."

"Where did it happen? Behind some club on Sixth Street."

"In public?"

"Yeah, sorta, I guess. I mean, we were out in the open, but nobody else was around."

He had a flash image of himself calling Pat and telling her that her baby boy was in jail for public lewdness. *Where were you, Dean?* she would have asked. Where *had* he been while his son was composing smutty letters and getting blow jobs in alleyways?

The self-accusations had to be shelved until later, too. "Those two times? That's it?"

"Yeah, she cooled it, dumped me."

"But you weren't ready to be dumped."

Gavin looked at him as if he was crazy. "Hell, no. She's hot."

"To say the least," Dean said in an undertone. "If there's anything else, you'd better tell me. I don't want any more ugly surprises, something the cops have discovered that you haven't told me."

Gavin wrestled with indecision for at least half a minute before he said, "She, uh . . ." He opened a desk drawer, removed a paperback copy of *The Lord of the Rings,* and took out a photograph that had been secreted between the pages. "She gave me this the other night."

Dean reached for the photograph. He didn't know which astonished him more, the girl's graphic pose or her shameless smile. He slipped the picture into his shirt pocket. "Get showered and dressed."

"Dad—"

"Hurry. I've been instructed to have you there by noon. A lawyer is meeting us there."

Finally, the gravity of his predicament seemed to have penetrated layers of adolescent insolence. "I don't need a lawyer."

"I'm afraid you do, Gavin."

"I didn't do anything to Janey. Don't you believe me, Dad?"

His sullenness had dissolved. He looked young and scared, and Dean experienced that same twinge in his heart that he had felt the night before when he watched him sleep.

He wanted to embrace him and assure him that everything would be all right. But he couldn't promise that because he didn't know it to be true. He wanted to tell him that he believed him implicitly, but, unfortunately, he didn't. Gavin had betrayed his trust too many times.

He wanted to tell him he loved him, but he didn't say that either. He was afraid that Gavin would rebuke him for it being too little too late.

Paris had been pacing the hallway for more than an hour, waiting. Nevertheless, she reacted with a start when Dean emerged through the double doors of the CIB, where he, Gavin, and an attorney had met with Curtis and Rondeau in an interrogation room.

He looked surprised to see her. "I didn't know you were here."

"I couldn't leave until I knew that Gavin was all right."

"So you know?"

"I was with Curtis listening to the tapes when . . ." She stopped, unsure of what she should say.

"When my son became a suspect?"

"As far as we know, no crime has been committed and Janey is with a friend."

"Sure. That's why Curtis is putting Gavin through the wringer."

She pushed him toward a bench and made him sit down. It was an ugly, sad-looking piece, a cheap metal frame supporting a blue vinyl cushion with the stuffing poking up through numerous cracks. Probably it had been mindlessly picked at by the restless hands of witnesses, suspects, and victims who had occupied this same bench while despairing over their fate or that of someone they loved. They wouldn't have been in this place unless their lives had been upended, perhaps permanently.

"How is Gavin handling it?" she asked softly.

"He's subdued. Not giving off any attitude, thank God. I think it's finally sunk in that he's in deep shit."

"Only because he exchanged sexually explicit emails with Janey. So did a lot of others."

"Yeah, but Gavin has demonstrated a real creative flare," he said with a bitter laugh. "Did they show you any of the stuff he'd written?"

"No. But even if I'd read it, it wouldn't have changed my opinion of him. He was a terrific little boy, and he'll be a fine young man."

"Two days ago I thought breaking curfew was a major offense. Now . . . this. Jesus." Sighing, he propped his elbows on his knees and covered his face with his hands.

Paris placed her hand on his shoulder. It was instinctive. He needed to be touched, and she needed to touch him. "Have you called Pat?"

"No. Why upset her if it turns out to be nothing except some dirty emails?"

"Which I'm sure is exactly what it'll turn out to be."

"I hope. Twice he talked us through his actions that night. The accounts didn't vary."

"Then he's probably telling the truth."

"Or his lie has been well rehearsed."

Staring straight ahead, toward the open staircase across the hall, he tapped his clasped fingers against his lips. "I talk to liars every day, Paris. Most people lie to one degree or another. Some don't even realize they're lying. They've said or believed something for so long that it becomes their truth. It's my job to filter out their bullshit until I get to the real truth."

When he paused, Paris remained silent, giving him an opportunity to organize his thoughts. The warmth of his skin radiated up through his shirt and into her palm where it still rested on his shoulder.

"Gavin admits to driving home drunk," he said. "He admits to stopping along the way to barf in someone's yard and to disobeying me by leaving the house in the first place.

"He owns up to liking Janey, or at least liking what they did together. He says he talked to her that night and tried to persuade her to go somewhere with him. She shot him down cold.

"He got mad, said things, some of which I can't believe came out of my son's mouth. He confesses to being furious when he left her, but he insists that he did. He says he joined a group of guys and remained with them, drinking tequila, until he left for home. He didn't see Janey again."

Turning his head, he locked gazes with her. "I believe him, Paris."

"Good."

"Am I being naive? Is that wishful thinking?"

"No. I think you believe him because he's telling the truth." She gave his shoulder a light squeeze of reassurance. "Is there anything I can do?"

"Have dinner with us tonight. Gavin and me."

Not expecting that, she quickly removed her hand from his shoulder and looked away. "I work at night, remember?"

"There's plenty of time to have dinner before you go to the station. We'll start early."

She shook her head. "I have something to do this afternoon that can't be postponed. Besides, I don't think it's a good idea."

"Because of what happened last night?"

"No."

"Yes."

Vexed by his perception, she said, "Okay, yes."

"Because you know that if we're together it's going to happen again."

"No it won't."

"It will, Paris. You know it will. Furthermore, you want it to just as much as I do."

"I—"

"Dean?"

Upon hearing his name, they sprang apart. A woman had just alighted from one of the elevators and was coming toward them. There was only one word to describe her: stunning.

Her tailored suit emphasized her curvy figure rather than detracted from it. Excellent legs were shown off by a fashionably short skirt and high heels. Lip gloss and mascara were her only makeup, and no more than that was needed. She wore no jewelry other than discreet diamond studs in her ears, a slender gold chain at her throat, and a wristwatch. Her pale, shoulder-length hair was parted down the middle, the style loose, classic, and uncomplicated. A California girl in a power suit.

Dean shot to his feet. "Liz."

She graced him with a dazzling smile. "Everything went so well in Chicago, I wrapped things up a day early. Made all my flight connections and thought I would surprise you with a late lunch. Ms. Lester told me I could find you here, and apparently I did pull off a surprise."

She hugged him, kissed him on the mouth, then turned and gave Paris an open and friendly smile. "Hello."

Dean made a terse introduction. "Liz Douglas, Paris Gibson."

Paris didn't remember coming to her feet, but she found herself standing face-to-face with Liz Douglas, whose handshake was firm, like a woman accustomed to conducting business primarily with men. "How do you do?" Paris said weakly.

"A pleasure to meet you. Are you a policewoman? Do you work with Dean?" She was trying to see past Paris's tinted lenses and probably had assumed she was an undercover officer.

"No, I work in radio."

"Really? Are you on the air?"

"Late night."

"I'm sorry, I don't—"

"No need to apologize," Paris told her. "My program comes on when most people are already in bed."

After a brief but awkward lapse in conversation, Dean said, "Paris and I knew each other in Houston. Years ago."

"Ah," Liz Douglas said, as though that was an explanation that clarified everything.

"You'll have to excuse me. I'm late for an appointment." Paris turned to Dean. "Everything will be fine. I know it will. Please tell Gavin hello for me. Ms. Douglas, nice to meet you." She walked quickly away, toward the elevators.

Dean called her name, but she pretended not to hear and kept

walking. As she disappeared around the corner, she heard Liz
Douglas say, "I get the distinct impression I interrupted something.
Is she in some sort of trouble?"

"Actually, I am," he replied. "Gavin and I."

"My God, what's happened?"

By then an elevator had arrived. Paris stepped into it and was
grateful to find herself the sole passenger. She leaned against the
back wall as the doors slid closed. She didn't hear any more of
Dean's conversation with Liz. But she didn't need to. The familiarity with which they'd kissed said a lot.

He would no longer need her hand on his shoulder. He had Liz
to console him now.

Gavin knew that if he lived to be a hundred, this would go down
as the worst day of his life.

For this visit to the police station, he had dressed in his nicest
clothes, and his dad hadn't even had to tell him to. They were
probably ruined now because for the past hour and a half he'd
been leaking sweat from every pore. The BO would never come
out.

On TV and in movies, suspects under interrogation made themselves look guilty with their body language. So he tried not to
fidget in the uncomfortable chair, but sat up straight. He didn't let
his eyes dart about the room, but looked directly at Sergeant Curtis. When asked a question, he didn't elaborate, but spoke truthfully and concisely, although the subject matter was embarrassing.

He took his dad's advice—now was not the time to withhold information. Not that he was trying to cover up anything. They already knew about the emails, the Sex Club, all that. He didn't
know Janey Kemp's whereabouts or what had happened to her. He
was as clueless about her fate as they were.

Yes, he'd had sex with her. But so had every guy he'd met since
coming to Austin, with the exception of his dad and the men in
this room.

All but one. And more than Curtis's persistent questions, it was
that one who was making him sweat. He'd been introduced as
John Rondeau.

The instant Rondeau walked into the room Gavin recognized
him. After all, he'd seen him just last night with two busty babes,
climbing from the backseat of a car. And it sure as hell hadn't been
a prayer group.

There was no mistaking that the young cop had recognized him, too. When he saw Gavin, his eyes had widened slightly but returned to normal in a nanosecond. Then he had clapped a warning stare on Gavin that made his scrotum shrink and snuffed any comment he might have made about having seen this guy before.

The others, including his dad, probably took Rondeau's stare as stern disapproval of the emails he had swapped with Janey. But Gavin knew better. Gavin knew Rondeau was threatening him with severe consequences if he betrayed his extracurricular activities to his superiors.

Gavin felt even more afraid when Curtis asked his dad to leave the room. Lately, his old man had been a real hard-ass, constantly riding him about one thing or another. It had gotten to where Gavin dreaded the sight of him, knowing he was about to receive a lecture on something. But he was glad to have his dad on his side today. And no matter how bad the situation became, Gavin knew he wouldn't abandon him.

He remembered once when they'd gone to the Gulf Coast for a long weekend. His dad had cautioned him about swimming out too far. "The waves are stronger and higher than they look from the beach. There's also a strong undertow. Be careful."

But he'd wanted to impress his dad with what a good swimmer and body surfer he was. Next thing he knew, he couldn't touch bottom and the waves just wouldn't let up. He panicked and floundered. He went under, knowing he was doomed to a death by drowning.

Then a strong arm closed around his chest and hauled him to the surface. "It's okay, son, I've got you."

He sputtered and struggled, still trying to find a footing.

"Relax against me, Gavin. I won't let you go. I promise."

His dad towed him all the way back to shore. He didn't bawl him out when they got there either. He didn't say, "Stupid kid, didn't I tell you? When are you going to listen and learn?"

He'd just looked real worried while he thumped him on the back until he'd coughed up all the seawater he'd swallowed. Then he had wrapped him in a beach towel and hugged him tight against his side for a long time. Not saying anything. Just staring out across the water, holding him close.

When the weekend was over and his mom had asked if everything had gone okay, his dad had winked at him while telling her that everything had been fine. "We had a great time." He never did tell her that Gavin would've been a goner if he hadn't saved him.

Gavin trusted him to be there to grab him if he sank today, too.

His dad was like that. A good person to have around during a crisis.

That's why it had stressed him when the detective asked his dad to wait outside while they talked to Gavin alone. "I'll leave, but only if the lawyer stays," his dad had stipulated.

Curtis had agreed. Before he left, his dad had looked at him and said, "I'll be right outside, son," and Gavin was confident that he would be.

After he left, Curtis had looked at him so hard, he'd begun to squirm in his seat despite his determination not to. He was beginning to wonder if the detective had gone mute by the time he said, "I know it's hard to talk about certain things in front of your dad. Girls and sex. Stuff like that."

"Yes, sir."

"Now that your father isn't here, I'd like to ask you some questions of a more personal nature."

More personal than they'd already been? You gotta be kidding me. That's what he'd thought, but he'd said, "Okay."

But the questions were basically the same ones his dad had asked him before they left the house. He responded to Curtis just as candidly. He told him about the times he and Janey had had sex.

"You didn't engage in any sexual activity with her that last night you saw her?"

"No, sir."

"Did you see her having sex with anyone else?"

What, did they think he'd watch? Did they really think he was that sick? "I wouldn't have gone up to her and started talking if she'd been with another guy."

"Did you touch her?"

"No, sir. I tried to take her hand once, but she pulled it back. She told me I was needy, and that my neediness had gotten to be a real pain."

"That's when you called her a bitch and so forth?"

"Yes, sir."

"What was she wearing?"

Wearing? He couldn't remember. When he called up an image of her, he saw only her face, the sultry eyes, the smile that was both inviting and cruel. "I don't remember."

Curtis looked over at Rondeau. "Can you think of anything else?"

"Where'd you get the picture of her?"

Gavin dreaded looking directly at him, but he did. "She gave it to me."

"When?"

"That night. She said, 'Get over it, Gavin.' Then she gave me the picture. A 'souvenir,' she called it. When I got to missing her, I could use it, you know, to get off."

"Did she tell you who took the picture?"

"Some guy she's been seeing."

"Did she say his name?"

"No."

"Did you ask?"

"No."

Curtis waited to see if Rondeau had anything else he wanted to ask, but when he sat back, satisfied, Curtis stood up. "That's it for now, Gavin. Unless you can think of anything else."

"No, sir."

"If you do, notify me or tell your father immediately."

"I will, sir. I hope she's found soon."

"So do we. Thank you for your cooperation."

As promised, his dad was waiting outside the CIB, but Gavin was surprised to see that Liz was with him. Immediately she rushed toward him. She asked if he was all right and smothered him in a hug.

"I've gotta go to the bathroom," he mumbled and moved away before anyone could stop him.

No one was at the urinals. He slipped into one of the stalls and checked for feet beneath the partitions. When he was sure he was alone, he bent over the toilet and vomited. He hadn't had much to eat today, just some cereal for breakfast, so mostly he spewed bile and then had the dry heaves until the blood vessels in his neck seemed on the verge of bursting. The spasms were so violent, they made his torso sore.

Fear had caused him to vomit once before. When he was fourteen, he had sneaked his mother's car out. She was on a date with the man she'd ultimately married. Since she had abandoned him to go to dinner with that loser, Gavin had felt it served her right if he drove her car illegally.

He'd gone only as far as the nearest McDonald's, where he'd scarfed down a Big Mac. On his way home, only a block from his house, a neighbor's new golden retriever darted right into the path of his car. The puppy had been the talk of the neighborhood. He was cute and friendly, and when Gavin had gone down to meet him a few days earlier, he had licked his face enthusiastically.

He had braked in time to prevent a tragedy, but he had come close enough to killing the puppy that as soon as he got home, he'd thrown up his ill-gotten meal. His mom never knew that he'd taken the car out, and the puppy had grown into a dog that still thrived. Beyond a guilty conscience, he hadn't had to face any consequences.

He hadn't been as fortunate this time.

He flushed the toilet twice before leaving the stall. At the sink he splashed double handfuls of cold water over his face, rinsed his mouth out several times, then bathed his face some more before turning off the faucet and straightening up.

Before he could even register that Rondeau was there, the cop had one hand on the back of his head and the other in an iron grip around his wrist and was pushing his hand up between his shoulder blades.

chapter nineteen

Rondeau shoved Gavin's face against the mirror. It struck with such impact, Gavin was surprised the glass didn't crack. He wasn't sure about his cheekbone. The pain brought unmanly tears to his eyes. His arm felt like it was being wrenched from his shoulder socket. Gasping, he said, "Let go of me, asshole."

Rondeau hissed directly into his ear, "You and I have a secret, don't we?"

"I know your secret, Officer Rondeau." His lips were smushed against the mirror, but he could make himself understood. "While you're off duty from the police department, you fuck high school girls."

Rondeau rammed his hand up higher between Gavin's shoulder blades, and in spite of Gavin's determination not to show any fear, he cried out. "Now let me tell you your secret, Gavin," he whispered.

"I don't have a secret."

"Sure you do. You'd had your fill of that little bitch's games. You figured it was time she was taught a lesson. So you arranged to meet her. She got abusive and you got mad."

"You're crazy."

"You were so enraged, so humiliated, you lost it, Gavin. In the state of mind you were in, I can't hazard to think what you did to her."

"I didn't do anything."

"Of course you did, Gavin," he said smoothly. "You had the perfect motive. She dumps you, then makes you a laughingstock. She ridiculed you on the message board, for everybody to read. A 'dickless dud.' Isn't that how she referred to you? You couldn't have that. You had to shut her up. Forever."

Rondeau's salesmanship made the scenario sound plausible. Gavin panicked at the thought of how many other policemen, including Sergeant Curtis, Rondeau could convince.

"Okay, she was making fun of me, and I was mad at her," he said. "But the other is crap. I was with friends that night. They'll vouch for me."

"A bunch of rednecks and jocks stoned on tequila and grass?" Rondeau scoffed. "You think anything they testify to will hold up in court?"

"Court?"

"I hope you've got another alibi lined up, Gavin. Something stronger than the testimony of those losers you hang out with."

"I don't need an alibi because I didn't do anything to Janey except talk to her."

"You didn't hit her on the head with a tire iron and roll her body into the lake?"

"Jesus! No!"

"You're not shitting bricks every waking moment, wondering when her body will be discovered? I'll bet I can find somebody who will testify to seeing you and Janey in a struggle."

"They'd be lying. I didn't do anything."

Rondeau stepped even closer, mashing Gavin's thighs against the sink. "Whether you did or not, I really don't care, Gavin. They can let you go, or they can send you away for the rest of your life, it makes no difference to me. But if you rat me out, I'll make sure you look guilty as shit. I'll lead them to believe—"

"What the hell is going on?"

Gavin felt the rush of air immediately after hearing his dad's booming exclamation from the doorway. He yanked Rondeau away from him and slammed him against the tile wall, then used his hand like a staple against Rondeau's neck to hold him there.

"What the hell do you think you're doing?" His voice reverberated off every hard surface of the room. "Gavin, are you all right?"

His cheek was throbbing and his shoulder hurt like hell, but he wasn't going to complain in front of Rondeau. "I'm okay."

His dad looked him over, as though to reassure himself that he wasn't seriously hurt, then turned back to Rondeau. "You'd better make this good."

"I'm sorry, Dr. Malloy. I've been reading that stuff your son wrote. It just . . . It's disgusting, some of it. I've got a mom, a sister.

Women shouldn't be talked about like that. When I came in here to take a leak, I saw him and just blew my cool, I guess."

Gavin wouldn't have wanted to be in Rondeau's shoes. His dad was practically breathing fire into his face and his hand hadn't relaxed its pressure on his throat. Rondeau's face was turning red, but he stood stock-still, as though afraid that if he moved, he could set off an eruption of wrath that he would be powerless to combat.

Finally, Dean lowered his hand, but his eyes were just as effective at keeping Rondeau nailed to the wall. His voice was quiet and controlled, but menacing. "If you ever touch my kid again, I'll wring your fucking neck. Do you understand me?"

"Sir, I—"

"Do you understand me?"

Rondeau swallowed, nodded, then said, "Yes, sir."

Despite his meekness, it was several moments before Dean released him from his stare and stepped back. He extended his arm toward Gavin. "Let's go, son."

Gavin glanced at Rondeau as he walked past him. The young cop might have convinced his dad that he'd experienced an uncontrollable surge of righteous indignation for which he was truly sorry.

But Gavin wasn't fooled. Rather than creating more trouble for himself, he would keep Rondeau's dirty little secret. What did he care if the cop led a double life that included screwing underage girls? The girls hadn't seemed to mind.

Once they'd left the rest room, Gavin took a glimpse at his dad. His jaw was clenched and he looked ready to make good on his threat to wring Rondeau's neck. He was glad that he wasn't on the receiving end of that simmering anger.

He figured that his cheekbone would soon be sporting a bruise, and possibly it was already beginning to discolor because the moment Liz saw them, she knew something had happened.

"What's wrong?"

"Nothing, Liz," Dean told her. "Everything's fine, but I have to skip lunch. Sergeant Curtis has paged me."

Apparently, while he was in the john heaving up his guts, his dad had filled her in on what was going on.

"There's somebody he wants me to talk to. I'm sorry you cut your trip short only to rush back to this mess."

"If it's your mess, it's my mess," she said.

"Thanks. I'll call you at home tonight."

"I'll be glad to wait until you're free."

Dean shook his head. "I have no idea how long I'll be. This could take the rest of the afternoon."

"Oh, I see, well . . ." She looked so disappointed Gavin felt sorry for her. "You're too valuable around here for your own good. Would you like me to drive Gavin home?"

Inwardly Gavin groaned, *Please no.* Liz was okay. She was certainly great to look at. But she tried too hard to make him like her. Often her efforts were so transparent that he resented them. He wasn't a little kid who could be won over with bright chatter and excessive interest in him.

"I appreciate the offer, Liz, but I'm going to send Gavin home in my car."

Gavin whipped his head toward his dad, thinking he must not have heard him correctly. But no, he was passing him his car keys. Two nights ago, he had made Gavin surrender the keys to his rattle-trap. Now he was entrusting him with his expensive import.

This demonstration of his trust meant more than when he had threatened Rondeau with death. Protecting your kid was required, but trusting him was a choice, and his dad had chosen to trust him when he had given him no reason to. If fact, he'd given him every reason not to.

It was something he needed to think about and analyze. But later, when he was alone.

"I'll call you when I'm ready to leave, Gavin. You can come back and get me. Does that sound like a plan?"

His throat was awfully tight, but he managed to squeak out, "Sure, Dad. I'll be waiting."

Even though her present situation was chaotic, Paris didn't use it as another excuse to postpone the necessary trip out to Meadowview.

And perhaps after kissing Dean last night, guilt also had motivated her to call the director of the perpetual care facility and tell him that she would be there at three o'clock.

When she arrived promptly, he was in the atrium entrance to greet her. As they shook hands, he looked abashed and apologized for the tone of the letter she had received the day before.

"In hindsight I wish my wording hadn't been quite so—"

"No apology necessary," she told him. "Your letter prompted me to do something I've needed to do for months."

"I hope you don't think I'm insensitive to your grief," he said as he led her down the hushed corridor.

"Not at all."

Jack's personal effects had been placed in a storage room. After unlocking the door, the director pointed to three sealed boxes stacked on a metal shelving unit. They weren't large and didn't contain much. Paris could easily have carried them all to her car, but he insisted on helping her.

"I'm sorry for any inconvenience my delay has caused you and the staff," she said as they placed the boxes in the trunk of her car.

"I understand why you'd want to stay away. The hospital couldn't hold good memories for you."

"No, but I never had to worry about the treatment Jack received here. Thank you."

"Your generous donation was thanks enough."

After settling Jack's outstanding medical bills, she had donated the remainder of his estate to the facility, including the sizable life insurance policy he had obtained when they became engaged. She was the beneficiary, but she could never have kept the money.

She and the director had parted company in Meadowview's parking lot, under a broiling sun, knowing it was doubtful they would ever see each other again.

Now the three boxes sat on Paris's kitchen table. There would never be a good time to open them, and she would rather have it over and done with than continue to dread it. Using a paring knife, she slit the packing tape on all three boxes.

In the first were pajamas. Four pair, neatly folded. She'd bought them for him when he was first admitted to Meadowview. They were soft now from being laundered countless times, but they still had the cloying, antiseptic smell she associated with the hallways of the hospital. She closed the box.

The second contained mostly papers, those notarized, triplicate documents from insurance companies, county courthouses, hospitals, medical and law offices, which reduced Jack Donner to a Social Security number, a statistic, a client, an entry for an accountant to tabulate.

As executor of his will, she'd had to deal with all the legalities inherent in a person's demise. All the wherefores and hereins were past tense now, the documents obsolete. She had no need or desire to read them again.

Only the third box remained. It was the smallest of the three. Even before opening it, she knew the contents would be the most

upsetting because the articles inside were Jack's personal posses-
sions. His wristwatch. Wallet. A few favorite books, which she
had read aloud to him during her daily visits to Meadowview. A
framed photograph of his parents, who were already deceased
when Paris met him. She had thought it a blessing that they hadn't
lived to see their only child so reduced.

Shortly after moving him to Meadowview, she had emptied his
house. His clothes she had given to a charity. Then, steeling herself, she had sold his furniture, his car, snow skis, bass-fishing
boat, tennis racquets, guitar, eventually the house itself, to pay the
astronomical medical bills that the insurance didn't cover.

So this was all that Jack Donner had owned when he died. He'd
been left with nothing, not even his dignity.

His wallet was soft from wear. His credit cards, long expired,
were still in their slots. Behind a plastic shield, her own face smiled
up at her. Noticing a sliver of paper behind the photo, she pinched
it out. It was a newspaper clipping that Jack had folded several
times so it would fit behind her picture.

She unfolded it and saw another picture of herself. Only this
one wasn't a flattering studio portrait. This one had been snapped
by a photojournalist. He had captured her looking tired, bedrag-
gled, and disillusioned as she stood gazing into the distance, her
microphone held forgotten at her side. The headline read, "Career-
making Coverage."

Tears blurring her eyes, she rubbed the edges of the clipping between her fingers. Jack had been proud of the job she'd done,
proud enough to save the newspaper article about it. At any point
in time afterward, had he realized the cruel irony of his pride in
her work on that particular story?

Funny, that a total stranger to them, someone they never even
met, would have such a catalytic impact on their lives. His name
was Albert Dorrie. He changed Jack's and her destiny the day he
decided to hold his family hostage.

It had been an uneventful Tuesday until the story broke just before
lunchtime. When those in the newsroom heard that a woman and
her three children were being held at gunpoint in their home, they
were galvanized into action.

A cameraman was assigned to go to the scene. As he hastily
gathered his equipment, the assignments editor ran a quick inventory of his available reporters. "Who's free?" he barked.

"I am." Paris remembered raising her hand like a schoolgirl who knew the correct answer.

"You've got to record the voice-over for that colon cancer prevention story."

"Recorded and already with the editor."

The veteran newsman rolled his cigarette, which was never lighted inside the building, from one side of his nicotine-stained lips to the other while contemplating her with a scowl. "Okay, Gibson, you get on it. I'll send Marshall to take over for you when he finishes at the courthouse. In the meantime, try not to fuck up too bad. Go!"

She piled into the news van with the video cameraman. She was hyper, anxious, excited to be covering her first late-breaking story. The video photographer facilely navigated Houston freeway traffic while humming Springsteen.

"How can you be so calm?"

"Because tomorrow there'll be some other nutcase, doing something equally psychotic. The stories are the same. Only the names change."

To some extent, he was right, but she figured his mellow mood was largely due to the joint he was smoking.

Barricades had been placed at the end of a street in a middle-class neighborhood. Paris leaped from the van and ran to join the other reporters who were clustered around the SWAT officer currently acting as spokesperson for the Houston PD.

"The children range in age from four to seven," Paris heard him say as she wedged herself into the mass. "Mr. and Mrs. Dorrie have been divorced for several months. She recently won a child custody dispute. That's all we know at this time."

"Was Mr. Dorrie upset over the custody ruling?" one reporter shouted.

"One would assume, but that's only speculation."

"Have you talked to Mr. Dorrie?"

"He hasn't responded to our attempts."

Paris's cameraman had caught up with her. Reaching through the crowd, he passed her a microphone that was connected to his camera.

"Then how do you know he's in there, holding his family at gunpoint?" another reporter asked.

"Mrs. Dorrie called in a 911 and was able to convey that message before she was disconnected, we believe by Mr. Dorrie."

"Did she say what kind of firearm he has?"

"No."

Paris asked, "Do you know what Mr. Dorrie hopes to gain by this?"

The SWAT officer said, "At this time, all I know for certain is that we have a very serious situation on our hands. Thank you."

With that, he concluded the briefing. Paris turned to the cameraman. "Did you get my question on tape?"

"Yep. And his answer."

"Such as it was."

"The newsroom called. They're gonna come to you live in three minutes. Can you think of something to say?"

"You focus the camera, I'll think of something to say."

She staked out an advantageous spot from which to do her live cut-ins. The Dorrie house could be seen in the background at the far end of a narrow, tree-lined street, which on any other afternoon would probably have been serene.

Now it was thronged with emergency vehicles, police units, news vans, and people who had come to gawk. Paris asked one of the Dorries' neighbors if she would talk to her on camera about the family, and the woman happily consented.

"I always thought he was a nice man," the woman said. "Never woulda thought he'd snap like this. You just never know about people. Most are crazy, I guess."

An hour into the standoff, Paris spotted Dean Malloy arriving in an unmarked car. He seemed impervious to onlookers and walked with confident determination as uniformed officers escorted him past the gaggle of reporters and toward the SWAT van that was parked midway between the barricade and the house. Paris watched him enter the van, then called her assignments editor and reported this update.

"Will you shut the hell up!" he shouted to the voices in the background. "Can't hear myself think." Then to Paris, "Who is he again?"

She repeated Dean's name. "He's a doctor of psychology and criminology, on staff with HPD."

"And you know him?"

"Personally. He's trained to negotiate with hostage takers. He wouldn't be here if they didn't think they needed him."

She went live with this breakthrough, scooping all the other stations.

By hour three of the standoff, everyone was growing a little bored and perversely wishing that something would happen.

Paris got a lucky break when she noticed a small woman standing at the edge of the crowd of spectators. She was being supported by a man at her side while she wept copiously but silently.

Leaving her microphone and cameraman behind, Paris approached the couple and introduced herself. Initially the man was antagonistic and told her bluntly to get lost, but the woman finally identified herself as Mrs. Dorrie's sister. At first she was reluctant to talk, but Paris eventually learned the stormy history of the Dorrie marriage.

"This background information could be very useful to the police," she told the woman gently. "Would you be willing to talk to one of them?"

The woman was wary and frightened. Her husband remained hostile.

"The individual I have in mind is not an ordinary policeman," she told them. "He's not a SWAT officer. His sole purpose in being here is to see that your sister and her children come out of this situation unharmed. You can trust him. I give you my word."

Minutes later, Paris was trying to coax a uniformed policeman to carry a note to the SWAT van and hand-deliver it to Dean. "He knows me. We're friends."

"I don't care if you're his sister. Malloy's busy and doesn't want to talk to a reporter."

She signaled her cameraman forward. "Are you rolling tape?"

"I am now," he said, swinging his camera up to his shoulder and looking into the eyepiece.

"Be sure to get a close-up of this officer's face." She cleared her throat and began speaking into the microphone. "Today Officer Antonio Garza of the Houston Police Department impeded efforts to rescue a family being held hostage by an armed gunman. Officer Garza declined to convey an important message to—"

"The hell you doing, lady?"

"I'm putting you on TV as the cop who screwed up a hostage rescue."

"Give me the friggin' note," he said, snatching it from her hand.

It was a long, agonizing quarter of an hour before Dean stepped from the van and walked toward the barricade. He batted aside microphones thrust at him as he scanned the faces in the crowd. When he saw Paris waving at him from outside her station's news van, he made a beeline toward her.

"Hello, Dean."

"Paris."

"I wouldn't ever take advantage of our friendship. I hope you know that."

"I do."

"I wouldn't have drawn you away if I didn't think this was vitally important."

"So your note indicated. What have you got?"

"Let's get inside."

They scrambled into the back of the van, where she had persuaded Mrs. Dorrie's sister and brother-in-law to wait. She made introductions. Space was limited even though the cameraman had remained outside. Paris didn't want to spook them with the camera and lights.

Dean hunkered down in front of the distraught woman and spoke quietly and calmly. "First of all, I want you to know that I'm going to do everything within my power to keep your sister and her family from getting hurt."

"That's what Paris said. She gave us her word that we could trust you."

Dean cast a quick glance at Paris.

"But I'm afraid the policemen will storm the house," the woman said, her voice breaking emotionally. "If they do, Albert will kill her and the children. I know he will."

Dean asked, "Has he threatened their lives before?"

"Many times. My sister always said he would wind up killing her."

He listened patiently to what she had to impart, interrupting only when he needed a point clarified, gently prodding her when she faltered. The van grew warm and stank of marijuana. Dean seemed unaware of the uncomfortable surroundings, of the sweat that beaded his forehead. His eyes never wavered from the sobbing woman's face.

He asked pertinent questions and must have committed her answers to memory because he wrote nothing down. When she had told him everything she knew that could be relevant, he thanked her, reassured her that he was going to bring her sister and the children out safely, then asked her if she would stay close by in case he needed to speak to her again. She and her husband agreed.

As they emerged from the stuffy van, Paris passed Dean a bottle of water. Absently he drank from it as they walked toward the barricade. A deep worry line had formed between his eyebrows.

Finally she ventured to ask if the interview had been helpful.

"Absolutely. But before it can help, I've got to get Dorrie to talk to me."

"You have his cell number now."

"Thanks to you."

"I'm glad I could help."

Garza and other uniformed policemen held back the crowd of reporters calling questions to Dean as he stepped through the barricade. He started to walk away, but paused long enough to turn back and say, "You did good, Paris."

"So did you."

She remained where she was, watching him until he disappeared into the SWAT van, then called her assignments editor and told him what had happened.

"Good work. Helps to have friends in high places. Since you've got a rapport with the head kahuna, stay put, see it through to the end."

"What about Marshall?"

"I've made it your baby, Paris. Don't disappoint me."

An hour later, she learned along with all the other media that Malloy was finally in conversation with Dorrie. He had persuaded the man to let him speak to Mrs. Dorrie, who had tearfully told him that she and the children were still alive, physically unharmed but terribly frightened.

Paris went live with that report at the top of the five o'clock news. She repeated it at six o'clock because there'd been no further developments and, at the conclusion of the newscast, did a general recap of the events that had taken place throughout the long day. She also fielded extemporaneous questions from the anchors.

Jack arrived at seven with burgers and fries for her and her cameraman. "Who's been smoking weed?" he asked.

"She has," the cameraman replied as he popped a french fry into his mouth. "Can't get her off the stuff."

But when he finished his meal and stepped from the van, he hesitated. "Jack, about the . . . uh . . ."

Jack smiled guilelessly. "I don't know what you're talking about."

The cameraman was visibly relieved. "Thanks, man."

When they were alone, Paris shot Jack a look of vexation. "A fine manager you'll make."

"A good manager instills loyalty." His easy grin turned to an expression of concern as he reached out and stroked her cheek. "You look exhausted."

"My blusher wore off hours ago." Recalling Dean's disregard for his personal discomfort, she added, "How I look on camera doesn't seem very important in light of what I'm reporting."

"You've done a fantastic job."

"Thanks."

"No, I mean it. The station is all abuzz."

That morning, when she'd left in the news van, she had approached the story as an opportunity to strut her stuff, win some attention, create the buzz Jack had mentioned.

Over the course of the day, that had changed. The turning point had been Dean's conversation with Mrs. Dorrie's sister. It had opened her eyes to the grim reality of the story, given names to the people involved, made it a human tragedy rather than a vehicle to propel her career forward. It seemed distasteful to benefit from the misfortune of others.

"Have you seen Dean any more?" Jack asked, breaking into her thoughts.

"Only once. He came out midafternoon to ask Mrs. Dorrie's sister about the children's favorite foods, toys, games, pets. He wanted to personalize his conversations with Mr. Dorrie."

Jack frowned thoughtfully. "It'll be personalized for Dean if this goes south."

"All he can do is his best."

"I know that. You know that. Everybody knows that except Dean. Mark my words, Paris. If five people don't walk out of that house, he'll beat himself up over it."

Jack hung around for another hour, then left with her promise to call him if the situation changed. It didn't. Not for hours. She was sitting in the passenger seat of the van, organizing her notes and trying to find a new angle to the story, when Dean tapped on the windshield.

"Has something happened?" she asked.

"No, nothing. Sorry if I alarmed you," he said, coming to stand beside the open window. "I just had to get out of that van for a while, get some fresh air, stretch my legs."

"Jack said to tell you to hang in there."

"He came around?"

"To bring us burgers. Have you had anything to eat?"

"A sandwich. But I could stand a drink of water."

She passed him a bottle. "I've been drinking from it."

"Like I care." He took a long swallow, recapped it, and handed it back to her. "I have a favor to ask. Would you call Gavin?

Whenever I'm involved in something like this, he gets scared." He gave her a fleeting smile. "Too many cop shows on TV. Anyhow, tell him you've talked to me and assure him that I'm okay."

Reading the question in her eyes, he added, "I've already spoken to him. So has Pat. But you know how kids are. He'll come nearer to believing it if it comes from someone not his parent."

"I'll be happy to. Anything else?"

"That's it."

"Easy enough."

His necktie had been loosened and his shirt sleeves were rolled back to his elbows. He propped his forearms in the open window, but turned his head in the direction of the house. He stared at it for a long while before he said softly, "He may kill them, Paris."

She didn't say anything, knowing that she wasn't expected to. He was confiding his worst fear to her, and she was glad he felt comfortable enough with her to do that. She only wished she could think of a reassurance that didn't sound banal.

"I don't know how a man could shoot his own children, but that's what he says he's going to do." Lowering his head to his clasped hands, he rubbed his thumb across his furrowed brow. "Last time I talked to him, I could hear one of the little girls crying in the background. 'Please, Daddy. Please don't shoot us.' If he decides to pull that trigger, there's not a goddamn thing I can say or do to stop him."

"If it weren't for you, he probably would have pulled the trigger already. You're doing the best you can." Then, without any forethought, she touched his hair.

He raised his head immediately and looked at her, possibly wondering how she knew that he was doing his best, or needing to hear that he was. Or maybe just to verify that she had touched him.

"Word filters back to us, you know," she said in a voice barely above a whisper. "From other cops. They all think you're incredible."

In a voice equally low, he asked, "What do you think?"

"I think you're pretty incredible, too."

She would have smiled, as one friend to another, but a smile seemed inappropriate for a multitude of reasons. The situation, for one. The tightness that had seized her chest until she could barely breathe, for another. But especially because of the intensity of feeling with which Dean was looking at her.

As on the night they met, the stare stretched into more than just an exchange between friends. Only this time it lasted even longer and the gravitational pull between them was much stronger.

She would have lowered her hand, which was still raised, an exposed culprit that had acted of its own volition. But lowering it would only have made its transgression more noticeable and lent it the meaning she didn't dare acknowledge.

Later she wondered if they'd have kissed if his pager hadn't beeped.

But it did and broke the spell. He checked the LED. "Dorrie's asking to talk to me." Without another word, he sprinted to the van.

It was midnight before he finally negotiated the release of the children. Dorrie was afraid that SWAT officers were going to rush the house. Dean assured him that he wouldn't allow that to happen if he would let the kids leave. Dorrie agreed on the condition that Dean come as far as the porch and carry them away from the house himself. Of course, Paris didn't know the terms of this negotiation until the crisis was over.

She was talking to Mrs. Dorrie's sister when the cameraman came jogging over to them and said, "Yo, Paris, Malloy is walking up to the house."

With her heart in her throat, she watched as Dean stood, his hands raised high into the air, at the edge of the porch. No one could hear what he and Dorrie said to one another through the door, but he remained in that vulnerable position for what seemed to her an eternity.

Eventually the door was opened from inside the house and a little boy slipped through, followed by an older girl carrying a smaller child. All were crying and shading their eyes against the bright lights aimed at the house.

Dean placed his arms around their waists and, carrying them against his body, delivered them to the Child Protection Services caseworkers who were standing by to receive them.

One of Dorrie's bargaining points, Paris learned later, was that the children were not to be handed over to his sister-in-law, who'd always hated him and had tried to turn his wife against him.

When Paris did a stand-up reporting the children's release, her voice was hoarse with fatigue and her appearance ragged, but a spirit of optimism had rejuvenated everyone at the site.

She concluded her stand-up by remarking on that mood shift. "For hours it seemed as though this standoff might have a tragic ending. But police personnel are now hopeful that the release of the children unharmed signifies a breakthrough."

Her last word was punctuated by two loud gunshots. The noise silenced Paris and other reporters doing similar stand-ups. In fact, she had never experienced a silence that sudden and that profound.

It was shattered by the third and final shot.

Paris stared at the clipping one last time, then refolded it exactly as Jack had done and replaced it behind her photograph in his wallet. She returned the wallet to the box, sick with the knowledge that if Jack had ever connected the night of the standoff to what transpired afterward, he might not have saved the clipping, but would have ripped it to shreds.

chapter twenty

She was a small woman. The hands twisting the damp tissue could have belonged to a child. Her legs were crossed at the ankles and tucked beneath the chair. She was as jittery as a piano student at a recital, awaiting her turn to play.

Curtis introduced them. "Mrs. Toni Armstrong, this is Dr. Dean Malloy."

"How do you do, Mrs. Armstrong?"

Curtis was being as gallant with her as he had been with Paris. "Can I get you something to drink?"

"No thank you. How long do you think this will take? I've got to pick up my children at four."

"I'll have you out of here well before then."

Prior to this meeting, Dean had been briefed for all of thirty seconds, the time it had taken him to walk to Curtis's cubicle after seeing Gavin and Liz off. He didn't have a clue as to why he'd been summoned to sit in on this interview. He remained standing, propping himself against the wall, for now a silent observer.

Mrs. Armstrong wasn't the shrinking violet her dainty appearance implied. It must have appeared to her that she was being ganged up on, because she put a stop to the pleasantries and cut to the chase.

"Mr. Hathaway said you had asked to see me, Sergeant Curtis, so I'm here. But no one has explained why you wanted to talk to me. Should I call my lawyer? Is my husband in some kind of trouble that I don't know about?"

"If he is, we don't know about it either, Mrs. Armstrong," Curtis replied smoothly. "But he has violated the terms of his probation, correct?"

"That's right."

"And Hathaway says you've recently noticed other troubling behavior."

She lowered her head. "Yes."

Curtis nodded sympathetically. "Hathaway called one of the SOAR officers, who then brought your husband to my attention."

Dean was beginning to see where this was going. SOAR—Sex Offender Apprehension and Registration—was under the auspices of the CIB. The detectives who specialized in sex offenses would know about Curtis's investigation. Too often those crimes and homicide overlapped.

"Could you please fill me in on the background?" Dean asked.

"Eighteen months ago Bradley Armstrong was convicted of molesting a minor and sentenced to five years' probation, mandatory group therapy, and so forth. Lately he's been skipping meetings.

"His probation officer scheduled two appointments with him today. He didn't show. Mrs. Armstrong notified his attorney, who went to his office—he's a dentist—to urge him to comply, get his act together. He'd split, although he had appointments with patients scheduled for this afternoon. Nobody knows where he is. He isn't answering his cell phone."

Toni Armstrong said, "I'm glad Hathaway called you. I'd rather Brad be arrested for violating his probation than . . . than for something else."

"Like what?" Dean asked.

"I'm afraid he's on the brink of committing another offense. He's doing everything he's not supposed to do."

Curtis, sensing that a rapport had been established, offered Dean his desk chair. Once he was seated, he said, "I know it's difficult for you to talk about this, Mrs. Armstrong. We're not trying to make the situation harder on you. In fact, we'd like to help."

She sniffed, nodding. "Brad is collecting pornography again. I found it in his office. I can't crack his computer because he's constantly changing the password to keep me out, but I know what I would find. It came out during his trial that he had bookmarked dozens of websites. And I'm not talking about artistic or elegant erotica. Brad goes for the very hard-core stuff, especially if the girls are in their teens.

"But that's not the worst of it. I haven't even told his probation officer all of it." She smiled at Dean wanly. "I'm not sure why I'm telling you. Except that I want Brad stopped before he gets into real trouble."

"What didn't you tell Mr. Hathaway?"

In fits and starts, she told them about her husband's frequent absences from his office and home, his lies, and his justifications for his actions. "All of which I know are signs that he's losing control over his impulses."

Dean agreed with her. These were classic bad signs. "Has he become defensive when you try to talk to him about it? Overly sensitive and angry? Does he accuse you of being suspicious, of not trusting him?"

"He turns every argument away from himself and tries to throw the blame on me for being unsupportive."

"Has he become violent?"

She related what had taken place in their kitchen last night.

When she finished, Dean asked quietly, "You haven't seen him since he stormed out?"

"No, but we spoke by phone this morning. He apologized, said he didn't know what had come over him."

"Has he ever been rough with you before?"

"Not even playfully rough. I've never seen him like that before."

Another bad sign, Dean thought.

She must have read the concern in his expression. Her eyes bounced between him and Curtis. "I still haven't been told why I'm here."

"Mrs. Armstrong," Curtis said, "does your husband ever listen to late-night radio?"

"Sometimes," she replied hesitantly.

"Has he ever disappeared before?"

"Once. Just after his patient's parents charged him with molesting their daughter. He was missing for three days before he was found and arrested."

"Where was he found?"

"In a motel. One of those residence places. He said he went into hiding because he was afraid no one would believe his side of the story."

"Did you?" Dean asked.

"Believe him?" Sorrowfully she shook her head. "That wasn't the first time a patient or coworker had complained about inappropriate behavior or touching. Different dental practices, different cities, even. But the same complaint.

"Brad's behavior leading up to that incident was similar to what it has been recently. Only this time, it's more pronounced. He's not trying so hard to hide it. He's more defiant, and that's making him reckless. That's why it was so easy to follow him."

"You followed him?"

Simultaneously with Dean's question, Curtis asked when this had taken place.

"One night last week." She rubbed her forehead as though ashamed of the admission. "I can't remember exactly. Brad had called from his office and said he wouldn't be coming home until late. He made up an excuse, but I saw through it. I asked a neighbor to watch my children.

"I got to his office before he left, so I was able to trail him from there. He went to an adult book and video store and stayed for almost two hours. Then he drove out to Lake Travis."

"Where specifically?"

"I don't know. I would never have found the area if I hadn't been following him. It wasn't a developed area. No homes or commercial buildings around. That's why I was surprised to see so many people there. Mostly young people. Teenagers."

"What did he do there?"

"For the longest time, nothing. He just sat in his car, watching. There was a lot of drinking, messing around, pairing off. Eventually Brad got out and approached a girl." She lowered her head. "They talked for a while, then she got into the car with him. That's when I left."

"You didn't confront him?"

"No," she said, smiling ruefully. "I was the one who felt dirty. I just wanted to get away from there, go home and take a long shower. Which is what I did."

In deference to her embarrassment, neither Dean nor Curtis said anything for a moment. Finally Curtis asked, "Could you identify the young woman you saw with him?"

She thought about it for a moment, then shook her head. "I don't think so. All that registered with me was that she was probably still in high school. It was dark, so I never got a good look at her face."

"Blond or dark hair? Tall, petite?"

"Blond, I think. Taller than me but shorter than Brad. He's five-ten."

"Could this be her?" Curtis reached for the picture of Janey Kemp that had run in the newspaper and held it out to her.

She looked at it and then at them individually. "Now I know why you wanted to see me," she said, her eyes filling with fear. "I read about this girl. A judge's daughter who's missing. That's it, isn't it? That's why I'm here."

Rather than answer her, Curtis said, "Did you ever tell your husband what you'd seen, that you had him cold?"

"No. I pretended to be asleep when he came in that night. The next morning, he was cheerful and affectionate. Teasing the kids, making plans with them for the weekend. Being the perfect husband and daddy."

She was contemplative for a moment. Dean sensed that Curtis was about to break into her thoughts with another question, but he subtly motioned for him to hold off.

Eventually Toni Armstrong raised her head and spoke directly to Dean. "Sometimes I think Brad actually believes his lies. It's as if he's living in a fantasy world where there are no consequences for his actions. He can do as he pleases without fear of getting caught or paying a penalty."

That was the most disturbing thing she'd told them. Dean doubted that she realized that, but Curtis did. When Dean glanced over at him, the detective was frowning thoughtfully.

He knew, as Dean did, that the profiles of serial killers and sexual predators typically included an elaborate fantasy life, one that was so compelling and so real to them that they acted it out. They often believed themselves to be above the laws of a society that had grievously wronged them, and answered only to a god who understood, and even sanctioned, their perversity.

Curtis cleared his throat. "I appreciate your time, Mrs. Armstrong. Since the subject matter is so upsetting, I especially appreciate your candor."

But she wasn't going to be whisked away that easily. "I've told you some awful truths about my husband, but he could not be involved in the disappearance of this young woman."

"We have no reason to believe that he is. None. As I said, we're following numerous leads." Curtis paused, then added, "With assistance from you, we could eliminate him as a suspect."

"How could I help?"

"By letting our experts try to crack his computer. Get into his files, see what they find. This girl was heavily into a website where sexually explicit messages are posted. She made a lot of contacts that way. If she and your husband never corresponded, then chances are slim that he knew her."

She thought about it, then said, "I won't agree to that until I've consulted Brad's attorney."

Curtis accepted the condition but didn't look happy about it.

Dean's opinion of Mrs. Armstrong went up another notch. She was no pushover. This toughness probably hadn't been in her nature before the difficulties brought on by her husband's addiction. She'd had to acquire it in order to hold on to her sanity and survive.

Curtis waited as she got out of the chair and walked her out of the cubicle. "Thank you for obliging us, Mrs. Armstrong. I hope your husband is located soon and that he gets the help he needs."

"He could not be the man you're looking for."

"Probably not. Besides, we're not sure that Janey Kemp has met with foul play. But, as you've no doubt learned, all prior offenders come under suspicion any time a sex offense is alleged. Your husband picked a bad time to miss an appointment with his probation officer, that's all."

That wasn't all, and she was smart enough to realize it. But she was also too polite to call Curtis a liar to his face. Instead, she told them good-bye.

"Nice lady," Curtis remarked once she was out of earshot.

"Intelligent, too." Curtis looked at Dean for elaboration. "Her husband is on a downward spiral, and she knows it. She also recognized your bullshit for what it was. In spite of what you told her, you obviously think there could be a connection between Armstrong's disappearance and Janey's."

"Can't rule it out." Curtis eased himself into his desk chair and indicated the other one to Dean. He took a Baby Ruth from a glass canister on his desk and offered one to Dean.

"No thanks."

As he unwrapped the candy bar, Curtis said, "Armstrong's own wife saw him solicit a minor for sex. He went to that remote place on the lake for that specific purpose. And how did he know to go there? Only one way."

"The Sex Club," Dean said.

"Exactly. He probably uses the message board like a menu. Whets his appetite by reading what's posted there, then goes out looking for the girl who posted it. And the girl Toni Armstrong saw him with matches Janey Kemp's general description."

"*Very* general," Dean said. "She described half the high school girls in and around Austin."

"All the same, it's a coincidence that cuts very close. You agree?"

Dean raked back his hair. "Yeah, yeah, I agree."

He had felt empathy for Toni Armstrong. He identified with hoping to God you were right to believe in the innocence of a loved one in whom you had little trust.

"If she doesn't volunteer his computer soon, I'm going to request a court order," Curtis told him. "Rondeau may be able to track Armstrong through Janey's email address book, but it'll take longer. In the meantime, I've put everyone on alert that I want to talk to Dr. Armstrong as soon as he surfaces. We've already put out an APB on his car."

"Speaking of which, any lab results back from Janey's car?"

Curtis grimaced. "Evidence overkill. They collected trace evidence of every fiber, either natural or manufactured, known to man. Carpet, clothing, paper. Every frigging thing. It'll take weeks to sort it all out."

"Fingerprints other than Janey's?"

"Only several dozen. They're searching for matches. Maybe we'll get lucky and one of them will be Brad Armstrong's. They also collected traces of soil, food, plants, and controlled substances. You name it, we found it, and we can readily identify it. But if we'd collected evidence from a KOA campground, it couldn't be more scattershot.

"The girl practically lived in her car. According to her friends, even her own parents, she entertained in it extensively. She ate, drank, slept, and screwed in it. The only thing we've matched with certainty is a human hair, and it matches one we took from her hairbrush in her bathroom at home. Oh, and a speck of dried fecal matter. Identified as canine, which makes sense because we also collected several dog hairs that match those of the family pet."

"I don't remember seeing or hearing a dog."

"Stays in the laundry room. The judge is allergic." Curtis finished his candy bar, wadded up the wrapper, and tossed it into the trash can. "That's it so far."

"Nothing was found that sheds light on what happened to her," Dean remarked.

"No sign of a struggle, like ripped clothing or scuff marks on the interior surfaces. Only one hair, not like a clump that had been pulled out. No broken fingernails that would indicate resistance. No blood. The gas tank was half full, so she hadn't run out. No malfunction of the motor. Sufficient air in all the tires. It appears she left the car under her own power and locked it behind her."

"Intending to come back," Dean added thoughtfully. "What about other tire tracks in the area?"

"You know how many people have signed on to the Sex Club website at one time or another? Several hundred. I think every last one of them was congregated there that night. Say two or three rode together, you've still got a hundred vehicles. We've made a few imprints and are running down the makes and models, but it's going to take days, if not weeks, which we don't have.

"And matching DNA samples, even once we've isolated them, takes time. A lot of time. It sure as hell can't happen in"—he consulted his wall clock—"less than thirty-six hours."

"What about the photograph she gave Gavin? Any leads from that?"

"Taken with a film camera, not digital. The film wasn't developed at your corner one-hour photo."

"Our guy has his own darkroom?"

"Or uses someone else's. I've got several people working that angle, trying to track down suppliers of photographic paper and chemicals, but again—"

"Time."

"Right. And our amateur shutterbug may not buy his products over the counter. He could get them by mail order or buy them online." His thinning crew cut certainly didn't need smoothing, but he ran his hand over it as though it did. "Something else to toss into the gumbo, remember Marvin the janitor?"

"What about him?"

"Aka Morris Green, Marty Benton, and Mark Wright. Along with Marvin Patterson, those are the aliases we know of."

"What's his story?"

"Real name Lancy Ray Fisher. In and out of JV court numerous times on petty charges. At age eighteen he did time in Huntsville for grand-theft auto. Got the sentence reduced by ratting out a cell mate who had boasted to Lancy Ray about a murder. But once free, assorted felonies followed, for which he served minimum sentences, usually by plea bargaining. Best known for bad checks and credit card theft."

"Where is he?"

"Don't know. We're still looking and so is his parole officer. He dove underground when we called ahead. Griggs and Carson got an ass chewing for that. Anyhow, Marvin's avoidance of us leads me to believe that violating parole isn't his only crime and that cleaning the toilets at the radio station isn't his sole source of income."

"Or that he's got something worse to hide," Dean said.

"We got a warrant and searched his place. No computer."

"He could've taken it with him."

"Could've, but he left behind other goodies."

"Like?"

Curtis ran down a list of electronics that would be hard to come by on an average janitor's salary. "Mostly sound equipment. Fancy stuff. We also carried out boxes of crap we're still sorting through. But here's where it gets really interesting. One of those felonies I mentioned? Sexual assault. His DNA is on record."

"If you could match him to trace evidence found in Janey's car—"

"If I had the time to match it, you mean."

Dean shared the detective's frustration. It was an upside-down case. They had good leads, but no crime and no victim. They were looking for an abductor without knowing for certain that Janey Kemp had been abducted. They were working under the assumption that she was being held against her will, that her life was in peril, but for all they knew—

A fresh thought struck Dean. "What if . . ."

Curtis looked at him, prompting him to continue. "Say it. I'm open to any ideas at this point."

"Is it possible that Janey herself is behind this?"

"For attention?"

"Or fun. Could she have put a male friend up to calling Paris just for kicks, just to see how far it would go and what would happen?"

"It's not that far-fetched an idea. But it's not original either. I went over to the courthouse this morning to talk to the judge and—"

"He's carrying on business as usual?"

"Right down to the black robe," Curtis said with dislike. "He clings to the notion that Janey is doing this to spite him and his wife. Come the election in November, the judge doesn't need any adverse publicity. Clean family image and all that. He thinks Janey is trying to scotch his chances to keep his seat on the bench."

"Damn."

"What?"

"I'm thinking like Judge Kemp now?"

Curtis chuckled. "And you could both be right."

They mulled it over for several seconds before Dean said, "I don't think so, Curtis. Valentino convinced me. Either Janey's anonymous prankster friend knows enough psychology to pass for the real thing, or he is."

"I have to think he is."

"Janey kept an appointment with this guy. They met in a designated place. She secured her car and rode away with him."

"It would appear," Curtis said.

"Which is consistent with Gavin's story."

The detective stared thoughtfully at the toe of his polished boot. "Gavin could've taken her somewhere in his car so they'd have privacy to thrash things out."

"And instead, Gavin thrashed her? Is that what you're thinking?"

Curtis looked up and shrugged as though to say, *Maybe.*

"After talking briefly to Janey, Gavin joined his friends. He gave you a list of names and numbers. Have you checked with them?"

"Working on it."

The detective's noncommittal answer irritated Dean even more. "Do you think he could disguise his voice enough to sound like Valentino? Don't you think I'd be able to identify my own son's voice?"

"Would you want to identify it?"

Dean could withstand criticism. Sometimes his analysis of a suspect, a potential witness, or a cop in trouble wasn't received well and made him unpopular with fellow officers. It was an accepted hazard of his job.

But this was the first time his integrity had come into question. Ever. And it made him madder than hell. "Are you accusing me of obstructing justice? You think I'm withholding evidence? Do you want a strand of Gavin's hair?"

"I may later."

"Any time. Let me know."

"I meant no offense. The thing is, you hold back a lot, Doctor."

"For instance?"

"You and Paris Gibson. There's more there than you let on."

"Because it's none of your goddamn business."

"The hell it's not," Curtis said, his ire rising to match Dean's. "This whole thing started with her." He leaned forward and lowered his voice so that anyone beyond the cubicle couldn't overhear. "You two were a dynamic duo during a standoff situation down in Houston. Made all the papers, TV news."

"People died."

"Yeah, I heard that. Tore you up pretty bad. You took some time off to get your head on straight."

Dean fumed in silence.

"Not long after that, Paris's fiancé, your best friend—something else you failed to mention—becomes incapacitated. She quits TV news and devotes herself to taking care of him, and you—"

"I know the history. Where'd you get your information?"

"I have friends in the HPD. I asked," he replied without apology.

"Why?"

"Because it occurred to me that maybe this Valentino business stems from all that."

"It doesn't."

"You're sure? Valentino's hang-up seems to be unfaithful women. Do you think an attractive and vital woman like Paris remained faithful to Jack Donner for the whole seven years she cared for him?"

"I don't know. I lost contact with her and Jack after they left Houston."

"Entirely?"

"She wanted it that way."

"I don't get it. You were going to be best man at their wedding."

"Your Houston source was very thorough."

"He didn't tell me anything that wasn't in print. Why did Paris ask you to stay away?"

"She didn't ask, she insisted. She was abiding by what she thought Jack would want. We'd been athletes together in college. Buddies, and all the physical rowdiness that implies. He wouldn't have wanted me to see him so debilitated."

Curtis nodded as though it was a valid answer, but maybe not a complete one. "And something else that strikes me as curious," he said. "The sunglasses."

"Her eyes are sensitive to light."

"But she wears them in darkness, too. She had them on last night when you arrived at the Wal-Mart store. It was the middle of the night and there wasn't even a full moon." Curtis fixed an incisive look on him. "It's almost like she's ashamed of something, isn't it?"

chapter *twenty-one*

Stan would rather have had an appointment with a proctologist than with his uncle Wilkins. Either way, he was going to get his ass reamed, but at least a proctologist would wear gloves and try to be gentle.

Their meeting place, the lobby bar of the Driskill Hotel, was in Stan's favor. Since Wilkins planned to fly back to Atlanta that evening, he hadn't booked a suite. *Thank God,* thought Stan as he entered the downtown landmark. It was unlikely that his uncle would flay and fillet him in a public arena. Wilkins hated scenes.

The hotel lobby was as tranquil as a harem during afternoon-nap time. The stained-glass ceiling provided subdued illumination. One tended to walk as quietly as possible across the marble mosaic floors. Nor did one wish to disturb a single glossy frond as one passed a potted palm. Sofas and chairs invited one to languish on the deep cushions and enjoy the flute solo filtering through invisible speakers.

But at the center of this oasis of cool serenity squatted a poisonous toad.

Wilkins Crenshaw was well under six feet tall, and Stan suspected he wore elevator lifts in his shoes. His gray hair had a yellowish tint and was so sparse that it barely concealed the age spots on his waxy scalp. His nose was overly wide, which matched fleshy lips, the lower one curling downward. He bore a resemblance to an amphibian of the ugliest genus.

Stan figured his uncle's appearance was the main reason he had stayed a bachelor. The only appeal Wilkins might hold for the opposite sex would be his money, which was the second reason he was still single. He was too stingy to share even a small slice of his financial pie with a spouse.

Stan also guessed that his uncle had been a nerdy outcast in the military academy to which he and his father had been sent by his grandfather. From there the brothers had been given no option other than attending the Citadel. Upon graduation each had served a stint in the air force. Then, having earned the appropriate degrees and done their patriotic duty, they had been allowed to join the family business.

At some point during these passages into manhood, the nerdy Wilkins had turned mean. He had learned to fight back, but his weapon of choice was brainpower, not brawn. He didn't use his fists, but he had a remarkable talent for instilling fear. He fought dirty and took no prisoners.

He didn't stand when Stan joined him at the small round cocktail table. He didn't even greet him. When the pretty young waitress approached, he said to her, "Bring him a club soda."

Stan despised club soda, but he didn't change the order. He would do his best to make this meeting as painless as possible. Smiling pleasantly, he began with flattery. "You're looking well, Uncle."

"Is that a silk shirt?"

"Uh, yes."

It was a family trait to dress well. As though to compensate for his physical shortcomings, Wilkins was always immaculately garbed and groomed. His shirts and suits were tailor-made, mercilessly starched and steamed. A wrinkle or loose thread didn't stand a chance.

"Do you go out of your way to dress like a queer? Or do you just come by that faggoty look naturally?"

Stan said nothing, only nodded his thanks to the waitress when she delivered his club soda.

"You must've inherited that flamboyant style of dress from your mother. She liked ruffles and such. The more the better."

Stan didn't dispute him, even though his shirt wasn't in the least flamboyant, not in style or color. And he seriously doubted his mother had ever worn a ruffle in her life. She'd never looked anything except perfectly correct. She'd had excellent taste and in his opinion remained the most beautiful woman he had ever seen.

But arguing any of this would be pointless, so he changed the subject. "Did your meeting with the GM go well?"

"The place is still making money."

Then why, Stan wondered, was he scowling? "The latest ratings were very strong," he remarked. "Up several points over the previous period."

He'd done his homework so he could impress his uncle with this quote. He only hoped Wilkins didn't quiz him by asking the dates of the last ratings period or to explain what a point was.

His uncle gave a noncommittal grunt. "That's why this business with Paris Gibson is so upsetting."

"Yes, sir."

"We can't have our radio station involved."

"It's not exactly *involved*, Uncle. Only peripherally."

"Even to a minor extent, I don't want us connected to something as unsavory as a teenage girl's disappearance."

"Absolutely not, sir."

"That's why I'm going to tear your fucking head off and piss down the hole if you had anything at all to do with making those phone calls."

Uncle Wilkins had learned something besides meanness from his days in the military. He'd learned to express himself in language that could not be misinterpreted. The crudeness of his statement was topped only by its effectiveness.

Stan quailed. "Why would it even cross your mind that I could—"

"Because you're a fuckup. You have been since your mother expelled you. From the moment you drew breath, she knew you were a mewling little turd. I think that's why, when she got sick, she just lay down and died."

"She had pancreatic cancer."

"Which gave her a good excuse to finally rid herself of you. Your father also knew you weren't worth spit. He didn't want to be burdened with you. That's why he sucked so hard on his pistol, it blew the back of his head off."

Stan's throat closed. He couldn't speak.

Wilkins was relentless. "Your father was weak to begin with and your mother made him weaker. He felt it was his duty to remain married to her even though it was her personal goal to fuck every man she met."

Cruelty was his uncle's lifeblood. Having experienced it for thirty-two years, Stan realized he should be used to it. He wasn't. He glared at Wilkins with unmitigated hatred. "Father had affairs, too. Constantly."

"More than any of us know, I'm sure. He poked every woman

he could in order to convince himself that he still could. Your mother didn't permit him in her bed. He seemed to be the only man she had an aversion to."

"Besides you."

Wilkins closed his hand so tightly around his glass of bourbon that Stan wondered why the crystal didn't break. He had scored a direct hit and it felt good. He knew exactly where his uncle's disdain for his mother was coming from. Countless times, Stan had heard her laugh lightly and say, "Wilkins, you're such a disagreeable toad."

Coming from his mother, who adored men, that was a colossal put-down. Moreover, she had never shown any fear of Wilkins, and that would be the ultimate insult. He thrived on making people afraid of him. With her, he had failed utterly. Stan delighted in reminding him of it.

A slurp of bourbon restored him. He said, "Considering your dysfunctional parents, it's little wonder you have problems with sex."

"I don't."

"All evidence being to the contrary."

Stan's face turned hot. "If you're talking about that woman in Florida—"

"Who you tried to hump over her fax machine."

"That's her version," Stan said. "It wasn't like that. She was all over me until she got cold feet, afraid someone was going to walk in."

"That's not the only time I've had to bail you out because you couldn't keep your pants zipped. Just like your father. If you had half the aptitude for business that you do for fornicating, there would be more money in the till for all of us."

That, Stan suspected, was the crux of Uncle Wilkins's animosity. He couldn't touch the sizable trust fund Stan's parents had set up for him, which included not only what he had inherited upon their deaths, but a large share of the corporation's earnings ad infinitum. The terms were irrevocable and irrefutable. Even Wilkins with all his power and influence couldn't invalidate his trust and steal his fortune.

"That time at the country club swimming pool, what were you trying to prove when you exposed yourself to those girls? That you could get it up?"

"We were eleven years old. They were curious. They begged me to see it."

"I guess that's why they went screaming to their parents. I had to shell out a few grand to keep the incident under wraps and to keep you from being permanently banned from the club. You got expelled from prep school for whacking off in the shower."

"Everybody whacked off in the shower."

"But only you got caught, which indicates an absence of self-control."

"Do you intend to parade all my adolescent indiscretions past me? Because if you do, I'm going to order a drink."

"We haven't got time for me to parade all your indiscretions past you. Not during this meeting." He checked his wristwatch. "I'll be leaving shortly. I told the pilot I wanted wheels up at six."

May you crash and burn, Stan thought.

"What I want from you," Wilkins said, "is a denial that you've been making dirty phone calls to that woman deejay."

"Why would I do that?"

"Because you're a sick little fucker. It cost me a fortune for your shrink to tell me what I already knew. Your parents created a mess—you. And left me with the job of cleaning it up. I'm just glad that—so far at least—all your 'indiscretions' have been with women."

"Stop it," Stan hissed.

He wished he had the nerve to leap across the table, take hold of his uncle's short, fat neck, and squeeze until his bulging frog eyes popped from their sockets and his tongue protruded from his fat lips. He would love to see him dead. Grotesquely, painfully dead.

"I didn't make those phone calls," he said. "How could I? I was in the building with Paris when those calls came through from public telephones miles away from the station."

"I've checked it out. It's possible to reroute calls, make it look like they're coming from one phone when they actually originate on another. Usually a disposable cell phone, one that's been stolen perhaps. Makes the calls virtually untraceable."

Stan was flabbergasted. "You checked out how it could be done, even before you asked me if I'd been doing it?"

"I haven't gotten to where I am by being stupid and careless like you. I didn't want one of your so-called indiscretions blowing up in my face. I don't want to be left looking like a schmuck for trusting you to keep your dick where it belongs. As it is, I've got to answer to the board of directors for paying you a salary when it's a challenge for you to replace a lightbulb."

Wilkins fixed him with an unwavering stare and held it until Stan said, "I didn't rig any phone calls."

"The only thing you're good at is tinkering with gadgets."

"I didn't rig any phone calls," he repeated.

Wilkins eyed him shrewdly as he took another drink from his glass. "This Paris. Do you like her?"

Stan kept his expression impassive. "Yes, she's okay."

His uncle's stare turned harder, meaner, and, as usual, Stan yielded to it. He always did, eventually. And he hated himself for it. He *was* a mewling little turd.

He fiddled with the soggy cocktail napkin beneath his untouched club soda. "If you're asking me if I've ever entertained sexual thoughts about her, then yes. On occasion. She's attractive and has that whiskey voice, and we spend hours alone together every night."

"Have you tried with her?"

He shook his head. "She made it plain she's not interested."

"So you did try and she turned you down."

"No, I never tried. She lives like a nun."

"Why?"

"She was engaged to this guy," he said in a tone that conveyed his exasperation over the uselessness of this conversation. "He was in a private hospital up near Georgetown, north of here. Very exclusive. Anyhow, Paris went to see him every day. People around the station told me she did this for years. He died not too long ago. She took it hard and still isn't over it. Besides, she's not the type who could, you know . . ."

"No, I don't know. Not the type who could what?"

"Who could be seduced."

Wilkins stared at him for an interminable length of time, then peeled enough bills from his money clip to cover their tab. He placed them beneath his empty glass as he stood up. Reaching for his briefcase, he looked down his wide, unsightly nose at Stan.

"'Seduce' is a word that means you have to persuade a woman to have sex with you. Not at all confidence inspiring, Stanley."

As his uncle moved away, Stan said under his breath, "Well, at least I'm not so butt ugly I have to pay for it."

Stan learned one thing from the meeting. There was nothing wrong with his uncle's hearing.

The mobile home was no longer mobile. In fact, it had been in place for so many years that one corner of it listed. In front, a cyclone fence enclosed a small yard where nothing grew except Johnsongrass and sticker patches. The only nod toward landscaping were two cracked clay pots from which sprouted faded plastic marigolds.

A neighbor kid had kicked a soccer ball over the fence and into the yard but had never bothered to retrieve it. It had long since deflated. A two-legged charcoal grill that had been bought at a garage sale years before had been propped against the exterior wall of the house. The bottom of it was completely rusted out. The television antenna on the roof was bent almost to a right angle.

It was derelict, but it was home.

Home to three neglected and foul-tempered cats who'd never been housebroken, and a slattern who was addicted to coffee and Winstons, which she continually puffed in spite of the wheeled oxygen tank to which she was connected by a cannula.

She was wheezing heavily when the door to the mobile home creaked open, causing a wedge of sunlight to cut across the picture on her television screen. "Mama?"

"Shut the goddamn door. I can't see my TV with that light shining on it, and my story's on."

"You and your stories." Lancy Ray Fisher, aka Marvin Patterson, came in and shut the door behind him. The room was plunged into foggy darkness. The black-and-white picture on the television set improved, but only slightly.

He went straight to the refrigerator and looked inside. "There's nothing in here to eat."

"This ain't the Luby's Cafeteria and nobody invited you."

He scrounged around until he came up with a slice of bologna. On top of the fridge there was a loaf of white bread. He pushed aside one of the cats so he could get to it, then folded the bologna into a stale slice. It would have to do.

His mother said nothing else until the soap opera went into a commercial break. "What're you up to, Lancy?"

"What makes you think I'm up to something?"

She snorted and lit a cigarette.

"You're going to blow yourself up one of these days, smoking around that oxygen tank. I only hope I'm not here when you do."

"Make me one of them sam'iches." He did and as he passed it to her, she said, "You only come around when you're in trouble. What'd you do this time?"

"Nothing. The landlord is repainting my apartment. I need a place to stay for the next few days."

"I thought you were hot and heavy with some new girlfriend. How come you ain't staying with her?"

"We broke up."

"Figures. She find out you're a con?"

"I'm not a con anymore. I'm an upstanding citizen."

"And I'm the queen of Sheba," she wheezed.

"I've cleaned up my act, Mama. Can't you tell?"

He held his arms out to his sides. She looked him up and down. "What I see is new clothes, but the man underneath 'em ain't changed."

"Yes I have."

"You still making them nasty movies?"

"Videos, Mama. Two. That was years ago, and I only did it as a favor to a friend."

A friend who had paid him in cocaine. For as much as he could snort, all he had to do was get naked and screw. But then Lancy had started screwing one of the "actresses" off the set as well as on, and the jealous director began complaining about the size of his "package." In a medium where size mattered, Lancy just wasn't making the grade. "Nothing personal, you understand."

But of course Lancy had taken it personally. They'd had a parting of the ways, but not before Lancy made the director bleed and beg that his own package be left intact.

That had been a long time ago. He didn't do hard drugs now. He didn't play in dirty videos. He had improved every aspect of himself.

But apparently his mother didn't think so. "You're just like your daddy," she said as she noisily chewed her sandwich. "He was a shifty bastard, and you got the same sneaky look about you. You don't even talk natural. Where'd you learn to talk so fancy all of a sudden?"

"I'm working at the radio station. I listen to people on the radio. I've picked up speech patterns from them. I've been practicing."

"Speech patterns, my ass. Wouldn't trust you as far as I could throw you."

She went back to watching her soap. Lancy moved down the narrow hallway, stepping around piles of cat shit, and squeezed into the tiny room in which he slept when he was between incarcerations or employment, or at times like this when he needed to disappear for a few days. This was his last resort.

He knew his mother searched the room each time he left, so

when he pried up the loose vinyl tile beneath the twin bed, he did so with the fear of what he would find. Or, more to the point, not find.

But the cash, mostly hundred-dollar bills, was there in the small metal box where he'd stashed it. Half of it rightfully belonged to a former partner, who'd been convicted of another crime and was now serving a prison sentence. When he got out, he would come looking for Marty Benton and his share of the loot. But Lancy would worry about that when and if the time ever came.

The amount had shrunk considerably from what it was originally. He'd used a sizable portion of it to buy his car and new threads. He'd rented an apartment . . . well, two, actually. He had invested in the computer that was now inside the trunk of his car.

His mother would rag him about throwing away good money on a foolish contraption like a computer when she was still watching her stories in black and white. She didn't understand that in order to succeed at any endeavor, legal or ill, a person had to be computer savvy. Lancy had trained himself to be. To avoid the old bitch's harping, he would take his laptop inside and access the Internet through his cell phone only when she was asleep.

He counted his cash, stuffed several of the bills into his pocket, then returned the rest to their hiding place under the floor. This was his emergency fund, and he hated like hell having to tap into it now. Although this definitely qualified as an emergency.

Shortly after being released from his last incarceration, he'd landed a good job, but had been too stupid to appreciate it. One of the dumbest things he'd ever done was steal from the company. Not that he had thought of it as stealing, but his boss sure as hell had.

If he'd asked to purchase the cast-off equipment for a nominal amount, the boss probably would have told him to take what he wanted, that he was welcome to it. But he hadn't asked. He had reverted to his old ways. Catch as catch can. Get it while the gettin's good. One evening before leaving work, he had helped himself to the obsolete equipment, thinking no one would miss it.

But somebody had. He, being the only ex-con on the payroll, was the first person the boss suspected. When accused, he confessed and asked for a second chance. No dice. He was fired and had escaped criminal charges only because he returned everything he'd taken.

The experience had taught him several lessons, primarily never to tell the truth on a job application. So when Marvin Patterson applied for the job at the radio station, he checked the No box to the questions about arrests and convictions.

Lousy as it was to mop up after other people, that job had been a boon. When he got it, he felt that fate, or his fairy godmother, or some power beyond himself had compelled him to steal that stuff. If he hadn't been fired from that first job, he wouldn't have had the way cleared for him to work at 101.3.

Not only had the janitorial job been gainful employment that kept his parole officer pacified, it had kept Lancy from having to deplete his stash. And, most important, it had allowed him to be near Paris Gibson every night.

Unfortunately, there was no returning to that job now. Nor could he go back to his apartment, write a check on Marvin Patterson's bank account, or use an ATM to withdraw from it, all of which were surefire ways of letting yourself be found when you didn't want to be.

The minute those cops called telling him to stay put, that they were on their way over to talk to him about harassing Paris Gibson with a dirty phone call, he knew his goose was cooked. Just like that, he'd become an ex-con again and had acted accordingly. He'd grabbed his cell phone, his computer setup, some clothing, and cleared out.

His first stop had been his second residence, a dump of a place that he kept leased under an assumed name. What might seem like an unnecessary luxury had proved itself to come in handy.

But as he approached the parking lot, he spotted a police car at the IHOP across the street. He had driven past without pulling in. He told himself it was probably just a coincidence, that if the cops were lying in wait for him to show up there, they wouldn't be in marked cars. But he was taking no chances.

He had destroyed Marvin Patterson's fake IDs. Hello, Frank Shaw.

He'd swapped the license plates on his car, too, switching them for some he had stolen months ago.

No matter what anybody said about reform and rehabilitation, no cop, or judge, or decent, law-abiding citizen was going to extend to an ex-con the benefit of the doubt. You could swear on the Good Book that you were a changed man. You could beg for an opportunity to prove yourself. You could promise to become a contributing member of the community. It didn't matter. Nobody gave a con a second chance. Not the law, or society, or women.

Especially women. They'd do all manner of sex with you but

got squeamish when it came to a criminal record. There they got finicky. There they drew the line. Did that make sense?

Not to Lancy. But whether or not it was reasonable, that was the rule. Since he didn't conform to the rule, he had tried changing himself into a man who did. He dressed better, talked better, treated women like a gentleman would.

So far, the transformation hadn't met with stunning success. He'd had a few promising prospects, but eventually they'd gone the way of his other relationships. It was like there was a stain on him that could be seen only by women.

He just couldn't make them like and respect him. Starting with his own mother.

chapter twenty-two

"We know this is last minute, but we're hoping you'll go to dinner with us."

Paris looked from Dean to Gavin. In seven years, he had grown tall, lean, and handsome. His hair had darkened slightly and the bone structure of his face was more defined, but she would have recognized him even on sight.

"This is a cliché," she said, "and you'll hate me for saying it, but I can't believe you're so grown up." She clasped one of his hands between hers. "It's so good to see you again, Gavin."

With a mix of embarrassment and shyness, he said, "It's good to see you, too, Ms. Gibson."

"When you were nine, Ms. Gibson was appropriate. Coming from you now it makes me sound ancient. I'm Paris from now on, okay?"

"Okay."

"How about dinner?" Dean asked.

"I've already got something started."

He raised his eyebrows expectantly, putting her on the spot and giving her little choice except to say, "There's plenty if you and Gavin don't mind eating in."

"It will be a welcome change." Dean nudged Gavin across her threshold. "What are we having?"

"You weaseled an invitation out of me and now you're choosy?"

"Anything but liver or rutabagas."

"Angel-hair pasta with pork tenderloin and veggies. No rutabagas."

"My mouth is already watering. What can we do to help?"

"Uh." Suddenly she felt at a loss. It had been so long since she had entertained, she'd forgotten how. "We could all have something to drink."

"Sounds good."

"I have a bottle of wine . . ." She gestured toward the back of the house.

Dean said, "Lead the way."

In the kitchen, she assigned him the job of opening the Chardonnay, while she poured a Coke over ice for Gavin. Dean made himself right at home. She and Gavin were more awkward with the situation. "There's a CD player in the living room," she said to him. "But I'm not sure I have any music you'll like."

"I'll like it. I listen to your show sometimes."

Pleased to know that, she told him where to find her CD player. He left the kitchen for the living room. As soon as he was out of earshot, she said to Dean, "Am I to acknowledge the bruise on his face or not?"

"Not."

It had been impossible not to notice the dark bruise and slight swelling beneath Gavin's right eye. Naturally she'd wondered how he had come to have such a painful-looking injury. But Dean seemed angry and upset about it, so she changed the subject by asking how Gavin's meeting with Curtis had gone.

"Curtis said Gavin stuck to his original story, telling him nothing that he hadn't told me. He and Janey argued, then he joined a group of friends. Never saw her again."

"Does Curtis believe him?"

"Noncommittal. He didn't detain Gavin, which I take as a positive sign. Also, Valentino has a mature voice. I don't think Gavin could pull that off, even if he tried. And where would Gavin be holding a girl hostage? He doesn't have access to a place. He would have had to kill her that night and— Jesus, listen to me." He braced his hands on the edge of the counter and stared into the bottle of wine.

"Gavin had nothing to do with Janey's disappearance. I just know that, Dean."

"I don't think he did either. But I also never would have guessed he was doing the other stuff. It's been disconcerting, to say the least, to discover that my son has been leading a secret life."

"To some extent, don't all teenagers?"

"I suppose, but I've made it easy for him. I wanted him to like living with me, so I've soft-pedaled the discipline. It didn't seem

like I was going easy on him, but I suppose I haven't been as diligent or consistent as I should have been. Gavin took advantage of
that."

Turning his head to address her, he added, "With all my psychological training, shouldn't I have realized that I was being
conned?"

Just then Gavin called from the living room, "Is Rod Stewart
okay?"

"Great," Paris called back. Then to Dean, she said, "Cut yourself some slack. It's a child's duty to try and bamboozle his parents. As for discipline, techniques from a textbook don't always
translate to real life."

"But how can it be this hard to get right?"

She laughed softly. "If it were easy, if one system worked for
every child, a lot of so-called experts would be out of work. What
would they discuss on afternoon talk shows? Think of the chaos,
to say nothing of the economic crisis, that well-behaved and obe-
dient children would create."

After winning a smile from him, she dropped the joking. "I'm
not making light of your concern, Dean. In fact, it's admirable.
Gavin may have gotten off track, but he'll turn out all right."

He poured wine into the two stemmed glasses she had set out
and handed one to her. "We can hope." He clinked their glasses.

She looked at him over the rim of hers as she took a sip. "He
comes by it naturally, you know."

"What's that?"

"Gavin isn't the only master manipulator in the Malloy family."

"Oh?"

"Very crafty of you, showing up here with him in tow after I
had already declined a dinner invitation."

"It worked, didn't it?"

"As a psychologist, how would you classify a man who uses his
child to get a dinner invitation out of a woman?"

"Pathetic."

"How about two-timing?"

Dean's smile faltered. "You're referring to Liz."

"Did you tell her about your dinner plans for tonight?"

"I told her I needed to spend time with Gavin."

"But you didn't mention me."

"No."

"She seemed to have a rightful claim to your evenings."

"She has had, yes."

"Exclusive claim?"

"Yes."

"For how long?"

"Couple of years."

That came as an unpleasant shock. "Wow. When I knew you in Houston, your affairs lasted no more than a couple of weeks."

"Because the woman I wanted was taken."

"We're not talking about that, Dean."

"The hell we're not."

"We're talking about you and Liz. A two-year relationship implies—"

"Not what you're thinking."

"What is *Liz* thinking?"

"Dad?" From the open doorway, Gavin hesitantly interrupted them. He was extending a cell phone to Dean. "It's ringing."

"Thanks." He reached for the phone and read the incoming number on the LED. "Gavin, help Paris."

He left the kitchen before answering the phone, causing Paris to wonder if the call had been from Liz.

"What would you like me to do?" Gavin offered.

"Set the table?"

"Okay, sure. My mom made me do it all the time."

She smiled at him. "I remember whenever Jack and I went to your dad's house for dinner and you were there, that was your chore."

"Speaking of, I, uh, haven't had a chance to tell you. I'm sorry about him, you know, dying."

"Thank you, Gavin."

"I liked him. He was cool."

"Yes he was. Now," she said briskly, "do you think we should use the dining room, or eat here in the kitchen?"

"Kitchen's okay with me."

"Good." She showed him where the napkins, dishes, and cutlery were kept and he began setting the table while she sautéed the vegetables and strips of pork. "Are you looking forward to school this year?"

"Yeah. Well, I mean, I guess. It'll be tough, not knowing anybody."

"I can relate. My dad was career army." She filled a pot with water to boil the pasta. "We moved all over the map. I went to three different elementary schools and two junior highs. Luckily he retired, so I got to attend only one high school. But I remember how hard it was to be the new kid."

"It sucks."

"You'll adjust in no time. I remember when you had to switch Little League teams, midseason. You went from being a Pirate to a—"

"Cougar. You remember that?"

"Very well. Your coach had to quit."

"His job transferred him to Ohio or someplace."

"So all the boys on his team were divided up among the others. You weren't at all happy about it, but it turned out to be the best thing that could've happened. The Cougars needed a good short-stop, and you filled that position. The team went on to be district champs."

"Just city," he said modestly.

"Well, to hear your dad talk, it was the World Series. For weeks all Jack and I heard from him was 'Gavin did this, Gavin did that. You should've seen Gavin last night.' Drove us nuts. He was so proud of you."

"I made an error in one of the playoff games. The other team got a run because of it."

"I was at that game."

"That's why it sucked so bad. Dad had invited y'all to come watch me. I'm sure he could've killed me, then died of embarrassment."

She turned away from the range and looked at him. "Dean was most proud of you then, Gavin."

"He was proud of me for screwing up?"

"Hmm. In the next inning, you hit a double that batted a runner in."

"I guess that made up for it."

"Well, yes, to the fans and your teammates. But when Jack thumped your dad on the back and told him that you had redeemed yourself, Dean said you had redeemed yourself by getting right back into the game. He was more proud of the way you handled the mistake than he was of your hitting a double."

Turning back to the stove, she put the angel-hair pasta into the boiling water. When she turned back around, Gavin was still frowning skeptically. She nodded. "Truly."

And when she said that, she experienced a moment of realization. *Listen to yourself,* she thought. After making a mistake, Gavin had gotten right back into the game. He hadn't slunk into the dugout and spent the remaining innings on the bench, grinding his cleats into the dirt while beating himself up over his error.

Last night Dean had said he hadn't let his guilt and regret eat him alive. He had let it go.

Maybe there was a lesson to be learned from these Malloy men.

Dean returned to the kitchen, interrupting her disquieting thoughts. "That was Curtis." He glanced at Gavin as if reluctant to talk about the case in front of him, but he continued without asking Gavin to excuse himself. "The case has gone stale on him."

"What's happening?"

"He's got intelligence officers trying to run down Lancy Fisher."

"Who?"

"You know him as Marvin Patterson." He gave them a brief summary of Marvin's colorful criminal career. "He's wanted for questioning. And so is a Bradley Armstrong, a convicted sex offender who has violated his probation and flown the coop. He's got men checking into the telephone angle to see if it can be figured out how Valentino is rerouting calls. And Rondeau . . ."

He paused to glance at Gavin, who ducked his head.

"He's still working the computer side of this thing. They didn't find a computer in Marvin's place, but they found discs and CDs, so more than likely he took a computer with him. All this to say that Curtis is stuck in neutral. Since nothing new has turned up, I suggested to him that we see if we can provoke Valentino."

"Into doing what?"

"Poking his head out."

"How?"

"Through you."

"Me? On the air?"

"That's the idea. If you sing Janey's praises, make her out as a victim, maybe he'll call you to justify himself. He may talk longer and inadvertently give us a clue to his location or identity.

"The point is to keep the emphasis on Janey," he continued. "Personalize her. Repeat her name frequently. Make him think of her as an individual, not just his captive."

She looked at him doubtfully. "Do you think that tactic will work with Valentino?"

"Not entirely, no. But it'll also offend his ego if this is all about her instead of him. He wants to be the star, the one everybody's talking about. So by making her the focus, he may not be able to resist coming out to say, 'Hey, look at me.'"

Paris glanced at the clock.

Dean spoke her thought out loud. "Right. We've got just over twenty-four hours to stop him from doing what he threatened. Tonight could be the last chance we'll get to change his mind. He shouldn't be nudged into doing something extreme, which could have tragic results. But possibly you could persuade him to release her."

"That's not an easy assignment, Dean. There's a fine line between goading and persuading."

He nodded somberly. "I almost regret coming up with the idea because of that."

"What does Curtis think?"

"He jumped on the idea. Gung ho on it. But I reigned him in, told him it wasn't going to happen unless you were one hundred percent comfortable with it."

He came to stand closer to her. "Before you make a decision, there's something else to think about, and it's no small consideration. In fact, it's a major one. Valentino started out angry with you. He's doing this to punish you as well as the woman who wronged him. If you begin pressuring him, on any level and in any manner, he's likely to get angrier and you'll be the target. He's already made one veiled threat."

"Are you trying to talk me out of it?"

"Sounds like that, doesn't it?" he said with a wry smile. "Don't give a thought to disappointing Curtis or me. Taking risks is part of our job, but you didn't sign up for it. This has got to be your call, Paris. You say nix it, it's nixed. Think about it. You can give me your answer after dinner."

"I don't have to think about it. I'll do or say whatever is needed to get that girl home safely. But I'll need your guidance."

He reached for her hand and gave it a firm, quick squeeze. "I'll be right there with you, coaching you on what to say. I'd be there with you anyway."

Aware of Gavin watching them with interest, she turned away from Dean, announcing, "The pasta's ready."

"Hello? Brad, is that you? If so, please talk to me."

He hadn't planned what he would say when his home phone was answered, but he had been compelled to call if only to assure himself that his family was still there. As soon as he heard one of their sweet voices, he figured he'd think of something appropriate.

But upon hearing the tremor in his wife's plea, Brad Armstrong couldn't say anything. Her evident distress undid him. His throat seized up and he couldn't speak. He clenched the phone in his sweaty hand and considered hanging up.

"Brad, say something. Please. I know you're there."

He expelled a breath that was half sob, half sigh. "Toni."

"Where are you?"

Where was he? He was in hell. This shabby room had none of the amenities of the lovely home she had made for him and the kids. There was no sunlight in this room, no good smells. Here the blinds were tightly drawn, blocking out all light except for what came from one feeble bulb in the lamp. The room stank, mostly of his own despair.

But his surroundings weren't the worst of it. The real hell was his state of mind.

"You must come home, Brad. The police are looking for you."

"Oh, God." He had feared it, but having his fear realized made his stomach roil.

"I went to the police station this afternoon."

"You did what?" he asked, his voice breaking. "Toni, why did you do that?"

"Mr. Hathaway had to report you to SOAR." She explained how she had wound up in the office of a detective, but he was so distraught he caught only a portion of what she said.

"You talked about your own husband to the police?"

"In an effort to help you."

"Help me? By sending me to prison? Is that what you want for me and our children?"

"Is that what *you* want for them?" she countered. "You're the one who's destroying our family, Brad. Not me."

"You're getting back at me for last night, aren't you? That's what this is about. You're still angry."

"I wasn't angry."

"Then what do you call it?"

"Frightened."

"Frightened?" he snorted. "Because I wanted to make love? From now on, should I alert you in advance that I want to have sex?"

"It wasn't about sex, and it certainly wasn't lovemaking, Brad. It was aggression."

He rubbed his forehead, and his fingers came away wet with sweat. "You don't even try to understand me, Toni. You never have."

"This isn't about me and my shortcomings as a wife and human being. It's about you and your addiction."

"All right, all right, you've made your point. I'll go back to group therapy. Okay? Call the police and tell them you made a mistake. Tell them we had an argument and this was your way of getting back at me. I'll talk to Hathaway. If I suck up to him, he'll be lenient."

"It's too late for apologies and promises, Brad."

The finality and conviction with which she spoke alarmed him to an even greater extent.

"You've already been given more chances than you deserve," she continued. "Besides, it's no longer in my hands or Mr. Hathaway's. It's a police matter now, and I have no choice but to cooperate with them."

"By doing what?"

"Giving them access to your computer."

"Oh, Jesus. Oh, Christ. You do have a choice, Toni. Don't you see that you're going to ruin me? Please, honey, please don't do this."

"If I don't give them permission to get into it, they'll get a court order or a search warrant, whatever is required. It's really not up to me."

"You could . . . Listen, I could tell you how to clear it so they couldn't find anything. Please, Toni? It's not hard. A few clicks of the mouse, that's it. It's not like I'm asking you to rob a bank or something. Will you do that for me, honey? Please. I'm begging you."

She said nothing for a time, and he held his breath hopefully. But tonight his wife was springing one ugly surprise after another on him.

"One night last week I followed you out to Lake Travis, Brad."

Blood rushed to his head as his penitence turned to rage. "You were spying on me. I knew it. You admit it."

"I saw you with a high school girl. You and she got into your car. I can only presume that you had sex with her."

"You're goddamn right I did!" he shouted. "Because my wife cringes every time I touch her. Who could blame me for getting laid where and when I can?"

"Have you ever been with that girl who's missing? The judge's daughter. Janey Kemp?"

His breathing sounded abnormally rapid to his own ears, and he wondered if it sounded that way to Toni—or to anyone else who might be listening in. That possibility struck terror in him. Why was she asking him about Janey Kemp?

"Do the cops have the house phone tapped?"

"What? No. Of course not."

"While you were making chummy with the cops, did you set me up to get caught? Are they eavesdropping on this conversation? Is this call being traced?"

"Brad, you're talking crazy."

"Wrong, I'm not talking at all."

He disconnected, then dropped the cell phone as though it had painfully stung his hand. He began to pace the stuffy, claustrophobic room. They knew about him and Janey. They had found out, just as he had feared they would.

That . . . that Curtis. Sergeant Curtis. Is that who Toni said she had talked to this afternoon? Wasn't he in charge of investigating Janey's disappearance?

He'd been afraid of this. As soon as he saw her picture on the front page of this morning's paper, he had known it was only a matter of time before the police would be looking for him. Someone would have seen him with Janey and reported it.

Now he would have to be very careful about where he went. If he was spotted, he could be arrested. That couldn't happen. That *could not* happen. In jail, other prisoners did terrible things to men like him. He'd heard stories. His own lawyer had told him about the horrors that awaited a sex offender in prison.

God, he was in a fix. And he had Janey Kemp to thank for it, the teasing little slut. Everyone was against him. Janey. His wife, the raging nag. Hathaway, too, who wouldn't know what to do with a boner if he ever got one, which was unlikely. The parole officer was jealous of Brad's success with women. Out of spite, he would happily hand him over in handcuffs to be taken straight to prison.

But Brad's rage was short-lived. His fear returned, overwhelming him. Sweating profusely, gnawing his inner cheek, he paced the room aimlessly. This business with Janey could spell real trouble for him.

He should've stayed away from her. He saw that clearly now. He had known her by reputation even before she approached him the first time. He had read the messages posted about her on the Sex Club website, knew she was as sexually adventurous as he. He also knew she was a spoiled, rich brat who treated former lovers like dirt and poked fun at them on the Internet message board.

But he had been flattered that one of the most desired girls in the Sex Club had come on to him. What was he supposed to do, turn her down? What man could? Even knowing that he might be dooming himself, he hadn't been able to resist her allure. It was worth the danger that being with her posed.

Indulging his fantasies came with accepted risks. He knew he was courting disaster each time he picked up a high school girl, or fondled a patient, or jerked off in a video store, but the risk of getting caught contributed to the thrill.

He constantly challenged himself to see how much he could get away with. Paradoxically, his desire fed on gratification. The farther his escapades took him, the deeper he wanted to explore. Novelty was fleeting. There was always another boundary to cross, one more step to take.

But as he agonized in his private hell, he realized that he might have carried *this* fantasy one step too far.

chapter twenty-three

"*Boo!*"

Paris, who had just stepped into the dark hallway from the snack room, reacted by sloshing hot tea over her hand. "Damn it, Stan! That wasn't funny."

"I'm sorry. Jeez. I wasn't really trying to scare you." He rushed into the tiny kitchen and tore several paper towels off the roll. "Need butter? Salve? The emergency room?"

She blotted the tea off her hand. "Thanks, but no."

"I can't see your eyes, but I get the impression you're glaring."

"That was a silly thing to do."

"Why're you so jumpy?"

"Why're you so juvenile?"

"I said I was sorry. I'm just feeling exuberant tonight."

"What's the occasion?"

"Uncle Wilkins is winging his way back to Atlanta. Anytime there are several states between us, it's cause for celebration."

"Congratulations. But, just for the record, I don't like being scared. I never think it's funny." Stan fell into step behind her as she made her way back to the studio. Once they were in the light, she saw the bruise. "Ouch, Stan, what happened to your face?"

Gingerly he touched the spot at the side of his mouth. "Uncle smacked me."

"You're joking, right?"

"No."

"He struck you?" she exclaimed, then listened with dismay as he told her about their meeting in the lobby of the Driskill.

At the end of his account, he shrugged indifferently. "What I said pissed him off. It's not the first time. No big deal."

Paris disagreed, but Stan's relationship with his uncle was none of her business. "All around me, men are getting punched today," she muttered, thinking of Gavin's unexplained bruise. She sat down on her stool and glanced at the log monitor to see that she still had over five minutes of music on deck.

Without being invited to, Stan took the other stool. "Are you spooked by this Valentino business?"

"Wouldn't you be?"

"Uncle Wilkins asked if I was your mystery caller."

She cut a glance toward him as she stirred a packet of sweetener into her tea. "You're not, are you?"

"As if," he replied. "Although I am sexually maladjusted. At least according to Uncle Wilkins."

"Why would he think so?"

"Bad genes. Mother was a slut. Father was a lecher. Uncle hires hookers he thinks no one knows about. I suppose he thinks the apple didn't fall too far from the tree. But aside from being a sexual deviate, he thinks I'm a royal fuckup."

"He told you that?"

"In so many words."

"You're a grown man. Why do you take that crap from him? You certainly don't have to stand for his slapping you."

Stan looked at her as though she was deranged. "How do you suggest I stop it?"

He had a knack for making her want to throttle him one minute and pat him consolingly the next. A lot of juicy gossip had been circulated when Stan's father committed suicide. If there was any basis to it whatsoever, the Crenshaw family was indeed dysfunctional on many levels. It wasn't surprising that Stan had psychological issues that needed sorting out.

As the last of the songs wound down, she signaled him to be quiet and engaged her mike.

"That was Neil Diamond. Before that Juice Newton was singing about 'The Sweetest Thing.' I hope you were listening, Troy. That song was a request for you from Cindy. I'll be taking other requests until two o'clock. Or, if you have something on your mind, I invite you to share it with me and my listeners. Please call."

From that she went directly into two minutes of commercials.

"Do you think he'll call tonight?" Stan asked after she'd turned off her mike.

"I assume you mean Valentino. I don't know. It wouldn't surprise me."

"No clues as to who he is?"

"The police are investigating several possibilities, but they have
little to go on. Sergeant Curtis is hoping he'll call tonight, maybe
say something that would give them fresh leads." She looked at
the blinking telephone lines on the control board. "I know another
call from him could be valuable, but it gives me the creeps to talk
to him."

"Now I really feel bad about scaring you. I was teasing."

"I'll survive."

"Holler if you need me." He headed for the door.

"Oh, Stan, Dr. Malloy will be arriving shortly. Would you
please keep an eye on the front door and let him in?"

Stan did an about-face and returned to the stool. "What's with
you and the studly shrink?"

Paris shushed him and answered one of the phone lines. "This is
Paris."

The male caller requested a Garth Brooks song from the sound
track of the movie *Hope Floats.* "For Jeannie."

"Jeannie sounds like a lucky girl."

"It's on account of you that we're together."

"Me?"

"Jeannie was offered this job out in Odessa. Neither of us had
told the other how we felt. You advised her not to leave before
telling me her feelings. She did, and I told her I felt the same, so
she stayed at her job here and we're getting married next year."

"I'm glad it worked out so well."

"Yeah, me, too. Thanks, Paris."

She inserted "To Make You Feel My Love" into the program
log and answered another line. The caller requested that she send a
happy birthday wish to Alma. "Ninety? My goodness! Does she
have a favorite song?"

It was a Cole Porter tune, but within seconds Paris had located
it in the computerized music library and programmed it to play behind the Brooks ballad.

After taking care of that business, she looked over at Stan. "Are
you still here?"

"Yes, and my question stands. And don't tell me you and Malloy are old friends from Houston."

"That's exactly what we are."

"How'd you meet?"

"Through Jack. Their friendship outlasted college."

"But it didn't outlast you." She whipped her head toward him. "Ah, just a wild guess, but a correct one, I see."

"Get lost, Stan."

"I take it that this is a sensitive subject."

Exasperated, and knowing that he would bug her about this until she was forthcoming, she asked, "What do you want to know?"

"If Malloy was such a good friend of yours and Jack's, I want to know why I never heard of him until last night."

"We drifted apart when I moved Jack here."

"Why did you move Jack here?"

"Because Meadowview was the best health care facility for his particular needs. Jack was unable to maintain a friendship. I was busy overseeing his care and establishing myself in this job. Dean had his own busy life in Houston, including a young son. It happens, Stan. Circumstances affect friendships. Haven't you lost touch with some of your friends in Atlanta?"

Undeterred, he said, "Jack was the reason you gave up a career in TV news and came to work at this dump?"

"Around the time of his accident, I made a career change. Okay? Satisfied? Therein lies the whole story."

"I don't think so," he said, his eyes narrowing on her. "It sounds logical, even plausible, but it's too pat. I think you're leaving out the shadings."

"Shadings?"

"The nuances that make for a really good story."

"I'm busy, Stan."

"Besides, nothing you've told me explains the electricity that was arcing between you and Malloy last night. It nearly singed my eyebrows. Come on, Paris, give," he wheedled. "I won't be shocked. You've glimpsed the ugly underbelly of my family and nothing could be more scandalous. What happened with the three of you?"

"I've told you. If you don't believe me, that's your problem. If you want shadings, invent your own. I really don't care as long as it keeps you occupied. In the meantime, can't you find something productive to do?"

She returned her attention to the board, the phone lines, the log monitor, and the studio information monitor, where a new weather report had been submitted by a local meteorologist.

Stan sighed with resignation and moved toward the door once

again. Speaking over her shoulder, Paris called to him, "Don't touch anything breakable."

But as soon as he walked out, her flippancy dissolved. She tossed her tea, which was now tepid and bitter, into the trash can. She wanted to choke Stan for resurrecting disturbing memories.

But she couldn't dwell on them. She had her job to do. Engaging her mike, she said, "Once again, happy birthday to Alma. Her request took us back several generations, but every love song is a classic here on FM 101.3. This is Paris Gibson, your host until two o'clock tomorrow morning. I hope you'll stay with me. I enjoy your company. I also enjoy playing your requested songs. Call me."

She and Dean had agreed that she wouldn't address any remarks to Valentino or mention Janey until he arrived. They'd left her house at the same time, but he was going to drive Gavin home before coming to the station.

Dinner had gone well. By tacit agreement, they didn't talk about the case in which they had all become involved. Instead their conversation touched on movies, music, and sports. They laughed over shared memories.

As they were leaving, Gavin thanked her politely for the dinner. "Dad's a lousy cook."

"I'm no Emeril either."

"You come closer than he does."

She could tell that Dean was pleased by how well she and Gavin had gotten along and how relaxed their dinner together had been. She had felt very mellow herself, and she had drunk only a half glass of Chardonnay—her limit on a worknight. Her enjoyment was lessened only by knowing that she'd kept them away from Liz Douglas for the evening.

During the next series of commercials, she cleared the phone lines. Each time she depressed a blinking button, she did so with dread, which made her angry with Valentino. He had made her afraid to do the work that had been her salvation. This job had kept her grounded during the seven years she had overseen Jack's health care. She'd been able to endure those interminable days spent at the hospital only by knowing that she could escape to the radio station that night.

She received a call from a young woman named Joan, whose personality was so bubbly Paris decided to put her on the air. "You say you're a Seal fan."

"I saw him once in a restaurant in L.A. He looked super cool. Could you play 'Kiss From a Rose'?"

Moving by rote, she slipped the request behind three songs already on the log.

What was keeping Dean? she wondered. He was putting up a good front, but she could tell he was deeply worried about Gavin's connection to Janey Kemp. Any parent who loved his child would be concerned, but Dean would blame himself for Gavin's misconduct and look upon it as a failure on his part.

Just as he had assumed blame when Albert Dorrie's standoff with Houston police resulted in tragedy.

There it was again. Another reminder. No matter how hard she tried to avoid it, her mind kept going back to that. To that night.

Dean showed up at her condo eighteen hours after Mr. Dorrie had made orphans of his three children by killing first his estranged wife and then himself.

He arrived unannounced and apologetic. "I'm sorry, Paris. I probably shouldn't have come over without calling first," he said as soon as she opened the door.

He looked as if he hadn't even sat down during the last eighteen hours, much less slept. His eyes had sunk into the dark circles surrounding them. His chin was shadowed with stubble.

Paris had rested very little herself. Most of the day had been spent in the TV newsroom, where she had edited together an overall perspective of the incident for the evening newscasts.

Tragically the story wasn't that unusual. Similar incidents happened routinely in other cities. It had even happened in Houston before. But it had never happened to *her*. She had never witnessed something like that up close and personal. Being on the scene and living through it was far different from reading about it in the newspaper or listening with half an ear to television news reports while preoccupied and doing something else.

Even her jaded cameraman had been affected. His ho-hum attitude was replaced by dejection when the news van followed the ambulance bearing the two bodies to the county morgue.

But no one who had experienced it took the calamity to heart the way Dean did. His despair was etched deeply into his face as Paris motioned him inside. "Can I get you something? A drink?"

"Thanks." He sat down heavily on the edge of her sofa while she poured each of them a shot of bourbon. She handed him a highball glass and sat down beside him. "Am I keeping you from something?" he asked dully.

"No." She motioned down at her white terry-cloth spa robe. Her face was scrubbed clean; she'd let her hair dry naturally after a long soak in the tub. He usually didn't see her like this, but she wasn't concerned about her appearance. Things that had seemed important twenty-four hours ago had paled into insignificance.

"I don't know why I came," he said. "I didn't want to be out, with people. But I didn't want to be alone either."

"I feel the same."

She had begged off spending the evening with Jack. He'd been desperate to cheer her up and help take her mind off what she'd been through. But she wasn't yet ready to be cheered up. She wanted time to reflect. Furthermore, she was exhausted. Going to a movie or even to dinner seemed as remote as flying to the moon. Even making small talk with Jack would have required energy she didn't have.

Talking didn't seem to be the purpose of Dean's visit. After those few opening statements, he sat staring into near space, taking periodic sips from his highball glass. He didn't fill the silence with pointless conversation. Each knew how rotten the other felt about the way the standoff had ended. She guessed that, like her, he derived comfort just from being near someone who had shared the tragedy.

It took him half an hour to finish his whiskey. He set the empty glass on the coffee table, stared at it for several seconds, then said, "I should go."

But she couldn't let him leave without offering some consolation. "You did everything you could, Dean."

"That's what everybody tells me."

"Because it's true. You did your best."

"It wasn't good enough, though, was it? Two people died."

"But three lived. If not for you, he probably would have killed the children, too."

He nodded, but without conviction. She stood up when he did and followed him to the door, where he turned to face her. "Thanks for the drink."

"You're welcome."

Several seconds ticked by before he said, "I caught your story on the six o'clock news."

"You did?"

"It was good."

"Trite."

"No, really. It was good."

"Thank you."

"You're welcome."

Holding her with a stare, his eyes seemed to implore her in a way that she knew her own must mirror. Emotions that she couldn't deny, but had held in rigid check for months, erupted inside her. By the time Dean reached for her, she was already opening her lips to receive his kiss.

Later, when she relived it and was able to be brutally honest with herself, she realized that she had wanted him to kiss her, and that if he hadn't initiated it, she would have.

She had to touch him or die. The need for him was that essential.

Dean must have felt the same. His mouth mated with hers possessively and hungrily. Pretense and politeness were shattered. The constraints of conscience snapped. Tension that had been building for months was given vent.

She threaded her fingers up through his hair. He unknotted the tie belt of her robe and when he slid his hands inside, she didn't protest but rose up on tiptoes to bring their bodies flush against each other. They fit. And the perfection of it brought a temporary end to the kissing and they just held each other, tightly.

Paris's mind spun with sensual overload. The cold metal of his belt buckle against her belly. The texture of his trousers against her bare thighs. The fine cotton of his shirt against her breasts. His body heat seeping into her skin.

Then his lips sought hers again. As they kissed, his hand moved to her breast. His thumb brushed her distended nipple, then he bent his head to take it into his mouth, sucking it with urgency. Gasping his name, she clutched his head against her.

As he lowered her to the floor, she undid the buttons on his shirt and pushed it off his shoulders, but that's as far as it got before he was kissing her again. Between her thighs she felt him grappling with his belt and zipper.

The tip of his penis nuzzled her pubic hair, probed, and then was inside her.

His fullness stretched and filled her. He settled his weight onto her and she absorbed it gladly, squeezing his hips between her thighs. The pressure was incredibly sweet. The sounds that rose up from her chest were a joyous mix of laughter and weeping.

He kissed away the tears that leaked from the corners of her eyes, then clasped her head between his strong hands and laid his forehead against hers, rolling it gently back and forth as they exchanged the air they breathed and the ultimate intimacy.

"God help me, Paris," he said raspily, "I just had to be inside you."

She slid her hands beneath his clothing and pressed his buttocks with her palms, drawing him even deeper into her. He hissed a swift intake of air and began to move. With each smooth thrust, the intensity of the pleasure increased. And so did the meaningfulness. Cradling her chin in one hand, he tilted her face up for a kiss.

He was still kissing her when she came, so that her soft cries were released into his mouth. Within seconds he followed her. And still, they clung to each other.

Their separation was gradual and reluctant. As the physical ecstasy began to recede, the moral significance of what they had done encroached. She tried to stave it off. She wanted to rail at the unfairness of it. But it was inexorable.

"Oh, Lord," she moaned, and, turning onto her side, faced away from him.

"I know." He placed his arm across her waist and drew her back against his chest. He kissed her neck lightly and brushed strands of hair off her damp cheeks.

But his hand froze in the act when her telephone rang.

Earlier she had set her answering machine to pick up, so she could monitor calls. Now Jack's voice blared from the speaker, making him a third presence in the room.

"Hi, babe. Just calling to check on you, see how you're faring. If you're asleep, never mind calling me back. But if you're up and want to talk, you know I'm willing to listen. I'm worried about you. Dean, too. I've been calling him all evening, but he's not answering any of his phones. You know how he is. He'll be thinking it was his fault that the standoff turned out the way it did. I'm sure he could use a friend tonight, so I'll keep trying to reach him. Anyway, love you. Rest well. 'Bye."

For the longest time, neither of them moved. Then Paris disentangled herself from Dean and crawled as far as the coffee table, where she pressed her head against the wood, hard enough to hurt.

"Paris—"

"Just go, Dean."

"I feel as badly as you do."

She looked at him over her shoulder. It was bare; she had

dragged her robe along behind her like a bridal train. Frantically she tugged up the sleeve to cover the exposed slope of her breast. "You couldn't possibly feel as badly as I do. Please leave."

"I feel bad for Jack, yes. But I'm damned if I regret making love to you. It was destined to happen, Paris. I knew it the minute I met you, and so did you."

"No, no I didn't."

"You're lying," he said quietly.

She snuffled a laugh. "A minor offense compared to fucking my fiancé's best man."

"You know that's not what this was. It would be much easier for us if that's all it was."

That was true. Behind the shame, her heart was breaking from the despair of knowing that it would never happen again. Perhaps she could have forgiven herself a simple tumble, a hormonal rush, a temporary fall from grace. But it had been far too meaningful to dismiss and forgive.

"Just leave, Dean," she sobbed. "Please. Go."

She laid her head on the table again and closed her eyes. Scalding tears rolled down her cheeks as she listened to the rustle of his clothing, the jangle of his belt buckle, the rasp of his zipper, and his muffled footfalls on the carpet as he walked to the door. She endured a purgatorial silence until she heard the door open, then close quietly behind him.

"Paris?"

With a start, she looked behind her, toward the studio door. Dean was standing there, as though he had materialized from out of her memory.

She'd been so lost in thought, it took several seconds for her to process that this was the here and now, not an extension of her reverie. She swallowed thickly and motioned him in. "It's okay. My mike's not on."

"Crenshaw said I could come in if I didn't make any noise."

He sat on the stool beside hers, and for one insane moment, she felt like throwing herself at him, taking up where they had left off in her recollection. His scruff that night had left whisker burns on her skin. Within a few days they had faded. But the sensual imprints made on her mind had never gone away. Last night's kiss had revealed how vivid and accurate they were.

"Nothing yet from Valentino?"

chapter twenty-four

Sergeant Robert Curtis was working overtime. He was ensconced in his cubicle inside the CIB, where only one other detective was burning the midnight oil, on a robbery case.

The radio on Curtis's desk was tuned to FM 101.3. He was listening to Paris Gibson's voice while reading the information he'd gleaned about her suspended television career and departure from Houston. His friends in the HPD had been thorough, faxing him everything that had ever been printed about Paris, Jack Donner, and Dean Malloy. It was interesting stuff.

The search of Lancy Ray Fisher's, aka Marvin Patterson, apartment had yielded some surprises, too, specifically, a box of cassette tapes, all of Paris Gibson's radio program.

Now, why, the detective asked himself, would a con cum janitor have such a burning interest in Paris that he would collect recordings of past programs when he could listen to her live every night?

Lancy's mother hadn't provided any insight.

An intelligence officer, having weeded through miles of red tape and reams of records, had located her. Currently she lived in a mobile-home park in San Marcos, a town south of Austin.

Curtis himself had made the thirty-minute drive there. He could have dispatched another detective to conduct the interview, but he'd wanted to hear firsthand why Mrs. Fisher's son, Lancy, living under the alias Marvin Patterson, was seemingly obsessed with Paris Gibson.

The interior of Mrs. Fisher's domicile was even worse than the exterior portended, and she was as untidy and inhospitable as her home. When Curtis showed her his ID, she was at first suspicious, then belligerent, and, finally, abusive.

She shook her head to answer him, but also to clear it of the persistent sensual tweaks. "Did you get Gavin home all right?"

"With orders that he's not to leave, and I don't think he'll disobey me tonight. It shook him up to be questioned at the police station today. He was certainly on his best behavior tonight. Of course, he was trying to impress you."

"Well, he succeeded because I was impressed. He's great, Dean."

He nodded thoughtfully. "Yeah."

She watched him for a moment, noticing the worry line that had formed between his eyebrows. "But?"

He brought her into focus. "But he's lying to me."

"Why don't you take your sorry ass outta here? I got nothing to say to no goddamn cop."

"Has Lancy been to see you recently?"

"No."

Curtis knew she was lying, but he got the impression that there was no love lost between mother and son and that she would welcome a chance to air her complaints. Rather than challenge the truthfulness of her reply, he remained quiet and tried to pick the cat hair off his trousers while she sucked on a cigarette and he waited until she decided to unload.

"Lancy's been a thorn in my side since he was born," she began. "The less he comes around me, the better I like it. He lives his life and I live mine. Besides, he's gone and got uppity."

"Uppity?"

"His clothes and such. Drives a new car. Thinks he's better'n me."

Which wouldn't be saying much, Curtis thought. "What make and model is his car?"

She snorted. "I can't tell one Jap car from another."

"Did you know he was working at a radio station?"

"Sweeping up is what he told me. He had to take that job after getting fired from his other one on account of stealing. That was a good job and he went and blowed it. He's dumb as well as no'count."

"Did you know he used an assumed name?"

"Wouldn't surprise me what that boy did. Not after he was a cokehead and all." Leaning forward, she wheezed in an undertone, "You know, that's why he did them dirty movies. To get dope."

"Dirty movies?"

"My neighbor lady? Two rows over? She come running over here one night not long ago, says she's seen my boy, Lancy, wagging his thing in some nasty movie she rented at the video place. I called her a fuckin' liar, but she said, 'Come see for your ownself.'"

She sat up straighter, striking the righteous pose of a recent convert with only contempt for the unshriven. "Sure enough, there he was, nekkid as a jaybird, doing such as I ain't never saw did before. I's embarrassed to death."

Curtis feigned sympathy for a mother whose son had gone astray. "Does he still work in the, uh, film industry?"

"Naw. Don't do drugs no more either. Leastways he says he don't. It was a long time ago. He was just a kid. But still." She lit another cigarette. Curtis would leave there feeling and smelling like he had smoked three packs himself.

"What name did he use when he made the movies?"

"Don't remember."

"What were the titles of the movies he was in?"

"Don't remember and don't want to know. Guess you could ask my neighbor. And how come an old lady like her is watching trash like that anyway? She ought to be ashamed of herself."

"Does Lancy have a lot of girlfriends?"

"You don't listen too good, do you? He don't tell me *nuthin'*. How would I know anything about girlfriends?"

"Has he ever mentioned Paris Gibson?"

"Who? That a boy or a girl?" Her puzzled reaction was too genuine to have been faked.

"Doesn't matter." He stood up. "You know, Mrs. Fisher, that aiding and abetting is a felony."

"I ain't aided or abetted nobody. I done told you Lancy ain't been here."

"Then you won't mind if I look around."

"You got a warrant?"

"No."

She blew a gust of smoke up at him. "Oh, what the hell. Go ahead."

It wasn't a large place, so except for having to avoid hissing cats and their droppings, his walk through it didn't take long. Nor did it take him long to determine that someone had slept in the spare bedroom. The narrow bed had been left unmade and there was a pair of socks on the floor beside it. When he knelt down to pick up one of the socks, he noticed the loose floor tile beneath the bed. It came right up with a little nudge of his pocketknife.

Replacing what he found there exactly as he'd found it, he rejoined Mrs. Fisher in what passed for the living room. He asked who the socks belonged to.

"Lancy must've left them last time he was here. Long time ago. He never did pick up after hisself."

Another lie, but he'd be wasting his time to dispute it. She would continue lying. "Do you know if Lancy has a computer?"

"He thinks I don't know about it, but I do."

"What about a cassette recorder?"

"Don't know about that, but all them modern contraptions are a waste of good money, if you ask me."

"I'm going to leave you my card, Mrs. Fisher. If Lancy comes here, will you call me?"

"What's he done?"

"Avoided questioning."

"'Bout what? Can't be anything good."

"I'd just like to talk to him. If you hear from him, you'd be doing him a favor to notify me."

She took his business card and laid it on the cluttered TV tray beside her reclining chair. He didn't quite catch what she muttered around the cigarette dangling from her lips, but it didn't sound like a promise to do as he asked.

He was anxious to get into the fresh air and away from the potential of being blown to smithereens when her oxygen tank exploded, but at the door he paused to ask one further question. "You said that Lancy got fired from a good job for stealing."

"That's what I said."

"Where was he working?"

"The telephone company."

As soon as he got into his car, Curtis contacted the San Marcos PD, explained the situation, and asked them to keep surveillance on Mrs. Fisher's mobile home. He then got another detective in his own unit busy running down Lancy Ray Fisher's employment record at the telephone company.

Traffic on northbound Interstate 35 was reduced to a crawl because of road work, so by the time he reached headquarters, the information he'd sought was already available. Fisher's employment records at Southwestern Bell were in his real name. He'd been an excellent employee until he'd gotten caught stealing equipment.

"High-tech stuff at the time," the detective reported. "More or less obsolete now because the technology changes so quickly."

"But still useable?"

"According to the expert, yeah."

Armed with that information, Curtis bumped Lancy Ray Fisher up to the viable suspect list and turned his attention to the materials he'd been faxed from Houston.

Included were copies of newspaper articles, transcriptions of TV news coverage, and materials printed off the Internet. They told a tragic story and filled in some of the gaps that Malloy had been averse to filling.

For instance, Curtis now understood why Paris Gibson wore sunglasses. She had suffered an injury to her eyes in the same auto accident that had robbed Jack Donner of his life—except for a beating heart and minimal brain function.

Paris had been riding on the passenger side of the front seat, with her seat belt buckled. When the car struck the bridge abutment at a high rate of speed, air bags deployed. But they weren't any help against flying glass from the windshield, which was supposed to have been shatterproof, but wasn't, especially not when the 185-pound driver of the vehicle was catapulted through it.

Jack Donner was not wearing his seat belt. The air bag retarded his ejection from the car, but didn't prevent it. He sustained severe head trauma. The damage was irreparable and extensive. He was rendered physically helpless for the remainder of his life.

His mental capacity was limited to reacting to visual, tactile, and auditory stimulation. The responses were feeble, on the level of a newborn, but enough to prevent him from being classified as brain dead. No one could pull the plug.

Reportedly, his friend Dr. Dean Malloy of the HPD had been first on the scene. He had been following Mr. Donner in his own car, had witnessed the accident, and had made the 911 call from his cell phone. By all accounts, he was a caring and self-sacrificial friend, who for days following the accident kept vigil outside Ms. Gibson's hospital room and Mr. Donner's ICU.

The last follow-up story on Jack Donner's tragic fate reported that Paris Gibson had recovered from her minor injuries and, having resigned from her position at the TV station, was moving Donner to a private nursing facility.

She was quoted as thanking all her friends, associates, and fans who had sent flowers and cards wishing her and her fiancé well. She would miss her job and all the wonderful people in Houston, but her life had taken an unexpected turn, and now she must follow a new path.

There was no mention of Dean Malloy in the final story, an omission that practically screamed at Curtis. When one disappears from the radar screen of a strong and lasting friendship, there's got to be a good reason.

No deep, dark mystery there. He'd seen the way Malloy looked at Paris Gibson and vice versa. With I-want-to-see-you-naked lust. But it was also the care they took *not* to look at each other that gave away a yearning that went deeper than just the physical. It was the avoidance that incriminated them. If this was visible to him after having known them for only two days, it must have been glaringly obvious to Jack Donner.

Conclusion: In a love affair, three was one too many.

As he listened to Paris's program, his anger mounted.

She made no mention of him, of Valentino.

But she talked endlessly about Janey Kemp. She went on about how badly her parents wanted her to be returned to them unharmed. Told about her friends, who were worried for her safety. Extolled her virtues.

What a farce! Janey had told him how much she despised her parents, and the feeling was mutual. Friends? She made conquests, not friends. As for virtues, she was without them.

But to hear Paris tell it, Janey Kemp was a saint. A beautiful, charming, friendly, kind American ideal.

"If you could only see her now, Paris," he said in a whispered chuckle.

Janey disgusted him so much now that he had stayed with her only briefly today. She didn't look beautiful and enticing anymore. Her hair, once bouncy and silky, had looked like old rope coiled about her head. Her complexion was sallow. The eyes that could be sultry or scornful at will were now dull and lifeless. Barely acknowledging his presence in the room, she had stared vacantly and unblinkingly, even when he snapped his fingers an inch from her nose.

She seemed half dead and looked even worse. A shower would improve things, but he just couldn't be bothered with carrying her into the bathroom to wash her.

He couldn't be bothered with much of anything except dealing with this jam he'd gotten himself into. Time was running out for him to arrive at a workable solution. He had extended to Paris a seventy-two-hour deadline, and if he had any character at all, any sense of pride, he really should stick to that timetable.

Janey had become more of a liability than he had anticipated. There also remained the question of what to do about Paris.

He really hadn't looked beyond bringing Janey here and using her the way she begged to be used. She was a whore who advertised her willingness to try anything. He had called her bluff, that's all. Her boasts hadn't been empty ones either. She'd proved herself to be a gourmand of debasement.

He hadn't seriously planned on this ending with her demise, any more than he had planned to kill Maddie Robinson. That's just the way his relationship with Maddie had evolved. She'd said, "I don't want to see you anymore," and he had made certain that she wouldn't. Ever. When you looked at it that way, she had decided her fate, not him.

As for Paris, he hadn't thought much beyond placing that first call and telling her that he had taken action against the woman

240 * SANDRA BROWN

who had wronged him. He had wanted to frighten her, rattle her, and hopefully make her aware of her intolerable smugness. Who was she to dispense advice on love and life, sex and relationships?

What he hadn't anticipated was that his phone call to her would launch a police investigation and become the media event that it had. Who would have thought everyone would get so uptight over Janey, when she was getting exactly what she had asked for?

No, it had grown into something much larger than he had bargained for. He felt himself losing control of the situation. To survive, he must get back that control. But where to start?

One way would be to release Janey.

Yes, he could do that. He could dump her near her parents' house. She didn't know his name. He could clear out this room so that if she ever brought the cops to the "scene of the crime," he would be long gone. He would have to stop going to the meeting places of the Sex Club or risk being seen by her, but finding action was never a problem. The Sex Club was only one resource.

It wasn't a perfect plan, but probably the best course of action left to him. He would call Paris tonight at the appointed time and tell her that he'd only wanted to toy with her, make her realize that she shouldn't play with people's emotions and hand out glib advice. *I never dreamed you would take me seriously, Paris. Can't you take a joke? No hard feelings, okay?*

Yes, that was definitely a workable plan.

" . . . here on FM 101.3," he heard Paris say, interrupting his thoughts. "Stay with me until two A.M. I just got a call from Janey's best friend, Melissa."

Melissa.

"Melissa, would you like to say something to the listening audience?" Paris asked.

"Yeah, I just, you know, want Janey back safe," she said. "Janey, if you can hear this and you're okay, come home. Nobody's gonna be mad. And if someone out there is holding my friend against her will, then I have to tell you that's totally uncool. Let her go. Please. We just want Janey back. So . . . I guess that's it."

"Thank you, Melissa."

Wait, was he supposed to be the *villain* of this piece? He hadn't done anything to Janey Kemp that she hadn't wanted done. And Paris wasn't the snow princess she wanted everyone to believe either. She was no better than anyone else.

He dialed a number he knew by heart, knowing that this call couldn't be traced to his cell. He'd made certain of that.

"This is Paris."

"The topic tonight is Dean Malloy."

"Valentino? Let me speak to Janey."

"Janey is in no mood to talk," he said, "and neither am I."

"Janey's parents wanted me to ask you—"

"Shut up and listen to me. If you and your boyfriend don't move quickly, you'll have *two* deaths on your consciences. Janey's. And Jack Donner's."

"I'd feel better if you stayed at my house until this is over. I've got an extra bedroom. Nothing fancy, but you'd be comfortable. And safe."

Dean had insisted on following her home and seeing her inside. As before, Valentino's call had been routed through a deserted pay phone, which provided no leads. The police were now convinced that he never went near those pay phones.

This call had been most disconcerting because he had sounded even angrier and edgier than before. He had alluded again to Janey's death. And of course the reference to Dean and Jack had been an alarming new element. Either Valentino was excellent at guessing, or he knew with certainty that Jack's death implicated her and Dean to some extent.

"Thanks for the offer, but I'll be safe here." She went through her front door ahead of him. Once inside, he switched on a table lamp. She immediately turned it off. "I feel like a goldfish with the lights on. They can see in."

Dean glanced at the squad car parked at her curb. "Griggs has a replacement, I see."

"His night off. Curtis told me the personnel would be different but that this team of officers was just as vigilant." As Dean closed the door, she asked, "What about Gavin?" Valentino had spoken about Dean with such disdain, they were concerned not only for his and Paris's safety, but for Gavin's as well.

"Taken care of. Curtis dispatched a squad car to my house. I called Gavin and told him to expect it."

"Liz?"

"I didn't think officers were necessary, but I called and gave her a heads-up. Told her to be sure her alarm was set and to call me if anything unusual happened."

"Maybe she's the one who should be staying in your spare bed-room."

Rather than picking up the gauntlet, he said, "That's another conversation, Paris."

She turned and headed for the kitchen. He followed. It was two-thirty in the morning, but they were too troubled to sleep. "I'm going to have some hot chocolate," she said. "Want some?"

"It's eighty degrees outside."

She gave him a take-it-or-leave-it look.

"Juice?" he asked.

While her water was heating in the microwave, she poured him a glass of orange juice and took a package of cookies from the pantry. "What do you think he's lying about?"

"Valentino?"

"Gavin. Earlier tonight, you told me you thought he was lying to you. We got busy with all the calls coming in and never got around to finishing the conversation."

He stared into his glass of juice for a moment, then said, "That's the hell of it. I don't know what he's lying *about,* I just know that he is."

After stirring a packet of instant cocoa mix into her cup of hot water, she motioned for him to bring the cookies and follow her into the living room. She took one corner of the sofa, he the other. The package of cookies was placed on the cushion between them. The lamp stayed dark, but the glow from the porch lights came through the front windows, so they could see well enough. She removed her sunglasses.

"Do you think he's lying about his activities that night?" she asked.

"By omission, maybe. I'm afraid that there was more to his meeting with Janey than he wants to share."

"Like that they had sex?"

"Possibly, and he doesn't want anybody to know."

"Because that would make his story of leaving her to join friends less credible."

"Right." Dean munched a cookie. "But realistically, how could he be Valentino? It doesn't sound like him. He doesn't know about us." He looked over at her. "That part, anyway. He doesn't have the technical skills to reroute telephone calls."

"I asked Stan about how that technology works."

"How would he know?"

"He likes gadgets, expensive toys. Don't give me that look," she said when his eyebrow formed an inquisitive arch. "He's not Valentino. He hasn't got the balls."

"What do you know about his balls?"

"Please," she groaned. "Do you want to hear this or not?"

He gave a noncommittal harrumph as he reached for another cookie.

She continued, "Stan said it wouldn't be hard to do. Anyone with access to some equipment could probably learn how to do it over the Internet."

"What about somebody who had worked for the phone company?"

"It would probably be a snap. Why?"

"Before becoming a janitor, Marvin Patterson was an installer for Southwestern Bell."

Dean had followed her home from the radio station in his own car. During the drive, he'd had a lengthy cell phone conversation with Curtis. He recounted for her now everything that the detective had learned about Lancy Fisher.

"He had a collection of audiotapes? Of my show? What could that mean?"

"We don't know," Dean replied. "That's why Curtis has intelligence guys out tapping all their informers, trying to find the shy Mr. Fisher. We've got plenty of questions for him, number one being why the preoccupation with you."

"Which comes as a shock. He never showed the least bit of interest in me. Kept his head down and rarely spoke."

"Strange behavior for a former actor."

"Actor? Marvin?"

"He appeared—all of him—in a couple of porno videos."

"What!" she exclaimed. "Are you sure we're talking about the same man?"

He told her what Curtis had learned from Lancy Fisher's mother. "None of which explains why he taped your show every night. Or so it seems. He had ninety-two cassettes in all. Not very good quality, Curtis said. Probably recorded directly off the radio. Hours of love songs and Paris Gibson's sexy voice. It could be that Marvin just jerked off while listening to you. But that's a lot of jerking off."

"Spare me that image, please."

"Did he ever—"

"Nothing, Dean. He never mumbled more than a few words to me. Never even looked me in the eye that I can recall."

"Then as far as this case goes, he may be as innocent as the driven snow. He may have disappeared only because he's an ex-con and as such has a natural aversion to police interrogations even if he's got nothing to hide."

He paused and watched her closely for several moments, long enough for her to ask, "What?"

"Curtis has become a regular Sherlock Holmes into our past."

She blew on her hot cocoa, but she'd suddenly lost her appetite for it. "What's the good news?"

"There isn't any. He told me straight out that he knew the facts behind your leaving Houston. The accident. Jack's head injury. Your resignation from TV. And so forth."

"That's all?"

"Well, he stopped with that, but the silence that followed was teeming with curiosity and insinuation."

"Let him insinuate all he wants."

"I did."

She set her cup on the coffee table, then with a heavy sigh laid her head against the sofa cushion. "I'm not surprised by his curiosity. He's a detective, after all. And he didn't even have to dig very deep. Just scratch the surface and there's my life for all to see."

"I'm sorry."

She smiled faintly. "Doesn't matter. Other aspects of this are more important. Namely, Gavin." Leaving her head against the cushion, she turned it to look at Dean. "What happened to his face today?"

"I didn't hit him, if that's what you're getting at."

Affronted by his tone and the statement itself, she shot bolt upright. "That's not at all what I was 'getting at.'" Retrieving her mug of cocoa, she angrily stalked from the room, saying as she went, "Lock the door on your way out."

chapter twenty-five

With jerky, angry motions, Paris rinsed out her cocoa mug, then switched off the light above the kitchen sink. When she turned, Dean was standing in the open doorway, silhouetted against the faint light coming from the living room.

"I'm sorry I snapped at you."

"That's not what made me mad," she said. "It's that you would think that *I* would think that you had hit Gavin."

"But I did, Paris."

The admission stunned her into silence.

"Not today," he continued. "Several days ago. He provoked me, I lost my temper and backhanded him across the mouth."

Her anger evaporated as quickly as it had formed. "Oh. Then I struck a nerve, didn't I?" After a beat, she added softly, "I know what happened that time at Tech."

He looked at her sharply. "Jack told you?"

"He told me enough. But only after I'd commented on your rigid self-control."

He slumped against the doorjamb and closed his eyes. "Well, my self-control failed me the other night with Gavin, and again today with Rondeau."

"Rondeau?"

He told her about the scene he'd interrupted when he went into the men's room. "He had Gavin's face shoved up against the mirror. That's what caused the bruise on his cheek. I wanted to kill the guy."

"I would have wanted to myself. Why would he do such a thing?"

"He said he had a mother and a sister, and the obscene messages that Gavin had left on the website offended him so much that when he saw him, he lost it. A sorry excuse that stank of bullshit."

"Does Curtis know about this?"

"I didn't tell him, and I can't see Rondeau confessing."

"You're going to let the matter drop?"

"No. Hell no. But I'll deal with Rondeau in my own way and without any interference from Curtis." He laughed without humor. "Going back to our detective friend, he's a dogged cuss. He's not going to give up until he knows everything about our 'cozy little trio,' as he put it."

"Meaning you, me, and Jack."

"He's not dense, Paris. He knows there's more to the story than what was reported in the media, and much, much more that we're not telling him."

"It's none of his business."

"He thinks it is. He thinks Valentino may harken back to that."

She tried to turn away, but he reached for her and turned her back around. "We've got to talk about this, Paris. We didn't address it when we should have, seven years ago. If we had, Jack might not have gotten drunk that night. We should have gone to him, sat him down, and told him—"

"That we had betrayed him."

"That we had fallen in love, that neither of us had set out to, but it had happened, and that's just the way it was."

"So sorry, Jack. Rotten luck. See ya 'round."

"It wouldn't have been like that, Paris."

"No, it would have been worse."

"Worse than what, for godsake? Worse than how it ended?"

He took a deep breath and continued in a quieter, more reasonable tone of voice. "Jack was smarter than you gave him credit for. And a lot more perceptive. He could tell we were avoiding each other. Didn't you know he would want to learn the cause of it?"

Of course, he was right. She had sold Jack short by thinking that if she pretended nothing had changed, he would never learn that everything had. His fiancée and his best friend had made love. Their relationships—hers with Jack, his with Dean, hers with Dean—had been irrevocably altered. They couldn't revert to the way things had been. She'd been naive to think they could.

"I thought . . . thought . . ." She lowered her head and massaged her temple. "I don't remember what I thought, Dean. I just couldn't go to him and say, 'Remember the night after the standoff, and I told you that I wanted to be alone? Well, Dean came over to my place and we had sex on the living room rug.'"

Instead she'd taken a more subtle approach and declined each time Jack tried to get the two of them together. Her excuses became increasingly lame. "Eventually Jack demanded to know why I didn't like you anymore."

"I had a similar conversation with him," Dean said. "He asked me if you and I had crossed swords during the standoff. Had the crisis brought out the cop in me and the reporter in you, and never the twain shall meet. I told him he was way off base, that we liked and respected each other a lot. So he put it to the test with that surprise dinner."

Yes, that fateful dinner, she thought. Jack had arranged for them to meet at one of their favorite restaurants. She and Dean had arrived independently, not expecting to see the other there.

Being face-to-face for the first time since that night was as awkward for them as she had feared it would be. Making eye contact was difficult, but she couldn't keep herself from looking at him, and each time she did, she caught him stealing a glance at her. Yet their conversation had been stilted and formal.

"That dinner was an endurance test for me," Dean said. "You had rebuffed all my attempts to talk to you."

"It had to be a clean break, Dean. I didn't trust myself even to talk to you on the phone."

"Jesus, Paris, I was dying on the inside. I needed to know what you were thinking. If you were all right. If you were pregnant."

"Pregnant?"

"We hadn't used anything."

"I was on the pill."

"But I didn't know that." He smiled with chagrin. "Selfishly, I hoped you had conceived."

She couldn't admit to him even now that she'd clung to the same vain hope and was disappointed when she'd gotten her next period. A baby would have forced her to tell Jack the truth. It would have been her and Dean's justification for having to hurt him. But it hadn't happened.

"I went through hell agonizing over the state you were in when I left you that night," he was saying. "And suddenly there you were, sitting three feet across the dinner table from me, and I still couldn't ask or say anything I wanted to.

"And that wasn't all. Deceiving Jack was killing me," he continued. "Every time he told another joke, or threw his arm around me and called me his good buddy, I felt like Judas."

"He was trying his best to make it a fun evening. Ever the social chairman."

Jack had seemed determined to ignore the awkwardness between them. He had drunk too much, talked too loud, laughed too hard. But during dessert, he finally gave up and demanded to know what was going on.

"Look, I've had it with you two, okay?" he'd said. "I want to know, and I want to know now. What happened to make you so uncomfortable around each other? I'm guessing that either (a) you had a tiff during that standoff, or (b) you've been seeing each other behind my back. So tell me what the squabble was about, or fess up."

Thinking he'd made a clever joke, he folded his arms on the table and grinned at them in turn.

But Dean didn't respond to Jack's grin, and she'd felt as if her face would crack if she attempted a smile. Their silence spoke volumes. Even so, it was several moments before realization struck Jack, and when it did, it was a painful thing to watch. His grin collapsed. He looked first at her, almost quizzically. Then he looked at Dean as though willing him to laugh and say something like "Don't be ridiculous."

But when neither of them said anything, he realized that out of his jest had emerged the truth. "Son of a bitch," he said. He surged to his feet and sneered at Dean, "Dinner's on you, friend."

Apparently Dean had been following her thoughts because he said, "I'll never forget the look on his face when he put it together."

"Nor will I."

"In my haste to follow him out and try to stop him from getting behind the wheel of his car, I knocked over my chair. By the time I got it upright, the two of you had disappeared."

"I don't remember running through the restaurant after him," she said. "But I vividly remember catching up with him in the parking lot. He yelled at me, told me to leave him alone."

"But you didn't."

"No, I begged him to let me explain. He only glared at me and said, 'Did you fuck him?'"

Dean dragged his hand down his face, but the gesture did little to rub the regret from his features. "From all the way across the parking lot, I heard him say that. I heard you telling him that he shouldn't drive, that he was too drunk and too angry."

Heedless of her pleas, Jack had gotten into his car. She'd run around to the passenger side and luckily had found it unlocked. "I got in. Jack ordered me out. But I refused and instead buckled my seat belt. He cranked the motor and floored the accelerator."

They were silent for a time, lost in the recollections of that horrible night. Dean was the first to speak.

"He had every right to be furious with us for sleeping together. If our roles had been reversed, I . . . God, I don't know what I would have done. Torn him limb from limb probably. He was hurt and angry, and if he'd wanted to kill himself over it, there's really nothing we could have done to stop him, that night or on any future night. We wronged him, Paris. We'll live with that for the rest of our lives. But he wronged you when he drove off with you in that car."

He placed his hands on either side of her neck and caressed it with his fingertips. "That's what I blame him for. He could have killed you."

"I don't think it was his intention to kill anybody."

"Are you sure?" he asked gently. "What did you say to each other during those two minutes between the restaurant parking lot and that freeway overpass?"

"I told him I was sorry that we had hurt him. I told him that we both loved him, that it had been an isolated incident, a physical release after a traumatic experience, that if he could forgive us, it would never, ever happen again."

"Did he believe you?"

A tear slid unchecked down her cheek and she said huskily, "No."

"Did *you* believe you?"

She closed her eyes, squeezing out fresh tears. Slowly she moved her head from side to side.

Inhaling deeply, Dean drew her to his chest and stroked her hair.

"Maybe I should have said more," she said.

"Lied to him?"

"It might have saved him. He was enraged. Beyond reason. I tried to get him to pull over and let me drive, but he speeded up instead. He lost control of the car. He didn't drive into that abutment on purpose."

"Yes he did, Paris."

"No," she said miserably, not wanting to believe it.

"If a driver loses control, he reflexively stomps on the brake. I was right behind you. His brake lights never came on." He tilted her head back, forcing her to look at him. "Jack loved you, I don't doubt that. He loved you enough to want you as his wife. He loved you enough to fly into a jealous rage when he found out that you'd been with me.

"But," he said with emphasis, "if he had loved you the way he should have, unselfishly and unconditionally, he never could have considered taking you out along with him. As pitiful as his last years were, I never forgave him for trying to kill you."

His saying that made her love him all the more. And she did love him. From the moment they met, she had realized that her loving Dean Malloy was inevitable. But yielding to it had been impossible then, and it was impossible now. Other people had always stood between them. Jack, certainly. Now Liz.

She worked herself free of his embrace and said, "You should go now."

"I'm staying here tonight."

"Dean—"

"I'll sleep on the living room sofa." He held up his hands in surrender. "If you don't trust me to keep my hands off you, you can lock your bedroom door. But I'm not leaving you alone as long as there's a lunatic out there harboring a grudge against you."

"I can't imagine how he knew that Jack's death is on my conscience."

"And mine."

"What happened between you and me is certainly not public knowledge, and I've never discussed it with anyone."

"He probably did some research on you and surmised the cause of Jack's accident, just as Curtis did."

"Jack's accident could have been caused by any number of things," she argued.

"But only one would have busted up our friendship. It's not that much of a mind teaser, Paris. Valentino has got an ax to grind with unfaithful women. If he's concluded that you cheated on Jack with me, then you personify his nemesis. Even if it were a wrong assumption, Valentino has made it his reality and that's what he'll act on." He shook his head stubbornly. "I'm staying."

He napped on the sofa until dawn, when he silently let himself out of the house. He waved to the two officers sitting in the patrol car still parked at the curb, making certain they were aware of his departure.

He had hardly slept. He looked and felt as if he had been up most of the night. But this was an errand that couldn't wait. He didn't want to postpone it even for the time it would take to go home for a shower and a shave.

He rang the bell twice before he heard the dead bolt click on the other side of the door. Liz peered sleepily through the narrow crack allowed by the brass chain lock, then closed the door only long enough to unlatch it.

"It's unforgivable of me to show up at this time of morning," he said as he stepped inside.

"I forgive you." She wrapped her arms around his waist and snuggled against him. "In fact, this is a lovely surprise."

He hugged her. Beneath the silk robe, which was all she had on, her body felt warm, soft, and womanly. But he wasn't in the least aroused.

She eased back far enough to look up into his face, while keeping her lower body pressed intimately against his. "You look a little the worse for wear. Long night?"

"You could say so."

"Something new with Gavin?" she asked, her concern showing.

"No. He's not totally out of the woods yet, and until he is, I'll be apprehensive. But he's not the reason I'm here."

Her ability to read people had taken her far in her career and it didn't fail her now. After studying him for a moment longer, she said, "I was going to offer you some TLC in bed. But I think I should offer to make coffee instead."

"Don't bother. I can't stay long."

As though to shore up her pride, she dropped her arms to her sides, straightened her posture, and shook back her tousled hair. "Long enough to sit down at least?"

"Of course."

She led him to her living room sofa, where she claimed a corner, tucking her bare feet beneath her hips. Dean sat on the edge of the cushion and propped his elbows on his knees. On the drive over, he had rehearsed several ways to broach the subject, but had ultimately decided that there was no graceful way. He respected her too much to lie. He had decided to be forthright.

"For a long time now—months anyway—I've allowed you to believe that we would eventually get married. It's not going to happen, Liz. I'm sorry."

"I see." She took a deep breath and let it out slowly. "Do I at least get to know the reason?"

"At first I thought I had a classic case of cold feet. After being a bachelor for fifteen years, I thought the idea of marrying again was causing me to panic. So I didn't say anything, hoping that the misgivings would go away. I didn't want to quarrel about it or upset you unnecessarily."

"Well, I certainly appreciate your sensitivity to my feelings."

"Do I detect some sarcasm?"

"Definitely."

"I suppose I deserve it," he said. "I've just broken what amounted to an engagement. You don't have to be nice."

"I'm glad you think so, because I'm working my way up to a hissy fit."

"You're entitled to one."

She glared at him angrily, but then the hauteur returned. "On second thought, I'm not going to get into a fight with you. Histrionics would make it easier for you to storm out of here and never look back. Instead I'm going to put you on the spot. Because I believe I deserve a full explanation."

Actually he *had* hoped for a fight, during which they would swap invective and destroy any affection they'd ever felt for each other. A fight would have been swifter, cleaner, less painful for her, and easier for him. But Liz had slammed shut that cowardly escape hatch.

"I'm not sure I can explain." He spread his hands wide, indicating how futile it was to try. "It's not you. You're as smart and beautiful and desirable as the day I met you. More so."

"Please spare me the I'm-not-worthy-of-you speech."

"That's not what this is," he said testily. "I mean all of that sincerely. It's not about you. It's about *us*. It just isn't where I am, Liz."

"You don't have to tell me that. Lately you haven't been that involved whenever we've made love."

"Funny, I didn't hear you complaining."

"You're trying to pick a fight again," she said sternly. "Don't. And don't be stung by the criticism. It's not your performance that's at issue. It's your emotional detachment."

"Which I acknowledge."

"Is it because of Gavin and his coming to live with you? The additional demands on your time?"

"Gavin provided me with a good excuse to pull back," he admitted. "I'm not proud of the fact that I used him."

"Nor should you be. But this isn't about him either, is it?"

"No."

"Someone else, then?"

He turned his head and looked at her directly. "Yes."

"You've been seeing someone else?"

"No. Nothing like that."

"Then what, Dean? What *is* it like?"

"I love someone else."

She was silenced by the simplicity of his statement. She stared at him for several moments, assimilating it. "Oh. You love someone else. Did you ever love me?"

"Yes. On many levels I still do. You've been an important and vital part of my life."

"Just not the grand passion of it."

"When we started seeing each other, I honestly thought . . . I hoped that . . . I tried . . ."

"You tried," she said around a bitter laugh. "Just what every woman wants to hear."

The sarcasm was back, but it was forced. She had picked up a throw pillow and was hugging it to her chest, literally and figuratively giving herself something to hold on to. He felt he should leave now before his brutal honesty wounded her pride more than it was already wounded.

But as he stood up to leave, she said softly, "The woman in the sunglasses. The one you were talking to at the police station. Paris?" Raising her head, she looked up at him. "Come now, Dean, don't look so shocked. If I were blind, I still would have known that you and she had been lovers."

"Years ago. Only once, but . . ."

"But you never quite recovered."

He matched her sad smile. "No. I never did."

"Just out of curiosity, when did you start seeing her again?"

"The day before yesterday."

Her lips parted in wordless surprise.

"That's right. This alienation of feelings, for lack of a better term, started long before she entered the picture. Seeing her just confirmed what I already knew."

"That you weren't going to marry me."

He nodded.

"Well, thank God you didn't." Tossing the throw pillow aside, she came to her feet. "I don't want to be anybody's second choice."

"And you shouldn't be." He reached for her hand and squeezed it. "I apologize for taking up two years of your biological clock."

"Oh, it's probably for the best," she said flippantly. "What would I do with a baby when I went on a business trip? Take it along in my briefcase?"

She was making light of it, but he knew she was deeply disappointed. Maybe even heartbroken. She was too proud to make a spectacle of herself by crying. And perhaps, just perhaps, she cared too much for him to lay a guilt trip on him.

"You've got a lot of grace, class, and style, Liz."

"Oh, yeah. Out the wazoo."

"What'll you do?"

"Today? I think I'll treat myself to a massage."

He smiled. "What about tomorrow?"

"I didn't sell my house in Houston when I relocated here."

"You didn't?"

"You assumed that I had, and I never set you straight. Maybe I felt intuitively that I would need a safety net. Anyway, as soon as I can arrange it, I'll move back."

"You're special, Liz."

"So are you," she replied gruffly.

He leaned forward and kissed her cheek, then headed for the door. When he reached it, he turned back. "Be well." And, saying that, he left.

chapter twenty-six

"Hello?"

"Is this Gavin?"

"Yes."

"It's Sergeant Curtis. Did I wake you up?"

"Sorta."

"Sorry to disturb you. I couldn't reach your dad on his cell. That's why I'm calling the house phone. May I speak with him, please?"

"He's not here. He stayed over at Paris's house last night." Gavin regretted it the instant the words were out. Being the suspicious person he was, Curtis would jump to the wrong conclusion.

"We had dinner at her place," he explained. "After her program, you know, because of Valentino's latest call, Dad thought she shouldn't be alone."

"Cops are guarding her house."

"I guess my dad didn't think that was enough."

"Obviously."

Gavin decided to quit while he was ahead, afraid he might say too much. Anyway, why was it Curtis's business where his dad spent the night?

"Okay then, I'll try and reach him there," the detective said. "I have her unlisted number."

"I could give him a message," Gavin offered.

"Thanks, but I need to speak to him personally."

He didn't like the sound of that. Did Curtis have to speak personally to his dad about something relating to him? "Any news on Janey?"

"I'm afraid not. I'll talk to you later, Gavin."

The detective clicked off before Gavin could even say good-bye. He got up and went to the bathroom, then looked through a window on the front of the house and saw that the police car was still parked at the curb.

Was he the only one who appreciated the irony of their protecting him from Valentino, while at the same time suspecting him of being Valentino?

It was too early to get up, so he went back to bed, but discovered he couldn't sleep. Until Janey was found, he was going to be quarantined at home. He might just as well resign himself to that. It could be worse, though. If not for his dad, they probably would have put him in jail.

Considering that his dad had caught him in several lies and discovered his membership in the Sex Club, he wasn't suffering overly much. Last night, with his dad and Paris, it hadn't been half bad.

He'd almost dreaded seeing her after so many years. What if she'd changed and now acted like an old person? He was afraid she'd have big, stiff hair and too much jewelry, that she'd be gushy and sappy, going on and on about how much he'd grown, make a big to-do over him like his mother's relatives always did at family get-togethers.

But Paris had been cool, just like he remembered her. She was friendly, but didn't overdo it like Liz did. She didn't talk down to him either. Even when he had known her before, she had talked to him like an equal, not like a kid.

Jack had always addressed him as Skipper, or Scout, or Partner, something cute, and had talked to him boisterously, like he was a baby who had to be entertained. Jack had been okay, but of the two, he had liked Paris better.

He had liked Paris better than the girls his dad had dated then, too. He remembered thinking that if Jack wasn't in the picture, how cool it would be if his dad liked Paris as a girlfriend.

His mom had thought that maybe he did.

She'd never talked to him about it, of course, but he had overheard her say once to a friend that she thought Dean had a "thing" for Paris Gibson, and that he only dated other women because she belonged to Jack Donner.

At the time, he'd been too young to understand the implications. Nor had he been particularly interested in the relationships between grown-ups. But after having seen how anxious his dad had been to get to her house last evening, how he'd checked himself out in the rearview mirror before they left the car, he thought his mom might have been right. He'd never seen his dad consult a mirror before meeting Liz.

For as long as he could remember, his parents had been divorced. As a kid, he had gradually begun to comprehend that his family wasn't like the ones in TV commercials where the mommy and daddy ate breakfast together, and walked on the beach holding hands, and rode in the same car, and even slept in the same bed. He noticed that in other houses on his block, the daddy was there all the time.

He asked questions of both parents, and after they had explained the meaning of divorce, he had fervently hoped that his parents would get back together and live in the same house. But the older he got, the better he came to understand and accept that a reconciliation was an extremely dim possibility. Dumb kid that he was, he had continued to hope.

His dad had dated lots of women. Gavin forgot most of their names because none had lasted very long. He'd heard his mom talking to his grandmother about the "flavor of the month" and knew that she was referring to his dad's girlfriends.

His mom hadn't dated nearly as much, so it was surprising that she was the one to remarry. Her remarriage had dashed all hope that his parents would, somehow, miraculously reunite. That's when he'd gotten really mad at her and had determined to make her life with her new husband miserable.

Looking back, it had been a stupid, childish way to behave. He'd been a real jerk. His mom must have loved the guy or she wouldn't have married him. She didn't love his dad anymore. Gavin had heard her tell his grandmother that, too. "I'll always love Dean for giving me Gavin," she had said, "but we made the right decision early on to split up."

He figured his dad didn't love his mom either, and maybe never had. He tried to picture his parents as a couple, and it just didn't look right. Like two pieces from different puzzles, they didn't fit. It hadn't worked originally and it never would.

Live with it, Gavin, he thought.

His mom was happy now in her second marriage. His dad deserved to be happy, too. But Gavin didn't think Liz was the one who was going to make him happy.

He drifted off, thinking about it, but before he was completely asleep, the doorbell rang.

Jesus! Why was everybody up so frigging early this morning?

He made his way to the front door and unlocked it. To his regret, he didn't check to see who had rung the bell before he opened the door. John Rondeau was standing on the porch.

Gavin's eyes darted past him to the squad car at the curb. He was comforted to see that it was still there. The cops inside were noshing on doughnuts. No doubt a gift from Rondeau.

"Don't worry, Gavin, your protectors are in place."

Rondeau's pleasant tone of voice didn't fool him. Not for a second. His cheekbone had finally stopped throbbing, but it was still sore and would remain discolored for days. Rondeau outweighed him by probably thirty pounds. He knew firsthand that the son of a bitch was capable of violence. But he'd be damned if he'd cower.

"I'm not worried about anything," he retorted. "Especially you. What do you want?"

"I wanted to add something to what I told you yesterday."

"If my dad finds out you're here, he'll whip your ass."

"That's why this is such a good time, because I know he's not at home." He was smiling, so to anyone looking, including the cops licking sugar glaze off their fingers, this would appear to be a chat between friends. "If you decide to tell anybody about my—"

"Crimes."

His smile only widened. "I was going to say extracurricular activities. If anybody hears about that from you, it won't be you I come after."

"I'm not afraid of you."

Ignoring that, Rondeau said, "I'll skip you and go straight for your old man."

"Is that supposed to be a joke? Because it's freaking funny." Gavin snorted derisively. "You're a computer geek."

"I'm working my way out of that unit and into the CIB."

"I don't care if they make you chief, you haven't got the balls to have a face-off with my dad."

"I wasn't talking about attacking him myself. That would be stupid because he would be watching for that. But what about some psycho jailbird he has to interview?

"Malloy goes into jail cells all the time, you know," he continued smoothly. "Talking to junkies and rapists and homicidal maniacs, trying to get information from them, manipulating them into confessing. What if one of them was tipped off that Dr. Malloy was coming on to his woman, making moves on her while he's in jail?"

"You're getting even funnier."

"Like the way he moved in on his best friend Jack Donner with Paris Gibson."

Gavin's next smart-alecky retort died on his lips. "Says who?"

"Curtis, for one. Says anyone with a grain of sense who can add two and two together. Your dad fucked his best friend's fiancée, which caused Jack Donner to try and commit suicide."

"You're making that up."

"If you don't believe me, ask him." Rondeau clicked his tongue against the roof of his mouth. "It's an ugly story, isn't it? But it fuels any rumor I might start among the jail population that Dr. Malloy, despite all his buddy-buddy tactics, is not to be trusted, especially with a lonely and susceptible female.

"You get my drift, Gavin? Cops get set up to die by other cops all the time. We're human, you know. We make enemies among ourselves. It happens," he said, shrugging. "He wouldn't see it coming, but he'd be just as dead and you'd be just as orphaned."

Fear struck Gavin's heart. "You get out of here," he said thickly.

In no apparent hurry, Rondeau pushed himself away from the doorjamb. "Okay, I'll leave you now. But I strongly urge you to think about what I said. You're nothing. You're dog shit on my shoe, not worth my time and effort. But if you rat me out," he said, poking Gavin's bare chest hard with the knuckle of his index finger, "Malloy goes down."

Paris's eyes came open slowly, but when she saw Dean sitting on the edge of her bed, she sat bolt upright. "What's happened?"

"Nothing new. I didn't mean to startle you."

She was relieved to know that there was no bad news, but her heart was still pumping hard from her initial fright and now from having Dean sitting on her bed. Not having quite regained her breath, she asked, "How was the sofa?"

"Short."

"Did you sleep at all?"

"Some. Not much. Mostly I worked, made some notes on Valentino's profile."

As tired as she'd been, it had taken her a long time to fall asleep, knowing that he was in the next room. It had hovered in her subconscious and had prevented her from getting a restful sleep. "I feel like coffee."

He nodded, but he didn't move and neither did she. The silence stretched out as they continued to gaze at each other across the narrow strip of bed separating them.

260 • SANDRA BROWN

"Should have locked my bedroom door after all?" she asked in a voice barely above a whisper.

"Definitely. Because, as it turns out, I can't keep my hands off you."

He reached for her and she stretched toward him, but just before their lips met, she said, "Liz—"

"Not a factor."

"But—"

"Trust me, Paris."

She did, giving herself over to his kiss—his untempered, possessive, delicious kiss. Placing her hands on his stubble-covered cheeks, she tilted her head to change the angle of their lips and invited more intimacy. He pushed aside the blanket and sheet covering her and pressed her onto the pillows, following her down, lying close beside her.

He drew back in order to look at her, taking in her unglamorous tank top and boxers. "Fancy sleepwear."

"Designed to inflame."

"It's working," he growled.

She explored his face with her fingertips, smoothing his eyebrows, stroking the straight line of his nose, then tracing the shape of his lips and touching the shallow cleft at the bottom of his chin.

"Your hair is grayer," she remarked.

"You're wearing yours shorter."

"I guess we've both changed."

"Some things have." His eyes moved to her breasts and when he caressed her through the tank top, her nipple tightened. "Not that. That I remember."

He kissed her again, except with more urgency than before. Splaying his hand over her bottom, he lifted her onto the erection that strained against his trousers.

A rush of fluid heat spread through her lower body and into her thighs. It had been years since she had experienced that aching desire to be filled. She sighed with joy over feeling it again, and moaned with longing to have that desire assuaged.

"We've waited long enough," he said, rolling back only far enough to reach for his fly. "Too damn long."

But they would wait longer. Her telephone rang.

Both froze. They locked gazes, and each knew without having to say anything that she must answer the call. Too many things were at stake. Dean flopped onto his back and blistered the ceiling paint with his curses.

Paris pushed her tangled hair from her eyes and reached for the cordless phone on her nightstand. "Hello?" She mouthed to Dean that it was Curtis. "No . . . no, I was awake. Is there news?"

"Of a sort," the detective said brusquely. "None about Valentino or Janey directly. Brad Armstrong and Marvin Patterson are still at large. But actually I'm calling for Malloy. I understand he's there."

With more composure than she felt, she said, "Just a moment. I'll get him."

She covered the mouthpiece as she extended the telephone toward Dean. He looked at her inquisitively, but she raised her shoulders, saying, "He didn't say."

He took the telephone from her and said a curt good morning to the detective. Paris got up and went into the bathroom, closing the door behind her. She showered quickly and put on a robe before going back into the bedroom. Dean was no longer there and the telephone had been returned to the battery charger.

She followed sounds into the kitchen. Dean was scooping coffee grounds into the paper filter. Hearing her behind him, he glanced at her over his shoulder. "You smell good."

"What did Sergeant Curtis want?"

"Coffee will be ready in a few minutes."

"Dean?"

"Gavin told him I was here. He had called my house because he couldn't reach me on my cell. When I went to see Liz this morning—"

"You went to see Liz this morning?"

"At dawn. I turned off my cell and forgot to turn it back on. As a courtesy to her, I didn't want a phone call to interrupt what I had to tell her."

Paris said nothing but felt the pressure of a dozen questions wanting to be asked. He calmly removed two coffee mugs from her pantry and only then turned to face her. "Which was that I wouldn't be seeing her again."

She swallowed hard. "Was she upset?"

"Mildly. But not shocked. She'd seen it coming."

"Oh."

He must have read her mind, because he said quietly, "Don't blame yourself for the breakup, Paris. It would have happened anyway."

"Are you . . . okay with it?"

"Relieved. I was unfair to her by letting it go on for so long."

The coffeemaker gurgled, signaling that the coffee was almost ready and giving her a graceful way to change the subject. She went to the fridge for a carton of half-and-half. "What did Curtis want?"

"Only to give me a status report."

"On the case?"

"No, on my employment with the APD. I've been placed on indefinite suspension."

chapter *twenty-seven*

"*H*i, Mama, it's Lancy."

"Christ, what time is it?"

"Nearly nine."

"Where're you at?"

Last evening he had returned to the mobile-home park through a back gate and had parked two rows away from the lane on which his mother's home was situated. Risking barking dogs and skittish neighbors who would welcome a chance to shoot first and ask questions later, he'd sneaked between the narrow lots.

His reconnoitering seemed a bit melodramatic, but it was a precaution that proved to be unwarranted. He spotted the unmarked police car immediately. It was parked about thirty yards from his mother's patch of lawn. Anyone inside the no-frills sedan had an unrestricted view of her front door. It was a good thing he had gone to her trailer and dipped into his piggy bank when he had.

He had slinked back to his car and returned to Austin because he didn't know where else to go. He had called a neighbor, who was as trustworthy as anyone among Lancy's few acquaintances. He confirmed what Lancy suspected—the police had tossed his place. "I saw them carrying out boxes of stuff," the neighbor reported.

The tapes of Paris Gibson's shows would be in those boxes. *Shit!*

Now, disregarding his mother's question, he asked, "Have any cops come around?"

"Guy named Curtis. From Austin."

"What did you tell him?"

"Nothin'," she grumbled, "'cause I don't know nothin'."

"Did he search the trailer?"

"He poked around. Found your socks."

"Did he take them with him?"

"What would he want your dirty socks for?"

"Go to the window and look out toward the south end of the street."

"I'm in bed," she whined.

"Please, Mama. Do me this favor. See if there's a dark-colored car parked down the street."

She griped and cursed, but the telephone clattered when she obviously dropped it on her bedside table. She was gone an inordinate amount of time. When she finally returned, she was wheezing like a bagpipe. "It's there."

"Thanks, Mama. I'll talk to you later."

"I don't want none of your trouble rubbing off on me, Lancy Ray. You understand me, boy?"

He replaced the greasy receiver on the hook of the pay telephone. Thrusting his hands in his pockets and hunching his shoulders, he walked down the breezeway of the residence motel. Beneath the bill of his baseball cap, his eyes furtively watched for squad cars that he expected to appear at any moment with a squeal of brakes and shouts for him to freeze.

After learning that he couldn't hide in his mother's place, he had returned to his secret apartment to spend the night. He'd driven past it once. There'd been no police car at the IHOP across the street or anywhere else that he could see.

He got in without being detected, but it was hardly a comfortable refuge. It stank. It was dirty. It made him feel dirty.

He'd been up all night, and it had been a long one.

"You're screwed, blued, and tattooed this time, Lancy Ray," he muttered to himself as he unlocked the door and once again slipped back into the dank, dark lair of a wanted man.

Curtis's shiny cowboy boots were propped up on his desk, his ankles crossed. He was concentrating on the hand-tooled pointed toe of one of them when a yellow legal tablet landed on the desk an inch away from it. He turned to find Paris Gibson standing behind him. Even though she was wearing her sunglasses, he could tell by her body language that she was in a major snit.

"Good morning," he said.

"You're going to kowtow to that egomaniacal fool?"

He removed his feet from his desk and motioned her into a

chair. She declined the offer and remained standing. He said, "That fool is a powerful county judge."

"Who has the police department in his pocket."

"It wasn't my decision to suspend Malloy. I couldn't even if I wanted to. He outranks me. I was just the messenger."

"Then let me rephrase," she said. "Judge Kemp has the *gutless* police department in his pocket."

Withstanding the insult, he addressed the issue. "The judge went straight to the top with his complaint. After he and Mrs. Kemp heard you talking about their daughter on the radio last night, he went into orbit. Or so I was told. He called the chief at home, got him out of bed, demanded that Malloy be fired for publicly maligning his daughter, dragging the family name through the dirt, and mishandling a delicate family situation, which should have been dealt with privately. He also cited conflict of interest since Gavin Malloy had been brought in for questioning."

"How did he know about that?"

"He's got moles within the department. Anyway, he threatened to sue everything and everybody if Malloy wasn't removed not only from the case, but from the APD. The chief wouldn't go that far, but he did agree that a temporary suspension was called for. Just until things cool down."

"Just to pacify the judge."

Curtis conceded with a shrug. "I got the edict from the chief before dawn this morning. He asked—make that *ordered*—me to notify Malloy since I was the one who'd brought him in to work the case. That was my punishment, I guess."

"I said nothing except flattering things about Janey last night," Paris argued. "In fact, I went out of my way not to allude to her bad reputation, the Internet club, any of that. We were trying to humanize her to Valentino, portray her as a helpless victim with friends and family who care about her."

"But the Kemps wanted to avoid all media, remember? Even a mention of Janey's disappearance. So your going on the radio, under the advice of the police department's staff psychologist, and talking about her, looked like defiance of their wishes."

"Dean told me that you were very keen on the idea."

"I admitted that to the chief."

"So why didn't the judge demand that you be fired, too?"

"Because he doesn't want to antagonize the whole department. He knows I've got a lot of friends on the force. Malloy hasn't been here long enough to cultivate that kind of loyalty.

"Besides, the judge wanted to get back at you, too. You and Malloy went to his house more or less as a team. He just didn't have the guts to criticize you publicly because of your popularity. It might be bad PR with voters to speak out against Paris Gibson."

"Leaving Dean the scapegoat," she concluded. "Has the media learned of his suspension?"

"I have no idea. If it gets out, you can bet Kemp will exploit it."

She sat down, but not because she was placated. He could tell that by her resolute expression as she leaned forward and spoke directly, to his face. "You go to your chief and tell him that I insist that he retract Dean's suspension. Immediately. Furthermore, if a story about it makes the news today, I'll be on the radio *tonight* talking about the self-serving political machine that drives this police department.

"I'll tell the public about the graft, officers receiving bribes in exchange for not making arrests when they're warranted, and about the department's blatant favoritism toward the wealthy and powerful.

"In four hours, I could do a lot of damage, more I think than even Judge Kemp could do. For all his chest thumping, I doubt if several hundred thousand people have even heard of him. But I have that many loyal listeners every night. Now, who do you think wields the most influence, Sergeant Curtis?"

"Your program isn't political. You've never used it as a soapbox."

"I would tonight."

"And tomorrow Wilkins Crenshaw would fire you."

"Which would win me even more public support and sympathy. It would become a media wildfire that I would fan for weeks. The Austin PD would have a tough time restoring John Q. Public's confidence."

Curtis couldn't see her eyes well behind the tinted lenses, but he could see them well enough. They weren't even blinking. She meant what she said.

"If the decision were up to me . . ." He raised his hands helplessly. "But the chief may not bend."

"If he refuses, I'll call a press conference. I'll be on television by noon. 'Paris Gibson goes public.' 'The first time seen on TV in seven years.' 'The face behind the voice revealed.' I can hear the promos now."

Curtis could hear them, too. "The story about Malloy may already have gotten out."

"Then your chief will issue a press release saying that it was a huge misunderstanding, overly eager reporting by someone misinformed, et cetera."

"Did Malloy send you to champion his cause?" She didn't even deign to answer and he didn't blame her. Malloy wouldn't stoop to that. Curtis had only taken the cheap shot because he didn't have any real ammunition against her arguments. "All right, I'll see what I can do."

"Take this with you," she said, pushing the legal pad toward him.

"What is it?"

"The work Dean was doing last night. He stayed up most of the night profiling Janey's kidnapper and rapist while the judge was plotting to have him discredited and fired.

"It should make for interesting reading. Your chief will realize what an asset he has in Dr. Malloy and what an egregious mistake it would be to take him off this case. Of course, Dean may tell you all to go to hell, and I wouldn't blame him. But you can try and persuade him to come back."

"You're pretty sure of our compliance."

"I'm sure only of how wise one becomes when it's a matter of covering one's own ass."

"I'll think about it and get back to you." Dean depressed the button on his cell phone, ending the call. "Meanwhile," he added under his breath, "go fuck yourself." Noticing Gavin's stunned reaction to his language, he chuckled. "Your generation didn't coin the phrase, you know."

They were having a late breakfast at a coffee shop when the chief of police himself called to nullify his suspension.

"Earlier this morning, he was ready to fire me," he told Gavin as he dug back into his omelet. "Now I'm an asset to the department. An excellent psychologist as well as a highly trained officer of the law. A cross between Sigmund Freud and Dick Tracy."

"He said that?"

"It was almost that ridiculous."

"If you're back on the case, won't Janey's dad be pissed?"

"I don't know how the department is going to deal with the judge, and I don't care."

"Do you want to keep working there?"

"Do you want me to?"

"*Me?*"

"Do you like it here, Gavin?"

"Does it matter?"

"Yes."

Gavin idly stirred his glass of milk with a plastic straw. "It's okay, I guess. I mean, it hasn't been too bad living here."

Dean knew that was probably as close to a yes vote as he was going to get. "I'd hate to leave this job before giving it a fair shake," he admitted. "I think I can do a lot of good here. Austin's a happening place. I like the city, the energy of it. Great music. Good food. Fine climate. But I also like having you living with me. I want you to continue to. So can we work out a deal?"

Gavin regarded him warily. "What kind of deal?"

"If I try out the job, will you try out the high school? I don't mean just attend it, Gavin. I mean really apply yourself, make friends, participate in school activities. You'll be required to put forth as much effort at school as I'll be putting into my job. Do we have a deal?"

"Can I have my computer back?"

"As long as I have access to it at any time. From now on, I'll monitor how much time you spend on it, and how you use it. That's a nonnegotiable point. Another condition is that you must take part in some school activity or sport. I don't care if you play croquet, so long as you don't spend all your free time locked inside your bedroom or just hanging out."

He gave Dean a fleeting glance across the table, then looked back down into his plate. "I was thinking about maybe going out for basketball."

Dean was pleased to hear it, but he didn't want to overreact and jinx it. "We've got the perfect driveway in back of the house for a basket. Want to see about putting one up so you can get in some shooting practice?"

"Sure. That'd be good."

"Okay, then. We understand each other. And just so you know, I broke it off with Liz."

Gavin's head came up. "You did?"

"Early this morning."

"That was kinda sudden, wasn't it?"

"Actually, I've been thinking about it for some time."

Gavin began playing with the straw again. "Was it not working out because of me? Because I live with you now?"

"It was because I didn't love her as much as I should have."

"You didn't want to make the same mistake twice."

It pained Dean for his son to think of his marriage to Pat as a mistake, although he was precisely right. "I suppose you could put it that way."

Gavin mulled it over for a moment. "Did Paris figure into it?"

"Hugely."

"Yeah, I thought so."

"Are you cool with that?"

"Sure, she's great." He took the plastic straw out of his glass and began bending and twisting it. "Did you sleep with her while she was engaged to Jack?"

"What?"

"You want me to repeat it?"

"That's a very personal question."

"That means yes."

"That means I'm not going to discuss it with you."

Gavin sat up straighter and looked at him with resentment. "But it's okay for you to pry into *my* sex life. I have to tell you what I did and who I did it with."

"I'm a parent and you're a minor."

"It's still not fair."

"Fair or not, you— Damn!" Dean said when his cell rang again.

He checked the caller ID, saw Curtis's number, and considered not answering. But Gavin had slumped into the corner of the booth and was staring sullenly out the window. It would probably be a one-sided conversation with him from here on anyway.

Dean answered on the fourth ring. "Malloy."

"You talk to the chief?" Curtis asked.

"Yes."

"You staying?"

Although he'd made his decision, he didn't see any reason to jump through hoops for them. "I'm considering it."

"Whether you do or not, I need you to come in."

"I'm having breakfast with Gavin."

"Bring him with you."

Dean's heart jumped. "What for? What's happened?"

"The sooner you can get here, the better. I just got some bad news."

Curtis didn't beat around the bush. "Your friend Valentino jumped his deadline. Janey Kemp's body was discovered half an hour ago in Lake Travis."

Reflexively Dean reached for Paris's hand and gripped it hard.

He'd been surprised to see her waiting in Curtis's cubicle when he and Gavin got there. She told him she had been summoned just as he had, with no more explanation than he had received.

Curtis had arrived a few minutes behind them. He'd asked Gavin if he would wait for them with another detective in one of the interrogation rooms. As his son was led away, Dean had a strong sense of foreboding. Justifiably, as it turned out.

"Two fishermen found her nude body partially submerged beneath the root system of a cypress tree. I was called immediately and rushed out there. Although she hasn't been officially identified, it's her.

"The crime scene unit is combing the place. The ME is examining the body, even before he moves it. Hopes to get something. She looks pretty bad," he said with a heavy sigh. "Bruises on her face, neck, torso, and extremities. What appear to be bite marks . . ." He glanced at Paris. "Several places."

"How did she die?" Dean asked.

"We won't know until the autopsy. The ME estimated that she hadn't been in the water more than six or seven hours, though. Probably put there sometime last night."

"If you had to guess . . ."

"I'd guess strangulation, like Maddie Robinson. The bruises on Janey's neck match the ones she had. On the other hand, the two could be unrelated."

"Sexual assault?"

"The ME will also determine that. Again, if I had to guess, I'd say very likely."

They were silent for a time, then Paris asked softly, "Have the Kemps been notified?"

"That's why I was late getting here. I stopped at their house. The judge was still fuming over the chief's reversed decision and thought I had come to make amends. When I told them about the body, Mrs. Kemp collapsed, but she wouldn't allow him to console her.

"Each blamed the other. They shouted accusations. It was an ugly scene. When I left they were still going at it. I'm meeting them at the morgue in an hour to get a positive ID, and I don't look forward to it."

He stared into near space a moment, then said, "They wouldn't win a popularity contest with me, but I have to admit I felt sorry for them. Their only child has been brutalized and murdered. God knows what she endured before she died. I couldn't help but think about my own daughter, how I'd feel if somebody did that to her, then dumped her in a lake for fish to feed on."

Dean saw from the corner of his eye that Paris had pressed her fingers vertically against her lips as though to forcibly contain her emotion. "Why did you want to see Gavin?" he asked Curtis.

"Will he submit to a lie detector test?"

"Bad time for a joke, Sergeant."

"I'm not joking. We're no longer shooting in the dark. I've got a dead girl. I've got to tighten the screws."

"On my son?"

"He was one of the last people to see her alive."

"Except the person who kidnapped and killed her. Have you checked out Gavin's alibi?"

"His friends, you mean? Yes, we ran down several of them."

"And?"

"Unanimously they vouched for Gavin, said he was with them. But they were drunk and high, so their memories were fuzzy. None could nail down the time he joined them or the time he left."

"You're only subjecting Gavin to this because he's the one suspect who's available," Dean said angrily.

"Unfortunately, you're right," the detective admitted with chagrin. "So far there's been no sign of Lancy Ray Fisher even though we've staked out his apartment and his mother's place. One interesting thing turned up on his bank statement, though. There were several canceled checks made out to a Doreen Gilliam, who teaches high school drama and speech."

He looked at them meaningfully before adding, "Ms. Gilliam moonlights by giving private lessons out of her home. Lancy, aka Marvin, has been taking speech and diction lessons."

"*Speech* lessons?" Paris exclaimed. "He rarely spoke."

Curtis shrugged.

"To aid in disguising his voice, maybe?" Dean asked.

"That was my thought," Curtis said.

"He worked for the telephone company and would have the know-how to reroute calls," Dean mused out loud. "And he's fixated on Paris or else why the tapes?"

"One of the first things I'm going to ask him when he's brought in," Curtis said. "Finding this body raises the bar considerably, so off come the kid gloves. With everybody. I hadn't heard back from Toni Armstrong, so I obtained a search warrant for their house. I made Rondeau personally responsible for cracking Brad Armstrong's computer. In my book, he's got a real good shot at being our man. His own wife testified that she caught him picking up a teenage girl.

"I've pulled in the sheriff's office, the Texas Rangers, and the Texas Highway Patrol. Every law-enforcement officer in the city and surrounding area is on the lookout for Armstrong as well as Lancy Ray Fisher. In any case, we're not putting the squeeze exclusively on Gavin."

"Is that supposed to make me feel better?" Dean asked. "My son being lumped in with a sex offender and a porn star? And since you can't find them, you're requiring Gavin to take a lie detector test."

"Not requiring, requesting."

Paris laid her hand on his arm. "Maybe you should agree to it, Dean. It will clear him."

He wanted to believe it would turn out like that. But Gavin was holding something back. It was only a gut instinct, but it was strong enough to make him afraid of the secret Gavin was keeping.

Curtis was frowning down at the folder on his desk that Dean guessed contained crime scene photos of Janey Kemp's body. "The evidence we have on Gavin is circumstantial. Nothing hard. You'd be within your rights to refuse the test." He looked up at Dean, and Dean recognized the detective's challenge for what it was.

"Fuck that. Gavin takes your damn test."

chapter twenty-eight

"Paris, it's Stan."

"Stan?"

"You sound surprised. You gave me your cell number months ago, remember?"

"But you've never called it."

"Only in case of an emergency, you said. I just heard about Janey Kemp on the news. I called to see if you're all right."

"I can't describe how awful I feel."

"Where are you?"

"At the downtown police station."

"I bet it's hopping. Did the body give up any clues to who did it?"

"I hate to disappoint you, Stan, but the only gruesome detail I know is that she's dead."

"Do you plan on doing your program tonight?"

"Why wouldn't I?"

"The GM notified Uncle Wilkins about the body. They discussed it and thought that, with everything that's happened, you might want to take the night off, replay a tape of an old show."

"I'll call the GM later and talk to him myself. But if anyone asks, tell them that I'll do the program live as always. Valentino is not going to scare me off."

"He's done what he said he was going to do, Paris. Do you think he'll call again?"

"I hope he does. The more he talks to me, the better chance we have of identifying him."

"Too bad you couldn't have caught him before he killed her." After a pause, he added, "Guess I shouldn't have reminded you of that, huh? I'm sure you already feel bad enough for being the one who set him off in the first place."

"I've got to go, Stan."

"Are you mad? You sound mad."

"I just don't want to talk about it anymore right now, okay? I'll see you tonight."

She clicked off. He wished he could have kept her talking longer because it tied up his phone line. If his uncle continued to get a busy signal, he might become discouraged and stop calling.

Ever since he'd learned that Janey Kemp's body had been discovered, Uncle Wilkins had been phoning periodically. He pretended to be concerned about the station's involvement, but Stan knew the reason for the frequent calls—Uncle Wilkins was checking up on him.

He should never have admitted to being attracted to Paris. You'd think that was all his uncle had heard during their meeting. He'd been referring to it ever since.

During their last telephone conversation, Wilkins had said in his most menacing voice, "If you've done anything perverse or inappropriate . . ."

"I've been an altar boy around her. I swear to God."

How could he have behaved otherwise with Paris? She wasn't rude, but she never acted particularly happy to see him. Sometimes, even when she was talking to him, she seemed preoccupied, as though she had something on her mind that was more important or interesting than him.

He was certain that if he'd ever made a move on her, she would have cut him off at the knees. She'd never invited even the slightest flirtation. In fact, she often looked through him, as though he wasn't there. Much like his parents, she treated him with a casual disregard that was as hurtful as an outright rejection. He was always an afterthought.

His chance for a romance with Paris had always been remote. But it had been totally squelched when Dean Malloy entered the picture. Malloy was an arrogant son of a bitch, confident of himself and his appeal to the opposite sex. He would never need to coerce a secretary into raising her skirt or cajole a date into bed.

Fact of life: Things came easier to men like Malloy.

Another fact: Women like Paris were attracted to men like that.

People like Paris and Malloy had never known a day of rejection. It would never occur to them that love and affection didn't come as easily to others as it did to them. They shone like bright little planets, without an inkling of what it was like to be someone who could only orbit around them. They had no idea the lengths to which someone would go to attain the adoration they took for granted.

No idea.

Gavin's head was bowed so low, his chin was almost touching his chest. "In the lake?"

"Her body is being transported to the morgue, where it will undergo an autopsy to determine the cause of death."

Gavin raised his head. The news of Janey's death had caused him to go pale. He swallowed with difficulty. "Dad, I . . . You gotta believe me. I didn't do it."

"I believe that. But I also believe just as strongly that you're keeping something from me."

Gavin shook his head.

"Whatever it is, wouldn't you rather tell me than have it come out during a lie detector test? What don't you want me to know?"

"Nothing."

"You're lying, Gavin. I know you are."

The boy surged to his feet, fists clenched. "You have no right to accuse someone of lying. You're the biggest liar I know."

"What are you talking about? When have I lied to you?"

"My whole life!" Dean watched in dismay as tears sprang to his son's eyes. Angrily, Gavin swiped at them with his fists. "You. Mom. Always telling me you loved me. But I know better."

"What's makes you say that, Gavin? Why do you think we don't love you?"

"You didn't want me," he shouted. "You got her pregnant by accident, didn't you? And that's the only reason you got married. Why didn't you just get rid of me and save yourselves the trouble?"

He and Pat had never specifically discussed how much they would tell Gavin if he ever asked this question. Perhaps they should have. She wasn't here to consult, so Dean was left to answer his son's tortured questions alone. Despite the embarrassment it might cause Pat, and himself, he decided Gavin deserved the unmitigated truth.

"I'll tell you everything you want to know, but not until you sit down and stop looking at me like you're about to go for my throat."

Gavin battled with indecision for several moments, then plopped back into the chair. His expression remained belligerent.

"You're right. Your mother was pregnant when we got married. You were conceived during a weekend fraternity party in New Orleans."

Gavin laughed bitterly. "Jeez. It's even worse than I thought. Were you college sweethearts at least?"

"We had dated a few times."

"But she wasn't someone you . . . not someone special."

"No," Dean admitted quietly.

"So I was a mistake."

"Gavin—"

"Why didn't you use something? Were you drunk or just stupid?"

"A little of both, I guess. Your mother wasn't on the pill. I should have acted more responsibly."

"Bet you shit when she told you."

"I'll admit that it came as a shock. For your mother as well as me. She was about to graduate and launch her career. I was beginning grad school. Her pregnancy was a hurdle neither of us had counted on at that time in our lives. But—and I want you to believe this, Gavin—abortion was never even considered."

He could tell by his son's expression that he wanted desperately to believe that, but was still finding it difficult to accept. Dean couldn't blame him. Perhaps he and Pat had been wrong to not discuss this with Gavin once he was old enough to understand how women became pregnant. If they had explained it to him, he wouldn't have developed insecurities about his self-worth, and harbored such resentment toward them.

"Nor was adoption discussed. From the start, Pat planned to have you and keep you. Thank God she paid me the courtesy of telling me that I had fathered a child. And when she did, I insisted that you have my name. I wanted to be in your life. Although neither of us wanted to marry the other, I wanted to make you legally mine. She finally agreed to go through with the ceremony.

"We didn't love each other, Gavin. I wish I could tell you otherwise, but it wouldn't be the truth, and that's what you've asked for and I think that's what you deserve to hear. We liked each other. We were companionable and respected each other. But we didn't love each other.

"We did, however, love you. When I held you for the first time,

I was nothing short of awed and overjoyed. Your mother felt the same. She and I lived together until you were born.

"During that time, we tried to convince ourselves that love would eventually blossom and that we'd come to realize we wanted to be together for the rest of our lives. But it wasn't going to happen and both of us knew it.

"We cried on the day we finally agreed that staying together would only make for three unhappy people and postpone the inevitable. It was in your best interest that we split sooner, before you could even remember, rather than later. So when you were three months old, she filed for divorce."

He spread his hands wide. "That's it, Gavin. I think it would help if you also talked to your mother about this. Understandably, she didn't want you to know because she didn't want you to think badly of her. I don't want that either. She wasn't a party girl who slept with every guy on campus. That weekend was the last fraternity party we would ever attend because we were both about to graduate. We got wild and crazy and . . . it happened.

"Your mother sacrificed a lot in order to raise you as a single parent. I know you're upset with her for marrying now, but that's just too damn bad. Pat's not only your mother, she's a woman. And if you're entertaining some childish fear that her husband is going to replace you in her life, you're wrong. Believe me, he couldn't. No one could."

"I don't think that," he said, speaking to his lap. "I'm not an idiot. I know she needs love and all that."

"Then maybe you should stop sulking about it and tell her that you understand."

He gave a noncommittal shrug of his shoulders. "I just wish you'd told me, you know, before now. I knew anyway."

"Well, if you knew anyway, and it didn't make a significant difference in your life, then why are you using it as an excuse now?"

His head snapped up. "An excuse?"

"Lasting marriages don't necessarily make for happy homes, Gavin. Lots of kids who live with both parents have a far worse childhood than you've had, and, believe me, I know this.

"You're using your accidental conception as an excuse to behave like a jerk. That's a cowardly cop-out. Your mother and I are human. We were young and reckless and made a mistake. But isn't it time you stopped brooding over *our* mistake and started accepting responsibility for your own?"

Anger infused Gavin's face with color. He breathed heavily through his nose. But tears had once again collected in his eyes.

"I love you, Gavin. With all my heart. I'm grateful for the mistake your mother and I made that night. I'd willingly die for you. But I refuse to let you use the circumstances of your birth to distract me from what is more imperative and, right now, considerably more critical."

He moved his chair closer to the one in which Gavin sat and planted his hand firmly on his shoulder. "I've talked to you frankly, man to man. Now I want you to act like a man and tell me what you've been holding back."

"Nothing."

"Bullshit. There's something you're not telling me."

"No there's not."

"You're lying."

"Get off my back, Dad!"

"Not until you tell me."

His features reflected the turmoil within as he wrestled with his fear and possibly his conscience. Finally he blurted out, "Okay, you want to know? I was in Janey's car with her that night."

Paris checked her wristwatch. She'd been waiting outside the CIB for over an hour. Dean's attorney, whom she recognized from the day before, had arrived. He'd disappeared through the doorway and into the department. Beyond that, she knew nothing of what was going on. She didn't know if they'd begun Gavin's lie detector test or not.

Lack of sleep was beginning to catch up with her. She leaned her head against the wall behind the bench and closed her eyes, but still she couldn't rest. Haunting thoughts crowded her mind. Janey Kemp was dead. A sick, twisted individual had killed her, but Paris felt partially responsible.

As Stan had so tactlessly reminded her, Valentino had been motivated by the advice she'd given Janey. If only she hadn't aired Janey's call-in that night, Valentino wouldn't have heard it.

But tragically, he had. Once he'd issued his threat to punish Janey, what could she, Paris, have done differently? What could she have said to prevent him from taking the final step and killing her?

"Ms. Gibson?"

She opened her eyes. Before her stood a petite woman who was evidently in distress. Her face, though very pretty, was drawn. She was holding her handbag in a death grip. The skin was stretched so tightly across her knuckles, they looked like bare bone. Anguish had reduced her from dainty to frail. Although she was putting up a brave front, she looked about as stalwart as a dandelion puffball.

Paris immediately tried to ease the stranger's apprehension with a smile. "Yes, I'm Paris."

"I thought it was you. May I join you?"

"Of course." Paris made room for her on the bench and the woman sat down. "I'm sorry, I . . . Have we met?"

"My name is Toni Armstrong. Mrs. Bradley Armstrong."

Paris recognized the name, of course, and immediately understood why the woman was discomfited. "Then I know why you're here, Mrs. Armstrong," she said. "This must be awfully difficult for you. I wish we were meeting under pleasanter circumstances."

"Thank you." She was hanging on to her composure by a thread, but she did hold on, and that earned her Paris's respect. "When the police searched our house, they overlooked this." She removed a CD from her handbag. "Since they confiscated Brad's computer, I thought I should hand this over, too. It could have something important on it."

A confusing thought caused Paris to frown. "Mrs. Armstrong, how did you recognize me?"

Even with all the news coverage the story of Janey's disappearance had generated, Paris's picture had been kept out of it. Wilkins Crenshaw had personally intervened and put pressure on the local media to not use her photograph. Paris had no delusions: He wasn't concerned for her. He wanted to protect the reputation of the radio station. In any case, the local media had agreed to extend that professional courtesy. She wasn't sure how long their largess would last.

Toni Armstrong nervously wet her lips and ducked her head. "This CD from Brad's computer was only the excuse I gave myself for coming to see Sergeant Curtis. The real reason is that I didn't tell him everything yesterday."

Paris said nothing, her silence inviting Toni Armstrong to continue.

"Sergeant Curtis asked me if Brad ever listened to late-night radio. I said yes, sometimes. He went on to ask something else and never came back to that subject. Your name wasn't mentioned, so I didn't volunteer that we—Brad and I—had known you from Houston."

Her eyes were imploring, almost as though willing Paris to remember on her own so she wouldn't be required to recount the circumstances under which they'd become introduced.

"I apologize, Mrs. Armstrong. I don't remember ever meeting you."

"You and I never actually met. You were Dr. Louis Baker's patient."

Suddenly Paris's memory crystallized. How could she not have remembered his name? Of course, Armstrong was an ordinary name. Neither Curtis nor Dean had mentioned that their suspect Brad Armstrong was a dentist.

"Your husband's a dentist? *That* dentist?"

Toni Armstrong nodded.

Paris inhaled a swift breath. "I'm so sorry."

"You don't owe me an apology, Ms. Gibson. What happened wasn't your fault. I didn't blame you. You did what you had to do. Brad felt differently, of course. He said that you . . . that you had flirted with him, led him on." She smiled sadly. "He always says that. But I never thought for a moment that you had encouraged him to do what he did."

Paris had gone to Dr. Louis Baker for some dental work, but when she arrived at the clinic, she was informed that he'd been called away on a family emergency. Her choice was to reschedule or let one of his partners treat her. The appointment had been postponed twice, she was already there, so she opted to see the other dentist.

She remembered Brad Armstrong as a nice-looking man with an engaging manner. Since she was scheduled for several procedures, some of which might be uncomfortable, he'd suggested using nitrous oxide to help her relax.

She'd agreed, knowing that "laughing gas" had no lasting effect as soon as one stopped inhaling it and that it was safe when administered in a clinical environment. Besides, if a numbing shot was required, she would just as soon not know when it was coming.

Soon she was feeling completely relaxed and carefree, as though she was floating. At first she thought she had only imagined that her breasts were being touched. The caress had been featherlight. Surely it was only a false physical sensation brought on by her state of euphoria.

But when it happened a second time, the pressure was distinctly firmer and applied directly to her nipple. There could be no mistake. She opened her eyes and, shaking off her lethargy, removed the small mask from her nose. Brad Armstrong smiled down at her, and the leering quality of his grin convinced her that she had imagined nothing.

"What the hell do you think you're doing?"

"Don't pretend you didn't enjoy it," he'd whispered. "Your nipple is still hard."

Even reclined in the dental chair as she was, she came off it like a shot, knocking over a metal tray of implements and sending it crashing to the floor. An assistant, whom he had sent out on a trumped-up errand, came rushing back into the treatment room. "Ms. Gibson, what's wrong?"

"Have Dr. Baker call me at his earliest convenience," she told her before storming out.

The dentist had called her later that day, expressing his concern. She reported what had happened. When she finished her story, he said with chagrin, "I'm ashamed to say that I thought the other woman was lying."

"He's done it before?"

"I assure you, Ms. Gibson, this will be the last time. You have my utmost apologies. I'll take care of it immediately."

Dr. Armstrong had been dismissed. For several days afterward, Paris had shuddered in repulsion whenever she thought about the incident, but after a time it had faded from her memory. She hadn't thought any more about it until now.

"I assume your husband blamed me for getting him fired."

"Yes. Although he's been forced out of other practices for similar incidents since then, he's always held a grudge against you. While you were still in Houston, he turned off the television set anytime you appeared. He called you ugly names. And when your fiancé got hurt, he said you deserved it."

"He knew about Jack, the accident?"

"And Dr. Malloy. He theorized that it was a love triangle."

Paris exclaimed, a soft "Oh."

"When we moved here and Brad discovered you were on the radio, his resentment flared up again." Mrs. Armstrong lowered her head and twisted the straps of her handbag. "I should have told Sergeant Curtis about this yesterday, but I was so afraid they would think Brad was involved with this missing-girl case."

"She's no longer missing." When Paris told her that Janey Kemp's body had been discovered, Toni Armstrong finally lost her valiant battle against tears.

chapter *twenty-nine*

Anytime John Rondeau crossed paths with Dean Malloy, he went out of his way to be nothing but pleasant. But Malloy treated him with patent animosity. Curtis had noticed. Rondeau had overheard him asking Malloy what the problem was. Malloy had replied with a gruff, "Nothing," and Curtis hadn't pressed him.

As far as Rondeau was concerned, Malloy could glower at him until hell froze over. It was Curtis he wanted to butter up, not Malloy. The psychologist had the higher ranking, but it was Curtis who could recommend Rondeau for CIB.

As for Malloy's kid, he had him right where he wanted him, which was scared out of his skivvies. The results of the lie detector test had been in his favor and had basically cleared him of suspicion. So, one might wonder, why was he still so fidgety?

He was sitting in a chair near Curtis's desk, his shoulders hunched in a self-defensive posture. A bundle of nerves, he couldn't sit still. His eyes darted about fearfully. He looked like he would disintegrate if somebody said "Boo!"

Only Rondeau knew why the boy still looked so scared, and he wasn't telling. Neither was Gavin. Rondeau was confident of the kid's silence. He had frightened him sufficiently that he wasn't about to tattle on him. Brilliant to think of threatening his dad, not him. That had done the trick.

It was crowded inside Curtis's cubicle, where they'd all gathered for a brainstorming session. Curtis was there, of course. Malloy. Gavin. And Paris Gibson.

Rondeau welcomed any opportunity to share space with her, though it was hard for her to notice him with Malloy stamping around repeating ad nauseam that he feared she would be next on Valentino's to-do list.

Rondeau had stumbled on to this meeting when he came to report to Curtis what he'd found on the CD Mrs. Armstrong had hand-delivered to Paris. It wasn't all that earthshaking, but he grabbed any opportunity to impress Curtis and bump up his chances of getting into the CIB.

Paris—innocently, of course—had stolen his thunder before his arrival. What Toni Armstrong had withheld from him while he was searching her house, she had imparted to Paris—her husband had fondled Paris when she'd been his patient.

Had Mrs. Armstrong shared this with him and he'd been the one to bring it to Curtis's attention, it would have been a real feather in his cap. As it was, he'd have to earn that feather by some other means.

"I've got a bad feeling about this guy," Sergeant Curtis was saying of the dentist. "Has he contacted his wife today?" he asked Paris.

"She says no. All her attempts to reach him have been unsuccessful."

"If he called her from his cell, we could place him using satellite," Malloy remarked.

"I'm sure that's why he hasn't done it," said Rondeau, hoping he'd made Malloy sound like a fool. His neck was still sore from Malloy's squeeze yesterday. He and Malloy were never going to be friends, but he didn't consider that any great loss.

"Have you checked out his phone records?" Malloy asked.

"Working on it," Curtis replied. "It'll look really bad for him if he's made repeated calls to the radio station." Turning back to Paris, he asked, "Mrs. Armstrong didn't recognize his voice on the tapes?"

"She's listening to them again, but I'm not sure how reliable her input will be. She's very upset. When I told her about Janey, she underwent an emotional meltdown that I think had been brewing for days."

"Would you recognize Brad Armstrong on sight?"

Paris frowned. "I don't think so. The incident happened a long time ago. I saw him only that one time, and I was high on nitrous oxide."

"Would a photograph be helpful?" Rondeau asked, nudging Malloy aside and wedging himself into the center of the enclosure.

"Possibly," Paris said.

He produced the CD that Toni Armstrong had brought from home and given to Paris. "Apparently Brad Armstrong scanned photos and burned them onto CDs. The ones we found during the search had porno shots taken out of magazines on them.

"But this last one has family photographs on it. I brought it back so it could be returned to Mrs. Armstrong, but it may be useful now. May jiggle your memory, Paris."

"Can't hurt to take a look," said Curtis. He booted up the computer on his desk, then stepped aside so Rondeau could sit down. He was aware of Paris moving in close behind him to get a better look at the monitor screen. He caught a whiff of a clean scent, like shampoo.

He executed the necessary keystrokes and within seconds a snapshot filled the screen. The family of five was posed in front of an attraction at a theme park. Parents and kids were wearing American clothing and American smiles, living the American Dream.

Rondeau turned toward Paris. "Look familiar?"

For several moments, she studied the man in the photograph. "Honestly, no. If I had spotted him in a crowd, I wouldn't have immediately recognized him as the man who fondled me. It was too long ago."

"You're sure you haven't seen him recently?" Malloy asked. "If he resented you as much as Mrs. Armstrong indicated, he might have been stalking you."

"If I have seen him, it didn't register."

Curtis, who was still studying the Armstrong family snapshot, said, "I wonder who took the picture."

"Probably he did," Rondeau said. "A guy who has a scanner and makes a CD photo album—"

"Would be into cameras," Curtis finished for him. He turned to Gavin. "Janey told you her new boyfriend took that picture of her, correct?"

The kid withered beneath the attention of everyone in the room. His left knee was doing a jackhammer number. "Yes, sir. When she gave me the picture, she said he'd taken that one and lots of others. She said he liked taking the pictures almost as much as the sex."

"I don't recall any camera equipment being found during the search of their house," Rondeau said. "But he's got to have a setup or he wouldn't have these family photographs. Some were taken with wide-angle or telephoto lenses."

"Has the lab turned up anything on that photo Janey gave Gavin?" Malloy asked.

Querulously Curtis shook his head. "The only prints on it belonged to Janey and Gavin."

"Sergeant Curtis?" Griggs poked his head in, interrupting.

"In a minute," the detective told him.

"What about the local outlets for photographic supplies?" Malloy asked.

"Still being investigated," Curtis said. "Running down their clients is a time-consuming process."

"You wouldn't think that many people had their own darkrooms," Malloy said.

"Mail-order customers. Faxed-in orders. People ordering online. It's a chore."

Griggs interrupted a second time. "Sergeant Curtis, this is important."

But Curtis's mind was moving down a single track. He addressed the detectives who had clustered just outside his cubicle. Some didn't work homicide cases, but he'd asked everyone in the unit for their cooperation and time if they could spare it.

"Somebody determine if there's a darkroom in Brad Armstrong's home. Garage, attic, toolshed, extra bathroom. I don't care how crude." One of the detectives peeled away from the group in a hurry.

"We need Brad Armstrong's telephone records ASAP. Find out what's taking so long." Another detective rushed away to carry out that assignment.

"Print out a picture of him—no family members, just him. Get it to all the TV stations in time for their first evening newscasts. He's wanted for questioning, got it? *Questioning*," he stressed to the detective who reached for the CD that Rondeau helpfully ejected from Curtis's computer.

"Also distribute it to the intelligence officers who're checking out those photo places," Curtis called out across the cubicles. "Have it faxed to all the other agencies that are helping us in the search."

That business dispatched, Rondeau said, "Sir, I apologize for not putting it together sooner."

"Never mind." Curtis, dismissing him in a way that stung, turned to Paris. "His wife will be our best source of information. Are you sure she'll cooperate?"

"Absolutely. Whether or not he's Valentino, she wants him to be found and has promised to cooperate in any way she can."

Curtis bobbed his head at a plainclothes policewoman. "Ask Mrs. Armstrong who takes their family photographs. Make it conversational."

While everyone was distracted, Rondeau looked over at Gavin Malloy and winked. The boy mouthed, *Get fucked*. Rondeau smiled.

"Sergeant?" Griggs was still making a nuisance of himself. "Excuse me?"

Finally Curtis turned to him and growled, "What is it, for christsake?"

"S . . . somebody to see you, sir," he stammered. "And . . . and Ms. Gibson."

"Somebody? Who?"

Griggs pointed across the tops of the cubicle walls. Curtis and Paris followed him through the maze of tiny offices to the double-door entrance where two uniformed patrolmen were holding a handcuffed man between them.

Paris exclaimed, "Marvin!"

Lancy Ray Fisher was seated at the table in one of the interrogation rooms. Paris sat across from him while Curtis stood at one end and Dean at the other. Even though they'd been focused on Dr. Brad Armstrong, the man she knew as Marvin Patterson remained a viable suspect.

He'd walked into police headquarters and introduced himself to the officers at the lobby desk. Recognizing him instantly, they had put his hands in restraints for his elevator ride up to the third floor. He'd put up no resistance whatsoever. Each time Paris and he made eye contact, he looked away quickly, appearing to be guilty of something.

She was surprised by how nice looking he was without his baggy coveralls and the baseball cap he wore to work. She'd never seen his face in full light. Nor had he seen hers, she reminded herself. Maybe that's why his glances at her weren't only guilty, but also curious.

"Should I get a lawyer?" he asked Curtis.

"I don't know, should you?" the detective replied coolly. "You're the one who called this meeting and insisted on Paris being in on it. You tell me if you need a lawyer."

"I don't. Because I can tell you right off, and it's the God's truth, I had nothing to do with that girl's kidnapping and murder."

"We haven't accused you of having had anything to do with it."

"Then why'd those guys downstairs pounce on me and put me in these?" He thrust his cuffed hands toward Curtis.

Unfazed, Curtis replied, "I'd have thought you'd be used to them, Lancy. You've been in them often enough."

The young man slumped back in his chair, acknowledging the verity of that.

"Marvin," Paris said, getting his attention, "they found tapes of my shows, a large number of tapes, in your apartment. I'd like to know why you had them."

"My real name is Lancy."

"I'm sorry. Lancy. Why did you collect all those tapes?"

Dean said, "To us, it looks like you have an obsessive interest in her."

"I swear, it's not what you're thinking."

"What am I thinking?" Dean asked.

"That it's for some kinky reason. It's not. I . . . I've been studying her." He looked at their baffled faces. "I, uh, I want to be like her. Do what she does, I mean. I want to be on the radio."

If he'd said he wanted to pilot a nuclear submarine through the capitol rotunda, they couldn't have been more astonished.

Paris was the first to recover. "You want a career in radio broadcasting?"

"I guess you think that's crazy, considering my criminal record and all."

"I don't think it's crazy. I'm just surprised. When did you decide on this career path?"

"A couple years back. When I got out of Huntsville and started listening to you every night."

"Why Paris, specifically? Why not another deejay?"

"Because I liked the way she talked to people," he said to Dean. Then he turned back to her. "It seemed like you really cared about the people who called in, like you cared about their problems." Looking abashed, he added, "For a while there, I had it pretty rough. Getting back into life on the outside. You were like my only friend."

Curtis was staring at him with a skeptical scowl. Dean, too, was frowning. But Paris gave him a smile that encouraged him to continue.

"One night this guy called, told you he'd been laid off from his job and couldn't find another. You said it seemed to you that his confidence had suffered, and that's when you should aim the highest, reach the farthest.

"I took the advice you gave him. I stopped trying to get penny-ante jobs and applied at the telephone company. They hired me. I was making good money, enough to pay for voice lessons. Better clothes. A good car. But I got greedy, lifted some equipment I knew I could hock fast. They didn't file charges but they fired me."

He fell silent, as though castigating himself for such a bad judgment call. Paris looked over at Dean. He lifted his shoulders as though to say that Lancy could either be telling the truth or telling a whopper.

"After a few weeks of unemployment," he continued, "I couldn't believe my good fortune when I saw the ad in the paper about a job at the radio station. I didn't care that it was cleaning out the crapper . . . uh, toilets. I wanted to be in that environment any way I could get in. So I could observe you. See how you work. Maybe even pick up some of the technology.

"I rigged a recorder up to my radio at home and had it timed to tape every show. During the daytime, I'd replay the tapes and try to imitate the way you talked. I practiced, trying to get your diction and the rhythm of your speech down. I took more lessons to get rid of my accent."

He shot her a grin. "As you can hear, that's going to take a lot more work. And of course I know I'll never be as good as you no matter how hard I work at it. But I'm determined to give it my best shot. I wanted to . . . I *had* to, what do they call it?"

"Reinvent yourself?" she guessed.

His eyes lit up. "Yeah, that's it. That's why I was using an alias. My real name sounds too much like where I came from."

Curtis tossed a folder onto the table and when Lancy saw that it was his criminal record, he winced. "I know it looks bad, but I swear to God I've put that life behind me."

"It's a long list of wrongdoing, Lancy. Did you find Jesus in Huntsville, or what?"

"No, sir. I just didn't want to be trash for the rest of my life."

Curtis harrumphed, unconvinced.

Lancy glanced around and must have realized that they were still skeptical. He wet his lips and in a tone of desperation said, "I wouldn't do anything to hurt Paris. She's my idol. I haven't made any threatening phone calls. As for that girl who turned up dead, I don't know anything."

Curtis propped a hip on the corner of the table and addressed the younger man in a deceptively friendly way. "You like high school girls, Lancy Ray?"

"Sir?"

"You dropped out of school at sixteen."

"I got my GED while I was in prison."

"But you skipped all the fun of high school. Maybe you're making up for what you missed."

"Like the girls, you mean?"

"Yeah, that's what I mean."

He shook his head emphatically. "I don't pick up underage girls and have sex with them. I'm not perfect, but that's not my thing."

"Do you like women?"

"You mean, over men? Hell, yes."

"You've got a handsome face. Good build. It can get awfully lonely in prison."

Self-consciously Lancy cast a look at Paris, then lowered his head and muttered, "They left me alone. I stabbed one in the . . . in the testicles with a fork. I got a year tacked onto my sentence for it, but they didn't bother me after that."

She was embarrassed for him. She hoped Curtis would let up, but she was afraid that if she interfered he would ask her to leave and she wanted to hear this.

Curtis said, "I met your mother yesterday."

Lancy raised his head and looked directly at the detective. "She's a cow."

"Whoa! Did you hear that, Dr. Malloy? Did that sound like latent hostility toward a female? A resentment—"

"I don't like my mother," Lancy said heatedly, "but that doesn't carry over into my sex life. If that was your mother, would you like her?"

Curtis persisted. "Do you have a girlfriend?"

"No."

"Want one?"

"Sometimes."

"Sometimes," Curtis repeated. "When you get a hankering for a girlfriend, what do you do?"

"What do you mean?"

"Come on, Lancy Ray." Curtis tapped the folder with a blunt index finger. "You were sent up for sexual assault."

"That was a bullshit rap."

"That's what all rapists say."

"This guy, this movie producer—"

"A pornographer."

"Right. We were making triple-X-rated skin flicks in his garage. He got upset when his girl started coming on to me. It was all right for us to . . . you know, while his camera was rolling. But not in private. So he and I got into it and—"

"And you cut him up pretty bad."

"It was self-defense."

"The jury didn't buy it, and neither do I," Curtis said. "When you finished with him, you started in on the girl."

"No, sir!"

He denied it so emphatically and indignantly that Paris had to believe he was telling the truth. "It was him. He worked her over good." He pointed to the folder. "All those things that were done to her, he did."

"They collected your DNA."

"Because she and I had been together earlier that day. He caught us. That's what started the fight."

"His testimony was corroborated under oath by two of the production crew and the girl herself."

"They were all junkies. He fed them dope. I didn't have anything to offer in exchange for them telling the truth."

Dean asked, "Why should we believe your version of this, Lancy?"

"Because I own up to all my other crimes. I did some awful things, but I never beat up a woman."

Paris leaned across the table toward him. "Why did you run away when the officers called to say they wanted to question you? Why didn't you tell them what you're telling us now?"

He sighed heavily and raised his cuffed hands to rub his forehead. "I freaked. I'm an ex-con. That automatically makes me a suspect. Then, I knew if they discovered that I'd been taping your shows, they'd for sure haul me in."

"Why did you leave the tapes behind?"

He smiled shyly. "Because I'm stupid. I panicked and got the hell out of there. Forgot them. Maybe I've lost my criminal instinct. I hope I have."

He had a safe-effacing manner that Paris liked. But Curtis didn't appear to be charmed by it.

"If you had admitted this to us the day before yesterday, we might have come closer to believing you."

Lancy looked at Paris and said earnestly, "I'm telling the truth. I don't know anything about this Valentino character or those phone calls. I don't know anything about Janey Kemp except what I've heard on the news. The only thing I'm guilty of is wanting to learn to do what you do."

"You've been working at the station for months," she said softly, "but you've never even engaged me in conversation. Why didn't you come and talk to me about your ambition? Ask for advice? Guidance?"

"Are you kidding?" he exclaimed. "You're a star. I'm the guy who pushes around the mop bucket. I'd never have worked up my nerve to talk to you. And if I had, you would have laughed at me."

"I would never have done that."

He searched her eyes, behind her lenses. "No, maybe you wouldn't have. I see that now."

"Where've you been all this time?" Curtis asked. "You didn't return to your mom's place or your apartment."

"I keep a . . . I guess you'd call it a—"

"Hideout?" Curtis prompted.

Lancy looked abashed. "Yes, sir. I'll give you the address. You're welcome to search it."

"You can bet we will," Curtis said as he hooked his hand beneath Lancy's arm and hoisted him from the chair. "And while we're at it, you'll be residing with us here."

chapter *thirty*

*I*t was a great bar for trolling.

It was on the lakeshore, a cedar-shingle place well known to the locals. Fishermen might stumble upon it, but it wasn't a watering hole that would attract tourists or country club golfers. The clientele was comprised mostly of construction workers, cowboys, and biker types. A white-collar professional would feel out of his element, so it was highly unlikely that Brad Armstrong would be spotted here by anyone he knew.

Peanut shells crunched underfoot as he made his way across the dim barroom. It was lighted only by neon signs, nearly all boasting the Lone Star flag and a brand of beer. The shaded fixtures suspended over the billiards tables provided supplemental lighting, but it was obscured by tobacco smoke.

The bubbling Wurlitzer in the corner emanated a revolving rainbow of pastel colors, but there was nothing subtle about the music blaring from it. It was old country, the twangy, wailing, woebegone kind, pre Garth, McGraw, and the like.

Customers drank beer from the bottle, Jack Daniel's, or Jose Cuervo straight. Which was what the girl was shooting when Brad joined her at the bar. He recognized her immediately. That she was here today, now, was a cosmic sign that he was doing nothing wrong.

He glanced down at the two empty shot glasses in front of her and motioned for the bartender to serve up two more. "One for me and one for the lady with the nipple ring."

She turned to him. "How'd you— Oh, hi. Coupla nights ago, right?"

He grinned. "I'm glad you remember."

"You're the guy with all the porno."

His face registered a crestfallen expression. "I was hoping you'd remember me for my . . . other memorable quality."

She licked her upper lip and smiled. "That, too."

"I wouldn't expect to find you in a place like this," he said. "You outclass it."

"I hang out in here sometimes." She cracked a peanut shell between her teeth and daintily ate the nuts. "Before the Sex Club starts gathering." She dropped the shell onto the floor and dusted off her hands. "You don't exactly blend either."

"I think we were destined to see each other again."

"Cool," she said.

Makeup had been slathered on to make her look legally old enough to drink. Either the bartender was fooled or, more likely, didn't care that she was underage. He served the tequila shots that Brad had ordered.

"What shall we drink to?"

She rolled her large, dark eyes toward the ceiling as though the answer might be written in the chemically polluted layer of smoke that hovered there. "How about body piercing?"

Leaning forward, he whispered, "I get hard just thinking about it." He clinked his glass to hers and simultaneously they tossed back the fiery liquor.

This was so damn easy, he thought. Didn't mothers warn their daughters against talking to strangers anymore? Didn't they tell them never, ever to go with a man they didn't know? What was the world coming to? It made him afraid for his daughters.

But thinking about his family killed the mood, so he tucked thoughts of them safely away and ordered another round of tequila shots.

After that one they agreed to leave. He smiled smugly as they passed the pool tables. He was the envy of tough guys with tattoos on their arms and knives attached to their thick leather belts. He'd been successful where apparently they had not. Maybe because his hair was clean.

"It's Melissa, right?" he asked as he held the car door open for her.

Her glossy red lips smiled over his remembering her name. "Where are we going?"

"I've got a room."

"Super."

Ridiculously easy.

Coming out this evening wasn't a wise thing to do, but he couldn't have stayed cooped up another minute or he would have gone crazy. He couldn't return home. Toni had been calling his cell phone at fifteen-minute intervals all day, begging him to come back. The police only wanted to talk to him, she said. *Right,* he thought. *They want to talk to me through iron bars.*

He hadn't answered his phone and he hadn't called her, knowing that the police had probably set up a system of tracking his cell by satellite. The discovery of Janey's body didn't bode well for him. News reports had said that an autopsy was being conducted. Hearing that had nearly sent him over the edge.

He'd fretted, stewed, paced, lambasted his wife for not understanding him, and Janey for being a cock teaser he couldn't resist, even his mother, who'd punished him severely for masturbating when he was little.

Truthfully, he didn't remember such a time, but psychologists had asked him during therapy sessions if he'd been so punished and he'd said yes because that seemed to be the expected and accepted explanation for his sexual preoccupation.

As the news reports went from bad to worse, actually including his name in them, his anxiety increased. He had tried to distract himself by looking at his pornographic magazines, reading the letters and "true" experiences submitted by subscribers. But soon familiarity had made them boring. Besides, his craving wasn't going to be satisfied vicariously.

He was aroused and needed relief. With the pressure he'd been under recently, who could blame him? He resolved that if relief wasn't going to come looking for him, he would have to go looking for it.

Now he'd found it.

"This isn't the car you were in the other night," Melissa remarked as she punched through radio stations until she found one playing a thrumming rap song.

The police would've spotted his car, so he had called and ordered one from a rental place that delivered. Not a chain outfit that required all kinds of documentation, but one that, according to their yellow pages ad, would take cash. That signaled to Brad a business that was light on rules and regulations. The only amenity promised was a working air conditioner in all their cars.

While waiting for it to arrive, he'd showered and dressed, splashed on the Aramis, and put a supply of condoms in his pants pocket.

As anticipated, the man who delivered the car looked as if his next stop might be a 7-Eleven store he could rob. Brad flashed him his driver's license and filled out a form with false information. He'd counted out the required deposit and added ten bucks for a tip. The man spoke only limited English and didn't seem to care one way or the other what day Brad promised to return the ten-year-old car to their lot.

"Had we met before?" Melissa asked him now. "Before the other night, I mean. You look familiar."

"I'm a famous movie star."

"That must be it," she said, giggling.

To distract her from that train of thought, he said, "Do you always look this sensational?"

"You think?"

Actually she looked like a whore. The dyed hair was spiked stiffer and higher than it had been the other night. Outside the dimness of the bar, her makeup looked even more garish. Her halter top was made of some flimsy fabric through which he could see her dangling silver nipple ring. Most table napkins were larger than her skirt.

In short, she was asking for it. She should thank him for saving her from being gang-banged by the rednecks in the bar.

He drew her eyes down to his lap. "See what you're doing to me."

She assessed the distention behind his trousers, then said, "Is that the best you can do?" and leaned back against the passenger door. She idly brushed her fingertips across the nipple with the ring piercing it.

The girl knew her stuff. His erection stretched. "I can't watch you and drive."

She gave the nipple ring a teasing yank.

He groaned. "You're killing me, you know that?"

"But you'll die happy."

He reached across the console and slid his hand beneath her skirt, felt the scratch of lace against his fingers, then worked his way past it.

"Hmm. Right there." Melissa closed her eyes. "Don't get stopped for speeding. At least not till after I come."

Gavin was waiting outside the CIB when Dean, Paris, and Sergeant Curtis emerged. His hope was riding on Lancy Ray Fisher. He shot to his feet, asking, "Was he the guy?"

"We don't know yet," his dad told him. "Sergeant Curtis is going to keep him here, ask him some more questions."

Paris glanced at her wristwatch. "If it's no trouble, I'd like to stop at my house before going to the station. I ran out in such a rush this morning."

"I'll drive you and drop Gavin at home on the way," Dean said. "We'll have our cell phones on, Curtis. If anything happens—"

"I'll call right away," he assured them. "I'm going to lean on Lancy Ray."

"With all due respect, I don't believe he's Valentino," Paris said.

The detective nodded. Gavin thought he looked very tired. A blond bristle had begun to sprout from his pink cheeks. "I'm still partial to Dr. Armstrong," he told them, "but I'm not ready to give up on Lancy Fisher just yet. I'll be in touch."

They were turning toward the elevators when Curtis spoke Gavin's name. His first thought was, *What now?* But he said, "Yes, sir?"

"I'm sorry I had to put you through that today. I know it wasn't any fun."

"It's okay," he said, not really meaning it. It hadn't been okay at all. He'd hated being made to feel guilty when he wasn't. "I hope you find out who did that to Janey. I should've told you from the beginning that she and I were in her car. But I was afraid you'd think, well, what you thought. I guess she met whoever killed her after she got rid of me."

"It appears that way. Are you absolutely certain she never mentioned who she was meeting afterward? A name? Occupation?"

"I'm positive."

"Well, thanks," Curtis said. "I appreciate your cooperation."

His dad nudged him toward the elevators and they left. Gavin sat in the backseat on the way home. Nobody said much, each seemed lost in his own thoughts. When they reached the house, a patrol car with two officers inside it was already parked out front. Inwardly Gavin groaned. He'd had his fill of policemen today. If he never saw one again—except his dad—it would be too soon.

"I don't need baby-sitters, Dad. Or am I still grounded?"

"You're grounded, but the cops are for your protection. They stay until Valentino is caught."

"He's not gonna—"

"I'm not taking any chances, Gavin. Besides, the guards are Curtis's mandate, not mine."

"You could call them off if you wanted to."

"I don't want to. All right?" When his dad was wearing that face, the argument was over. He nodded grudgingly. Then his dad reached over the seat and laid his hand on his shoulder. "I was proud of the way you conducted yourself today."

"At the risk of sounding patronizing, so was I, Gavin," Paris told him.

"Thanks."

"Call my cell immediately if anything happens. Promise me you will."

"I promise, Dad." He climbed out. "'Bye, Paris."

"'Bye. See you soon, okay?"

"Yeah, that'd be great."

He shuffled up the walkway. They didn't pull away until he had let himself in. Unlike his mom and dad, the two of them looked right together. He sorta hoped it would work out between them.

He waved at them from the front door before shutting and bolting it, effectively becoming his own jailer.

"Penny for them."

Paris looked across at Dean. "My thoughts? I was thinking about Toni Armstrong. I feel for her. I like her."

"So do I. Brave lady."

"I think she loves her husband. Deeply. Under the circumstances, that must be very conflicting." Curious, she asked, "From a clinical standpoint, when is a person considered a sex addict?"

"Tricky question."

"I'm sure you can address it, Dr. Malloy."

"All right. If a guy gets twelve hard-ons in a day, I'd congratulate him and probably urge him to try for thirteen. If he *acts* on twelve hard-ons in a day, I'd say that's a little excessive and we could have a problem."

"You're being facetious."

"Somewhat, but there's a basis of truth." His grin relaxed and he became serious. "Sex can become an addiction like anything else can. When the compulsion outweighs common sense and caution. When the activity begins to have a negative effect on one's work, family life, relationships. When it becomes the governing force and the exclusive means of personal gratification."

He glanced at her, and with a nod she prompted him to continue. "It's the same point at which a social drinker becomes an alcoholic. The individual loses control over the craving. Conversely, the craving gains control over the individual."

"Like making him willing to sacrifice a wife and family to get his thrills."

"That doesn't mean that Brad Armstrong doesn't love his wife," he said. "He probably does."

Reflecting on that, she stared through the front windshield. Even behind her sunglasses, she had to squint against the setting sun, which was doing a bang-up job of it. She wondered what Judge and Marian Kemp were doing just now. This spectacular sunset would go unnoticed by them.

"They have a funeral to arrange."

"I'm sorry?" Dean said.

"Thinking out loud. About the Kemps now."

"Yeah," he said with a sigh. "I can't imagine how devastating it would be to lose a child. I've counseled cops who did, but to my own ears, every word I said to them sounded like so much crap. If anything happened to Gavin . . ." He stopped, as though unable to articulate the dreadful thought. Then he said quietly, "I want to be a good parent to him, Paris."

"I know."

"Because of my own dad."

"I know that, too."

"How much did Jack tell you?"

"Enough."

He had told her that Dean's relationship with his father had been volatile. Mr. Malloy had a fierce temper, and Dean usually caught the brunt of it. Sometimes his dad's rages had turned violent.

"Did your father beat you, Dean?" she asked.

"He could give me a hard time, yeah."

"Is that a gross understatement?"

He shrugged with an indifference she knew was phony. "I could take his shit," he said. "When he started in on my mom, that's what I couldn't take."

According to Jack, the defining incident had taken place when Dean's parents visited him for homecoming weekend his sophomore year at Texas Tech. During a party at the fraternity house, Dean's father had picked an argument with him. Dean tried to ignore it, but his father became increasingly vituperative and wouldn't be put off.

His mother, embarrassed for her son, tried to intervene. That's when Dean's father began disparaging her. His words were humiliating and cruel. Heedless of his friends and the other parents looking on, Dean took up the banner for his mother. His dad threw a punch. Before it was over, Dean was straddling Mr. Malloy's chest and, in Jack's words, "pounding the shit out of him."

After that night their relationship became even more antagonistic, and it remained so until his father died.

"I went a little crazy that time at Tech," he said now. "I'd never been like that before, and I haven't lost my temper like that since. If Jack and some of the others guys hadn't pulled me off him, I might have killed him. I wanted to kill him.

"I hated like hell that it happened, because of the embarrassment to my mom. But at least it made the old man think twice before he lit into her again, especially if I was around." He glanced at Paris; she'd never seen him look as vulnerable. "But it scared the hell out of me, Paris. I can't even describe it. A red rage? It consumed me, blotting out everything else.

"My dad launched into fits like that all the time. That night I learned that whatever caused him to be the way he was, it's inside me, too. It came out that once. I live in fear of it happening again."

Reaching across the console, she laid her hand on his arm. "He provoked you in the meanest way. You reacted. But that doesn't mean that you have this latent rage that can ignite in an instant. You're not like him, Dean," she said with emphasis. "You never were and never could be.

"As for Gavin, it's allowed to get angry with him. Kids anger and disappoint and make their folks crazy. That's what they do. It's inherent in being a kid. And it's all right for you to get mad at him when he does.

"In fact, Gavin might doubt that you love him if you didn't get mad at him. He needs to know you care enough to get angry. He's going to test you often, just to reassure himself that you still care." Then she laughed. "Listen to me. You're the psychologist and the parent. I'm neither."

"Everything you're saying is right, though, and I need to hear it."

She smiled at him gently. "As long as you praise him at least as much, if not more, than you punish him, you'll be fine."

He mulled it over for a moment, then winked at her. "Smart as well as beautiful. You're a dangerous woman, Paris."

"Oh yeah, that's me. A regular femme fatale."

"Maybe that's what attracted Lancy Ray Fisher. Your element of mystery appealed to his criminal instinct."

She rolled her eyes. "He wants my job."

"So he says."

"You think he's lying?"

"If he is, he's convincing. He's either sincere or a damn good con artist."

"That was my impression, too."

"What's it like to be someone's idol?"

She gave him a sad smile. "I don't recommend that anyone pattern his life after mine."

Just then his cell phone rang. He answered it with one hand. "Malloy . . . Huh, speak of the devil. No, Paris and I were just talking about him." He mouthed *Curtis* and she nodded.

"What about Lancy's home away from home?" He listened for a moment, then said, "Probably not a bad idea." Curtis had more to tell him, then Dean signed off with, "Okay, stay in touch."

After disconnecting, he updated Paris. "He 'drilled Lancy Ray good,' is the way Curtis put it. But Lancy is sticking to his story."

Officers sent to the apartment where he had been holed up reported that Lancy had been there, but it didn't appear that anyone else had.

"No sign of Janie being held captive there?" Paris asked.

"None. No amateur photo lab. Nothing naughtier than one issue of *Playboy*. So Curtis is hotter than ever for the dentist. He's about to have a heart-to-heart with Toni Armstrong."

"Hmm, what a dilemma for her. On the one hand, she wants her husband apprehended so he can get help, but on the other, she's incriminating him."

"He incriminated himself."

"I know that. I'm thinking as she will. She loves him and wants him to be healed, but if he's beyond healing, how long can she be expected to stand by her man?"

"Good question, Paris."

Too late she realized that what she had said about Toni Armstrong could apply to herself.

Dean pulled his car to a stop at the curb in front of her house. Cutting the engine, he turned to face her, ready to speak, but she cut him off before he could.

"Jack needed me."

"*I* need you."

"Hardly in the same way."

"That's right. You were with him out of obligation. I want you to choose to be with me." He held her stare for several seconds, then pushed open his car door and got out.

As they went up the walkway, she stopped to collect her mail, which had been neglected for the last two days. Once they were inside the house, she tossed the bundle onto the entry table. "Lord knows when I'll get to that. My desk at work is even—"

That was all she had time to say before Dean pulled her into his arms and kissed her. While doing so, he removed her sunglasses and dropped them on the table. Then he embraced her tightly, drawing her up against him. Immediately responsive, her arms slid beneath his to encircle his torso. She dug her fingertips into the muscles of his back.

As his mouth fused with hers, he gathered up the fabric of her skirt until he could stroke her bare thigh. Her insides melted, but she pulled her mouth free of his kiss, gasping, "Dean, I've only got an hour."

"Then that'll be a record for us. So far our sexual encounters have lasted no longer than three minutes." He buried his face in her hair. "This time, I want to see you naked."

Laughing deep in her throat, she moved her head against his. "What if you don't like what you see?"

"Not a chance in hell."

He pushed his hands into her panties and gripped her ass. She made a low sound of pleasure but the voice of reason was louder. "What if Curtis calls?"

"I've learned to live with disappointment. But all the more reason for us to get busy."

Taking her by the hand, he walked purposefully toward the bedroom, dragging her along behind him. A girlish giggle bubbled up from Paris's chest. Her heart began to race. She felt terribly wicked and wonderfully, gloriously alive.

Dean was laughing, too, as he dealt with the stubborn fabric-covered buttons on her top. "Damn these things."

She was more deft. His shirt was soon open and she pressed a kiss against the warm skin just below his left nipple, feeling his heart beating against her lips.

Finally having succeeded with the buttons, he removed her top and unclasped the front fastener of her brassiere. Then his hands were on her, kneading her breasts with his strong fingers.

She watched his face as he looked down at her. His expression was at once passionate and tender as he saw her nipples responding to the glancing touches of his fingertips. His eyes met hers for barely a second before he dipped his head and took one into his mouth.

She unbuckled his belt and lowered his zipper, then worked her hand into the waistband of his underwear. He was velvety smooth, hard, throbbing with life. She rolled her thumb across his glans and he shuddered.

"Paris, stop," he said, stepping out of her reach. "If you . . . You can't do that. I'll come. And I want this to last."

She shrugged off her bra, then reached behind her to unfasten her skirt, pushed it past her hips, and stepped out of it. Feverishly, his eyes moved over her. In one swift motion, he removed his slacks and underwear. She gazed at him with frank appreciation, but when she reached for him again, he staved her off.

Then he dropped to his knees and kissed her through the silk bikini. His hands splayed over her bottom as he held her against his face. The heat and moisture of his breath filtering through the fabric made her weak. He kissed her again. And again. She closed her eyes and used his shoulders to brace herself.

Then the silk seemed to dissolve because the barrier was no longer there. His lips were hot and quick on her a heartbeat before she felt his tongue, separating and seeking and stroking. She gave herself over to the pleasure, and it was immense.

But she retained enough control to beg him to stop when it became critical. He came to his feet and enfolded her in his arms. They held one another tightly, her breasts crushed against his chest, his sex making a deep impression in the softness of her belly.

Finally, they lay down face-to-face on her bed, virgin until now. Her hand coasted over his torso, down past his navel, and into the dense hair surrounding his sex. She drew her finger up the length of his penis. He covered her hand with his and guided it up and down. "Jesus," he groaned.

"I can't quite believe this is happening."

"Me neither." He kissed her nipple, caressed it with his tongue. "I keep thinking that I'll wake up."

"If you do, please leave me in the dream."

He separated her legs and positioned himself between them, then entered her by degrees, giving her body time to accommodate him, pausing to test each new sensation before pressing deeper, until he was sheathed snugly and completely inside her.

Soaked in pleasure, they kept from moving as long as they could endure it, but it only got better when he withdrew, then thrust into her.

chapter thirty-one

Dean shook water from his ear as he raised his cell phone to it. "Malloy."

"Curtis."

"What's up?"

"What's that noise?"

"The shower," Dean replied, turning to wink at Paris, who was rinsing the shampoo from her hair. Head thrown back, soapy water streaming over her breasts and funneling between her legs. God, she was gorgeous.

"You're showering?"

"So I can look as fresh as you. What's up?" he repeated.

"One of the other detectives has been chatting with Lancy Ray. Remember when Paris asked him why all the subterfuge, why he hadn't just come to talk to her?"

"He was shy."

"That . . . and he didn't want to move in on another guy's territory."

"What guy?"

Paris looked at him with puzzlement as she stepped from the shower. He handed her a towel.

"Stan Crenshaw," Curtis said.

That was possibly the only statement that could have diverted his attention from Paris's naked form. "Pardon me?"

"That's right. Lancy Ray was operating under the misconception that Stan and Paris are lovers."

"Where'd he get that?"

"From Crenshaw."

Dean cupped the cell phone's mouthpiece and told Paris to

hurry and get dressed. His urgency must have communicated itself to her, because she rushed back into the bedroom. "Tell me," he said to Curtis.

"Crenshaw told the janitor not to bug her. Made up some bull-shit about it being company policy that he was the only one allowed access to her, told him she didn't like people staring at her because of her sunglasses, that she liked the darkness for reasons that were nobody's business.

"Lancy Ray wanted to keep his job, so he went along, kept his distance and rarely even spoke to her for fear of Crenshaw getting jealous and having him canned. He said the guy was jealous of anyone who went near her."

"Why didn't Lancy tell us this the first time we talked to him?" Dean asked as he struggled to dress himself with one hand.

"He took it for granted that everyone knew they were a couple."

"My ass. There's something about Crenshaw that isn't right. I knew it the night I met him. He took that proprietary stance with me, too, but I thought he was just a prick."

"Maybe he is just a prick."

"And maybe not. I want him turned inside out, Curtis. I want to know every fucking thing about him, and I don't care who his uncle is or how much money he has."

"I hear you. This time I'm skipping Uncle Wilkins. We're going straight to the Atlanta PD, the district attorney's office, the damn governor of Georgia if necessary. One good thing, he's carrying on business as usual. He's at the radio station. Griggs and Carson are there and just called in."

"We'll be on our way momentarily. Tell those rookies to keep him there if he tries to leave. Have you checked his phone records?"

"Under way."

"Who's doing the digging into his background?"

"Rondeau volunteered."

"Rondeau." Dean made no effort to mask his displeasure.

"He's going to run a thorough computer check."

"He was supposed to have done that already."

"I told him to go deeper this time."

"Would've been nice if he'd dug deeper the first time."

"What's with you and him? I sense tension."

"He's cocky."

"That's it? You don't like his personality?"

"Something like that. Look, we gotta run."

"Maybe Paris shouldn't do her show tonight. Give us a chance to check out Crenshaw."

"Tell her that. She's determined. Besides, I'm not budging from her side. Later."

Before the detective could say more, Dean hung up and hustled Paris out of the house. Once in the car, she asked for details. "From what I could gather, his call was about Stan."

He filled her in on what Lancy Ray Fisher had divulged. She let out an incredulous laugh. "I can't believe it."

"It's not funny."

"No, it's hysterical."

"I don't think so."

"Dean," she said, giving him a fond smile, "in light of recent, ahem, events, I can understand your male posturing. I'm flattered. I wish there were a dragon you could slay for me. But don't waste the machismo on Stan, for heaven's sake. He's not Valentino."

"We don't know that."

"*I* know. He's a prick, just as you said. And it upsets me that he misled Marvin—Lancy. And God knows who else. But he hasn't got the brains or the balls to be Valentino."

"We'll soon see," he said as he whipped his car into the station parking lot.

Griggs and Carson waved from the front seat of the squad car as she unlocked the door. As usual, the building was dark and the offices deserted. Harry, the evening deejay, gave her a thumbs-up through the window of the studio as they went past. Dean had learned the layout of the building and led the way through the dim hallways.

They reached her office, to find Stan seated at her desk, feet propped on the corner of it, desultorily sorting through her mail.

"Stan Crenshaw, just the person I wanted to see," Dean said as he strode in.

Stan lowered his feet from the desk, but they'd barely touched the floor before Dean took him by the front of his shirt and hauled him up from the chair.

"Hey!" Stan objected. "What the hell?"

"We need to have a little talk, Stan."

"Dean." Paris laid her cautionary hand on his arm. He released his grip on Stan's shirt.

"You've been telling lies about Paris."

Taking umbrage, Stan pulled himself up straighter and smoothed his hand over his rumpled shirt. But he might just as well have tried to defy a redwood, and he seemed to realize it. His gaze shifted to Paris. "What's your boyfriend talking about?"

"Lancy said that you told him—"

"Who the hell is Lancy?"

"Marvin Patterson."

"His name is Lancy?"

"You told him that you and Paris were sleeping together."

His head swiveled back to Dean. "No I didn't."

"Didn't you insinuate that you and she were more than coworkers? Didn't you warn him to back off, leave her alone, and not even talk to her?"

"Because I know how she is," Stan declared.

"Is that right?"

"Yeah, that's right. I know she's a private person. She doesn't like to be bothered by other people, especially while she's concentrating on work."

"So you told him to lay off in order to protect her privacy?"

"You could put it that way."

"I don't need you to screen the people I associate with, Stan," Paris said. "I didn't ask you to and I dislike the fact that you did."

"Well, gee, I'm sorry. I was trying to be a friend."

"Only a friend? I don't think so," Dean said. "I think you've been entertaining fantasies about Paris. You've deluded yourself into believing there's a romance between you two somewhere in your future. You're jealous of any other man who expresses an interest in her, even a platonic one."

"How do you know Marvin's interest is platonic?"

"He said it was."

"Oh, and he's to be believed over me? A janitor who's using an alias?" He made a scoffing snort. "You're the one who's delusional, *Doctor*." He headed for the door, but Dean's next words halted him.

"That possessiveness could be a strong motivator."

Stan turned around quickly. "For what?"

"Let's see, creating an ugly situation for which Paris would be partially blamed. Placing her job at risk. Placing her life in jeopardy. Shall I go on?"

"Are you talking about that Valentino business?" Stan asked angrily. "Paris brought that on herself."

"I see. It's her fault that Valentino kidnapped and murdered a seventeen-year-old girl."

"A girl who went asking for trouble."

With deceptive calm, Dean sat down on a corner of her desk. "Then your opinion of women is basically low?"

"I didn't say that."

"No, you didn't come right out and say it, but I sense a large chunk of hostility against the fairer sex lodged deep inside your psyche, Stan. Like a seed caught between two molars. It bugs you like hell, but you can't get it out."

"Wooooo." Stan waggled his fingers an inch from Dean's face. "Don't try that psychological hocus-pocus voodoo on me. There's nothing wrong with me."

Dean's jaw bunched with anger, but his voice remained calm. "So I'm to believe that all your dealings with women have been perfectly normal and problem free?"

"Has any man's dealings with women been perfectly normal and problem free? Have yours, Malloy?" He cut his eyes to Paris. "I think not."

"You're not Dean," Paris said quietly. "He doesn't have your history."

His mocking smugness vanished. In the next heartbeat, he was seething. "Did you tell him about the harassment charge?"

Dean turned to her. "The *what?*"

"At his previous job, a female employee accused Stan of sexual harassment."

Dean gave her a look that said he couldn't believe she hadn't shared this information with him before now. She realized that she'd been wrong not to. Probably she also should have told him about Stan's promiscuous parents and his overbearing uncle's cruelty.

Dean turned back to him. "Obviously you do have issues with women, Stan."

"She was the office whore!" he exclaimed. "She had slept with every other guy who worked there. She gave head to the anchorman under the desk during a newscast. She kept coming on to me and when I responded, she turned into a vestal virgin."

"Why?"

"Because she was more greedy than horny. She saw a way to get her hands on some of my family's money. She cried foul and my uncle paid her to shut up and go away."

Dean assimilated that, then said, "Let's go back to when you 'responded' to her."

"Wait, how come I have to answer your questions?"

"Because I'm a cop."

"Or because you've been in Paris's pants yourself?"

Dean's eyes narrowed dangerously. "Because if you don't answer my questions I'm going to take you downtown and lock you up until you get talkative. That's my official, professional answer. Off the record, my personal answer is that if you say anything like that about Paris again, I'm going to take you outside and smear some of your pretty face on the parking lot."

"Are you threatening me?"

"You bet your skinny ass I am. Now stop dicking around and tell me what I want to know."

Despite what he'd said, Dean wasn't performing a hundred percent in an official capacity. He wasn't interrogating Stan in the calm, confidence-inspiring manner he usually used with suspects. But Stan probably wouldn't have responded to his usual approach. Taking a harder line with him seemed to be working.

Stan glared at Dean, fired drop-dead looks at Paris, but crossed his arms over his chest as though to protect himself. "I'm going to file charges of police brutality. My uncle will—"

"Your uncle will have more than me to worry about if it turns out you're Valentino."

"I'm not! Don't you listen?"

"When that woman said no to you, did you go ahead and complete the act?"

Stan's eyes darted between them. "No. I mean, yeah. Sort of."

"Well, which is it? Yes, no, or sort of?"

"I didn't force her, if that's what you're getting at."

"But you completed the act?"

"I told you she was the—"

"'Office whore.' So she was asking for it."

"Right."

"For you to rape her."

"You keep putting words in my mouth!" Stan cried.

"And you're going downtown with me. Right now."

Stan backed away from him. "You can't . . ." He looked frantically at Paris. "Do something. If you let this happen, my uncle will have your job."

She didn't even consider questioning Dean. Frankly, she was now afraid of Stan. Perhaps she had misjudged him. She had always thought of him as a worthless, maladjusted screwup, but basically harmless. Maybe he *was* capable of committing the crimes against Janey Kemp.

If he proved not to be Valentino, she would have to face Wilkins Crenshaw's wrath. Undoubtedly it *would* cost her her job. But she would rather lose her job than her life.

Dean took Stan by the arm and turned him toward the door. Stan began to struggle and Dean had his hands full trying to restrain him without handcuffs. When his cell phone rang, he tossed it to Paris so she could answer it for him.

"Hello?"

"Paris?"

She could barely hear over the crude invective Stan was screaming at Dean. "Gavin?"

"I've gotta talk to my dad, Paris. It's an emergency."

Gavin had been whiling away his time watching television, which was the only privilege his dad hadn't revoked. He'd put his favorite movie into the VCR, but the challenges confronting Mel Gibson seemed tame compared to what was happening in his own life.

He was worried about his dad and Paris.

He hadn't felt nearly as dismissive as he'd acted when his dad said that Valentino might come after them. This guy really could intend to harm them and didn't seem afraid to try. He shouldn't be underestimated. Who'd have thought he would murder Janey?

When the house phone rang, he welcomed the distraction. He rushed to answer and did so without even checking the caller ID. "Hello?"

"Why haven't you been answering your cell phone?"

"Who is this?"

"Melissa."

Melissa Hatcher? Oh, great. "I haven't had my cell on. It's been kinda hectic—"

"Gavin, you gotta help me."

Was she crying? "What's the matter?"

"I need to see you, but there's a cop car parked in front of your house, so I drove on past. You gotta meet me."

"I'm not supposed to leave."

"Gavin, this is no bullshit," she fairly shrieked.

"Just come over."

"With cops there? I don't think so."

"Why not? Are you high?"

She blubbered and sniffed, then said, "Can I sneak in through the back?"

He didn't want any part of her crisis, whatever it was. Having to take a lie detector test would clear up a guy's thinking and rearrange his priorities, but quick. He'd made a promise to himself that if he came out of this mess reasonably unscathed, he would cultivate a new circle of friends.

Another major infraction, and he could find himself on his way back to Houston. He didn't want to return to his mother's house. Now that things were square between him and his dad, he looked forward to staying with him, maybe until he graduated from high school.

It was definitely in his best interests to tell Melissa he was busy and hang up. But she sounded really strung out. "Okay," he said reluctantly. "Park on the street behind us and walk between the houses. There isn't a fence. I'll let you in through the patio door. How soon can you be here?"

"Two minutes."

He checked to make certain that both policemen were in the squad car at the front curb, and that one wasn't making his hourly tour around the house, then went into the kitchen and watched for Melissa. When she emerged from the hedge of oleander bushes that separated the two properties, she looked like a trick-or-treater.

Tears had left tracks of black eye makeup down her cheeks. Her clothes looked more like a costume than anything a normal person would wear. It was a mystery to him how anyone could run in the platform sandals she was wearing, but she managed. She skirted the pool and clopped across the limestone terrace. He opened the sliding glass door and she flung herself against him.

He pulled her inside and closed the door. Supporting her against his side, he half-carried her into the den, where he lowered her into a chair. While she babbled incoherently, she continued to clutch at him.

"Melissa, calm down. I can't understand a thing you're saying. Tell me what's going on."

She pointed to the wet bar across the room. "I gotta have something to drink first."

When she tried to get up, Gavin pushed her back down. "Forget it. You can have some water."

He took a bottle from the mini-fridge, and while she drank from it, he remarked, "You're a freak show. What happened?"

"I was . . . was with him."

"Who?"

"The guy . . . the . . . the dentist. That Armstrong."

Gavin felt his jaw drop open. "What? Where?"

"Where? Uh . . ."

She looked around the room as though Brad Armstrong might be standing in a corner of it. Gavin wanted to slap her. How could anybody be so damned dense?

"*Where,* Melissa?"

"Don't holler at me." She rubbed her forehead as though trying to massage the answer out. "A motel. I think the sign out front had a cowboy, or a saddle, something like that on it."

A motel in Austin with a western theme. That narrowed it down to several hundred, he thought caustically. "If you met him there—"

"I didn't. He picked me up in a bar on the lake and drove me there. I was shit-faced. I'd been drowning my sorrow, you know, over Janey, with tequila shots. He showed up, bought me a drink."

"And you went to a motel with him?"

"It wasn't like I didn't know him. I was with him a few nights ago and we hit it off."

"Where was this?"

"That, uh, oh, you know the spot. Where we all go sometimes."

He anxiously motioned for her to continue.

"We did it in his car."

"What kind of car?"

"Today or then? They were different."

"Today."

"Red, I think. Or maybe blue. I wasn't paying much attention either time. He was nice to me. Really got off on my pierced nipple. It's new." She grinned at him and proudly raised her top.

"Nice."

Actually he thought she was grotesque. He'd never liked her much, had never been attracted to her, but just then, she repulsed him. He also began to question whether she was really hysterical or if this was all an act, a ploy to get inside his house, or more. She was jealous of Janey and could be trying to get some of the attention her murdered friend was receiving.

He pulled her top back into place. "Are you sure it was Brad Armstrong you were with, Melissa?"

"Don't you believe me? Would I go out looking like this on purpose?"

She had a point. "When did you learn that this was the guy the police are looking for?"

"We drove to this motel. Got in bed. He's humping away when I happen to glance across the room at the TV set. It was on, but the sound was muted. And his picture is on the screen. Big as Dallas. Everybody and his dog is out looking for him, and he's balling *me*."

"What did you do?"

"What do you think? I got him off me. I told him I had to leave, remembered I was late for an appointment. He put up an argument. Tried to talk me into staying. The more he talked, the crazier he got. First he called me a tease, then he said I was a cruel bitch, then he totally wigged out. Grabbed me and shook me and said I could go when he was good and finished with me."

She held out her arms to show Gavin the bruises beginning to appear on her biceps. "I'm telling you, Gavin, he went completely nuts. Slapped me, called me a cunt, said I was as much a cunt as Janey Kemp had been. That capped it for me. I started screaming bloody murder, and he let me go. I grabbed my clothes and hoofed it."

"How long ago?"

"Since I ran out? Maybe an hour. I flagged down a guy in a pickup truck and hitched a ride back to my car, then I drove straight here, saw the cop car. All this time I'm trying to reach you on your cell phone. Finally remembered your home number. You know the rest." She gave him an imploring look. "I'm in a bad way here, Gavin. Just one shot of something, please?"

"I said no." He squatted down in front of her. "Did you talk to him about Janey?"

"You think I'm stupid? I didn't want to wind up like her."

"Did you see any pictures of her around?"

"He had the newspapers."

"Any regular photographs?"

"No. But when I first got there, I wasn't looking, and later all I wanted to do was split."

"You said that when you met him earlier this week, he looked familiar. Had you ever seen him with Janey?"

"I'm not sure. Could be I've just seen him lurking in the crowd. He visits the Sex Club website and—"

"He said that?"

"Yeah. And the other night he had this huge stash of porn. He likes to party."

When Gavin reached for the cordless phone and began punching in numbers, she sprang from the chair. "Who're you calling?"

"My dad."

She grabbed the phone from him. "He's a cop. I don't want to get involved with the police. No thank you."

"Then why'd you come to me?"

"I needed a friend. I needed help. I thought I could get it from you. Of course, I didn't know you had dorked out since the last time I saw you. No booze, no—"

"There's a manhunt on for this guy." Angrily Gavin snatched the phone back. "If he's the one who killed Janey, he's gotta be caught."

Her facial features collapsed and she began to whimper and wring her hands. "Don't be mad at me, Gavin. I know they've gotta catch him, but jeez . . ."

He softened. "Melissa, the reason you came to me, out of all your friends, is because you knew I would call my dad. Deep down, you wanted to do the right thing."

She pulled her lower lip through her teeth. "Okay. Maybe. But give me time to flush some stuff. On top of everything else, I don't need to get busted for possession. Where's the bathroom?" He pointed her toward the powder room in the hallway even as he redialed his dad's cell phone number. It rang four times before it was answered.

He could barely hear the hello above the yelling and what sounded like scuffling in the background.

"Paris?"

"Gavin?"

"I've gotta talk to my dad, Paris. It's an emergency."

chapter thirty-two

"This is Paris Gibson. I hope you're planning to spend the next four hours with me here on 101.3. I'll be playing classic love songs and taking your requests. The phone lines are open. Call me.

"Let's start off our time together with a hit from the Stylistics. It's what falling in love should be about, 'You Make Me Feel Brand New.'"

She shut off her mike. The phone lines were already lighting up. The first caller requested B. J. Thomas's "Hooked on a Feeling." "Since tonight's theme is how we feel when we fall in love."

"Thanks for calling, Angie. It'll be up next."

"'Bye, Paris."

She was going through her normal routine, although tonight wasn't at all normal or routine. It had been almost an hour since Dean had left in a rush to meet Gavin and Melissa Hatcher at the downtown police station.

Immediately after hanging up with Gavin, Dean had dialed Curtis and capsulized Melissa's story. Curtis milked him for information and immediately acted on it.

"It shouldn't be long till we have him in custody," Dean told Paris after concluding his conversation with Curtis. "We can start at the bar where he picked up Melissa. She has an approximate idea of how long it took Armstrong to drive from there to the motel, so that gives us a radius to search within. It's a wide area, but not as wide as before."

Paris had asked him if someone had told Toni Armstrong about this development.

He nodded somberly. "Curtis was with her when he took my

call. Their attorney had joined her there." Then he hugged Paris tightly. "He'll soon be in custody, and you'll be safe. It'll be over."

"Except for the memory of what he did to Janey."

"Yeah." He sighed his regret, but his mind was clicking along at a mile a minute, in cop modality. "Curtis says the squad car remains outside until we've got Armstrong. Besides, Griggs practically considers himself your personal bodyguard." He looked over at Stan, who'd been momentarily forgotten. "I guess this lets you off the hook, Crenshaw."

"You're going to regret the way you treated me."

"I already do. I wish I'd kicked your ass while I had a good excuse." He kissed Paris swiftly on the mouth, then rushed out.

Stan followed him from her office, leaving in a huff. She let him go without saying anything. He would pout, but he would survive, and in the meantime she had a program to prepare for. Making amends with Stan could wait until she had more time and he was in a more receptive mood.

Now, at half past the hour, she engaged her mike. "I'll be back after the break with more music. If you have a request, or just something on your mind you'd like to share, call me."

She cut her mike and, sensing a presence, turned on her swivel stool. Stan was standing directly behind her. "I didn't hear you come in."

"I sneaked in."

"Why?"

"I figured as long as you and your boyfriend regard me as a creep, I should behave like one."

It was a typically childish, peevish, Stan-like thing to say. "I'm sorry your feelings were hurt by Dean's allegations, Stan. But admit it. For a while there, you looked like a plausible suspect."

"For rape and murder?"

"I said I was sorry."

"I thought you knew me better than that."

"I thought I knew you better, too," she exclaimed, losing patience with him. "If your behavior had been above reproach, no one would have suspected you. But aside from the sexual harassment charge in Florida, you've been lying about me, telling people we were lovers."

"Only Marvin, or whatever his name is. And not in so many words."

"Whatever you said, you managed to get your message across. Why would you lead anyone to believe that?"

"Why do you think?"

His voice cracked and he suddenly appeared to be on the verge of tears. The emotional display made her embarrassed for him. "I had no idea you felt that way about me, Stan."

"Well, you should have, shouldn't you?"

"I never looked at you as a . . . in a romantic context."

"Maybe those damn sunglasses keep you from seeing what should be obvious."

"Stan—"

"You only saw me as an incompetent whipping boy for my uncle, and a fag."

It was an uncomfortable truth that she couldn't deny, but she did apologize. "I'm sorry."

"For godsake, that makes three times you've said you're sorry. But you don't really mean it. If you wanted to change the way you feel about me, you could. But you don't want to. Especially now that you've got your boyfriend back. He slobbers over you, doesn't he? And you—who have always maintained a hands-off policy—you're suddenly in heat.

"I think you came here straight from bed, didn't you? When have you ever come to work with wet hair? Having fun, Paris? Isn't it nice there's no inconvenient fiancé to eliminate this time?"

"That's a tacky and extremely insensitive thing to say."

Leaning toward her, he smirked. "Did I prick your conscience?"

She had to curl her fingers into fists to keep from slapping him. "You don't know anything about that or about me. This conversation is over, Stan."

She turned back to the control board, checked the countdown clock, looked at the blinking telephone lines. She depressed one of them. "This is Paris."

"Hi, Paris. My name's Georgia."

"Hello, Georgia." She breathed slowly and silently through her mouth in an effort to calm her anger and focus on the business at hand.

"I've been having some doubts about my boyfriend," her caller said.

Paris listened while the young woman whined about her boyfriend's fear of commitment. During the monologue, Paris glanced over her shoulder. The studio was empty. As when Stan had come in, he'd left just as stealthily.

• • •

"We've got him!" Curtis shouted from his cubicle in the CIB. "They'll have him here in ten minutes."

Dean met the detective in the narrow passageway between offices. "Did he put up any resistance?"

"The arresting officers got the motel manager to open the door of his room. Armstrong was sitting on the bed, his head in his hands, crying like a baby. Kept saying over and over, 'What have I done?'"

Dean moved toward the exit. "I want to tell Gavin."

"Thank him for me. The lead he gave us narrowed the playing field considerably. And stick around, will ya? I'd like for you to be in on the interrogation."

"I plan to be. I'll be right back."

Gavin and Melissa Hatcher were seated on the same bench outside the CIB where he and Paris had been sitting . . . when was it? Only yesterday? God, so much had happened since then, with the case, with them.

As the double doors swung shut behind him, he gave Gavin and Melissa a thumbs-up. "He's just been arrested. They're bringing him in now. You did well, son." He placed his arm across Gavin's shoulders and gave him a brief hug. "I'm proud of you."

Gavin blushed modestly. "I'm just glad they caught him."

Turning to the girl, Dean said, "Thank you, too, Melissa. Coming forward took a lot of guts."

When Dean had arrived at the police station, Melissa and Gavin were already with Curtis. He and several other detectives were listening to her detailed account of the time she'd spent with Brad Armstrong.

Although she seemed to enjoy being the center of attention, she had looked a fright. Since then, she had washed the streaked makeup off her face and brushed her hair so that it no longer radiated from her head like spikes on a medieval mace. Someone, probably a policewoman, had located a cardigan sweater for her to put on over her sheer halter top, which had proved to be a distraction even to seasoned detectives.

Now she beamed at Dean's compliment, but then wet her lips nervously. "Do I have to see him?"

"We need you to officially identify him as the man who assaulted you."

"It wasn't exactly assault. I was wasted, but I knew what I was doing when I left the bar with him."

"You're a minor. He had sex with you. That's a crime. He also struck you and tried to hold you against your will. We can hold him on those charges while we're waiting for Janey's autopsy report from the medical examiner. I know it won't be easy for you to see him again, but your help is essential. Have your parents arrived?"

"Not yet. They freaked out when I called them, but they weren't as pissed as I would have thought, I guess since I coulda turned up dead, too. Is it okay if Gavin stays with me?"

"If you want him to. Gavin?"

He raised his shoulders in a shrug of consent. "Sure."

"Okay then, Dr. Malloy," Melissa said. "Bring on the pervert. I'll stay as long as you need me."

"This is Paris."

"It's me."

Merely the sound of Dean's voice caused her heart to flutter and brought on a silly smile. "Did you lose the hot-line number I gave you? Why are you calling on this line?"

"I thought I'd see what it was like to be an ordinary listener."

"You might be a listener, but you're certainly not ordinary."

"No? Glad to hear it." There was a smile behind his voice, too, but it soon turned serious. "They've arrested Armstrong. He's due here any minute."

"Thank God." She was relieved, but her heart immediately went out to his wife. "Have you seen Toni?"

"Just a few minutes ago. She's distraught, but I think she's glad we got him before he could hurt anyone else."

"Or himself."

"The possibility of suicide had occurred to me, too. You're getting as good at my job as I am."

"Not even close. Oops, hang on a sec. I've got to do a station ID." She dispatched her business, then came back on the line. "Okay, I've got a few minutes."

"I won't keep you. I promised to call as soon as I knew something."

"And I appreciate it. My program will go a lot smoother now that I know he's been apprehended. I couldn't concentrate, and every time I answered a phone line, I held my breath, afraid it would be him."

"You don't have to worry about that now."

"Is Gavin still with you?"

"He's keeping Melissa company. What he did was great, huh?"

"I thought so."

"Me, too. Shows maturity and a sense of responsibility."

"And trust in you, Dean. That's the most significant breakthrough."

"After a few derailments, I think we're on the right track now."

"I'm sure of it."

"Speaking of misguided youths, Lancy Ray Fisher was released."

"I'm thinking of hiring him."

"I beg your pardon?"

She laughed at his shocked tone. "I've never worked with a producer, although management has offered me one. It would be a good way for Lancy to learn, get some experience."

"What would Stan think about it?"

"It's not his decision to make."

"Any backlash over what happened earlier?"

She hesitated, then said, "He's brooding, but he'll get over it."

Dean had enough on his mind without her telling him about her most recent altercation with Stan. It had made her uneasy. After everything that had been said, could they mend fences and resettle into a comfortable working relationship? Unlikely.

However, the prospect of dissidence in the workplace didn't upset her as it would have even a week ago. Then, her life had revolved around her job. Anything that affected it had a profound effect on her, because that's all she had. That had changed.

As though following her thoughts, Dean said, "I want to spend the night with you."

The declaration evoked memories of the abbreviated but precious time they'd spent in bed earlier this evening and sent a tingle through her all the way down to her toes. "I'm supposed to disconnect callers who say things like that."

He chuckled. "I want to, but unfortunately I don't know how long I'll be needed here."

"Do what you need to do. You know I understand."

"I know," he said, sighing. "But tomorrow night is a damn long time to wait."

She felt the same. With as much professionalism as she could muster, she said, "Caller, do you have a request?"

"In fact I do."

"I'm listening."

"Love me, Paris."

She closed her eyes and held her breath for a moment, then said softly but emphatically, "I do."

"I love you, too."

John Rondeau took the stairs rather than waiting for the elevator. His email exchanges with a counterpart in the Atlanta PD had yielded new information on Stan Crenshaw, which he was eager to share with Curtis. Rather than forwarding it by email or telephoning, Rondeau wanted to deliver it in person.

But when he reached the CIB, it was humming with activity. For the number of personnel bustling about, it could have been high noon rather than nearing midnight. As a policewoman barreled past him, he hooked his hand in her elbow, bringing her to an abrupt halt. "What's going on?"

"Where've you been?" she said, frowning at him as she extricated her arm. "We got Armstrong. They're about to bring him in."

Rondeau spotted Dean Malloy in conversation with Toni Armstrong and a gray-suited man who had "lawyer" stamped all over him. He found Curtis in his cubicle, hunched over his desk phone and rubbing his palm back and forth across his burred head.

He was saying, "No, Judge, he hasn't confessed, but there's a lot of circumstantial evidence pointing to him. We're hoping the autopsy will produce some DNA, although the body was washed—"

He stopped speaking, apparently having been interrupted. He rubbed his head a little more briskly. "Yes, I'm well aware of how long DNA testing takes, but maybe when Armstrong knows that we're submitting his for a possible match, he'll crack. I certainly will, Judge. By all means. As soon as I know more. My condolences again to Mrs. Kemp. Good night."

He hung up, stared at the receiver for several seconds, then looked up at Rondeau. "What?"

Rondeau raised the file folder he'd brought with him. "Stan Crenshaw. The guy has been a deviant since grade school. Raising girls' skirts. Indecent exposure. Interesting reading."

"I'm sure it is, but he's not Valentino."

"So what do I do with this? Ditch it?"

Standing, Curtis shot his monogrammed cuffs and smoothed down his necktie. "Leave it on my desk."

"Somebody should look at it," Rondeau insisted.

A sudden shift in the atmosphere indicated that something momentous was happening beyond the walls of Curtis's cubicle. Rondeau followed him out. They wended their way into the center of the CIB.

Rondeau recognized Dr. Brad Armstrong from the family snapshots taken off the CD. Flanking him were two uniformed policemen. Handcuffed, he stood with his head down, his aspect that of a defeated man. He was ushered into an interrogation room. Malloy, the attorney, and Toni Armstrong crowded in. Curtis was the last to enter the room. He closed the door behind him.

Rondeau, feeling rebuffed, tapped the folder against his open palm. If Curtis thought he had Valentino, then he should probably just let it drop and forget Stan Crenshaw.

But what if, after interrogating Armstrong, Curtis determined they had the wrong guy? What if the result of the autopsy cast doubt on or even refuted the circumstantial evidence against him? What if his DNA didn't match any samples they collected from Janey's remains, if they even could since her body had been chemically cleansed?

Reaching a decision, Rondeau left the CIB in a hurry. As he went through the double doors, he spotted Gavin Malloy and a girl seated together on a bench in the vestibule. He had missed seeing them when he came in. From the open staircase, he had turned right to enter the CIB. They were seated to the left of the stairs. At the sound of the doors closing, the girl turned her head toward him.

Oh, shit!

He didn't know her name, but he'd seen her plenty of times. If she recognized him, he'd be up shit creek.

John Rondeau made a dash for the stairs.

"Hey, Gavin, who's that guy?"

"Huh?"

The past few days had caught up with him. His head had been resting against the wall, and he'd been dozing.

Melissa nudged his elbow. "Hurry! Look!"

"Where?"

He raised his head, blinked open his gritty eyes, and looked in the direction of Melissa's pointing finger. Through the metal railing of the staircase, he caught a glimpse of John Rondeau's head just before he cleared the landing below and disappeared.

"His name is John Rondeau."

"Is he a cop?"

"Computer crimes," he muttered. "It was him who ratted out the Sex Club."

"Seriously? Because I've seen him somewhere. In fact, I think I might've balled him."

Terrific, Gavin thought. If she placed Rondeau as someone who hung out and partied with the high school crowd, then blabbed about it, Rondeau might think he was the one who'd fingered him.

"No way. He's got one of those faces that always remind you of somebody else." It wasn't a very good explanation, but it was all he could think of.

Melissa frowned thoughtfully. "Guess I'd have to see his cock to know for sure. But I could swear . . ."

Just then they heard a ping signaling the arrival of an elevator. They turned in time to see a nice-looking, well-dressed couple step around the corner and into their view.

Melissa stood up.

"Your folks?" Gavin asked, surprised by how presentable and respectable they appeared. He'd been expecting the Osbornes, not June and Ward Cleaver.

Awkwardly, Melissa wobbled toward them on her platform sandals, self-consciously tugging down her short skirt. "Hi, Mom. Hi, Dad."

Their arrival couldn't have been better timed. Gavin wanted nothing more to do with Rondeau, and that extended even to talking about him. He hated being the keeper of the cop's dirty little secret, but, remembering Rondeau's threat toward his dad, Gavin would carry that secret to his grave.

chapter *thirty-three*

"*I*'m sorry, Toni. I'm sorry. Will you ever be able to forgive me?"

Dr. Brad Armstrong seemed more concerned about his wife's opinion of him than he did about the serious allegations being made against him, which could potentially cost him his life. He appealed to her plaintively and somewhat pathetically.

"Let's get through this first, Brad. There'll be plenty of time later to talk about forgiveness."

She was stoic, her voice calm, which was amazing in light of the ordeal confronting her. She was probably being held together with the emotional equivalent of Scotch tape, but she remained intact. Dean gave her a "hang in there" nod as she left the interrogation room, leaving her husband alone with him, the attorney, and Curtis.

Curtis identified everyone present for the benefit of the tape recorder, then began by telling Bradley Armstrong everything they knew about him and why they considered him a suspect in the kidnapping and murder of Janey Kemp.

"I didn't kidnap that girl."

His earnest denial didn't impress Curtis. "We'll get to that. First let's talk about the time you molested Paris Gibson." Armstrong grimaced. "I see you remember the incident," Curtis remarked. "To this day you resent Ms. Gibson, don't you?"

"She got me fired from a lucrative practice."

"Do you deny touching her inappropriately?"

He lowered his head and shook it.

"Answer audibly for the recorder, please."

"No, I don't deny it."

"Have you called her radio show recently?"

"No."

"Ever?"

"I may have."

"If I were you, I wouldn't hedge on the easy stuff, Dr. Armstrong," Curtis advised. "Have you ever called her while she's on the air? Yes or no?"

The dentist raised his head and sighed. "Yes, I called her, said something rude, and hung up."

"When was this?"

"Long time ago. Shortly after we moved to Austin and I realized she had a radio program."

"Only that once?" Dean asked.

"I swear."

"Did you know that there was some involvement between Ms. Gibson, Dr. Malloy, and a man named Jack Donner?"

Dean looked at Curtis and was on the verge of asking him where the hell that question had come from, but Armstrong answered before he had a chance. "It was on the news down in Houston."

Then Dean realized the validity of the detective's question. Valentino had said Jack's death was on their consciences, indicating that he was acquainted with their history.

"When you called her, where did you call from?"

"My house. My cell phone. I don't remember, but I certainly never called her about Janey Kemp."

Curtis had learned that Armstrong's cell and home phone records didn't list any calls to the radio station, but he'd only requested records going back several months. Armstrong could be telling the truth, or he could have used a public telephone to make the Valentino calls, or he could have an untraceable cell.

Curtis asked if he had disguised his voice when he called.

"No need. She would never have recognized my voice. We only met that . . . that once."

"Did you identify yourself to her?" Curtis asked.

"No. I just said, 'Screw you,' or something to that effect, then hung up."

"Where'd you get Valentino?"

He glanced at his lawyer, then at Dean, as though seeking an explanation.

"What?"

"Valentino," Curtis repeated.

The news stories had cited Paris Gibson's telephone warnings as a key element in the case, but the caller's name had been withheld to prevent chronic confessors from gumming up the investigation with false leads.

"You pick that name up from the silent movie actor?" Curtis asked. "And why seventy-two hours? Did you pluck that deadline from thin air? Why not forty-eight, which is closer to what it turned out to be, isn't it?"

Armstrong turned to his attorney. "What's he talking about?"

"Never mind. We'll come back to that," Curtis said. "Tell us about Janey Kemp. Where did you meet her?"

With his attorney closely monitoring every word, Armstrong admitted that he'd frequented the Sex Club website and had eventually begun joining its members at the specified meeting places. "I invented reasons to leave the house."

"You lied to your wife."

"That's not a crime," the attorney said.

"But engaging in sexual activity with minors is," Curtis fired back. "When did you first meet Janey, Dr. Armstrong?"

"I don't remember the exact date. A couple months ago."

"What were the circumstances?"

"I already knew who she was. I'd noticed her, asked around, and learned that her user name for the website was pussinboots. I'd been reading the messages she left on the boards, knew she was . . ." He stammered over his next word, then rephrased. "I knew she was sexually active and willing to do just about anything."

"In other words, she was prey to predators like you."

The lawyer ordered him not to respond.

Curtis waved a semi-apologetic dismissal of the statement. "The night you met Janey, did you have sex with her?"

"Yes."

"Janey Kemp was seventeen," the attorney stipulated.

"Barely," Curtis said.

In an anguished voice, Armstrong said, "You've got to understand, that's what these girls were there for. They came looking for it. I never had to coerce a single one of them into having sex with me. In fact, one—not Janey, another one—charged me a hundred dollars for five minutes of her time, then went right on to her next customer. She said she was working toward a Vuitton handbag."

"You have proof of this?"

"Oh, sure, she gave me a receipt," Armstrong replied sarcastically.

Curtis failed to see the humor in this and remained stone-faced. Dean believed the dentist was telling the truth about the prostitution because it coincided with what Gavin had told him.

Curtis continued the questioning. "On the night you met Janey, you had sex with her where?"

"In a motel."

"Where you were found tonight?"

He nodded. "I keep an efficiency apartment there."

"Which you rent for that purpose?"

"Don't answer," the attorney instructed.

"Did you take pictures of Janey?" Curtis asked.

"Pictures?"

"Photographs. Different in subject matter from the kind you take of your family vacations," the detective added dryly.

"Maybe. I don't remember."

Curtis narrowed his gaze on him. "Your den of iniquity is being searched even as we speak. Why don't you tell us what we might find and save us all some time here."

"I have some porno magazines. Videos. I've taken pictures of . . . of women on occasion, so maybe, yeah, there might be some pictures of Janey."

"You develop these pictures there in your makeshift darkroom?"

He looked genuinely mystified. "I don't know how to develop film."

"Then where'd you have your pictures of 'women' developed?"

"I send the film to a lab out of town."

"What lab?"

"It doesn't have a name. Just a post office box. I can give you that."

"Let me guess. This is a film-developing outfit that caters to specialized customers like you?"

Shamefaced, he nodded. "I don't use it often, but I have."

Armstrong's answers to this line of questioning were inconsistent with what Janey had told Gavin about her new boyfriend's passion for photography. Either he was telling the truth or he knew how to lie convincingly.

Curtis must have thought so, too, because for the time being he let the subject drop and asked about the last time Armstrong had seen Janey.

"It was three nights ago. I guess it was the night she disappeared."

"Where'd you see her?"

"At a spot on the shore of Lake Travis."

"You went there for the specific purpose of meeting her?"

Armstrong answered, "Yes," before his attorney could caution him not to. Too late Armstrong saw his lawyer's raised hand. "It's not a crime to make and keep a date," he said to him.

The lawyer addressed Curtis. "I'm only agreeing to let my client go into detail here because he adamantly denies anything beyond having congress with the victim, who was a consenting adult. This isn't to be considered a confession to any allegation of kidnapping or murder."

Curtis nodded and motioned for Armstrong to continue.

"Janey was waiting for me in her car."

"What time was that?" Dean asked, remembering that Gavin had said that he, too, had been in Janey's car and that she had seemed to be waiting for someone else to join her.

"I can't remember exactly," Armstrong said. "Around ten, maybe."

Curtis asked, "What did you do in her car?"

"We had sex."

"Intercourse?"

"Fellatio."

"Did you use a condom?"

"Yes."

"Then what happened?"

"I . . . I wanted to stay with her for a while longer, but she said there was something she had to do. I think she was waiting to see someone else."

"Like who?"

"Another man. She insisted I go on my way, but she promised to see me the following night, same place, same time. When I left, she was in her car, listening to the CD player. I went the next night. She wasn't there. I didn't know about her disappearance until I read about it and saw her picture in the newspaper."

"Why didn't you come forward then?" Curtis asked.

"I was scared. Wouldn't you be?"

"I don't know. Tell me. Would I?"

"I'd violated the terms of my probation. A girl I'd had sex with several times had gone missing." He raised his shoulders in a gesture of helplessness. "You do the math."

Curtis snickered. "I've done it, Dr. Armstrong. My tally says you wanted more of Janey than she was willing to give you that night. Things got rough. You tend to get rough when a woman doesn't give you what you want when you want it, isn't that right?"

"Sometimes I get angry, but I'm working through it."

"Not fast enough. In the meantime, your anger got the best of you, and before you knew it, you were choking Janey. Maybe she died right then, maybe she just became unconscious and died later.

"In any case, you panicked. You took her to that swell room you've got in that lousy motel and tried to figure out what to do with her, but in the end you rolled her body into the lake and then crawled into your hidey-hole and hoped to God you'd get away with killing her."

"No! I swear I didn't force her into doing anything, and I sure as hell didn't murder her."

The attorney was massaging his eye sockets as though wondering how in the hell he was going to construct a defense out of his client's frantic denials. Curtis looked as stern and unyielding as a cigar store Indian.

"I don't think you did it intentionally," Dean said quietly.

Armstrong turned to him with the desperate expression of a drowning man in search of a lifeline.

The role of good cop fell to him because he played it well. Let Curtis be the hard-ass. For the next several minutes, Dean would be Brad Armstrong's best friend and only source of hope. He folded his arms on the table and leaned into it.

"Did you like Janey, Brad? I assume it's okay if I call you Brad."

"Sure."

"Did you like her? As a person, I mean."

"Truthfully, not much. Don't get me wrong, she was something else." Suddenly cautious, he glanced at his attorney.

"Sexy and willing?" Dean prompted. "The kind of girl we all wanted to date in high school?"

"She was just like that. But I didn't particularly like her personality."

"Why not?"

"Like most girls with her looks, she was conceited and self-absorbed. She treated people like dirt. You either played her way or she didn't play at all."

"Did she ever turn you down?"

"Only once."

"For another guy?"

He shook his head. "She said she was PMSing and not in the mood."

Pal to pal, Dean smiled at him. "We've all been there."

Then he sat back and folded his arms across his chest, his smile reversing into a frown. "The problem is, Brad, that most guys would blow it off. Oh, there'd be some frustration and maybe some hard cussing, but eventually your average guy would go have a beer or two, watch a ball game, maybe even find a more accommodating girl. But you take rejection hard. You can't tolerate it. Which causes you to lash out, doesn't it?"

He swallowed hard and mumbled, "Sometimes."

"Like you did tonight with Melissa Hatcher."

"I haven't had time to confer with my client about Melissa Hatcher," the lawyer said. "So I can't allow him to talk about her."

"He doesn't have to say a word," Dean said. "I'm going to talk to him." Then, without waiting for the attorney's permission, he continued. "This girl advertises the merchandise. She's advertised it to me, to Sergeant Curtis here, and all the detectives in this unit. Any man would take the way she dresses as a 'come and get it.'"

"So who could blame me for—"

"Do not say a word," Brad's lawyer snapped.

Ignoring the lawyer, Dean kept his attention riveted on Armstrong. "Unfortunately for you, Brad, the state of Texas blames you. If you penetrate the sexual organ, mouth, or anus of a child, it's called 'aggravated sexual assault.' Correct?" he asked, turning to the attorney, who nodded curtly.

"How old is Melissa?" Brad asked.

"Sixteen until next February," Dean told him. "She claims you had sexual contact and intercourse."

"What if . . . what if . . . it was consensual?" Armstrong asked, seeming not to hear the admonitions of his attorney instructing him not to say anything.

"Doesn't matter," Curtis answered. "You're a convicted sex offender. Under Chapter Sixty-two that makes what you did indefensible."

Armstrong buried his head in his hands.

Dean said, "Your previous conviction for indecency with a minor was a third-degree felony. This is the big time, Brad. It's a first-degree felony."

"Not to mention capital murder," Curtis chimed in.

Without acknowledging Curtis's statement, Dean proceeded.

"You've paid dearly for your inappropriate and illegal behavior. You've lost jobs, the respect of your colleagues. You're in danger of losing your family."

The man's shoulders rose and fell in a harsh sob.

"Yet in spite of the costly consequences of your unacceptable behavior, you haven't stopped it."

"I've tried," he exclaimed. "God knows, I've tried. Ask Toni. She'll tell you. I love her. I love my kids. But . . . but I can't help myself."

Dean leaned forward again. "That's precisely my point. You can't help yourself. Melissa got you so hot tonight that when she said no, you flipped out. You grabbed her, shook her, slapped her around. You didn't want to, but you couldn't control the impulse, even knowing how much you were going to regret your actions later.

"Your desire to sexually dominate this girl shot your conscience and common sense all to hell. You had to have her, simple as that. Nothing else mattered. Not the punishment you would face when caught. Not even your love for Toni and your children could stop you. It's a compulsion you haven't learned to contain. It caused you to do what you did to Melissa tonight, and what you did to Janey."

"Do not respond," the lawyer said.

Dean lowered his voice another degree and spoke to Armstrong as though they were the only two people in the room. "I have a clear picture of what happened three nights ago, Brad. Here's this sexy, desirable girl who you thought was as enamored of you as you were of her. She'd been seeing you regularly, and you thought exclusively.

"That night, she goes down on you. And it's great, but you know she's insincere. You know she's a liar and a merciless tease. You know that she's waiting for her new interest to come along and replace you.

"When you confront her about it, she tells you to get lost. You've become jealous and possessive, and she can't stand your whining any longer. Did you honestly believe that she would give up other men for *you?* she asks. You poor, delusional slob.

"You get furious. You ask yourself, where does she get off treating me like this? Calling up Paris Gibson and talking about me on the radio? Who does she think she is?"

Dean's gaze held the suspect mesmerized. "When you got into Janey's car that night, I don't think you had already plotted her kidnapping and murder. I think you'd planned only to confront her, have it out with her, clear the air.

"And maybe if she hadn't mocked you, that's the way it would have ended. But Janey laughed in your face. She emasculated you with her ridicule, insulted you in a way you couldn't tolerate. You lost it. You wanted to punish her. And that's what you did. You devised a punishment of sexual abuse, befitting what she'd done to you. You hurt her until you decided you'd had your vengeance, to hell with the deadline you gave Paris, and then you choked her to death."

Armstrong stared at Dean in stunned horror. He looked over at Curtis, whose visage remained unmoved and unchanged. Then, folding his arms on the table, he laid his head on them. In a tormented, cracking voice, he groaned, "Oh, God. Oh, *God.*"

Curtis and Dean honored the attorney's demand to have a few minutes alone with his client and left the room. Curtis was smiling and rubbing his hands together, relishing the coup de grace.

"He hasn't signed a confession yet," Dean reminded him.

"It's a matter of pen and paper. By the way, you're good."

"Thanks," Dean said absently. This had been round one of what would probably be a lengthy and exhausting interrogation, but several things about it were nagging him. "I didn't ask him specifically if he'd heard Janey on the radio talking about the jealous lover she was about to dump."

"But you alluded to it and he didn't deny it."

"He denied calling Paris about Janey."

"Before we even asked, which says 'guilty' to me," the detective argued.

"He knew about Paris's connection because it was in the news. His phone records refute the allegation that he called her."

"There are several ways he could have placed those calls without it showing up on records."

"Making weird phone calls hasn't been part of Armstrong's MO before. Why now?"

"Maybe he needed a new thrill. The Valentino phone calls spiced things up for him, and at the same time wreaked havoc on Paris. He wanted to get his kicks and get revenge. The calls accomplished both."

That made sense, but only after you massaged it into place. "Valentino's calls have a meanness to them that I just don't see in Armstrong. He's sick, but I don't think he's evil."

Curtis frowned at him irritably. "Forget motivation for a moment and consider some facts."

"Such as?"

"His occupation. He's a dentist."

"The chemical scouring," Dean said, musing out loud. The medical examiner had been able to confirm that, like Maddie Robinson, Janey's body had been astringently washed.

"Right. It's the kind of thing a medical man would do."

"It's the kind of thing a meticulous psychopath would do, too. Someone with a compulsion for scrubbing away his guilt."

"Armstrong straddles both categories."

Dean glanced over his shoulder at the closed door of the interrogation room. "Janey was restrained. She was tortured. She had bite marks, for godsake."

"We'll get impressions of his bite for comparison."

"My point is, none of Armstrong's priors involved violence or even hinted at a propensity for it. He was a creep, but he wasn't a violent creep."

"What is this, Malloy?" Curtis asked crossly. "His own *wife* told us that his violent tendencies had been escalating. *You* said that was a natural progression for his particular psychosis. Are you second-guessing yourself?"

"I know what I said, and I was right."

"Okay then. He knocked Melissa Hatcher around tonight."

"There's a wide gulf between knocking a woman around and torturing one before squeezing the breath out of her."

"Not in my book. And probably not in the book of the woman being knocked around."

"Don't be obtuse, Curtis," Dean said angrily. "I'm not excusing either. I'm just saying—"

"Ah, shit, I know what you're saying," Curtis grumbled, then expelled his frustration on a gust of breath. After a short pause that allowed tempers to cool, he asked, "Any more misgivings?"

"The photography."

"Armstrong admitted that he might have taken some pictures of Janey."

"'Some.' 'Might have.' He talked about the photography as though it was no big deal. Janey indicated otherwise. Before we start on Armstrong again, do you mind if I get Gavin in here and ask him more about this?"

Curtis shrugged. "I'm for whatever will help nail this guy."

Dean stepped into the corridor and motioned for Gavin. He got up, leaving Melissa sitting with a couple Dean assumed were her parents.

"What's up, Dad?" he asked. "Has he confessed?"

"Not yet. In the meantime, I'd like you to talk Sergeant Curtis and me through everything Janey told you about Valentino. Any detail you can remember. All right?"

"I already have, a dozen times."

"One more time. Please."

They found Curtis pouring himself a cup of coffee. He offered them one, but they declined. Curtis took a sip from his Styrofoam cup, then said, "At the risk of beating a dead horse, even an off-handed remark Janey might have made could be important, Gavin."

"I wish I could remember something else, sir. She told me the guy was older. Older than us, I mean. That he was cool, knew how a woman liked to be treated."

"We're mainly interested in the photography," Dean told him.

"She said he was a camera freak," Gavin said. "Lights, lenses, an elaborate setup. He posed her himself. Moved her around, you know, her arms and legs. Head. Everything."

"Could she have been exaggerating to impress you? Make you think of her as a model, like in *Penthouse?*"

"It's possible," he replied. "But if she was exaggerating, she sure did her homework, because she knew a lot about it. She mentioned shutter speeds, stuff like that. Said he tinkered with gadgets to get each picture just right, and would get mad if she didn't co-operate."

"He didn't just fire off a few naughty snapshots," Dean said to Curtis. "If you study the picture that Janey gave Gavin, you can tell it was taken by an amateur trying to be artistic."

"And you don't think Armstrong is capable of that?"

"Capable," Dean said. "But if you're out cheating on your wife, who is more than likely waiting up for you, do you take that much time with photography?"

While Curtis was still mulling that over, he happened to glance beyond Dean's shoulder. "What are you doing here?"

Dean turned to see who had caused Curtis's distraction and saw Officer Griggs coming toward them. The rookie's grin dissolved under Curtis's frown and tone of stern disapproval.

"I . . . I was given the all clear, sir. Told it was okay to leave. But I was anxious to know if Armstrong had confessed, so instead—"

"You left Paris out there alone?" Dean asked.

"Well, sir, not—"

"Who told you to leave?"

"John Rondeau."

From the corner of his eye, Dean noticed Gavin's reaction to the mention of Rondeau's name. He reacted not with the expected dislike, but with alarm.

"Gavin? What is it?" His son stared back at him, whey-faced. *"Gavin?"*

"Dad . . ." The boy had to swallow hard before he could continue. "There's something I've gotta tell you."

chapter thirty-four

Through the glass-block walls, the blue-white fluorescent lighting of the radio station's lobby relieved the surrounding darkness, but only marginally. Downtown city lights were obliterated by hills. The moon was too slender to shed significant light. At this time of night, only an occasional car sped past on the narrow state highway. The nearest commercial building was a convenience store a half mile away, and it had closed at ten.

From the vantage point of the FM 101.3 building, nothing was visible except hills dotted with cedar trees, limestone boulders, and an occasional herd of beef cattle. It was an ideal spot for the transmission tower that intermittently blinked its red lights as a warning to low-flying private aircraft.

Rondeau dawdled beside his car until the taillights of Griggs's patrol car disappeared behind a hill. He frowned with contempt for the officers driving away. Sure, he had wanted them to leave. But shouldn't they have verified the order, which he told them had come straight from Curtis, rather than taking his word for it? That kind of carelessness was unacceptable. Tomorrow he would report them. It wouldn't win him their regard, but one didn't advance one's career by making friends.

He started toward the entrance, carrying with him the folder of information on Stan Crenshaw. It painted a disturbing portrait of a man whose dysfunctional family and personal insecurities had led to sexual malfeasances dating back to childhood, which were credible harbingers of Valentino's aberrations.

What offended Rondeau most, however, was the injustice it signified. Crenshaw had gotten away with his misconduct. His uncle had bought him out of every scrape. By doing so, Wilkins Crenshaw had slowly created a monster capable of kidnapping, raping, torturing, and murdering a lovely young woman.

Because of his myopic focus on Brad Armstrong, Sergeant Curtis had dismissed the juicy contents of this folder. Initially Rondeau had taken offense at the snub, but it had actually worked to his advantage. Unwittingly, Curtis had handed him a golden opportunity to become everyone's hero.

Rather than press the buzzer, he knocked on the glass door.

He didn't have to wait long before getting his first look at the singularly unimpressive and unimposing Stan Crenshaw. He appeared out of a shadowed hallway off the lobby and approached the door warily, peering through the glass that, with the darkness beyond it, Rondeau knew would be reflecting like a mirror. Crenshaw did all but cup his hands around his eyes in order to see who had knocked.

He assessed Rondeau with the condescension of the born rich, then looked beyond him toward the parking lot, where the squad car was conspicuously missing. "Where're the policemen?"

Rondeau, already tasting success, held up his badge.

"That, of course, was Johnny Mathis with his classic, "Misty." Definitely music to nuzzle by. I hope you have someone near you tonight as you listen to 101.3, classic love songs. This is Paris Gibson bringing you up to midnight with Melissa Manchester's 'I Don't Know How to Love Him.' The phone lines are open. Call me."

When the song began, she disengaged her mike. Two of her phone lines were blinking. She pressed one of the buttons, but got a dial tone. Mentally she apologized to the caller who obviously had given up on being answered.

She pressed the second blinking light. "This is Paris."

"Hello, Paris."

Her heart actually stopped before a burst of adrenaline restarted it with the hard, fast pounding of a sprinter coming off the blocks. "Who is this?"

"You know who it is." His laugh was even more frightening than his whispery voice. "Your faithful fan Valentino."

Frantically she looked over her shoulder, hoping that perhaps Stan had silently rejoined her in the studio. She would have welcomed his sneaking up on her now. But she was alone in the room. "How—"

"I know, I know, your boyfriend thinks he's nabbed his culprit.

His egotistical bungling would be comical if it weren't so pathetic." He laughed again, and it caused goose bumps to break out on her arms. "I've been a bad boy, haven't I, Paris?"

Her mouth had gone dry. Her heart continued to thump against her ribs and her pulse vibrated loudly against her eardrums. She ordered herself to calm down and *think.* She must alert Dean, Sergeant Curtis, Griggs outside, someone, that they had the wrong man in custody and that Valentino was still at large. But how?

What was she thinking? She had a microphone at her fingertips! Hundreds of thousands of people were tuned in.

But even as she reached for the mike switch, she reconsidered. Should she blurt out over the airwaves that the Austin PD had blundered? What if this call turned out to be a hoax, someone playing a cruel trick on her? What if she started a public panic?

Better to keep him talking until she could figure out what to do. "On top of everything else, you're a liar, Valentino. You moved up the deadline."

"That's true. I have no honor."

"You killed Janey before giving me a chance to rescue her."

"Unfair, wasn't it? But I never claimed to be honorable, Paris."

"Then why did you call me in the first place? If you intended to kill her all along, why set up this elaborate telephone campaign?"

"To rock your world. And it worked, didn't it? You feel positively rotten over your inability to save that slut's life."

Paris refused to buy into his baiting. She'd been down that path, and Janey had died anyway. The only way she could redeem herself would be to identify this son of a bitch and see him brought to justice, and that couldn't be done by arguing with him.

She could dial Dean on her cell phone, but—damn!—it was in her office, in her handbag. Could she create a technical problem that would alert Stan? Soon the Manchester song would end. It was the last in a series. Dead air would bring Stan into the studio to see what the problem was.

While she brainstormed, Valentino rambled. "She had to die, you see, for fucking me over. She was a heartless bitch. I enjoyed watching her die slowly. I could tell when she realized that she would never get away from me. She knew she wasn't going to survive."

"That must have been a real head trip for you."

"Oh, absolutely. Although it was actually heartrending the way her eyes silently pleaded with me to spare her life."

That statement made Paris forget her recent resolve not to be riled by anything he said. "You sick bastard."

"You think I'm sick?" he asked pleasantly. "I find that strange, Paris. I tortured and killed Janey, yes, but you tortured and killed your fiancé, didn't you? Wasn't it torture for him to learn about your unfaithfulness with his best friend? Do you think of yourself as sick?"

"I didn't drive Jack's car into a bridge abutment, he did. The accident was his fault. He determined his fate, not me."

"That sounds like a rationalization," he said in the reproving tone of a priest in the confessional. "I don't see the difference between your sin and mine, except that your fiancé's torture lasted much longer and he died much more slowly. Which makes you much crueler than me, doesn't it? And that's why you must be punished.

"Would it be just to let you go on your merry way and live happily ever after with Malloy? I don't think so," he said in a nasty singsong. "That is not going to happen. You will never be together because you, Paris, are going to die. Tonight."

The line went dead. Instantly she reached for her hot-line phone. No dial tone. Nothing. Silence. In quick succession, she tried all the phone lines, but to no avail. They were dead.

Realization crept over her like an encroaching shadow. Either he had the access and ability to disable computerized telephone equipment from off the premises or—and this is what she feared—he had simply interrupted telephone service from inside the building.

She shot from her stool. Yanking open the heavily padded door, she shouted down the dark corridor, "Stan!"

The Manchester song was winding down. Racing back to the control board, she punched her mike button. "Hello, this is Paris Gibson." Her voice sounded thin and high, not at all like her normal contralto. "This is not a—"

The sound of a high-pitched alarm interrupted her.

She swung her gaze toward the source. The sound was coming from the scanner, which recorded everything that went out over the air. You never knew it was there, really. The alarm only alerted you to an interruption in transmission.

Terror seizing her, she punched her mike button repeatedly, but, like all the others on the board, it refused to light up.

Again she lunged for the door. "Stan!" The echo of her scream seemed to chase her as she ran toward her office. Her handbag was where she'd left it on her desk, but it had been toppled onto its side. The contents had been spilled onto her desk. With shaking hands, she riffled through cosmetics, tissues, loose change, hoping to find her cell phone, but knowing it wouldn't be there.

It wasn't.

And something else was missing—her keys.

Frantically she searched through the mail scattered across her desk and even dropped to her knees and looked beneath it, but she knew that both her key ring and her phone had been taken by the same individual who had cut the phone lines and shut down transmission. All lines of communication had been severed by the man who had killed Janey and had promised to kill her.

Valentino.

Her breathing was so harsh, she couldn't hear anything else. She held it for several moments in order to listen. She crept to the open door of her office but hesitated at the threshold. The hallway, as always, was dim. Tonight the familiar darkness gave her no sense of security and comfort. It had a sinister quality, maybe because the building was as silent as a tomb.

Where was Stan? Hadn't he noticed that they weren't broadcasting? If he had checked the studio and discovered she wasn't there, why wasn't he going through the building calling for her, checking to see what had happened?

But even before her mind could completely form that question, it had arrived at the answer: Stan was unable to come and check on her.

Valentino had dispatched him, possibly even before he had called her. He could have been in the building for quite some time before she'd know of it, sealed as she'd been inside the soundproof room.

How had Valentino gotten past Griggs and Carson? Once he had, how had he opened the door to the building? A key was needed to unlock the dead bolt from either side. Had he persuaded Stan to open the door? How?

Questions for which she had no answers.

She was tempted to slam her office door, lock herself inside, and wait for help to arrive. Already, listeners all over the hill country would be wondering what had caused the station to go off the air. Dean might even know. Sergeant Curtis. Soon somebody would be rushing to her rescue.

But in the meantime, she couldn't hide herself in here. Griggs and Carson could be hurt. And Stan.

She stepped out into the hallway. Putting her back to the wall so she could see in both directions, she inched along it, toward the front of the building. As she moved along the corridor, she turned off every light switch she passed. One distinct advantage she had over Valentino was knowing the layout of the building. She was accustomed to navigating it in semidarkness.

Moving quickly, but as silently and cautiously as possible, she made her way toward the entrance. She approached each intersection of hallways with the fear of what awaited her around the corner, but when she turned the last one, the stretch of hall between her and the well-lighted lobby was clear. She raced down it and across the lobby, intent on launching herself against the door and pounding on the glass in order to get the attention of the policemen guarding her.

But the squad car wasn't there and the front door was bolted.

With a soft cry, she backed away from the door until she came up against the receptionist's desk. She rested against it to catch her breath and decide what to do.

Suddenly her ankle was grabbed. She screamed.

She looked down to see a man's hand reaching from beneath the desk. But before she could even try to work herself free of his grasp, the fingers relaxed and the hand fell lifelessly to the grimy carpet.

Stumbling over her own feet, she rounded the desk but drew up short when she saw the form lying facedown on the floor. She dropped to her knees and took the man by the shoulder, turning him over.

John Rondeau groaned. His eyelids were fluttering but remained closed. He was bleeding profusely from a wound on his head.

Gladness surged through her as she gasped his name. "John. Please, wake up. Please!" She slapped his cheek smartly, but he only groaned again, his head lolling to one side. He was unconscious.

Just beyond the reach of his outstretched hand lay an official-looking file folder. She read the name typed on the identifying tab: *Stanley Crenshaw.*

Her stomach dropped. "Oh my God."

Stan? It had been Stan all along?

But why not? she reasoned. His ineptitude could be an excellent guise. He had the time and opportunity to commit the crimes. His days were free and so were his nights before and after her program. He had just enough technical knowledge to reroute telephone calls. He was an electronics and gadget junky. Surely among all his toys was camera equipment he could easily afford. He was attractive enough to lure a thrill-seeking teenager.

And he had a lifetime's worth of anger and resentment pent up, more than sufficient motivation to kill a woman who had spurned him. And with chilling clarity, Paris realized that just tonight she, too, had rejected him.

"Help will be here soon," she whispered to Rondeau. He didn't respond. He'd slipped deeper into unconsciousness. The policeman was out of commission and she was on her own.

But she wasn't going to wait for Valentino to find her. She was going to find him.

Quickly, she patted down Rondeau's clothing. She didn't know if computer cops were armed or not, but she hoped so. She didn't like guns, was revolted by the whole idea of guns, but she would use one if she had to in order to save her life.

She exhaled her relief when she felt a bulge beneath his jacket. She flipped it back only to discover that the holster clipped to his belt was empty.

Stan must have had the same idea. He was armed.

After murmuring another assurance to Rondeau that he would be all right—which she hoped was true—she cautiously abandoned the false security of hiding behind the desk.

As she left the lobby, she switched off the fluorescent lighting, although it occurred to her that Stan knew the building as well as she, so the darkness was no longer her exclusive advantage.

Actually, she wasn't going to hide any longer. She and Stan were in the building alone together, as they had been hundreds of nights before. She wasn't going to play a childish cat-and-mouse game with him. If she went on the offensive and confronted him, she was confident she could talk to him long enough for rescue to arrive.

The engineering room was empty, so was the men's rest room and the snack room. All the offices, including her own, were deserted. Gradually she made her way to the very back of the building, where there was a large storeroom. The door to it was closed.

The metal knob felt cold in her hand when she grasped it and pushed the door open. She was met by the dank smell of disuse and oldness. The room was cavernous, darker even than the rest of the building. The open doorway cast a wedge of light across the concrete floor, but it was so faint as to be negligible.

Paris hesitated on the threshold until her eyes could adjust to this deeper darkness. When they did she noticed the walk-in closet where Lancy/Marvin's custodial equipment and supplies were stored. The door to it was ajar. Listening intently, she was certain she heard the sound of breathing coming from inside it.

"Stan, this is silly. Come on out. Stop this craziness before anyone else is hurt, including yourself."

Gathering all her courage, she entered the storeroom. "I know you've got a gun now, but I don't believe you'll shoot me. If you had wanted to kill me, you could have on any given night."

Had the breathing inside the closet become more agitated? Or was she imagining it? Or was it an echo of her own breathing she was hearing?

"I know you're angry with me for spurning your affections, but until tonight, I didn't even know you felt that way about me. Let's talk about it."

As she tiptoed across the concrete floor, toward the closet, her ears strained to listen for the merest sound beyond the walls, indicating the arrival of help. Even now, were marksmen taking up positions? Were special tactical officers scaling the exterior walls to get onto the roof? Or had she seen too many action movies?

When she was still a few feet from the partially open closet door, she paused. "Stan?" Reaching far out in front of her, she pushed the door open all the way.

No gunshots shattered the stillness. She reminded herself of what he had done to Janey. Now that he knew he was caught, he would be desperate, conscienceless, capable of anything. The situation required training she didn't have. Dean did.

Dean. In fear and longing, her heart silently cried his name as she took the final step that placed her in the open doorway.

At the sight of Stan, she stared in bafflement.

He was breathing heavily through his nostrils because his mouth was sealed closed with duct tape that had also been used to bind his ankles and wrists. His legs were bent so that his knees were up under his chin, and he had literally been stuffed into the industrial-size stainless-steel sink.

"Stan! What . . ." She was reaching out to tear the tape off his mouth when his eyes, already wide with terror, looked beyond her and stretched even wider.

She spun around.

"Surprise!" John Rondeau said.

But it was Valentino's voice.

chapter thirty-five

"Fuck it, fuck it," Dean repeated as he punched the rubberized digits on his cell phone.

He was steering his car with one hand and using his cell phone with the other. Several times he had redialed the hot-line number Paris had given him. She didn't answer. He dialed the radio station call-in number repeatedly, but kept getting the standard recording saying that Paris would be with him as soon as possible. He called her cell number, but got her voice mail.

"Why didn't you tell me about Rondeau?" Curtis, who was riding shotgun, was also on his cell phone. He had been put on hold, awaiting more information on John Rondeau.

"You heard it when I did."

The detective had been standing right beside him when Gavin revealed what he knew about Rondeau. It would be difficult to say who had moved first. Dean remembered shoving Curtis out of his way as he ran for the exit.

He had gained a little ground when Curtis shouted over his shoulder for units to be dispatched to the radio station. "SWAT, too! Now, now, move it!"

Dean wasn't going to hang around and see that the sergeant's orders were carried out, and apparently Curtis shared his urgency. They burst through the double doors and clambered down the staircase, taking two or three stairs at a time until they reached the garage level. Dean's car was parked the closest. The way he was pushing it now, they would beat the squad cars to the radio station.

"You failed to tell me Rondeau had accosted your kid in the bathroom."

"It was personal. I thought he was just an asshole."

"An asshole with—" Curtis broke off and listened. "Yeah, yeah," he said into the phone, "what've you got?"

While Curtis was getting the scoop on John Rondeau, Dean dialed Paris's numbers again. When he got the same result, he cursed lavishly and pressed his foot harder against the accelerator.

In what seemed like a direct correlation to his stamping on the gas pedal, the car radio went silent. Since his ears had been attuned to listen for Paris's voice, the sudden static hiss was as jarring as a blood-curdling scream.

The implication splintered his control. Viciously he punched the buttons on his radio dial. All other stations came through loud and clear. The radio wasn't malfunctioning; 101.3 had stopped transmitting.

"The station just went off the air."

Curtis, who'd been absorbed in his conversation, turned his head. "Huh?"

"She's off the air. She's stopped broadcasting."

"Jesus." Then into his cell phone Curtis said, "That'll do for now." He clicked off.

"What? Talk to me," Dean said as he took a corner practically on two wheels.

"No father in the Rondeau household. Ever. They're checking now to see if he died during John's infancy, or if there ever was a Mr. Rondeau. No significant male role model, like an uncle, scoutmaster—"

"I got it, go on."

"Mother worked to support John and his sister, older by one year."

"What have they got to say about him?"

"Nothing. Both are deceased."

Dean whipped his head toward Curtis. "He referred to them in the present tense."

"They were murdered in their home when John was fourteen. He discovered the bodies. Sister had been drowned in the bathtub. Mother had an ice pick shoved straight through her medulla while she was napping."

"Who did it?"

"Unknown. It's a cold case."

"Not anymore." Dean's fingers tensed around the steering wheel.

"We don't know that," Curtis said, reading Dean's thought.

"He was interrogated, but never really considered a suspect. Mom and kids were devoted to each other. Mother worked hard to support them. Brother and sister were latch-key kids. Reliant on each other. Very close."

"I'll bet," Dean said tightly. "Real close."

"You're thinking incest?"

"Valentino's behavior is symptomatic. Why wasn't all this in Rondeau's record?"

"The facts are. APD carefully screens every applicant."

"But no one looked beyond the tragedy of his losing his whole family. Nobody was looking for incest. What happened to young John after the double murder?"

"Foster care. Lived with the same couple until he was old enough to go it alone."

"Other children in that home?"

"No."

"Luckily. Did he get along with the foster dad?"

"No record of any problems. They doted on him."

"Especially the wife."

"Don't know," Curtis said. "But they gave him a glowing review. Said he was an ideal child. Respectful. Well behaved."

"A lot of psychopaths are."

"He had an excellent academic record," Curtis continued. "No problems at school. Went to two years of college before he applied to the police academy. Wanted to become a cop—"

"Let me guess. To prevent other women from dying the way his mother and sister had."

"More or less." Curtis glanced at him. "One tiny detail . . ."

"Yeah?"

"When she died, the sister was five months pregnant."

Dean risked giving him a questioning look.

"No," Curtis said. "They checked. It wasn't Rondeau's baby."

"I could have told you it wasn't," Dean said grimly. "That's why he killed her."

Curtis's cell phone rang. "Yeah," he snapped.

Dean could see the lights on the broadcast tower. What were they, a mile away? Two? He was tailgating the SWAT van. It had caught up with them several miles back and Dean had let it pass them.

The van was speeding, but Dean willed the driver to move it even faster. They were the two lead vehicles in a motorcade that included several police units. Bringing up the rear was an ambulance. He tried not to think about that.

Curtis ended his call. "They went into Rondeau's apartment. Wasn't much of a place, but he had some fancy photographic equipment. Albums chockfull of dirty pictures. Lots of Janey. Long blond hairs visible on the bedding. He's our guy."

Dean stared straight ahead, clenching his teeth so hard it made his jaw ache.

Curtis checked the pistol he carried in a belt holster, and a second one in an ankle holster. "You got a piece?"

Dean gave him a brusque nod. "I started carrying when he started threatening Paris."

"Well enough, but listen to me. When we get there, you're gonna keep out of the way and let those guys up there do their job." He nodded toward the SWAT van. "You got it?"

"I got it. Sergeant."

The reminder of their respective ranks wasn't lost on Curtis, but he didn't back down. "You go in there half cocked, you'll do something that would fuck up our arrest and he'd walk on some legal bullshit technicality."

"I said I got it," Dean said testily.

"So you're cool?"

"I'm cool."

Curtis slipped the pistol back into his ankle holster, muttering, "Like hell you are."

Dean said, "Right. If he's hurt Paris, I'm going to kill him."

She gaped at John Rondeau's grinning face, but her astonishment was only momentary. Then she reacted swiftly. With all her strength she pushed against his chest, but he shoved her against the metal shelving in the closet even as he fired his pistol at Stan.

The report deafened her. Or maybe it was her own scream.

Rondeau slapped her. "Shut up!" Grabbing her by the hair, he dragged her from the closet and kicked it closed with his foot. Then he pushed her with such impetus that she pitched forward onto the concrete floor.

"Hello, Paris," he said in the chilling voice she now knew well.

"Did you kill him?"

"Crenshaw? I hope so. That was the point of firing a bullet straight into his heart. What a loser. But stronger than he looks. He actually gave me this," he said, indicating the bleeding scalp wound. "He was obliging at first. Showed me how to stop transmission. At gunpoint, of course. Then he made this ridiculous but very valorous attempt to protect you by hitting me with a bottle of Snapple." He was still speaking in Valentino's voice.

"The voice . . . that's quite a trick."

"Isn't it? On the outside chance that any of my cop buddies were also Paris Gibson fans, I didn't want them to identify my voice when I called in."

"You were Valentino from the start." Her mouth was so dry, her tongue was sticking to the roof of her mouth on each word.

"Yes. That takes us back to . . . Let's see." He scratched his cheek with the barrel of his pistol. "Sometime before Maddie Robinson came along."

"So that makes two women you've killed."

He smiled indulgently. "Actually no, Paris."

"More than that?"

"Un-huh."

Keep him talking. The longer he talks, the longer you'll live. "Why did you kill them?"

Resuming his normal voice, he said, "Because they didn't deserve to live."

"They cheated on you like Janey did."

"Janey, Maddie, my sister."

"You murdered your sister?"

"It wasn't *murder.* I meted out justice."

"I see. What happened? What did your sister do to you?"

He laughed pleasantly. "Everything. We did everything to each other. I slept between them, you see. Between her and my mother. Get the picture?" He bobbed his eyebrows up and down.

He'd wanted to shock her and he had, but she tried to keep her expression impassive. She wouldn't give him the satisfaction of seeing her revulsion.

"We kept it all in the family. Our little secret," he said in a stage whisper. " 'Don't tell,' Mommy warned us. 'Because if you tell, they'll take you away and lock you up where they keep bad little boys and girls who play with each other's pee pees. Promise? Good. Now suck Mommy's titties and she'll do something extra-special nice to you.' "

Nausea rose in Paris's throat.

He continued in his blasé manner. "But then we begin to grow up. Sis gets an after-school job at a record store. She's there every afternoon instead of at home with me doing what we loved doing best. She starts staying later at the store so she can be with one of the guys who works there. She doesn't have time for me anymore.

"She's never in the mood. She says she's too tired, but it's really because she's fucking him all the time. And Mommy thinks it's grand, the way Sis has fallen in love. 'Isn't it romantic and aren't you happy for her, Johnny?'"

He lapsed into a brooding silence, then his chest heaved as though he were about to cry. "I loved them."

Taking advantage of his preoccupation, Paris glanced toward the door, gauging the distance.

His laughter brought her eyes back up to him. "Don't even think about it, Paris. This little stroll down memory lane hasn't distracted me from what I came to do."

"If you kill me . . ."

"Oh, I am going to kill you, but it'll be blamed on Stan Crenshaw."

"He's dead."

"As a doornail. I had to kill him. See, when I got here, I found you already dead, choked to death by Crenshaw, who'd been a twisted, sick fucker from the time he was a kid. It's all there in his file, the recipe for a sexually deviant psychopath.

"Anyhow, I sized up the situation and tried to apprehend him. During the ensuing struggle, he managed to get in one good one on my noggin, which, by the way, inspired that little trick I played on you. Clever, wasn't it? You were completely taken in, weren't you?"

"Yes," she admitted.

"Sorry, but I couldn't resist. Especially the bit with your ankle," he said, chuckling. "Where was I? Oh, yes, the way I'll tell it is that I was finally able to subdue Crenshaw and was binding his ankles and hands with duct tape I found in the closet when he attempted to escape. Sadly, I had no choice but to shoot him."

"Very tidy," she said. "But not perfect. The crime scene experts will find discrepancies."

"I've got answers for any questions that could arise."

"Are you sure you've thought of everything, John?"

"I've done my research. I'm a good cop."

"Who preys on women."

"I never 'preyed' on them. My mother and sister were hardly victims. They were my coaches. Every woman I've been with since has benefited from what they taught me, and all were willing partners. I wasn't even particularly attracted to Maddie at first. But she kept after me. Then she was the one who wanted to break if off. Go figure." He shook his head with disbelief.

"And if you're referring to the girls in the Sex Club as prey, you haven't been paying attention. They're whores looking for adventure. I have no inhibitions. They love me," he whispered, waggling his tongue at her.

Again, she swallowed her nausea. "Apparently Janey didn't love you."

"Janey didn't love anybody except Janey. But she loved what I did to her. She was a heartless little bitch who used people's emotions for target practice. And you sympathized with her, Paris. You put her on the radio to complain about me. Do you know why? Because you're exactly like her.

"You play with people's emotions, too. You think you're hot shit. You've got Malloy, even Curtis, panting after you, begging for any crumb of attention you might toss them."

Suddenly he checked his wristwatch. "Speaking of Malloy, I'd better get down to business. You've been off the air for five minutes."

Five minutes? It seemed like an eternity.

"Folks are going to start noticing, and I'm sure your psychologist friend will come charging in here like the cavalry and—"

From the front of the building came what sounded like an explosion of breaking glass, followed by shouting voices and running footsteps.

Paris kicked Rondeau in the kneecap as hard as she could.

His leg buckled beneath him and he screamed in pain.

Paris scrambled to her feet and made a dash for the door.

She didn't hear the gunshot until after she felt the impact of it.

It was more forceful than she could ever have imagined. The searing pain that followed stole her breath and almost caused her to black out instantly, but adrenaline kept her running, through the door, out of his line of sight, where she collapsed.

She tried to cry out and alert the police to her location, but she was unable to utter more than a faint moan. Blackness closed in around her, until the dim corridor elongated and narrowed, like the tunnel of a nightmare.

Dean would be leading the charge. Even Rondeau had said so. She must warn him. She tried to pull herself up, but her limbs had turned to jelly and she wanted badly to throw up. She opened her mouth to call out, but her well-trained, carefully cultivated voice failed her completely.

Rondeau was coming nearer the door. She could hear his groans of pain as he hopped across the cement floor of the storeroom. Soon he would reach the hallway. He would have the advantage over anyone coming around the blind corner at the end of it.

"Dean," she croaked. Once more she tried to stand. She made it as far as her knees, but she swayed unsteadily, then collapsed against the wall, hard. The resultant pain was like a branding iron burning through flesh, all the way to the bone. She left a blood trail on the wall as she sank to the floor.

Though her ears were ringing, she could tell that the shouting voices were coming closer. Flashlight beams crazily crisscrossed on the walls at the end of the hallway.

But hearing another sound, she turned just as Rondeau appeared in the storeroom doorway. He grunted with pain as he braced himself against the doorjamb. She took satisfaction from the odd angle at which his right leg was bent. His face was bathed in sweat and twisted into an ugly mask of rage as he glared down at her.

"You're just like them," he said. "I've got to kill you."

"*Freeze!*" The shout ricocheted off the walls like the beams of the flashlights.

But Rondeau didn't heed the warning. He raised his pistol and aimed it directly at her.

The barrage of gunfire was deafening and filled the corridor with smoke.

As she fell forward, Paris wondered vaguely if she was just losing consciousness, or dying.

chapter thirty-six

"Who actually brought him down?"

"Call it a group effort. Rondeau gave us no choice. Several of us hit him."

Paris leaned back against the hospital bed pillow, relieved by Curtis's answer to her question. She wouldn't have wanted Dean to carry the burden of taking John Rondeau's life. She learned later that he'd been the first one into the hallway, as she had known he would be. But Curtis and several SWAT officers were there, too. Any of the bullets fired at Rondeau could have been the fatal one.

This morning Curtis was looking even spiffier than usual, as though he had dressed up to pay her this visit. He was wearing a gray western-cut suit. His boots had an extra sheen. She could smell cologne. He had brought her a box of Godiva chocolates.

Yet his demeanor was all business. "Rondeau was computer savvy enough to learn how to reroute calls," he told her. "Our guys finally traced that last call to a cell phone. But he had planned on that, too. The phone was unregistered. A throwaway. That part of it was easy for him."

"He could change his voice at will, too. It was eerie."

Sometimes minutes would pass without her thinking of Rondeau and that agonizing period of time with him in the storeroom. Then, without warning, a recollection would thrust itself into her consciousness and she would be forced to relive the terrifying moments.

When she described this phenomenon to Dean, he assured her that each day the recollections would become less frequent and her memory would dim a bit more. Although she would never entirely forget the experience, it would sink into her subconscious. His counsel had a footnote: He would see to it that she lived in the present, and for the future, not linger in the past.

"Rondeau wanted to move to CIB," Curtis was saying. "He had already approached me about it. Said he wanted to work in the child abuse unit."

"Where he would have unlimited access to child pornography."

Curtis nodded, his disgust plain. "He went to the radio station that night to fulfill his personal agenda, and at the same time distinguish himself as a police officer by delivering Valentino.

"With you and Crenshaw dead, he might have pulled it off. Janey's body rendered none of the perp's DNA. Apparently he'd learned about an agent that served that purpose in a homicide case in Dallas." He shook his head with chagrin. "His police work taught him well."

"About Stan, have you received any updates on his condition?" she asked.

"Elevated to fair."

Miraculously Stan had survived the gunshot to his chest and the delicate surgery that had removed the bullet. He'd had a collapsed lung and extensive tissue damage, but he would survive. When he was stable enough to be moved, Wilkins Crenshaw had flown him by private jet to Atlanta.

"I asked his uncle to call me as soon as Stan is able to talk on the phone," she said. "I want to apologize."

"I'm sure he won't hold a grudge against you. He'll be too grateful to be alive."

"Rondeau told me he had shot Stan straight through the heart."

"If that's where he was aiming, he should've spent more time at the practice range," Curtis said with a grim smile. "Lucky for you he didn't."

She'd been told that her blood loss was significant because the bullet had entered her back just below her shoulder socket and had gone straight through. She would bear an ugly scar and her scorching tennis serve was a thing of the past, but she was alive.

If the bullet had cut a path a few inches lower, her life would have been over. Dean had advised her not to dwell on that either, although it was the common reaction of a survivor.

"Don't examine the reasons for your life being spared, Paris. To do so is futile. You could never arrive at an answer. Just be grateful you're here. I am," he'd said, his voice made husky by emotion.

Curtis brought her back to their conversation by saying that the incestuous relationships of Rondeau's boyhood had left him angry. "I don't think even he knew how angry he was," he said. "He'd learned to hide it well, but he harbored a deep-seated rage against women because of what an abusive mother had done to him."

"Dean explained it to me."

"I'm paraphrasing him," Curtis admitted. After a beat, he asked if she'd seen that morning's newspaper. "Judge Kemp is using Janey's murder as part of his campaign platform."

"That goes beyond tasteless."

"Some people," the detective snuffled with contempt.

"What's going to happen to Brad Armstrong?" she asked. "Will he go to prison?"

"He has to face the aggravated-sexual-assault charge, which carries a stiff sentence if he's convicted. But Melissa Hatcher admitted that she went with him willingly and engaged in numerous acts before she called a halt. He might plead to a lesser charge in exchange for a lighter sentence, but I predict that he'll serve time. Hopefully he'll use that time to get himself straightened out."

"I wonder if his wife will stay with him." Her eyes strayed to the floral arrangement Toni Armstrong had sent.

"Remains to be seen," Curtis said. "But if I was a gambling man, I'd say yes." They were quiet for a moment, then he slapped his thighs and, with a sigh, stood. "I should shove off and let you rest."

She laughed. "I've rested until I'm blue in the face. I can't wait to be released."

"Anxious to get back to work?"

"By next week I hope."

"Your fans will be happy. So will the hospital staff. They said every flower within a hundred-mile radius is in the main lobby downstairs."

"Dean wheeled me down there yesterday to see them. People have been exceptionally kind."

"Speaking for myself, I've missed listening to you." His entire scalp flushed a bright pink as he added, "You're a class act, Paris."

"Thank you. So are you, Sergeant Curtis."

A bit awkwardly, he reached for her right hand and gave it only one swift shake before releasing it. "I'm sure I'll be seeing you around. I mean, now that you and Malloy . . ." He let the sentence trail off.

She smiled. "Yes, I'm sure I'll be seeing you around."

• • •

Dean arrived just as she was adding the finishing touches to her makeup.

"Paris?"

"In here," she called from the small bathroom. He moved in behind her and their eyes met in the mirror above the basin. "How do I look?"

"Luscious."

She frowned dubiously at her reflection. "Hair styling isn't easy to accomplish one-handed. At least it's my left one that's out of commission."

He reached for her right hand, the back of which was bruised from the IV port that had been removed only the day before. He kissed the discolored spot. "To me you look fantastic."

"Your opinion definitely counts." She turned to face him, but when he only pecked her lips, she looked up at him with disappointment.

"I don't want to hurt you," he explained, indicating her bandaged arm and sling.

"I won't break."

With her right hand, she pulled his head down and gave him a real kiss, which he responded to in kind. They kissed with sexual passion, as well as with the desperation of knowing that they'd almost lost each other for the second time.

When they pulled apart, she said, "I received a get-well card from Liz Douglas. Very gracious of her under the circumstances."

"She's a lady. There was only one thing wrong with her. She wasn't you."

They kissed again, then, leaving his lips against hers, he whispered, "When we get home . . ."

"Um-huh?"

"Can we go straight to bed?"

"Will you do—"

"Everything. We're gonna do everything." He gave her a hard, quick kiss, then said, "Let's get out of here."

They gathered the last of her personal things and placed them in a tote bag. She put on her sunglasses. He ordered her into the hospital-mandated wheelchair and pushed her to the elevator.

As they were riding down to the ground floor, she said, "I expected Gavin to be with you."

"He sends his regards, but he left for Houston this morning to spend the weekend with Pat. He hopes to patch things up with her. Maybe even offer an olive branch to her husband."

"Good for him."

"He didn't fool me."

"You don't believe he's sincere?"

"Oh, he's sincere about setting things right with them. But he chose to go this particular weekend so we'd have time alone." As the elevator doors slid open, he leaned down and whispered directly into her ear, "I owe him."

Returning his grin, she said, "So do I."

"You are going to marry me, aren't you?"

Feigning affront, she said, "I wouldn't consent to a honeymoon otherwise."

"Gavin will be glad. He wants to make friends at his new school, and he told me what an advantage it would be to have a stepmom who was famous and also a total fox."

"He thinks I'm a fox?"

"Cool, too. You've got his unqualified approval."

"It's nice to be wanted."

Humor aside, Dean stepped around to the front of her chair and leaned down until his face was level with hers. "I want you."

They had an audience comprised of hospital staff and visitors in the lobby. Unmindful of them, he reached for her hand again and this time pressed her palm to his lips. They exchanged a look rife with meaning and implication, then he let go of her hand and said, "Ready?"

"Ready."

"Be forewarned, Paris. You'll be running a gauntlet. There are cameras galore outside that door. Every news outlet from Dallas to Houston to El Paso has a reporter and a photographer here to cover your hospital release. You're big news."

"I know."

"And that's okay?"

"It's okay. In fact"—she removed her sunglasses and smiled up at him—"it's time I came out into the light."

Grinning, he pushed the wheelchair toward the automatic doors. They slid open and camera strobes began to flash.

Paris didn't flinch.

acknowledgments

I really hate having to ask people for help and information. An autographed copy of the book and an acknowledgment in the back of it seem insufficient thanks for all the trouble these professionals went to on my behalf.

Public Information Specialist C, Laura Albrecht of the Austin Police Department never lost patience with me, even when I continued calling her with just "one more question." She opened doors that would ordinarily have been closed. Thanks also to the detectives of the Centralized Investigative Bureau, who all too frequently go unrewarded and unrecognized for the difficult job they perform. They were cordial and informative even after I explained to them that there was a rotten cop in my story.

In my next life, I want to be a drive-time deejay like Bill Kinder of KSCS-FM. Unlike me, he gets to talk to his fans every weekday. They call in by the hundreds. What a kick! He made it look easy to do a dozen tasks at once. He never broke stride, not even to answer my questions. If I got the radio technology all wrong, it's no fault of his.

A few unfortunates work with me on a daily basis. My agent, Maria Carvainis, deserves more gratitude than I'll ever be able to express. Amie Gray's middle name should be Britannica for her diligent fact checking and her gleaning of information on the most outlandish topics. I also wish to thank Sharon Hubler for the years that she streamlined my life. Without her I would often have been at the wrong place at the wrong time, doing the wrong thing. I wish her much happiness in her new life.

And to the dear man who lives with me: Michael, my thanks and my love, always.

Sandra Brown
1 April 2003